D0160685

PRAISE FOR *ANGEL*

"The line between good and evil becomes blurred in this twisted tale of fire and angels."—*Booklist*

"Thought-provoking blasphemy and gore-on-the-floor horror, with an urban cop twist. High-quality creepiness and more ideas than a dozen other horrors."
—Kim Newman, author of *Anno Dracula*

"[The] final showdown with the angel is satisfyingly spectacular."—*Publishers Weekly*

"An efficiently crafted, tightly plotted thriller about the devastating side effects of a skirmish in the long war between Heaven and Hell. *Angel* is a fine display of Kilworth's considerable powers as a storyteller, fleshed out with an abundance of gritty detail and twisting through chichanes and abrupt reversals with a verve that burns through the pages."
—*Interzone*

GARRY D. KILWORTH

A TOM DOHERTY ASSOCIATES BOOK
NEW YORK

ANGEL

This is a work of fiction. All the characters and events portrayed in this book are fictitious, and any resemblance to real people or events is purely coincidental.

ANGEL

Copyright © 1993 by Garry D. Kilworth

Cover art by Dave Kramer

Edited by David G. Hartwell

A Tor Book
Published by Tom Doherty Associates, Inc.
175 Fifth Avenue
New York, NY 10010

Tor Books on the World Wide Web:
http://www.tor.com

Tor® is a registered trademark of Tom Doherty Associates, Inc.

ISBN: 0-812-54284-3
Library of Congress Card Catalog Number: 95-53297

First U.S. edition: May 1996
First mass market edition: January 1997

Originally published in Great Britain by Victor Gollancz

Printed in the United States of America

0 9 8 7 6 5 4 3 2 1

This one is for my friend, Christian Lehmann, doctor, writer, and fellow collaborator

For the Angel of Death
spread his wings on the blast.

—Lord Byron

1

Two o'clock in the morning in San Francisco.

The policeman's name was Reynolds but because of his shock of red hair the boys at the station called him Foxy. Reynolds didn't like it much, he preferred to be called Ray, but he found out early in his career that the guy who is given a nickname has very little to do with its choosing. If the guys wanted to call you Dumbo or Goofy, they would do it, and the more you lost your cool over it, the more likely it was they would keep it up. It was best to wear a resigned expression and smile it off.

Foxy was off duty and on his way home, which took him through a dubious neighborhood where he parked his car and lit up a cigarette. He needed to think over his marriage, which had begun derailing itself. The cause and effect he knew was in himself: in his need for alcohol to blur the day's events before going home. Clementine knew that he had to work long shifts, and tolerated the cop's lifestyle, but she would not put up with his off-duty hours being eroded by booze. So here Foxy was, trying to choose between a happy marriage and the life of a single, drunken cop. Most people would not have found the choice difficult, but Foxy, with his dire need for a drink after work, could not contemplate life without either his wife or his bourbon. He was perched on the horns of a dilemma, and they were hurting him badly.

It was a chill, depressing morning and the mist was clinging to the walls of the alleys, drifting down the gutters to mingle with fumes from the effluence around the drains. A man stood on the corner of the street, looking up at the lighted window of a sleazy apartment building, just a few feet from Foxy's car. He looked like a mary, with his long eyelashes and nails. There were other lights on, but he seemed concerned only with this one room. The rigidity of his expression showed the intensity of his interest. He might have been taken for a voyeur, except there was nothing to see, not even a silhouette on the blind.

"WHADDYA TAKE ME FOR?"

The shout, from one of the other apartments, was muted, as if the caller had his head under a pillow, or some thick blankets. There were other noises, from other rooms. This was a neighborhood that was never quiet: at least a third of its inhabitants was always awake, kept that way by the barking of the dog nobody was supposed to be allowed to keep in the building, by the eternal moving of furniture above, by the clattering of dishes and cutlery, and, worst of all, the laughter. *He-he-he-he-he-he-he-he.* Some unknown castrato, laughing in a high-pitched voice at something others could not see, could not hear—laughing at nothing.

Laughter. *Murmur murmur murmur.* Laughter. *Murmur murmur murmur.* Laughter.

Just when the neighbors thought the insane laughter had died, it began again, shrill and persistent, drilling through the thin walls. No one could understand why someone hadn't killed him before tonight. With a laugh like that, he *deserved* to die. It drove everybody mad, it had everybody yelling, SHADDUP

FOR CHRIST'S SAKES WHAT'S SO GODDAMN FUNNY
YOU KNOW WHAT TIME IT IS YOU ASSHOLE? until
there was pandemonium and even Laughing-boy was screaming for quiet. QWAI-YET! Jesus!

This was a neighborhood that had a shift system for an-
noying those who were trying to sleep. Those who couldn't
sleep kept those who wanted to awake, so in the end nobody
slept and peace only descended with the dawn, when everyone
was out of their mind with frustration.

The watcher was silent, however, and maintained his vigil
without moving, though it was bitterly cold. The one remaining street light that hadn't been broken threw a dirty yellow
light from its dirty glass bulb onto the face of the watcher.

A woman seeing him there, whether hooker or society host-
ess, would have agreed he was a beautiful young man. His eyes
were pale gray, his full lips the texture of pink rose petals. His
flawless complexion was as soft as the skin of women who ad-
vertise cold cream on the TV. Perhaps it was not a man at all
but a woman in a man's clothing? Or a transsexual? But somehow Foxy sensed a hardness beneath the soft-looking exterior,
a terrible physical strength, that made him think this was not a
woman. He couldn't explain why, because he had met some
tough females in the course of his work, but this one just felt
like a man.

The man turned and looked at Foxy with languid unin-
quisitive eyes for a minute or two before turning away again,
and fixing his stare on that certain window. Foxy felt a sudden
tremor of fear run through him when those gray eyes settled
on his own. Something was deeply wrong and the cop in Foxy
felt urged to accost the guy, find out what he was doing there
so early in the morning. However, some feeling held him back.
That feeling was probably fear, though the policeman would
not admit it to himself.

Foxy told himself he was glad the man had not attempted

to speak to him. Foxy, unhappy with questionable genders at any time, would have hesitated before challenging this man about anything, anything at all. Still the physical appearance of the man fascinated him, held his attention as well as his unacknowledged fear. He saw before him the type of beauty English poets used to describe: the kind of good looks which frightened his manhood back into its shell.

The man stepped a few paces forward and Foxy was able to study the movements of the figure inside the white suit. As he had guessed, it was trim and athletic: a dancer's body. Even through the cloth he could see the ridged muscle: smooth, elongated, not bulging rocks. The fingers that rested on the wall, right where a piece of graffito said RED SCORPIONS RULE, were long, slim and almost translucent.

When he moved it was with the grace of a cheetah. There was a power in that movement, as if a great engine was purring away beneath the rib cage. An engine of grace. Foxy got a chill feeling, of something savage beneath the comeliness, just looking at this character.

Foxy stared, wondering what the hell this mary was doing just standing on the street at three thirty in the morning. Maybe he was watching his own window. Maybe someone was up there with his wife. Or more likely his boyfriend. Maybe there was going to be a murder. Foxy tried to care, but couldn't summon the energy to concern himself. His energy was all wrapped up in leaving the force, opening a restaurant. That was all he dreamed about. Him and Clem with their own bistro. Foxy fancied himself a chef. He had studied *cordon bleu* cooking at night school, all last year, and had been practicing since. People said he was pretty good, that you couldn't tell the difference between one of his dinners, and one at Rannouf's, *the* French restaurant, on the corner of Williams and Venus. Foxy didn't want a restaurant, as such, with all the snooty stuff that went with such a place: what he wanted was a bistro, plain and simple. A place where he could put some can-can posters on the wall, with "Moulin Rouge" in balloon letters, like the kind painted by that French artist with the baby legs.

The man on the sidewalk moved to the doorway of the building and entered.

The screaming and shouting between the apartments continued unabated. Somewhere on the roof the alley cats were calling each other out, adding their own brand of noise to the discord. It was bedlam, but normal. Soon some uniformed cops would drive by, look up at the tenement, shake their heads and keep on going before they got a call and became involved in a domestic fight. At least if they were six blocks away, and got the call, there was a chance the ruckus would be over by the time they reached the apartment concerned. Someone would have hit someone, maybe killed someone, but it would have quietened down somewhat. There would be blood and tears, but a lull in the storm.

Foxy stubbed out his cigarette in the car's ashtray, and reached forward to start the engine. His hand never reached the key. Instead, he was blinded by an intense white light. There was the sound of a muted explosion, and glass rained on the roof of Foxy's Ford, like out-of-season hail. Through the bright haze, Foxy saw flames belching from the building, which appeared to spread very rapidly.

He heard the crackle and crack of metal and stone under sudden intense heat, followed by the roar of the fire rushing down hallways, devouring oxygen, eating inflammable objects in its path. Through the shattered window came a long whiplash of flame, which flayed the building opposite above Foxy's head.

Foxy was stunned by the sudden ferocity of the fire, the swiftness of its progress and how quickly it reached such intensity. He was shocked at the speed at which it spread. It was as if hell had burst a blister, right there in that room: exposed an open wound which revealed the heart of its furnace.

Christ, he thought, another incendiary bomb! It had to be the mary that had been standing on the sidewalk.

I saw the bastard. I saw the bastard go in. I could've reached out and touched him.

He felt for the catch on the door, and fell out of the car onto the sidewalk. Getting to his feet, he stumbled along, half blind, feeling his way using the wall. The screams coming from the building were different now. No one was shouting SHADDUP WILLYA SHADDUP! Instead they were shrieking HELP ME SOMEBODY FOR GOD'S SAKES HELP ME!

Someone staggered from the doorway ahead, his clothes on fire. Foxy couldn't reach him: the heat drove the policeman back. He could smell his hair singeing, his skin burning. The figure fell with a moan to the concrete and writhed around like a wounded snake, then finally lay still. The crackle of burning timber, the fumes of melting plastic and flaming rubber flowed out into the street. Foxy paused, began a coughing fit, as the gases went down into his lungs. For a few seconds he convulsed and heaved, until he managed to stagger across the street to cleaner air, and propped himself up against a post.

The heat reached him even there, with its red-hot fingers. It burned the side of his face and once more he had to retreat to find a cool doorway. He stared at the conflagration, amazed at how quickly the inferno had got out of all control. Like many people, Foxy was terrified of fire. Fire was a live thing, an entity that knew no boundaries, no friends, no aliens. Fire was the ultimate destroyer of life and property. It formed many of his nightmares.

Then something happened which caused a bolt of fear to sear through Foxy's body. Like something from a dream, out of the doorway of the flaming building stepped the man in the white suit. Foxy couldn't be sure, because his vision was still blurred, but he could have sworn the man's clothes were smoking, perhaps burning. Yet the guy did not even pause in his stride, stepping over the body on the ground, and walking purposefully along the street.

"Hey, you!" Foxy yelled. "Stop right there!" He fumbled for his gun. "Freeze!"

But in his confused state he mishandled his weapon, and it fell with a clatter to the sidewalk. The figure half turned, stared. A strong draft of wind came down the funnel of the street to feed the fire and carried with it an odor which for a moment overpowered the smells of the fire. It was a scent which seemed incongruous with the situation. It was a smell which Foxy normally associated with one of those candlelit dinners which Clementine arranged for them, when she was in a romantic mood.

Then the figure moved on, swiftly, before Foxy could gather his mental reserves. Across the street his car was already in flames, the sounds of shrieking metal mingling with the screams of the hurt and dying.

There was no phone nearby. There was nothing more Foxy could do, except listen to these terrible cries, and hope that the ambulance and fire services would be along soon. He sat on the steps of the house outside which he was forced to wait, knowing what he was going to say to Clementine when he finally got home that night.

Clem, I've had enough. I'm leaving the force.

In a short while he heard the wail of the sirens.

2

The yellow truck with the Nebraska plates was stuck across the railroad tracks. There was no sound from its engine. A locomotive was hurtling down the line toward it. Inside the cab of the truck, the driver was frozen to the wheel. The passenger was also in a petrified state. Neither made a move to open their doors and escape from the oncoming train. They simply sat there, waiting for the impact.

The locomotive continued, without slowing down, toward the vehicle directly in its path. A crash was inevitable. Still there was no stirring from the interior of the truck. Suddenly, just before the impact, a hand reached down out of the sky, and eight-year-old Jamie Peters, god of this universe created by him, saved from certain damage the yellow truck and its two plastic inhabitants.

A detective sergeant was observing him from the other side of the room: his dad, Dave Peters.

"One day you're going to let those guys down."

"Naw. I'm real quick, Dad. I can do it a split second before the crash."

"Superman, huh? Well, I'm telling you, one day—"

There was a ring at the doorbell. Jamie said, "That's Mom," and ran to open the apartment door. Dave listened, to make sure he was right. He heard Celia's voice, then went back to thinking about what Foxy had told him.

There had been a fire the previous evening in a downtown district. Three people had died. It was another case of arson. In fact Foxy, from Dave's precinct, had been a witness and could describe the arsonist, though he hadn't been able to make an arrest. It was a sophisticated burning, according to Forensics, the starter probably being an incendiary device of some kind, though the investigators admitted that no residue casings had been found. It was the only way they could account for the sudden intensity of the ignition. Metal objects in the starter room had been twisted into weird and wonderful shapes as if someone had molded them like putty. The ignition flash had blinded Foxy, and the doer had got away during the time it took him to recover.

That no bomb debris had been discovered did not worry Bates of Forensic, who guessed that the casing and primer had probably melted in the intense heat of the fire, which had been fed by cheap synthetic furniture and had reached furnace temperatures. By the time Bates had been able to enter the smoking, gutted building, the incendiary casing was probably a dribble of alloy among all the other melted and twisted hunks of metal on the site. It was unusual not to find any starter debris, but not impossible.

The report on the crime was buried in the middle of the newspaper, among petty crimes, arson being a frequent news item in these firestorm days. It was the most common cause of accidental death, murder and manslaughter in the city, topping both traffic-death figures in the state of New York and the numbers of people who died from gunshot wounds in the state of Texas.

Dave sighed, knowing there was probably no immediate resolution. The politicians in their ivory towers were going berserk trying to find an answer to the situation. The mayor's son himself was one of the most recent victims, having been caught in a conflagration when a night club burned to the ground. What the press had not discovered, and what the police had managed to conceal from them, was that the young man's body was found fused with that of a stripper, in what remained of her dressing room. Their genitals were "locked together" as Dave's partner, Danny Spitz, put it, "tighter than a rivet in its hole."

Dave threw the paper aside at his wife's dramatic entrance through the doorway.

Celia Peters staggered into the living room and collapsed in a heap on the floor. Her hat fell off, and rolled over to the sofa, where it stopped. Celia liked hats, even when they were out of fashion. She lifted one leg, kicked, and her shoe went flying in the same direction as the hat. The second shoe hit a lampshade, which wobbled, until Jamie rushed over and steadied it.

Dave Peters stared at his wife's upside-down face.

"Tough morning's shop at the supermarket, huh?"

She sneered at him with her famous Mexican sneer.

"Listen, you cops don't know what tough is. Come with me next Saturday, and I'll show you *real* low-life vermin. They may look like nice women from good homes, but underneath, they're killers. You got to have elbows as sharp as knives to get to the bread, and the fruit counter—forget it . . ."

He laughed and reached down to pull her to her feet.

"I thought you wetbacks were used to that kind of hassle?" he said.

"Wetbacks? Watch it, gringo, my old man's a pistol-packing cop. How was your morning, husband? Pretty rough having to sit in that chair reading the newspaper, while I'm out having a good time."

"Somebody has to stay and look after Jamie. You know," he said as she sat opposite him, "I think that kid's got criminal tendencies . . ."

Jamie smiled at his father, knowing he was being kidded.

". . . he likes to crash trucks."

"Not me," cried Jamie. "I save 'em."

"You set them up, *then* you save them."

"So long as he saves them. Look, hon," said Celia to her husband, "how about a cup of coffee for a lady back from the wars?"

Dave climbed to his feet. "Coming right up, ma'am."

He left the room and went to the kitchen.

Detective Sergeant David Wilson Peters was a tall man, a little too willowy to be called tough. He had a kind of Jimmy Stewart leanness about him, and he tended to stoop slightly when he was talking to someone smaller. It was only when you stared into his eyes, that you realized he could give you trouble, even though you might be several pounds heavier. They were not so much hard, those eyes, as uncompromising. They were the eyes of a man who has his own code of conduct all sorted out, with no woolly edges, and if you were on the right side of the law, you saw in them a man you could trust. If you weren't, you saw that he was the type of cop you could beat to a pulp, and he would still get off the floor and fight like hell.

Celia Peters, on the other hand, was small and feisty, with the eyes of a puppy or a panther, depending on which mood you caught her in. She had seven brothers and three sisters, all small and feisty, who still lived down in Mexico City. Dave had met her while he was on vacation, and they married after three weeks. Her brothers and sisters visited every so often, but, much to Dave's relief, usually one at a time. He liked them, but when they got into a bunch they chattered in their own language, and it nearly drove him out of his head. The time he liked to hear Mexican-Spanish was when he was making love to Celia, and she got so distracted when she climaxed that she slipped into her mother tongue. It amazed him then, and he had to admit, turned him on. He never told her this, because it might make her self-conscious, and stop doing it.

"Here's the coffee," he said, coming back with two cups. "What would you like, Jamie? Lemonade?"

"Coke."

"No Coke," said his mom, "there's too much caffeine in it. Do you want to end up like your mother and father, drinking coffee till it comes out of your ears? Go get some lemonade."

"Aw, Mom."

"Let him have a mix," said Dave. "Half and half."

Celia glared at him, shook her head as if to say "You can't win" and then nodded. Jamie ran from the room to the refrigerator. They heard him clattering with the bottles. Celia didn't like cans of anything, because they were made of aluminum, deposits of which over a lifetime were believed to cause senile dementia. She had all steel pans in the kitchen, plastic toothpaste tubes, and would not use foil for wrapping up the sandwiches. Celia was into alternative therapies, like homeopathy and acupuncture, and against red meat, white bread, sugar, chocolate, and would not have a smoker in the house. She had her vices, though. She drank coffee by the gallon, and she was addicted to late night TV.

Dave sipped his coffee and said, "How about we take in a movie this afternoon?"

"Jamie should get some fresh air."

"Okay, we'll walk to the movies, and take deep-breathing exercises as we go, filling our lungs with all the 'Frisco traffic fumes."

"Funny. Let's go to Golden Gate park first, give him a run, and then to the movies early evening."

"Great idea."

As they left the apartment block, they heard the wail of sirens. Another fire, thought Dave. When was this current spate of arson going to stop? Sure, these things went in cycles, and a downturn always came round eventually, but this had been going on for over six months. And not only in San Francisco, but in other cities in the States too. A year ago arson had been a big problem in European cities: London, Paris, Rome. They still had fires over there, but not nearly as many as American cities were getting. The whole scene seemed to have crossed the Atlantic to the USA.

The trouble with crime of this kind, Dave thought dispassionately, was that it became fashionable. One or two big blazes, and the eyes of all the fire-bugs in the country lit up, and sales of matches and cigarette lighters began to climb. If he had been a gambling man, or had a few dollars to spare, he could have made a fortune on the stock market.

Now all the copycats were out of their dark holes and torching the cities of New York, San Francisco, others. Some of them would be old-time offenders, the kind that liked playing with matches, the sort of people who needed therapy more than they needed jailing. But there would be others. People with hate in their hearts for the whole human race: the sociopaths and psychopaths. People with revenge on their minds, evening up ancient scores with their enemies. People who wanted to collect the insurance on their failing businesses. People who created diversions with fires, while they robbed some other part of the city. The whole thing blossomed like an ugly scarlet bloom, until the fire department was working night and day, losing men to the fumes and flames, getting stretched beyond their capabilities of dealing with calls. And the police too, working over-overtime, pulling in suspects, questioning them, writing out reports, getting the shit thrown at them from the politicians.

The movie was a family comedy with, of course, a happy ending, and Dave came out of the cinema feeling good and warm inside. He had Celia on his arm, and Jamie holding his hand. They were almost skipping along the sidewalk, Celia laughing gaily, and Jamie peeking up at his parents, knowing everything was all right, his face suffused with pleasure.

When they got back to the apartment, Jamie tried to push his luck, and stay up that extra hour, but Celia was having none of it.

"Bed, young man, you've had a good long day. Don't spoil it. Your father will come and read to you in a minute."

Although Jamie could read by himself, he still clung on to the storyteller in his father, who (Dave freely admitted) liked the sound of his own voice. He enjoyed making up the different voices and accents, British, Italian or French, as well as Deep South. At that moment they were halfway through Harper Lee's *To Kill a Mockingbird* which was, on one level, too adult for Jamie, but he could identify with Scout and the other kids in the story, and Dave hoped the racial message was going in subliminally, if not consciously. He had no qualms about indoctrinating his kid with worthwhile values.

Jamie dropped off to sleep half-way through a chapter, and Dave finished it himself, reading silently. Then he put out the light, kissed his son on the cheek, and joined Celia in the living room.

"Hell of a kid you've got there," he said.

She looked up from her own novel.

"Thanks. You too. You want to watch some TV, or what?"

"No," said Dave. "I think I'll get an early night. Danny and me are on a stakeout tomorrow. I may not see you for a couple of days."

Her brow wrinkled and she tucked her feet under her skirts.

"Don't you get relieved?"

"Sure, eventually. You know how it is at the moment, with all these fires. The guys are running every which way, and the manpower . . ."

"Oh, *God*," she muttered.

"No, listen, hon, it'll probably be okay, and I'll get back by Tuesday morning, but I'm just giving you the worst scenario. Two days. That's the worst."

She bumped her head against his arm.

"Damn you, Peters." She smiled, and added, "And don't think I don't know why you're going to bed early. You know I don't like staying up without you."

He put on his best innocent look.

"I don't know what you mean. If you want to come to bed at the same time, that's great, but I'm sure I've got no ulterior motives. Look into my eyes, and tell me what you see. Pure innocence?"

"Ulterior motives," she said.

Actually, Celia went into the bedroom first. She liked to get ready as if she were going straight to sleep, with one of her full-length nightdresses on, and her raven-black hair tied up at the back, knowing that it would only take about five minutes for the nightdress to be decorating a bedpost, and the hair to be flailing loose over the pillows.

They made love gently tonight, without the sense of urgency that sometimes overtook them. Dave found his wife's body a continuous source of wonder. She was so rounded, so soft, he couldn't imagine what kind of delicate business went into the making of a woman. It didn't matter if they went at it hell for leather, until the bed had to be completely remade afterwards, or they took it slowly, looking into each other's eyes, he was filled with spiritual love for her. Sometimes he held her face in his hands as she climaxed, and it was the face of an angel surprised by ecstasy. Sometimes though, she was a demon, using her Spanish to urge him on, telling him *now now now now*, until he nearly went out of his mind with passion, and they finished hot-skinned and breathless, and he would say something like, "Were there any dirty words in there? Were you talking dirty? God, I wish I could speak Spanish." And she would smile one of her mysterious smiles and leave him guessing.

They never asked if it was good for one another, knowing that sometimes it was out of this world, sometimes it was good, sometimes not so good, but it was always worth the effort. Knowing that there would always be a next time, and that each next time would be subtly different from the last, or any other occasion.

When he switched out the light, she curled into a fetal position with her back to him, and he put his right arm around her, hugging her to him, thinking, If anything ever happens to Celia, I'm lost forever.

In another household, Ray Reynolds was having a heart to heart with his wife. She was persuading him to remain on the force for just a while longer, just until they got their mortgage into shape, and some of the furniture paid for.

Ray's wife Clementine had hair of burnished copper: a bouncy woman with a mass of freckles gathering to a dense multitude around the bridge of her retroussé nose. During the day the hair was up in a thick ponytail, but sometimes, in the evening, it was unleashed and spread over her shoulders in a Pre-Raphaelite loveliness that took Ray's breath away.

Between Ray and Clementine, both with obvious Celtic ancestry, their two kids didn't stand a chance. The children were called names like Carrots and Red at school, just as their dad had a nickname at work.

"It's your genes," said Carol, the older of the two, "you gave them to us straight. You could've diluted them a bit, if one of you had married someone else."

"But I love your dad, and he loves me."

"I know," said Carol miserably, "it's too late now."

"When you're older," said Ray, "you'll think it's great. The men will go crazy over you, like I did over your mom."

"Well, one thing," Carol retorted, "I'm not marrying any redhead . . ."

This conversation had been over just an hour before, and the kids were now in bed, and hopefully asleep. Ray had told his wife about the fire early that morning, and had made his bid at leaving the force, but she told him it would put them into too many "difficulties." Then she had another go at him about his drinking, and he told her she couldn't have it both ways. If he stayed on the force, he would keep drinking, because that's what the job did to him.

Clementine retorted, "You're a cliché, Ray. The drinking cop. One day you'll put the barrel of your thirty-eight in your mouth and I'll be a widow."

He was sitting on the floor at her feet, facing the TV, his head on her knees. She had been stroking his hair, but had stopped. Ray sat bolt upright.

He cried, "Don't *say* that."

Clementine's voice softened.

"Ray, I don't want you to hurt yourself. I'm just trying to shock you into a realization. And I don't want you to be unhappy. I love you. The kids love you. The booze will help you toward those things, not me. Six months, Ray. Six more months and we'll be on our feet. Stay away from trouble. Take that desk job you were offered at the station. Never mind if the boys sneer at you for driving a desk. You've got a family to think of. They're not going to bail you out of debt or visit you in the psychiatric ward."

Ray nodded, his head down.

"Yeah, that's what I'll do. I'll take the desk job. Safe."

She hugged his head. "That's my baby."

He sighed. "Yeah, I don't want to see another fire like that one this morning. Jesus, the stench of those burning bodies—"

He stopped, abruptly, remembering something about the time of the fire, about the incident.

"What is it?" Clem asked.

He shook his head.

"I dunno, but this morning, I could've sworn I smelled something . . . what are those nuts you put on the rainbow trout when you grill them?"

"Almonds?"

"Yeah, almonds. I could've sworn I smelled almonds, coming from the doer, the guy that started the fire."

"Maybe it was his aftershave?"

"Who the hell wants to walk around smelling of almonds?"

3

The two cops were parked a street back from Fisherman's Wharf. One was drinking coffee and studying the dashboard while the other was staring intently through the windscreen.

Detective Danny Spitz licked the edge of his plastic coffee cup, a habit that always irritated the hell out of Sergeant Dave Peters.

"Do you have to do that?" he asked, gripping the wheel of the car and shifting his position so that his head wasn't brushing the drooping sunshield. The trouble with police vehicles was that when you put them in for repair or servicing, they never fixed the things you would have done yourself, like a broken sunshield hanging right before your eyes. Any other cop would have snapped the damn thing off, and thrown it in the trunk, but Dave was not any other cop. He was an angel compared to most of them. Wrong was wrong. You didn't take graft, free meals or damage public property. A police car was public property.

"What? Do what?" cried Danny, knowing exactly what was

getting under Dave's skin. When you got a coffee from the machine, it always left a film of raw powder round the rim, and Danny liked to lick it off.

Dave ignored him, and went back to studying the character standing in the doorway of the amusement hall. Alternately picking his teeth with a matchstick, and performing surgical operations on his auricle region with the same blunt instrument, the guy was obviously undeterred from this activity by the bitter taste of ear wax.

Dave let his gaze wander from the revolting character to some still-smoking ruins two blocks down the street. Seven shops and eighty-one apartments had gone up in that particular conflagration. It never ceased to amaze Dave that a single match-head flame could cause so much damage, so much loss of life. All over the city there were charred gaps in the landscape, often visible in a place like San Francisco with its several heights. Some of these gaps were huge, some just single buildings. Not that they were all started by matches. Gasoline bombs, incendiary devices, oil fires—every inflammable substance known to man, it seemed, had been used at some time or another.

San Francisco residents were particularly chary of fire: in 1906 the three-day fire that raged following the earthquake had all but destroyed the entire city. Only dynamite had saved them from complete annihilation. Explosives had been used recently, to blow fire-breaks between the closely knit buildings. The fire a few weeks back in Noe Valley had needed a few pounds of plastic explosive to prevent its further spread. Residents do not take kindly to having their perfectly sound homes blown to matchwood and lawsuits were falling like confetti on the heads of the city fathers.

Danny Spitz suddenly growled like a terrier, bit a chunk out of his plastic cup with a *crunch,* spat it out the window, and looked defiantly at his partner. Dave continued to ignore him, knowing Danny was bored, was trying to get some sort of response. Danny was like a child in many ways, though he would turn twenty-eight come July. Unlike a child, he was prematurely bald on the crown of his head, and this coupled with his rounded features, gave him a monkish appearance. The boys at the station called him Friar Tuck, but never to his face because he had the temper of a witch crossed in love. Some cops were given two nicknames: one which was used openly, and another which was used when they weren't around. The open and generic name for Danny and Dave as a team was "the D&D." Under the counter they were Friar Tuck and Mother Teresa.

The guy they were watching, whose name was Caspar Greenaway, a bearded white Caucasian in a leather raincoat and jeans, suddenly straightened up. He almost came to attention in his worn Nikes as a Ford drew up to the sidewalk. Greenaway flicked away his match and leaned forward. Words were exchanged, and a furtive movement took place.

"That's it," said Danny, "he's taken the stuff. Let's go get the bastard. You take the pusher in the car, I'll get Greeny."

"Right," growled Dave. He gunned the engine, skidding the car across the street, to stop at an angle in front of the big Ford. Both cops leapt out, and immediately Greenaway took off down the street, heading south. Danny went after him while Dave went to the car window, hand on his gun which he had not yet drawn.

"Can I see your driver's license, please, sir?"

"Fuck you," cried the driver, a black youth.

The young man started to reverse the Ford, and went straight into another car which was coming to rest at the curb behind him. He panicked, fumbling with the gears, and the Ford shot forward ramming the police car. It leapt back again, then forward, crunching each time. Dave drew his police special and flipped his badge in front of the Ford's windscreen.

"All right," he yelled, "that's enough. Now unless you can drive this sucker sideways, you'd better step out nice and slow, hands where I can see them, Petey."

The youth got out of the car with his hands in full view, crying, "Who th'hell gave you th'idea you can call me by ma fust name? Only my momma calls me Petey, not some asshole cop."

Dave shoved him against the wall of the amusement hall and kicked his heels back.

"This asshole cop will call you what he likes, when he likes, until you stop peddling dope and become a useful citizen, Petey my boy. Then he'll call you sir and mister if you like, but you have to *earn* respect, you little creep."

Danny had arrived back, with Greenaway in tow.

"Don't struggle or I'll crack you one," said Danny, breathlessly, his hand gripping Greenaway's collar.

"Okay," said Dave to the two men, "you have the right to remain silent—"

"Bullshit," interrupted Greenaway. "Big bust. A coupla ounces. Why ain't you two out chasing fire-starters? They're the bad guys now. You should be ashamed of yourselves, busting us while people are getting burned to death . . ."

After the pair were handcuffed and shoved into the police car, Dave had to deal with the irate driver of the vehicle that had parked behind Petey Jakes. The man was screaming about compensation, suing the police department, and personally kicking Petey up and down a football stadium. It took ten minutes to calm him down.

They took their suspects to the station and booked them, first making sure that the Marlboro pack that had changed hands contained crack, and not cigarettes. They had made that mistake before, and come away with their tails between their legs. The damage to their own vehicle was another depression in the front fender, which already had so many craters it could have doubled for the topography of the moon.

Greenaway's accusation turned out to be prophetic. Danny and Dave were summoned before the Captain to learn that they had been put on fire-chasing patrol.

"The whole issue is getting out of hand," said Captain Reece. "Three more fires this morning. We're pulling them in, but we can't keep up with them. Look at that one there . . ."

The two men turned to see a woman sitting by a detective's desk. She was tall and willowy, with long, straggly, mousy-blonde hair and large glasses. She had that faded look of a garment that has been put through a washing machine too many times. Dave sensed she had been through some pretty harrowing experiences.

"What is she, a librarian or something?" asked Danny, obviously having come to his own conclusions.

"She set light to her boyfriend's apartment," replied Reeves. "Nobody was hurt, but that was just lucky. She looks like a quiet one, doesn't she?"

"They're the worst," said Danny, unnecessarily.

The Captain shook his head slowly.

"I don't understand these people, I really don't. That woman's got everything going for her. She's not a bad looker, if she straightened her back a bit and wore some decent clothes. She's got a degree in theology, lectures at the university when she's not starting fires."

Dave coughed and said, "Maybe she likes the clothes she wears. Maybe that's why she wears them."

The Captain looked at him closely, his brow knitted in puzzlement.

"What?"

"You said, 'If she wore some decent clothes.' They look okay to me."

Reece shook his head wonderingly.

"Sometimes, Peters, you amaze me. What the hell have her clothes got to do with the fact that she's an arsonist?"

Dave shrugged. "That's what I was thinking, but you brought it up, not me."

Reece stared at him, stone-faced, for a long while, until even

Danny began to get uncomfortable. The Captain and Dave Peters were so far apart in thinking, they might have been Neanderthal and Cro-magnon man, meeting on a bridge in time.

"Okay," grunted Reece at last, "let's get down to business. I was just trying to show you what we were dealing with here—not street-wise punks, or mobsters, but ladies with degrees in theology. We've also picked up a banker, a housewife and a kid of thirteen. Fire seems to fascinate across the spectrum. It's got to stop. The city is going up in flames and the mayor with it. I'll be surprised if he doesn't spontaneously combust before the month's out. You two get out there and stop it happening, hear me?"

"We hear you," said Danny, eager to get out of the office. "Come on, Dave, let's to it."

Dave was thinking that the arson attacks were increasing in frequency. Earlier, Reece had dumped some computer stats on his desk, which read like a horror story.

In 1980 there had been fifteen fires per thousand people in the USA, at a cost per fire of $2,000. That was approximately 3,000,000 fires at a total cost of $6 billion. The USA led the table for fires in that year, but not for costs. Though in West Germany there were only two fires per thousand head of population, West German fires cost their country $14,000 each: seven times as much as U.S. fires. America had many more small fires than somewhere like Germany, whose fires were big and expensive.

In 1990 the situation in the U.S. had not changed a great deal, with 3,200,000 fires, though the costs had risen with inflation. Fires, like shoes, do not go down in price, but keep pace with the rising cost of living.

But since the date of the first reported "white fire," in 1996, the annual fire rate had leapt to an incredible 21,000,000, at a total crippling cost of $102 billion, the higher sum reflecting the inflation rate, but also how stretched were the fire departments. Hidden in there somewhere were also the higher costs of buildings and goods going up in smoke: such as newly built Japanese department stores full of overpriced articles.

Presumably in giving Dave the data, Reece was trying to tell the D&D something: like, *catch the doers.*

It was as if a fire fever had gripped the public, and that everyone who had a grievance of any kind, sought to bring notice to that complaint by setting fire to something. Never before in the city had there been so many fires in so short a time. It appeared to be a disease which had reached epidemic proportions and in whose grip the city was powerless. There was indeed speculation among the medical profession that perhaps a virus was responsible: a biological newcomer that attacked a certain area of the brain and caused the victim to act on a previously latent urge to torch the environment, a fascination with a primal force.

A group of psychiatrists had proposed the alternative idea that it was not improbable that somewhere in the minds of modern men there were secret forbidden desires, inherited from prehistoric ancestors, which were being unlocked by the pressures and stress of contemporaneous society. These learned gentlemen pointed out that the captivation with fire was deeply embedded in the brain, and that throughout history people had worshiped fire as a source of mystery. Emperors had started conflagrations in their own backyards, conquerors had razed enemy cities to the ground, warriors had set forests and vast areas of grassland alight, kings and commoners had burned people at the stake, from martyrs to witches. In England they still celebrated the foiling of a seventeenth-century gunpowder plot to blow up Parliament, by burning effigies of a political criminal named Guy Fawkes (an explosives doer) on thousands of bonfires throughout the land.

These theories apart, it was certain that more people were

indulging in the childlike games of starting fires, some of which got out of control by accident, and others which were deliberately intended to destroy life and property. The fire-starters were of all ages, ranging from infants to geriatrics. They lit their matches and lighters and set fire to anything, even to their own houses.

That evening, as Dave was driving home, he heard a bulletin on his car radio. A large new Japanese department store had erupted in flame that afternoon. There were still people trapped inside, but the fire department said there was little hope they were still alive. A spokesman was being interviewed.

"The fumes from stuff like plastic furniture . . . hell, they don't stand a chance. I sent men in there, but you can't see a thing. Lost one man already . . ."

The loss of life was sickening, and Dave turned off the radio, rather than hear any more. What he really needed, he decided, was a long vacation. If he and Celia, and Jamie, of course, could get away somewhere—but it was impossible at the moment. Maybe in the summer. They could go to Alaska. Most of the time Celia wanted to visit her folks in Mexico, but it was time to start branching out.

When he got back to the apartment, he found that Celia and Jamie were out somewhere, so he made himself a sandwich and switched on the TV. She was probably visiting her best friend Susan, on the other side of the park, and wouldn't be back until about seven. He sometimes enjoyed a quiet half-hour, when he got in from work, without having to talk about his day and listen to Celia tell him about hers. He enjoyed that well enough, later, but he needed wind-down time first, and that wasn't always possible. She was usually a little too eager, and Jamie would want to show him things too. Work he had done at school.

Dave settled down in front of a sitcom, prepared to put up with the canned laughter, letting the inane jokes wash over him.

Then the news came on, and he was shown a raging inferno: the store that had been fired earlier in the day. It was grisly. There were smoking bodies on the sidewalk. Others had tried to jump, from too high up, and had hit the sidewalk like dummies, crumpling sickeningly on impact. One man was shown leaping out of a tenth-story window. Trying to run in mid-air, his legs bicycling on nothingness, his face revealed his terror, until he whacked into the concrete and ended his terrible fall.

Dave picked up the phone and dialed Danny's number. When Danny answered, Dave said, "Have you seen the news?"

"Yeah," said Danny. "Look what Reece's gotten us into."

"I don't wanna do this, I really don't. There's too much pain in it."

Danny said, "What about me? I'm Catholic."

Dave, who was a nothing, though married to a Catholic, said, "What's that got to do with anything?"

"Hell's fire and all that. It scares the shit out of me. It gives me a taste of what's coming after I wave farewell to the flesh."

"Come on, Danny, you go to confession at least three times a week."

There was a long pause at the other end, then Danny said, "Sure, but you know, I think I'm going to get it on the job one day, and I sin every morning. I'm a morning man, Dave. My dates are usually too drunk to do it when we get back to my place, so we do it in the morning. Chances are, I'll get it during the day, before I can get to confession in the evening, and I know I'll get it in the heart or head, so there won't be time for the last rites."

"You've got too much imagination," said Dave, getting confused between which was sex and which was death, since Danny would not mention either, but used *it* for both. Maybe he didn't know the difference himself. Maybe he thought they were one and the same thing.

"I knew you wouldn't understand," said Danny accusingly.

"That's the trouble with having an atheist for a partner." He sounded hurt, so Dave soothed him with some comforting words, sounding like a priest himself, then rang off.

He went into the kitchen and made himself a coffee, glancing at the clock and thinking that his family was a little late in getting home. Perhaps Celia had decided to go on to her art class, leaving Jamie with Susan?

He picked up the phone and rang Susan. Her husband Bill, an advertising executive, answered.

"Hello?"

The voice was cautious. You didn't give away your name or your number until you received a positive identification from the other end.

"Dave Peters, Bill—is Celia there?"

"Just a minute, Dave."

There was some shouting in the background, then Bill came on the phone again.

"Susan said they left each other at eleven this morning. Celia was going shopping, or something. Susan had to get back to pick up Angela. Anything wrong?"

Angela was Bill and Susan's three-year-old.

"Naw, shouldn't think so," said Dave, his heart pattering none the less. "She probably got caught up somewhere. See you, Bill."

"Yeah, take care of yourself."

Dave wandered back into the kitchen, wondering what he should do. He did not want to go chasing around in the car: he had panicked before when Celia had not been home. That time she had been at the hairdresser's, and he had missed her note on the fridge door. He went now to look in the same place, and saw the note attached by the little Mickey Mouse magnet. He gave a sigh of relief.

"Must be blind," he muttered, wondering why he hadn't noticed it before, but he had not needed to go to the fridge, either for his honey sandwich or his coffee, which he took without milk.

He opened the note.

Darling, it read, *I'll probably be home before you, but in case I'm not, don't touch the chocolate cake. It's for tonight. Love, love, love—Celia.*

P.S. Can the bank buy me a new dress? That new store, Mitsumaki, is having a sale.

An alarm sounded in his head. He tried to get a grip on his emotions. He told himself to think logically.

"They didn't go there," he said aloud. "They didn't go there, because she asked me about the bank. She's going tomorrow, or some time. She definitely says, 'Can the bank stand me a new dress?' " She wants to know *before* she goes to buy it." He stared around the kitchen, wildly, his eyes resting on the clock.

7:10.

"Come home, Celia," he whispered. "Come home now."

4

Danny Spitz patronized three different churches, visiting each once a week. He was too ashamed to use just one, since he had sins to confess every other day that never varied. Even so, each of the priests despaired of him, though individually they believed Danny was confessing only to them, and were unaware that he spread his confessions around, sharing them among the clergy.

Danny knew he was going to hell, but he couldn't help it. He was drawn, though, to give him his due, *resistibly*, toward casual sex. Neither fear of the priests, nor fear of hell, nor fear of death through the most dreaded of social diseases could prevent him from going to what he believed was eternal damnation. He was a lost man.

Danny: "Forgive me Father, for I have sinned."

Priest: "Again? Is it a different sin from the last several times?"

Danny: "No, Father, it's the same sin."

Priest *(despairingly):* "Daniel, Daniel, when are you going to get married?"

Danny: "Nobody wants me, Father. I'm—I'm—I look like some kind of monk. The boys all call me Friar Tuck. It's this premature baldness, and I look porky, only . . . look, Father, I can't help it if the Lord made me oversexed."

Priest: "If he did, which I doubt, it's up to you to be strong enough to resist temptation. Don't you think a lot of men would like variety? They don't succumb, Daniel."

Danny (*wondering if the priest meant himself*): "I know I'm weak, Father. I'm truly repentant."

Priest (*firmly*): "We all are, the morning after. What we have to do is stop ourselves before it happens."

Danny: "I'm sorry."

Priest: "If you don't think well of yourself, how can you expect a woman to respect and admire, even *love* you? Daniel, you're basically a good man. Why don't you try asking one of them? Perhaps they'll surprise you."

Danny: "I don't really know any girls. Is this a confession, or what, Father? I can get therapy from the police psychoanalyst."

Priest: "I'm trying to help you. Penance doesn't seem to be doing it. If you don't know any girls, where do you find your— the women who sin with you?"

Danny: "They wouldn't make good wives, Father, they're hookers. I told you that. They don't do it for nothing. I'd have to *pay* one of them to marry me."

Priest: "They're still women, Danny, and a hooker would be better than this weekly debauchery. All right, what shall we give you . . . ?"

A conversation similar to this one went on every other day or so, and drained Danny of any spiritual energy. Sometimes he went straight from confession to a bar, where he knew that after a couple of drinks, he would pick up a bargirl or hooker, take her home, and sin the pants off her. This was one of those nights.

Once he had finished four double bourbons in a row, he felt warm and glowing, and the recent confession was a dim memory, way back in his past. When he began to feel pleased with himself, he was in his most dangerous mood. It meant the drink had given him the self-confidence to approach a woman.

"Have I had enough?" he asked the bartender, turning his glass upside down.

"You've had four doubles, that's one over enough."

"Thanks, Frank, I can always count on you to be honest. Are all barmen as honest as you?"

"Only with cops."

Danny giggled.

"Hey, hey, Frank. Not in here. Some hooker might be listening in, and then where will my comfort come from tonight? Who would go to bed with a cop?"

"You don't look like a cop, you look like a—'

"Yeah, yeah, we all know what I look like. That's what turns 'em on, Frank. They like jumping in the sack with a holy man. Gives 'em a thrill."

Over by the juke box, a frizzy-haired blonde was talking to a small man with a button nose and horn-rimmed glasses. She looked up from her conversation and smiled. Danny smiled back, then climbed down from his stool. He lurched over to their table and said, "Mister, I hope you're not going to bed with this hooker, because I'm just about to bust her."

He flashed his badge, letting his jacket fall open to reveal his gun.

"This is my wife," cried the little guy, a bit too quickly.

"Yeah," said the woman, "the creep's my old man." She drew on her cigarette and smiled. "You want something, Danny?"

"I was just wondering."

"Okay, give me a minute to powder my nose, willya?"

The little man stared from one to the other of them. It took him a couple of minutes to realize he had been ousted. When it finally clicked, he looked aggrieved.

"What about me?" he asked her, as she stood up and walked toward the ladies' room.

"Tomorrow, Benny. Anyway, you can't afford it tonight. I know when pay day comes—once a month—which is about as often as you do. Once a month, Benny. Just after my period."

She turned in the doorway, bumping the door open with her backside, and gave him a false grin.

Danny swayed over the table, looking down at the guy. He thought he saw something in the man's eyes: a relief at having been let off the hook. Maybe he was suffering from the same sort of compulsion as Danny? Went through the same torment every time? Maybe the little guy was actually grateful that he did not have to go to bed with Rita tonight? Danny decided he would like to talk to a soulmate. They might be able to help each other: a kind of Sex Anonymous.

"Hey," Danny said after a moment, "you a Catholic? How do you handle it?"

The guy blinked rapidly.

"Where do you get off, mister? I ain't a Catholic, I ain't a cop, and I wanted Rita tonight. You cops think you can push everyone around?"

Danny was disappointed. It was no good talking to a Protestant. They didn't suffer the same guilt pangs as a Catholic. The Protestant God was a little more forgiving, more tolerant. He let you do more or less as you pleased, so long as you didn't kill anyone or bed another man's wife. Protestant hell had a few more creature comforts than Catholic hell. You probably got TV, bedside lamps, curtains and a long exercise period while they stoked up the coals.

The little man broke the silence, which he thought he had engineered by standing up to Danny.

"You can't push everyone around," he said emphatically.

Danny came to life again.

"Nope, just little guys like you. Aw, come on, I ain't gonna hurt her. You can go with her tomorrow night, after you've been paid." A dark thought came to him, and he frowned as he realized they pretty much shared Rita between them.

He said, "There's nothing wrong with you, is there? You use a condom?"

"Mind your own business," said Benny, finishing his drink.

Rita came out of the toilets. This time her smile was genuine.

"C'mon, fuzz-man. Let's go."

"Does he use a condom?" asked Danny, as she hooked her arm through his and led him toward the door.

"Who, Frank? How the hell would I know?"

"No, not Frank, that guy, Benny whatsisname. You go with him sometimes. Do you make him use a—"

"Danny boy, you know I *always* insist on it. A girl can't be too careful these days. Who the hell wants to die?"

He felt a little happier.

"Okay, then. You want to come to my place for the night?"

"Danny, you don't like it in the car, you don't like it at the hotel, you don't like it at my place, so where else would we do it? Anyway, I like your apartment, baby. It's nice."

"If I make you breakfast in bed, do I get a discount?"

"No discounts. I got to live, honey. I need the rent. What you get is a freebee special, you know what I mean?" and she gave his arm a squeeze.

"Oh, yeah," he said, sobering a little. "I like that, don't I?"

"You sure do, honey."

Back at the apartment, Danny made himself one more small drink, gave one to Rita, then the pair of them went into the bedroom. He undressed himself, because something in him disliked the idea of someone taking off his clothes. It wasn't that he didn't find it sensual, but he hated hands fiddling with his tie and shirt buttons. When Danny undressed he took the lot off in one go. He undid two shirt buttons, loosened his tie, and then peeled off his shirt, undershirt, tie and sweater, all in one movement. Next he levered off each shoe with the opposite foot, without untying the laces, unzipped his pants, and off came slacks, shorts and socks. All that was left was his gunbelt, which he kept around his waist because Rita always said it turned her on.

Rita peeled off her own clothes, one at a time, taking it slowly for his benefit. She left her bra on until she was between the sheets, because she had a thing about sagging breasts, but Danny never mentioned it because he was basically a kind man and he knew she would be hurt.

There was a warm softness, a puppy-fat pudginess to Rita that Danny liked. She always smelled good too, of talcum powder and cheap scent admittedly, but even inexpensive eau de cologne smelled good after the precinct house locker room, where he had had his shower.

"Oh, *ramrod*," she said, feeling him under the sheets, and his penis went as hard as a chisel in her rough-skinned hand as she deftly rolled a condom on it.

"The priest says I got to get married," he told her.

"What?" There was a long silence, then, "Danny," she said throatily, "you ain't asking *me*, are you? Wait till we've finished, then see if you like asking. That's your sex drive talking, not you."

"Would you say yes, if I asked you? Afterward?"

"Danny, I don't want to hurt your feelings, honey, but I been married twice before, and it didn't work. I loved the guys when I married 'em, and I hated 'em within a month. It just ain't right for me. You, I like you, despite you being a cop. You're a nice guy. Don't ask me, I might say yes, and I don't want to end up hating you, Danny. You pay most of my rent."

He laughed.

"You're all right, Rita."

"Yeah, sure, heart of gold. Now are you going to jab me in the stomach with that all night, or put it somewhere more useful?"

His hand went down beneath her soft rounded belly, and found the hair beneath. It felt moist. This surprised him.

"Hey, is that my gun belt doing that to you?"

She smiled.

"Naw, it's all this soft talk you're giving me. Kind of takes me back to when I used to do it for nothing—the good old days, when I really liked it, and didn't have to fake it. I'm enjoying it tonight, Danny, really I am."

"No shit?"

"Put it in me now, Danny, before I start breathing hard, and really lose my professionalism."

When they had finished, he kept his arms around her, and went into a doze. He was dreaming that Rita was standing in a doorway, with hot-pants on, and calling to him. But instead of saying, "Hey, big boy, you with the muscles, wanna show a girl a good time?" she was cooing, "You look like a nice man. You have an intelligent face. I like sensitivity in a guy . . ."

Danny was suddenly wide awake, aware of someone sitting on the side of his bed. He could hear breathing, feel the depression on the edge of the mattress. Rita was snoring gently, still in his arms.

He began to sweat, the terror gripping his stomach, giving him the cramps. This had been an imagined nightmare for many years: the ex-con come to exact his revenge from the cop who put him away. It happened. Not often, but it happened. Charlie Bateman had been chopped up with an axe in his bed by an escaped con with a grudge. *God*, he thought, *I'll never sin again. Just help me this time. I promise. I don't want to die, not like this.*

For a long time he just lay there, rigid, unmoving, every muscle in his body aching with the tension. At any second he expected hands around his throat, or the cold ring of a gun muzzle on his temple. Who had threatened him in recent years? John Smithson? Tacket Rudermann? Oh, God, oh, *God*, not Jimmy, the fucking ice pick maniac? Not him, please, God.

The figure on the bed remained motionless.

Danny eased his right arm from underneath Rita, and gradually slid his hand toward his gun, blessing the woman beside him for being turned on by a naked cop wearing a police special. His hand was shaking, as it found the holster and his fingers inched up it like a spider. He wondered if he were still asleep, and in the middle of some nightmare. Maybe this *was* punishment for sinning, long overdue?

He found the butt, his hand slippery with perspiration. When he had the weapon firmly in his grasp, he pointed it up through the sheet and blankets, toward the dark shape that was evident now that his eyes had got used to the lack of light. Through his fear came some elation. At least he would take the shit with him, if he had to go.

"Don't move you bastard, or I'll blow your fucking head off, I swear," Danny growled.

Rita stirred, and said, "Wha— . . . ?"

Danny pulled his other hand from underneath her and fumbled for the sidelight. There was a sobbing sound, coming from the dark shape now, and Danny's heart flipped. What the fuck was going on here?

"I swear I'll pull the goddamn trigger," he cried. Then his fingers found the switch and the room lit up.

Looking down on him, face ravaged and stricken, was Dave. Danny was shocked by his partner's appearance. He was gray and ugly, and his features looked as if someone had stamped all over them. There was a lump on his head, and bruises around the cheeks.

Dave and Danny had keys to each other's apartments, just in case anyone ever came after one of them. There was a telephone code they had worked out, so that the one on the outside would know what was going on, and could get in and rescue the other. It had never happened, but Dave always said that they could afford to be paranoid.

Rita was awake now, staring at Dave, saying nothing.

Danny said, "What in the Jesus has happened, Dave? Somebody get to you?"

Dave fell forward, sobbing violently, into Danny's arms.

"She's dead, Danny. They killed her. My baby boy. They killed them both. My God, I can't stand it."

His body jerked with the sobs, and Danny rocked him, holding him, strange feelings going through him. Had *they* broken into Dave's apartment? Who? An ex-con? Burglars?

"I'll make some coffee," whispered Rita. "You find out what this is all about."

"It's my partner," Danny explained.

She slipped out of bed and took Danny's robe, which hung on a hook behind the bedroom door. Then she was out of the room, and padding down the hall in her bare feet. A moment later Danny heard the clatter of cups. Dave was still crying, making noises like words, but no sense. He let him weep, hugging him and rocking the man like a baby.

"Is it Celia?" he finally asked. "And Jamie?"

"Yes." Dave pulled away now, sitting up, staring into the middle of the room, as if there were something significant there.

A lump formed in Danny's throat. God, not Dave's family. Jesus, the guy *lived* for his family.

Dave suddenly stood and walked to the window.

"That fire at the Japanese store? Celia was there, with Jamie. Shopping for a dress. I had to go to the morgue and identify the contents of her purse. There was stuff that didn't get burned."

Danny leaned forward, his head in his hands.

"Oh, my God, Dave. I'm so sorry."

"It's just that . . . I can't believe she's gone, you know. I've been sitting at home, thinking, any minute now I'll hear the key in the lock, and there she'll be, saying, sorry I'm so late, darling, I called in to see someone . . . God, I don't know. I think I'm going crazy. I can't—how the hell can I go on, Danny? I love her. I love my boy. Both of them gone, just like that. Why *both* of them, Danny? Not Celia, for Christ's sake, she never hurt anyone. Why did they do this to me? Why?"

He turned and banged his face savagely against the wall and Danny suddenly realized where the lumps and bruises had come from. He got out of bed and pulled on his shorts and slacks, then took Dave by the arm.

"They didn't do it to get at you, Dave. It was an accident, the fact that she was there. Come and have a cup of coffee, or a drink. Look, Rita's made some coffee. Come on, man, let's talk. We got to talk this out."

He led him into the living room, where Rita was sitting on the sofa smoking a cigarette. She looked up, questioningly, as they entered the room.

Danny said, "His wife and kid . . ."

She bit her lip and nodded.

Dave was sobbing again, and Danny left him in Rita's arms while he made two stiff drinks. He was beginning to wish it had been an ex-con on his bed. It would have been easier to handle than this.

It's gonna be a long night, he thought to himself, *and a long lifetime afterward.*

When he came back with the drinks, Dave was sitting up again, not looking like Dave at all: his face had lost control of its muscles and gone slack. There were pouches under the eyes and his cheeks hung like those of an old man. His color was sickly gray.

"Here, drink this, partner," he said. "This shouldn't have happened to you. There's no justice. God, I never seen you look like this before, Dave. You look so bad. I wish I could do something."

He was talking, just talking.

Dave ignored the hand with the Scotch, wrapped his arms around himself and began rocking backward and forward. Danny put his own arms around his friend as though he were a small distressed child. The two of them rocked together while Rita looked on, a helpless expression on her face, obviously embarrassed to be witnessing such raw emotion from two men. She wasn't paid to do this kind of thing. She wasn't a doctor, she was a whore, and though she was used to soothing away hurts, the wounds were never as deep and as savage as this. This stuff was too heavy for a hooker.

After a while, Danny began to feel self-conscious, and was aware that Dave smelled of stale sweat and his breath was sour. When he let his friend go, however, and stood up, he felt more self-conscious than ever.

Dave came out of his trance.

"Why Celia?" he said. "Why not some useless bitch out on the street?"

Rita moved away from him, sharply. Dave looked across at her and suddenly became very rational, realizing what he was saying, and seeing the hurt in her eyes.

"Oh, no . . . I'm sorry, I didn't mean that. I don't know what I'm saying . . ."

"It's okay," she said. "I understand. You lost your wife. That's tough."

"And there's my kid too, don't forget my kid. I was playing with Jamie only—God when was it?—yesterday, today? I don't know what the time is. What's the time, Danny? Celia and me, we congratulated each other on what a great kid he is, the center of my life you know, and I didn't even mind him waking me up off night shift. I'd have killed for that kid. He's gone and he hadn't even really started living, so fresh and shiny, and excited by things . . ."

Danny couldn't think of anything to say.

"It's a nightmare, Danny," Dave went on. "There was nothing left of her, just a black burned thing like some voodoo doll or something. You're a religious man, Danny, you got to give me something . . ."

"Only her body has gone, Dave. Her soul is with God. You got to cling on to that, because it's true. Celia hasn't gone, not forever. She and Jamie are waiting somewhere, and you'll all be together again some day, that's a fact. I wouldn't give you any shit, you know that, Dave, you're my partner. I believe in this. Celia had a beautiful spirit, and it's still there, and she's only sad because of you, Dave. You're the only thing that's making her sad, because Jamie's with her, and they're both happy. That's why you got to snap out of it and start to pull yourself together, you understand what I'm saying?"

Danny said what he said with real conviction, because he actually believed it. Dave's face became more composed and Danny saw his friend begin to relax. Rita came out of the bedroom, fully dressed, carrying a sleeping bag.

Dave said quietly, "Thanks, Danny," and to Rita, "I'm sorry, I don't know . . ."

"It's okay," she said, "but I'm going now. I'll see you later, Danny. Take care of yourself. You too, Dave."

Even before she had gone Dave was slumped over the sofa, in a fitful sleep, the sleeping bag draped over him. Danny said goodbye and locked the door behind her.

5

Malloch, like all his kind, was a chameleon. His physical appearance mirrored those of the human beings around him, and fooled everyone but his own kind. Being vain, Malloch and his compatriots were all beautiful creatures, in their mortal form.

Malloch knew he was being pursued along Turk Street after running the switchback Leavenworth Road all the way from Russian Hill, and he knew who was after him.

Malloch had once had great powers, but here on earth they were mostly gone from him. The only advantages he had over a mortal were a preternatural strength and self-healing powers which would ensure immortality. His flesh, bone and even brain tissue could heal itself within seconds. Provided his whole body did not undergo some basic thorough molecular change, such as being subjected to great pressure or heat, he was safe from death.

Against his enemy and the devastating weapon he carried, Malloch had no defense except to hide himself among the millions of humans and hope that he could remain undetected.

He came to a restaurant with a few people at the tables and went to go inside. The doorman stepped forward, placed a hand on his shirtfront.

"I'm sorry, sir. You can't go in without a tie. If you would step over to the hat check . . . ?"

Malloch took the man by his throat and squeezed. The doorman fell choking and spluttering to the sidewalk, and Malloch stepped over him, to walk across the restaurant, through the kitchens, and out the back exit.

There was a fence behind the restaurant, over which Malloch climbed, anxious to find some place where there were many mortals among whom he could hide. In an empty place, his enemy could detect him immediately, but the more people around him, the more his differences were less apparent. He gave off a radiance of evil that on its own was like a beacon in the night. Mortals had evil in their souls, some more than others. Their emissions were small compared to his, but with enough of them around him Malloch's dark radiance could be swamped sufficiently to confuse his hunter. This method of camouflage was especially effective in a place where the mortals were engaged in evil acts, or where the corrupt and depraved might gather together.

His second line of defense was to move quickly, from one place to another, so that his enemy could not home in at all on the signals he sought.

There was much fear in Malloch's empty breast, and this terror filled the shell of his earthly form. On the spiritual battle plains he had been a great warrior, a destroyer, a force of mighty power. Here on earth all that power had been taken from him, and he had been forced to take on a shape that would allow him to mingle with the detestable mortals.

Fear had been his undoing. He had run, deserted his leader, and along with others had scattered for regions where they could hide. They were legion, but their numbers were being cut with every breath. There was no safe place to hide in his own time and space. That left only one place to go: the world of the mortals.

A single enemy soldier, without higher authority, had taken it upon itself to follow them to earth. This soldier was of high rank, indeed from the First Triad, but had not distinguished itself enough in battle to earn itself a personal name. Now it had found itself a purpose and seemed determined to root out every last one of the enemy deserters from the universe. There was no compromise in this creature, no forgiveness, no mercy. It was not that it hated Malloch and his kind: it had simply set a task.

Malloch found a nightclub in the backstreets, a sleazy joint where the strippers were overflowing their skimpy panties, and the main business was conducted in the dirty toilet at the back. It was a place which dispensed illegal sex and killer drugs; where mobsters met to work out deals; where crooked cops negotiated with gangsters; where murder contracts were made; where death was dispensed like medicine.

Inside, Malloch took a table in the shadow of the stage and waited in fear.

Malloch sensed his enemy out in the street, striding purposefully along the sidewalk. When this terrible creature reached the door of the nightclub, it paused for a few moments. Malloch's heart stopped, while his enemy stood examining the atmosphere inside the club, searching for something with its feelings. If it suspected Malloch was in there the creature would probably burn the whole nightclub to the ground with white fire, occupants and all.

Malloch knew that his enemy would receive a blanket radiance of evil from the nightclub, full of pimps, thugs, robbers, murderers, and the unfiltered sludge of mankind. In one corner of the room, hidden by a tablecloth, a whore was playing with a john. Out at the back, in the toilets, drugs were being exchanged for money. In the alley beyond the toilets a drunken businessman was being kicked savagely in the head and relieved of his watch and wallet. The whole area was swamped with crimes and criminals.

Finally, the creature outside moved on, and Malloch heaved a sigh of relief.

Malloch even managed to smile as a girl came to his table.

"Want some company, baby?" she said.

Malloch nodded, "Why not?"

He bought her and himself a drink and began to relax.

Her hand went down to his thigh. She was small, dark and pretty, and Malloch was immediately interested in what she had to offer, being capable of enjoying her physically. Had he been his enemy he would have been asexual in mortal form, but as a creature from the opposite side he was better equipped than most men.

The girl's eyes widened as she found what she was looking for. "Wow," she breathed. "Big."

He moved her hand back to her own lap. Malloch was no exhibitionist.

She pouted and said, "Aw, don't you like me, honey?"

"You're okay, but not here. I've got somebody after me, and I don't want to be caught with my pants down, if you see what I mean."

"Sure." She looked around the room nervously. "Who's out to get you? The cops or the mob?"

"Neither. This is just one guy, but he's worse than both. Don't worry about it, he's gone by."

"Gone where?"

"Away, down the street."

"Oh. It's just that I can't handle any violent shit. My boyfriend beats me up if I get any bruises."

"That sounds logical," said Malloch.

She nodded, missing the point entirely.

"Listen," she said wistfully, "you sure you don't wanna get it on? You're awful pretty."

Malloch smiled.

"I know I am, but we'd have to go someplace else." His lust was beginning to fade. She was not *that* attractive to him and the streets were still a source of danger.

"Okay, but if we're gonna get it on it's gotta be soon, or my boyfriend will be over here and there'll be trouble, 'cause, you know, I'm a working girl."

Malloch followed her eyes across the room and saw a pimp looking at them. There was no malice in the man's face at the moment, but Malloch knew that if he did not go out the back with the girl soon, the pimp would saunter across and ask her what the fuck she was doin', sitting there having a good time while there were other johns just scratching their balls. The pimp was around six feet two of hard-looking muscle, and no doubt he liked using his fists, especially on his whore.

The girl plucked at the sleeve of his jacket.

"You're awful pretty," she said again. "Most of the johns I get ain't gentlemen like you—they're ugly fuckheads with bulging guts and three chins, an' they grab at you like you was meat or somethin'." She smiled.

"I know."

"Sure, so let me know when you're ready to leave. Thanks for the drink. I gotta work till then." She paused and looked into his eyes. "You know, decent men like you shouldn't come into places like this, you might get hurt. There's some bad guys in here, would stick you with a knife as soon as look at you. You be careful, you hear?"

"I promise," answered Malloch, and the girl left him to go to a table where a guy with several chins and a bulging gut was waiting to grab her breasts and shove his hand up her skirt the moment she sat down.

Suddenly, a shadow fell over Malloch's table, and he felt a prickle of alarm go through him.

When he turned, he saw that it was only the pimp.

"Wassamatta?" said the man, grinning broadly. "Don't you like my Ruby?"

"I haven't seen your ruby," snapped Malloch, "but if you get it out I'll tell you if I like it or not."

The pimp's smile disappeared instantly.

"Fuckin' smart guy, eh? You know what I mean, shithead. The girl. What was wrong with her?"

Malloch knew what the pimp was seeing: a pale slim young man, probably just out of college, soft-skinned and effete, maybe even effeminate. A silken, beautiful youth from a good family, out on the wicked town with Daddy's allowance. The pimp would be wondering where the Porsche was parked, and whether he could get his hands on the keys while Ruby was shattering the boy's virginity into irreparable pieces.

"Nothing was wrong with the girl. It's you that bothers me. I mean, you probably stick it in her when you feel like it, and I wouldn't want to go anywhere your dick has been, if you see what I'm getting at."

The pimp's eyes widened.

"You little shit!"

His hand went into his pocket and came out with a switch-blade. There was a *snick* and a flash of light as the blade sprang into view. The pimp made a darting move toward Malloch's throat, the knife glinting like a snake's head.

The only thing Malloch was worried about was his eyes, because they couldn't be replaced, but the pimp didn't know this and went for the heart.

Malloch's arm was quicker. Before the blade was half-way to its target, a slim-fingered hand grasped the pimp's wrist. Malloch gave the thick forearm a short sharp twist. There was a loud crack. The pimp went white, and gasped, his eyes bulging. The knife fell to the floor with a clatter. Someone screamed. Chairs scraped, as people moved away from the fight. The pimp reeled. His hand dangled obscenely from his forearm.

"You fucker!" he shrieked. "You've busted my arm!"

Malloch stood up, intending to leave.

"Think yourself lucky it wasn't your neck."

There was fight left in his adversary yet. The pimp tried to kick him in the genitals, the boot lashing out. Malloch caught his foot, held it for a second, then gave it a twist. There was another sharp crack like a branch snapping. The pimp fell on the floor, screaming and thrashing in pain, while bouncers began to move in from the four corners of the room. Malloch picked up one of the sturdy tables, broke off a leg. He waited for the first bouncer to reach him, then stepped smartly sideways, and delivered the man a swift and terrible blow to the kidneys. The bouncer's eyes bulged. There had been no time to avoid being struck. Malloch moved with the speed of a savage animal. The bouncer jack-knifed sideways, his head almost touching his right shoe.

The other bouncers stopped in their tracks.

"Wise move," said Malloch.

He threw the table leg like a javelin, at the wall between two of them, where it thudded into the plaster and buried itself a foot deep.

"Now, much as I'm enjoying myself, I have to go. As you can see, I'm stronger than I look, so please don't try anything foolish. Goodnight, Ruby," he bowed slightly in the girl's direction, "it was a pleasure."

He strode out of the room, people parting before him like waves on the Red Sea.

Once out in the street again, however, he was fearful, and made his way across the city to a safe house, where detection would be difficult. One could never afford to relax properly while on the run, and all that Malloch could hope for was that his enemy would be kept busy destroying less cunning deserters than himself, or would get the call to return home.

Somewhere in the city a building let out a loud *whumph*, there was instant brightness, and darkness fled from the streets.

His enemy was at work.

6

Dave is woken by Celia with a kiss, and he opens his eyes to see her all dressed and ready to go out. She looks darkly beautiful, her curvaceous Latin figure revealed by a shape-hugging suit. Her long black hair is in a single plait, coiled on the crown of her head and held in place with a slim comb. She has on her red lipstick, too, which means the trip is going to be serious, a money-spending spree of some sort. Dave sits up in bed and rubs his eyes. They feel sore, as if he's been crying. His tie and shirt are draped over the chair next to the bed, but he can't see his slacks.

What's going on? he says.

Come on, sleepy-head, she laughs, it's time to go shopping. You promised to take me to that new Japanese store, for a dress, don't you remember? Jamie's with Sue this morning, so we're free to do as we please. Better bring your credit cards, buster, because Celia is going *wild* today.

Okay, sure, I remember.

Something is bothering Dave, but he can't figure out what it is. It's like a fly buzzing around inside his skull, worrying the hell out of him. He climbs out of bed and goes to the bath-

room for a shave. He steps into the hall and the next minute
he and Celia are walking along the sidewalk and up the con-
cave steps into a department store. Dave still has on his shorts
and feels embarrassed, but no one seems to mind. Even Celia
laughs at his shyness.

You've got a shirt and tie on, haven't you? What are you
worried about, you big bear? I've hardly got anything on at all.
Look at me. Miss Skimpy, 1990.

Which is true. Her suit has gone. Now she's clothed in only
her best silk underwear, the set he had bought her for Christ-
mas last year. This doesn't seem right, either, and Dave tries to
shield her body from male stares as they stroll through the
store. He sees himself punching a few noses before the morning is out. Dave doesn't approve of men looking at his wife like
she's a picture in a girlie magazine. Celia's olive breasts are overflowing the top of her bra and Dave asks her to tuck them in,
as they are attracting too much attention, but Celia just gig-
gles.

Celia asks an assistant where to find the dress department,
and is told that the only ones they have left are in the store window.

Well, cries Celia, we'd better get to them before they all go,
my husband doesn't like me walking around like this. He's the
jealous type.

I am not, protests Dave, but any guy would be put out if
his wife walked around like that.

She pulls Dave's hand and leads him to the front of the
store, and steps into the window alcove.

There are no dresses, but there is a bed.

C'mon, whispers Celia into his ear, let's make love, you big
bear.

She pulls off her panties and lies on the bed. Passers-by have
stopped and are staring in at them, their mouths moving
silently, the glass too thick to hear what they are saying.

Jeez, Celia, we'll get arrested, says Dave.

Don't be silly, they can't arrest a cop, laughs Celia. Come on, don't be a bore. Who cares what they think? Show them what kind of man I've got.

He waits until the window is empty of people watching, then he lies down on the bed with her and she parts her trembling legs. As he enters her, he can feel her skin getting warm, like it always does when she gets excited. She has often told him she will catch fire one day, she gets so hot and excited. He cups her head in his hands as they move into a rhythm, and the years flee from her face, leaving the nineteen-year-old he had met and fallen in love with, down·in Mexico.

Baby, she says anxiously, I love you.

I love you, too, he murmurs.

Oh, God, I love you, she cries.

The tears begin to run down her cheeks, the way they always do when she becomes too emotional and cries during lovemaking. Suddenly, there's steam on her face. The tears sizzle on her flesh, which becomes hotter by the minute.

God, I can't stand it, she cries, I'm going to catch fire, Dave. Help me!

But she has said that before, many times, and anyway he can't stop himself, he just has to keep going, there's no turning back now.

He kisses her lips and burns his own.

Dave hears a thumping on the window and looks up, to see that the gawping faces of voyeurs have returned, and the sneers have changed to looks of horror. They point toward Celia, gesturing wildly.

Dave feels a burning sensation in his genitals and looks down on his wife.

Her cheek has begun to smoke, then holes appear, combusting slowly at the edges like paper soaked in saltpeter. The glowing rings widen quickly, before he can do anything to stop them.

CELIA!

It is all too quick, too fast, and he can't stop. He feels himself coming to a climax, and he knows the faster he pumps, the quicker she burns. Blisters come up all over her body, burst, and spread in fiery rings.

NO, NO, he screams. He goes faster and faster, moving in and out of her so swiftly the friction is burning his genitals. I'M SORRY, he cries, the tears streaming down his cheeks. I can't help it, Celia, I can't help it.

Gradually she turns to charcoal, then to ashes, until he is jabbing at gray dust, and when he looks up, there is Danny at the window, his face full of rage.

You bastard, mouths Danny, you couldn't stop, could you? Not even to save your own wife. You killed her, Dave. You murdered Celia. God, you're disgusting.

I'm sorry, whispers Dave. I didn't mean to. I'm so sorry.

Dave woke up with a start, sitting upright in bed, the sweat pouring from his body. He looked toward the window, where the hotel's dark curtains were holding back the sunshine, stopping it from entering and disturbing his rest. A thin ray had found its way through a chink, and sliced like a laser beam across his pillow, right where his eyes had been.

Christ, another dream, he thought.

He reached for a cigarette and lit it with trembling hands, the perspiration soaking into the paper and tobacco. He took a deep pull, and then coughed, still unused to smoking after such a long lay-off.

Guilt, he thought. I'm punishing myself. For what? For letting Celia go shopping? No, for all those times when I was mean to her. For all those times when I could have been just that bit better, arrived home a little earlier, spent just that little bit more time with her. For all those times I criticized her when she wanted approval. For all those times I could have said, "I love you," instead of moaning about the boys at the station, or the job, or not having enough money to make our lives more comfortable.

"What a waste," he said out loud.

The cigarette went out when it reached the damp ring of sweat, and he tossed it into the washbasin. He climbed wearily out of bed, feeling he had never been to sleep at all, and opened the curtains. Washington lay beyond the glass. He had come here to get away for a few days, and was staying at a small hotel on the east side. Washington had been chosen because of its distance from San Francisco, its plain face and because he had never been here with Celia. There were no memories out there waiting to pounce. It was not that he wanted to *forget* Celia, far from it, but he wanted to be the one with his hands on the memory controls. He was safe from surprises in Washington.

Dave showered, shaved and then dressed. He was on the top floor of a four-story building, and he used the stairs to reach the lobby below. There was a sign telling him which way to go for breakfast, and he followed the arrow to a small, dusty room at the back of the hotel. There were three other people in the room: a man who was working out of a briefcase, taking sips of coffee in between writing furiously, and an elderly couple who spoke with an English accent, probably tourists.

"What can I get you?" asked the waitress.

"Just coffee," replied Dave.

"No eggs?"

"Coffee."

"We got flapjacks."

"Coffee."

"Okay," the waitress gave a shrug, and flounced across the room to the English pair, who gave her the smiles and chit-chat she had been expecting from Dave. They were in Washington, they said, to see their son who worked here. The son's apartment was too small for him to have his parents stay there, so they had come to the hotel.

Dave lost interest after that.

A copy of the *Washington Post* was on the next table and Dave reached across and grabbed it, reading the headlines. More fires. There had been a big one in New York, at a museum, and a lot of exhibits had been destroyed.

Dave's heart felt like a lead weight in his chest. He was full of despair. What the hell was he going to do without Celia and Jamie? Was it worth going on at all? Surely the best thing would be for him to go up onto some roof and step out into space. Within seconds they could be together again.

Or he could go back to San Francisco and help Danny do battle with the fire-starters.

"Terrible state of affairs, isn't it?"

Dave looked up to see that the Englishman had stopped by his table and was staring at the headlines. Dave wanted the man to go away, but was too polite to be brusque.

"Yes, it is," said Dave, and without being able to help himself, added, "I've just lost my wife. She died in a fire in a department store."

Somehow it felt good to unburden himself to a complete stranger, even though he was in grave danger of bursting into tears again. The Englishman, whose wife seemed to have left the room, appeared to be uncomfortable.

"I'm sorry. I didn't mean to intrude on your private thoughts . . ."

"No, no, it's okay. It's my fault. I didn't mean to embarrass you—it just comes out. It's too recent, I suppose. I can't make any sense of it yet."

"May I sit down?" asked the man. "I'm waiting for my wife to fetch her handbag from our room."

"Be my guest. Join me in a coffee."

"Thank you, I will." A hand came forward. "Alex Wingman."

Dave shook the hand.

"David Peters."

The older man poured himself a coffee after reaching for a clean cup from a neighboring table. He sugared it twice and then sipped.

"I just love your American coffee," he said. "You and the Italians, you really know how to make it."

Feeling he was now trapped into talking, Dave asked without enthusiasm, "What do you do, Mr. Wingman?"

The other man leaned back in his chair. He ran his gnarled fingers through his white hair. He seemed to understand that Dave was not really interested in the answer and was only being polite, for the answer was brief and to the point.

"Not much, now. I'm retired. Used to be a schoolteacher, in Yorkshire. That's one of our counties. Largest county in England—the equivalent to your Texas, only pocket-size. Actually, you could get five Englands into Texas and over forty Yorkshires, but I expect you're used to being told things like that."

Dave laughed, despite himself.

"Not really, I don't meet many tourists. I'm a plainclothes cop."

"Really? How interesting. But you were saying, before I sat down, that you couldn't make any sense of your wife's death. I'm afraid that's one of the things I found it hard to come to terms with . . . the *why* behind my own wife's death. Oh," he said, "the lady I'm with at the moment, Jean, is my second wife. Liz, that's my first wife, died in a motor accident twelve years after we married. I still dream about it, the accident, I mean. I was the driver of the car."

Wingman's face showed signs of stress, and Dave thought, Jesus Christ, will I be like this, still mourning Celia after God knows how many years?

Wingman smiled gently. "Ah, I know what you're thinking, but these are momentary lapses. I don't go around thinking about her all the time. In fact you could say I am a reasonably happy man. I've found another nice person, to share what's left of my life with me, and we do very well together. What I wanted to say to you, is, *don't* try to make any sense out of it all. You'll go mad, if you do. I had a mental breakdown, quite a serious one, because the only sense you can put into a premature death is to blame yourself in some way. Don't do it, Mr. Peters, it's not worth it. It's a strange thing, but if you had hated your wife and had shot her deliberately, you would probably be blaming *her*, not yourself, for her death. My guess is you had nothing to do with the fire, or her being there, but you keep saying to yourself, 'If I had only done this, or said that, or stayed home, it would have been all right.'"

Dave's eyes widened a fraction.

"Ah, I'm right, aren't I?"

They talked some more on the same subject, and by the time the man's wife had joined them, Dave was feeling a lot less like suicide. The couple were mild and pleasant, not electric personalities, but nice people. The three of them went for a walk together, through a park, and inevitably the conversation got around to talking about the fires.

Jean Wingman asked him a direct question.

"Would you say we lived in a moral world, Mr. Peters?"

Dave shrugged. "Well, you're asking a policeman. I mean, my friends outside the force would say that most of the people they know are reasonably moral, but in my business we see the sick side of society—the running sores of humanity. We see the drug pushers, pimps, gangsters, wife-beaters, child-abusers, killers, maimers . . ."

Wingman said, "And what about on a larger scale? The big canvas? Is the world moral out there?"

Dave considered the question, calling to mind the wars going on in the Middle East, Africa and South America. Then there were the military regimes and dictators, throwing innocent people into jail without trial, torturing children, murdering, raping, pillaging, all in the name of power. There were probably monstrous crimes going on in some dark corner of the earth, which would only be revealed when someone found a mountain of skulls, or stumbled upon concentration camps full of emaciated creatures that were once human beings. There were respected politicians out there, lying through their teeth to save their worthless skins, and huge multinational companies willing to risk the lives of babies to sell their goods. There were dealers on the stock market interested only in money, no matter who or what was ruined in the process of them gathering their fortunes. There were immensely rich men who would sell their daughters to add one more buck to their wealth.

Was it a moral world?

"Not really," he replied, weakly.

Jean smiled at him.

"Well, take heart, young man, there are millions of gentle, compassionate people out there, in the majority by far. It's just that *good* seems to be a passive quality, and *evil* tends to swagger around and create havoc. These fires, terrible as they are, perhaps have some purpose. Perhaps they make us pull up short and say, 'Hey, is this the way the world is supposed to be? We should do something about changing it.' That's no comfort to a man who has just lost his loved ones, I know, but it's the best I can offer."

Dave stared at her kindly features and, strangely enough, he did feel a lot better. There was bitterness in plenty in his breast, and a lot of darkness, but he felt he could cope with it now. There were no more thoughts of suicide, only of getting even, of putting things to rights. It was his job to stop the fires from happening. It was his job to catch the people who were doing it, and put them where they belonged, whether that was behind bars, or in a hospital where they could get help.

"Thanks, Jean," he said, giving her wrinkled fingers a squeeze.

Wingman laughed and said, "Watch it, young man, I'm the jealous type."

"I can see that," said Dave. "And so you should be, with a gorgeous lady like this at your side. C'mon, it's nearly time for lunch. Let me buy you both a meal, and we can talk some more. I don't want to let you go just yet."

He took them to a French restaurant and the three of them idled away the next two hours in talk. Dave found it easier to bare his soul to strangers than he had to talk to Danny about how he felt. Danny was too close to him and knew too much already, whereas Dave wanted to tell someone how he had met his wife, what they had in common, where they differed, who her family was, what his son had been like, what sort of grades Jamie was getting at school. He wanted to talk over the history of his family, get it out in the open, examine it, just say their names over and over again, Jamie, Celia, Celia, Jamie. My wife did this, my son did that.

And they were good listeners, they knew the right questions to ask, they knew that definite answers were not required. When he left them at the end of the day, Dave was beginning to wonder if someone had sent them to him, to get him to lance his sores and let the poison out. By the following morning, he was ready to go back home, not cured, but at least he was sitting up in bed and taking notice, instead of lying with his face to the wall, wanting to die.

7

The next day Dave packed his bag, left the hotel and took the train back to San Francisco.

He would not live anywhere else, even though it was now a city full of memory traps, waiting to snap shut on his brain with their sprung metal teeth. San Francisco was the greatest city in the world, so far as Dave was concerned, and he would hardly change an inch of it. When he had been in the army he had even managed to get himself stationed at the Presidio, where he could wake up in the morning to the sight of Alcatraz and the smell of the ocean. Mario's coffee bar had still been within reach from there. It was difficult to live without a regular imbibing of Mario's espresso.

He loved the undulating streets, the streetcars, the busy harbor. The only thing he did not like was that damn bridge. *The* bridge. He could never understand why most people thought it beautiful. It was an eyesore, so far as he was concerned, but he was aware that he was in a minority—perhaps of one. Maybe there was some kink in the part of his brain that should appreciate geometric beauty.

At Oakland he had to change to a bus. He found a phone and dialed his own apartment number, hoping to catch Danny there. Danny was living in both apartments, to keep the place looking occupied.

There was noise and bustle on the concourse of the station, and this was distracting. A child was running between the public telephones, unhooking them and leaving them dangling. The mother was chasing the kid, trying to grab him by the coat, and, as he dashed past Dave, the detective was tempted to catch him but resisted, knowing that this was how lawsuits were born. Mothers can beat their own kids to death, but let anyone else so much as lay a finger on them, and they scream for the lawyers.

The first terrible shock: suddenly, there was Celia's voice in his ear!

"Hi, this is Celia Peters . . ."

Dave's heart soared and he almost swooned with happiness.

"Celia?" he yelled excitedly. "Celia, where have you been, darling? Oh, God, *Celia* . . ."

". . . Dave and I aren't home right now, but if you leave a message after the beep, we'll get back to you."

The second terrible shock: it was only Celia's voice, not her, not the real Celia.

It took several seconds to get through to Dave. It was a recording. He crashed. He felt worse than death, worse than when he had heard Celia was in the fire, worse than at the morgue, confronted by two blackened pieces of charcoal they told him were his loved ones.

He smashed the phone against the side of the phone booth, stopping the careering child in its tracks, so that it stood and stared at Dave in amazement. The mother grabbed the boy, glanced fearfully at Dave, and dragged the kid away. It protested, digging in its heels and screaming. Dave dropped the phone and put his hands over his ears.

The message on his answering machine had never been changed. Celia was still there, telling callers she would get back to them as soon as she could. Bizarre. How many of his friends had rung him with condolences, only to get the same message? Why hadn't someone told him? It was worse than receiving mail for her, posted before her death.

Gradually, he regained his composure. A woman came up and asked him if he was all right. She must have been an out-of-towner because city people passed by, not getting involved, especially with a nut. He told her he was okay. He'd just received bad news over the phone. He put the telephone gently back on the cradle, noticing that he had cracked the receiver. Then he walked away quickly, before some cop or member of the station staff called for reinforcements and decided to tackle him.

As he left the station the newsstand headlines told him that the Opera House in Paris had gone up in flames with the loss of thirty-five lives. The dead were all members of the cast, it being a rehearsal luckily, not a performance. In London, the crypt of St. Martin-in-the-Fields in Trafalgar Square had belched fire at three o'clock in the morning. A single charred corpse was found on the hot flagstones down there, the molten brass of a memorial floorplate mingling with the juices of the cadaver.

To top it all, on his way out into the street, there was a nut screeching about the end of the world.

"Fire is a cleanser," shouted the nut into Dave's face. "It comes to every decadent society, to wipe away the sin of the old order, to make way for a new!" He pointed a grubby finger at a spot between Dave's eyes. "Sodom and Gomorrah!" he cried. "San Francisco, Alexandria, Ancient Rome, London, Dresden, Hiroshima, Nagasaki. Evil cities, all. All destroyed by fire. *And there appeared unto them cloven tongues like as of fire, and it sat upon each of them.* Acts two, verse three."

Dave shook his head sadly.

"You don't believe me, friend? San Francisco is a place of evil. Pimps, gamblers, junkies, harlots . . ."

Why did these nuts always use that word *harlot*, which wasn't ever used in the street, and only appeared in the oldest of books? It was never hookers, whores or prostitutes—always *harlots*.

"I would argue with you, but I haven't got the time."

"We are being incinerated in a hell of our own making. Mephistopheles told Dr. Faustus that hell is here on earth, and we are all in it."

"Well, good for him," said Dave. "Now will you get out of my way, or do I walk over you?"

"The Good Book says that Satan will be destroyed in a lake of fire . . ."

The man's eyes were glazed, and Dave realized he could not see the people around him. He was in some hell of his own, with flames licking at his legs, and demons with forked tridents and arrowhead tails running this way and that, gathering sinners for him. In a way Dave envied him. It must be nice, he thought, to live in a world—even a fantasy world—where good and evil were easy to define, easy to recognize, and no gray shaded areas in between. Black and white. Simple as that.

" *'Wherein the heavens shall pass away with a great noise, and the elements shall melt with the fervent heat, the earth also and the works that are therein shall be burned up!'* "

Dave raised his eyes to that same heaven.

He pushed the nut gently aside and managed to reach the sidewalk without being accosted again.

He saw Danny waving to him from across the street. His partner had anticipated his return after all, and had a car and was waiting for him. That felt good. He crossed through a gap in the traffic, hoping he didn't get picked up for jaywalking.

The two men hugged, Danny getting embarrassed and letting go first.

"How are you, Dave?"

"After six weeks away? Good as new."

"Yeah, sure. Anyway, let's go get a drink. You coming back on the job?"

"You bet your ass."

He saw the look in Danny's eyes and knew that his partner had been hoping for that answer. Danny was never any good on his own.

Once they were in a bar, Danny asked the inevitable question.

"Now, how you *really* feeling?"

Dave answered honestly.

"Not good. Like shit. I don't suppose I'll be able to give another answer for a long time to come, but I'm not rotting away inside anymore, Danny. I feel pretty desperate sometimes, close to despair, especially at night, but . . . well, there you go. I guess I've got to go on. The only other choice is to die, and I've decided against that—oh, yes, I thought of it, pretty seriously, but it's passed. The death-wish has passed. It's just that life is a fraction more appealing than death at the moment."

Danny nodded at his drink.

"Well, you know how I feel, Dave."

"That I do, Danny. Now what have we got? You picked up any good collars lately?"

"An insurance job. We caught 'em with their hands still smelling of gasoline. A warehouse on the waterfront. We also caught the guy who was setting fire to dealers—oh, yeah, you weren't in on that. About a month ago. This guy was waiting for stockmarket dealers outside their homes, catching them on the way to work in the mornings, coming out of the office in the evening. He carried a Coke can full of gas and threw it over his victims, then set light to them."

"Jesus Christ! Makes a change from torching winos."

"Yeah, usually the head, so the hair caught fire. We had

some pretty nasty cases—guys going blind, couple actually snuffed it, their hearts gave up. One caught it with his mouth open and his throat was burned out. Twelve victims altogether. I went undercover, posed as a dealer—"

"What, *you?*" laughed Dave. "You couldn't deal a deck of cards."

"Sez you. Anyway, nice coat and suit, looking like a king, I was coming out of the offices of Rheinholt, Baker and Johnson, when this shit stepped out from behind my Rolls-Royce—"

"Rolls-*Royce?*" cried Dave, delighted.

Danny gave him a big grin.

"Yeah. I saw a hand holding a Coke can. I didn't even look at the guy's face, I just kicked it under his chin, hoping to God it wasn't full of Coca-Cola. Fortunately, it was gasoline, and the guy was covered in it. He ran, I chased, cornered him in an alley. He drew a knife, I drew my Zippo—"

"Shit, you didn't!" shouted Dave, delighted by the story, even though Danny had probably pepped it up.

"I drew my Zippo and said, 'Make your move, you fucker,' and he fell on his knees, begging me not to set light to him, as he had his mohair coat on. Anyway, we booked him, and I had to quit wearing expensive clothes and riding around in the hired Rolls and go back to the old jalopy."

"That's some story, partner."

"It happens to be true, ask any of the boys. Turned out the guy had lost a lot of money on the market, and like many others, he couldn't find it in himself to blame number one. It was *them,* those bastards out there, who were responsible for his loss of fortune. So he went out to get even. He got burned so why shouldn't they? Literally."

They had another drink, then Danny said, "You want me to drive you home now?"

"My *apartment,* Danny. It ain't home anymore."

When they got back to Dave's apartment he said to Danny, "I'm okay, you know."

"Sure. Sure, you are."

"I mean it. I'm fine."

"Okay," Danny looked down at his feet. "Anyway, say, I got myself a regular girlfriend now."

Dave smiled.

"Really, do I know her, or . . .?"

"Or is she some hooker? She's not a hooker, she's a nice girl. Been in a bit of trouble, yeah, but basically a nice lady. You'll meet her tonight, if you want to come out to dinner with us."

"I dunno, Danny, I got some things to do. Who is she, anyway?"

Danny's eyes lit up with excitement.

"You remember the girl with blondish hair, when we were sitting in Reeves's office?"

"No, I don't."

"Yeah, you do. Tall and willowy. She was being booked for setting fire to her boyfriend's bed. You gotta remember. The captain pointed her out . . ."

Dave recalled the woman now.

"Mousy-colored hair and big glasses."

"*Blonde*. It's definitely blonde hair."

"Whatever. Love is color-blind," said Dave. "You mean you're going out with a fire-starter? Isn't that a bit unethical?"

Danny bristled.

"Nah, shit. She's been to court and got probation. She was assigned to that asshole Manovitch and he tried to jump her. Used his position as probation officer to threaten her—said if she didn't come across he'd trump up a way to put her inside. She came to the precinct house and reported it, and the captain told me to lean on Manovitch, which I did with pleasure."

"She's still his?"

"Sure, but if he so much as lays a finger on her, I'll bust him for corruption. He knows that. He's been as good as gold since then."

"He's *still* operating?"

"Now, Dave, don't go all sanctimonious on me. You know it's difficult to nail these guys without proof. We tried to wire her, but he's a fucking eel, that one. It didn't work. We got something, but not enough. He knows we're standing on his toes, and he won't try it on with her again."

"What about the next one? Maybe a teenager this time."

"I told you. I spoke sharply to him."

"Well, I'll have a little word in his ear too."

Danny sighed, knowing it would be no good telling Dave to lay off. In any case, he reasoned that it would do Dave good to have something to think about other than his wife and kid.

"So," Dave said, "you and this Miss What's-her-name are getting it on?"

"Vanessa, her name's Vanessa Vangellen, and . . . we haven't been to bed yet. I just sort of take her out now and then, to the theater, to dinner, you know."

"Vanessa? Really. Vanessa Vangellen. She sounds pretty up-market for you, Danny. No wonder you haven't made your move."

Danny looked abashed.

"Now, don't go getting sarcastic, Dave, I can do without it. It's not me, it's her. She says she likes me as a friend, but that's all at the moment. I'm hoping it'll change. I mean, she's no great looker, any more than I am, so she can't afford to be too choosy. She's kinda nice, though, and I think we could make it together."

"What does she do? For money?"

"She lectures on theology."

Dave whistled.

"Brains as well as plain looks."

They parted later, with Dave promising he would be in to work the next day. He fixed himself a final drink, before staring at the answering machine. He did not change it. He never did change it himself. He left her voice on the tape, and sometimes, when he was out with Danny and feeling low, he would make an excuse to phone someone, and call his own number, just to listen to her voice again.

One day, the voice was Danny's.

"Dave, if that's you I know you're going to be angry, but I think this has got to be done. It's not healthy. You can hit me if you want to . . ."

Danny had obviously let himself into the apartment and changed the recording, after having listened to the message himself, and putting two and two together.

Dave never mentioned it again.

8

Vanessa Vangellen faced Stan Manovitch across the broad desk covered with the coffee-ring stains and map-like areas where the varnish had peeled. There was a picture on the wall behind his head, of some Canadian forest during fall. One of those bland panoramic scenes that they churned out like wall-paper for the cheap market stalls. It depressed her. The fiery colors of the leaves depressed her.

The office stank of stale cigar smoke. It seemed to seep from the cracks in the old leather of Manovitch's chair. A smouldering butt was on the ashtray between her and the probation officer, its smoke making her eyes sting. There was ash down Manovitch's waistcoat.

Vanessa set her narrow face in a particular way, so as to give the man on the other side of the desk no doubt how she felt about him. His pale blue eyes were staring at that expression in distaste, his thick-lipped mouth wet at the corners.

"So you snitched on me, huh?"

"I informed the police that I was being subjected to sexual harassment from my probation officer. You're lucky I didn't call your wife."

"I could get you back for that."

She glared at him with hot eyes.

"I shall have to report that particular remark too."

His hands came up and made pushing movements against the air.

"Just don't give me any more aggravation, Vanessa. And for the record, I don't give a damn what you tell my wife. We have that kind of relationship. I know one thing, she wouldn't go whining to the police if some guy like me made a pass at her. She'd take it as a compliment. Don't you feel just a little guilty, going to the cops and ratting on me? I mean, ours is not a society that approves of snitches. I'm just curious, you understand."

"What are you trying to do to me? You want to make me as crazy as the rest of the people you bully? I'm not one of your criminals. The psychiatrist—"

"Yeah, yeah, you got off light because of the shrink's report, but that don't mean you're totally innocent, otherwise the judge wouldn't have given you probation. I don't have to come on to you to give you a hard time, you know, and no matter who you run to with your tales, so long as I'm seen to be doing my job, it'll be all right with them. You think Spitz scares me? Is that it?"

He shuffled some papers on his desk and the gesture left her in no doubt as to the answer. Danny Spitz worried the hell out of this guy, which was strange because Danny was short and cute in a funny kind of way.

"Something going on between you two?" Manovitch asked with a smile.

He had caught her with her guard down, daydreaming, and she was infuriated with herself for letting it happen. She was also incensed by Manovitch's coarse manner, and by his assumptions. Why did men like this think they could say what they wanted to people in their care? He was supposed to be helping her, not trying to mess with her head. He was the sick one, not her.

"How did you ever get to be a probation officer? You're so ill-mannered—and brutish. Don't they have some kind of filter system to catch people like you?"

He shook his head and smiled.

"You're all mouth, ain't you? Not that I would complain about that . . ."

She caught the inference immediately and it made her feel like vomiting.

He smiled again.

"You see, Vanessa," he said softly, leaning on his elbows across the desk, "ladies like you don't have any defense against men like me. We win every time. I can humiliate you into the dirt, and you'll have to keep coming back for more. There's not a damn thing you can do about it."

She stared at his greasy scalp with its thin hair smarmed down to cover the baldness. He was utterly repulsive. He looked like her father.

There was the soggy butt-end of a cigar in Manovitch's right hand, nestled between the stubby fingers now, and it was still alight. She snatched it out of his grasp and pressed the lighted end against her wrist.

"Hey!" he yelled, his chair scraping backward.

There was a short sizzling sound, then the smell of burned flesh.

She tossed the cigar butt back onto his desk, and shouted, "THIS MAN BURNED ME!"

Someone walking past the office tried to peer in through the fogged glass.

"Jesus Christ!" whispered Manovitch, the sweat beads breaking out in his broad forehead. "What the hell are you trying to do?" His hands were on the arms of his chair, as if he were about to launch himself through the ceiling. Vanessa bored into him with her eyes.

"You think they'll believe you when you tell them I burned *myself*?"

He shrugged, wilting a little under her gaze.

"Don't fuck with me again," she said. "Ever."

The shadow behind the door moved closer, as if the person were listening, trying to make out what was going on. Manovitch stared at the glass, his face wet with perspiration. Finally, the figure moved off, walking down the corridor. Vanessa could hear the *clip-clip-clip* of a woman's high heels.

"Okay, okay," he said, becoming brisk and businesslike, "now you have a job to go to? They didn't ask you to leave, after you went to court?"

Though she was used to it, the pain had made her eyes water, and she looked away, out of the window so he wouldn't see. She did not want to give him the satisfaction of knowing how much it hurt. She didn't have to fight an irresistible need to look at the wound, like a person normally would, because she knew what it would look like. Small burns healed quite quickly, though they were intensely painful at first, and in a week or so's time the scar would be just one of a number.

"No, they understood."

"Good, fine. Well, if you leave San Francisco you have to inform me where you're going, and who you intend to see, you understand that?"

"You told me that last time."

"Fine, just so long as you understand. I'll want to see you again Friday, okay? Good. Friday, then."

When she was out on the street she let the air out of her lungs. That bastard! How did they get away with it? Vanessa suspected that most of the women he tried it on with would be too scared to report it. He probably had a seventy to eighty percent success rate. Well, this was one person he couldn't threaten and, if she ever got the opportunity, she would see him repaid for that burn.

She looked at it now that she was out of his sight, and the

wound wasn't too bad. She had known worse. Her long sleeves covered it, so that wouldn't be a problem.

Vanessa went first to a restaurant and had several coffees, until her hands stopped shaking. Then she caught a bus home.

Her apartment was a small cubbyhole affair. There were two rooms, one of them a living room cum kitchen, and the other a small bedroom, large enough only for a single bed with leg space down each side. Vanessa hated beds that were pushed against the wall. You were forever pulling them out to make them, and at night you could wake up in the pitch black with your face pressed against the plaster, thinking you were in some kind of tomb. It would make her panic, she knew, so she always gave herself space either side, be it ever so narrow.

Vanessa was not a tidy woman. She threw her bag on the floor, kicked off her shoes, and went into her bedroom. The bed was unmade, so she pulled the sheets up to the pillows, hiked her skirt up to her thighs, and then lay on top.

She suddenly started thinking about Tom, because, she supposed, she was missing sex with him. Should she phone him? You couldn't really telephone a man whose bed you had set on fire. He had called the police straight away too, which had banished any thought that he might love her. You didn't immediately hand over someone you loved to the law, no matter what they might have done. You asked for explanations, tried to understand, promised to help, something like that. You didn't shout, "You crazy bitch, what have you done?" and then call the cops.

Vanessa reached up her skirt and pulled down her tights, throwing them into a corner, then took off her glasses, hooking them carefully over the bedhead.

Well, no, it was not a good idea to call Tom. Should she call Danny? Not really, it wasn't friendship she wanted, right at that moment. Best to take a few painkillers with a hot drink and go to bed, sleep it off.

She dozed for a while, having funny half-awake dreams.

When she woke up fully, she had a shower and changed into black slacks and sweater, having abandoned the idea of an early night. It was nine o'clock in the evening. She decided she did want to talk to someone, after all, and she had decided to call on Danny, rather than phone him. She knew he often went to confession on a Wednesday, but that would have been around six o'clock. He would be home by now.

She put on some flat shoes, tied her hair back with an elastic band, slipped on a short coat, and left the apartment.

She took a cab to Danny's address, went inside the building, and rang the bell. It was a long time in being answered, and she rang twice more, seeing a light under the door. There was also a radio or TV on, though he may have left it that way on purpose to deter burglars.

Finally the door opened.

A tall man stood before her, in a dressing gown and pajamas.

It wasn't Danny.

She stepped back, confused, and looked at the number on the apartment door. It was the right one.

"Yes?" said the man, rubbing sleep from his eyes.

"I'm sorry, I thought—doesn't Danny Spitz live here?"

The man stared at her and some sort of recognition came into his eyes.

"You're Vangellen," he said. "Vanessa Vangellen?"

"Yes."

"I'm—well, look, this *isn't* Danny's apartment, it's mine. Danny was house-sitting for me while I was away. I'm his partner, Dave Peters. Has he spoken about me?"

Relief entered Vanessa's system.

"Of course—David Peters. Yes, of course he's spoken about you, but I expected God or something, the way he talks. You look like an ordinary man."

This made him laugh.

"Look, Danny's not here right at this moment. Didn't he take you to his place? I guess not. He was probably showing off. My apartment's much larger than his, I'm—I was married, so we needed the extra room, for . . ."

His face seemed to crumple a little, and she had heard the story from Danny, so she knew what was happening.

"It's okay," she said quickly. "I just wanted to talk with him about something. Nothing, in fact," she confessed. "I just wanted to talk to *someone*. This sounds a bit confused, but I was feeling a little lonely, and Danny's been a friend lately, I hope I can call him that . . ."

The door was opened wider and Dave Peters gestured with his arm.

"Come on inside, out of that cold hallway. Let me make you a drink or something."

She stepped inside, feeling the warmth of the room flood over her.

"I wouldn't mind a coffee, but I don't want to intrude."

"It's okay. I can sleep at any time. Forgive the dressing gown," it was a dull plaid affair, "it belonged to my father and I keep it for sentimental reasons. Getting a bit threadbare now. I'll go and change."

"That's not necessary," she assured him quickly.

"Yes, yes, it is. I feel uncomfortable like this."

"Shall I make the coffee, then? I know where it is."

"Sure, I won't be long. Yell if you can't find anything."

He left her and went into another room. She found the kettle and put on some hot water, knocking her wrist on the edge of the work surface. The burn pained her and brought tears to her eyes for a moment. She didn't rub it, knowing it would only aggravate the wound. Instead, she found some butter in the fridge and smeared that on. It was a nostrum, but it would do no harm. She liked to use fairy remedies sometimes. They reminded her of her mother.

By the time she had made the coffee, he appeared in the

doorway, tall and good-looking now that he had combed his hair and had on a smart shirt and slacks.

"Ready," she said.

Manovitch lay on his back in the half-light, smoking a cigar and staring at the strange ceiling. A car went by outside, its lights sweeping across the room and illuminating the fake night sky twinkling above his head. This irritated him, for some reason, and he would have spat if he hadn't been so dry.

Who the hell would paper a ceiling with midnight blue wallpaper covered in stars? he asked himself. There were some weird tastes around. Some weird ideas about style. The room stank of dog too. There was some fat retriever-type animal out in the hall, banished there for the night, who normally spent the same hours sleeping on top of the bed. She said it made her feel safe. That made Manovitch laugh, because if a burglar came through the window, the dog would've been first out of the doorway. It was that kind of mutt.

Beside him, softly snoring, was a thick-limbed woman, not his wife. A mother on probation for abusing her child. She wasn't a bad woman, compared with some, she just couldn't cope with three children under five years of age, and she had exploded, unfortunately for the two-year-old. Manovitch had found her too easy to get into bed to satisfy him. No wonder the bitch had three kids with only a year between each. Well, she only had two now. The middle kid had been taken away from her.

Manovitch pulled on the cigar, the glow lighting up the room as oxygen rushed to the burning red-hot end. He remembered the incident in his office that afternoon. How could he forget it? He reminded himself not to smoke when Vangellen came in to report again.

That cow Vangellen, now she was something else. No wonder she hadn't flinched when he'd asked about Spitz. It wasn't

Spitz she was laying, it was Peters, his partner. Shit, the guy's wife had only been dead a couple of months, and already he was letting loose on the singles.

Manovitch had waited outside her apartment this evening, until she left. Then he followed her, hoping to confirm his suspicions about Spitz. Well, he'd been wrong, but not dead wrong. If she thought he was going to lie down for this, she had another think coming. He'd get even somehow. Manovitch was not a man to reject. Trouble was, if he was scared of Spitz, he was *terrified* of Peters. He didn't mind admitting it. So he had to bide his time, wait around a while, then hit the fuckers when they were least expecting it.

He recalled the time he had been screwing around with that girl from the typing pool, whose husband was a rookie cop. The young husband had come to Manovitch and threatened to bust his lights if he didn't stay away from his wife. That was a few years ago now, when Manovitch was in his mid-thirties. He hadn't liked people who threatened him then, either.

In those days there was a spate of murders down by the waterfront. It was thought that the Chinese were doing it, because it involved butcher's knives and meat cleavers. The Chinks' favorite weapons.

Manovitch had lured the kid cop down to the waterfront, and then took his head half off with a chopper. It had been easy, the boy being a rookie. He hadn't even drawn his gun when he saw that it was a white man standing in the shadows. He had just obeyed the beckoning finger, and *whap*, no more face. Manovitch had paid his debt, and the Chinese were in big trouble for whacking a cop. That was okay. He was no friend of the ethnics. They could drown in shark's fin soup for all he cared. Then he had the terrible job of consoling the rookie's widow. That was a *real* bitch.

These thoughts made Manovitch feel a lot better. He drew on his butt again, and then glanced sideways at the matted black hair on the pillow, the open mouth. Christ, she was ugly. No wonder it had been easy. He was no oil painting himself, he knew that, but she took the prize. Still, waste not, want not. He gave her a dig in the ribs with his elbow. She snorted, half waking.

"Whad is it, angel?" she murmured, thickly.

"Don't bother to wake up," he told her, "just roll over."

9

Sirens sounded during the night: fire, police, ambulance. Dave fell from the edge of his bed, staggered to the window to look out upon a city with at least three big blazes in progress, the sky lit up from beneath as if it were a stage, and the moon and stars actors. It might have been a poetically inspiring scene, those fires flowering among the dark buildings of a desert city, if people out there were not dying.

Getting out of bed he realized he was very drunk. He couldn't remember doing the drinking, but his brain felt as though it was wrapped in barbed wire, the way it always did when he had gone too far down the bottle.

He staggered to the kitchen and made himself a cup of coffee, knowing it would keep him awake but needing the caffeine. He had run out of milk, and vaguely wondered why, but took the coffee black anyway. In the darkness of the kitchen he did not so much brood, as reflect on what life had been like a few months ago. There was the kitchen mixer, caught in a ray of moonlight from the gingham-curtained window. It hadn't been used since Celia had gone. Half the things in the house hadn't been touched since then. It was a mess, mostly in the corners you couldn't see.

A man carries a slowly evolving picture, he thought, of how it's all going to be until the day he dies. He sees himself growing old, his wife aging with him, and their son reaching manhood, marrying, producing grandchildren for them. Pictures. How many of us see those pictures mature to match those in our heads? Jamie might have been caught up with drugs, become a junkie. Or Celia a drunk. Or himself snagged by some irrational wild affair into which men often throw themselves during their mid-life, with tragic consequences. Or perhaps Celia would have been the one to have the affair, some grand obsession, and Jamie caught on booze, himself hooked on crack? Who the hell could tell what the future might bring? He didn't think any of those things likely, but he didn't know for sure.

The kitchen began to spin.

What he should be doing, he knew, was not sitting and sipping coffee, dreaming of what might have been, but thinking over what wonderful times they had had together, and thanking God, thanking *someone*, anyway, that they were no longer suffering. Perhaps if they had lived, crippled in body and mind, it might have been much worse for them all. They might have ended up hating one another.

Was that selfish? After all, he was alive, and well.

He noticed the hump in the bed when he returned, and for a moment something stirred within him. It was the same kind of feeling he got when he woke each morning, forgetting Celia was gone.

"What the hell's going on?" he said, the words coming out a little slurred, despite the coffee.

The hump stirred slightly, the face coming into view. It was a woman, someone Dave did not immediately recognize. She smelled of whiskey and remained asleep. She looked familiar, though he couldn't say why.

Dave continued to stare at her, then suddenly remembered.

The Vangellen woman. She had stayed. He felt so groggy and unstable it was all he could do to fall into bed beside her, thinking that it could all be better sorted out in the morning, when the effects of the drink had worn off.

When he woke again, she was propped up beside him, naked and smoking a cigarette, the bedcovers thrown back on her side. She seemed quite uninhibited, though this might have been forced: a pose for him to wake up to.

Her stringy hair was tickling his face.

She was wearing her glasses. It seemed strange, a naked woman wearing glasses. Quite out of his experience. They were usually desperate for you to see them without glasses.

It took him a few seconds to register that he was in his own bedroom. Then he remembered the previous evening, some of it, and a strong feeling of disappointment in himself overcame him.

"How the hell did that happen?" he said.

She turned and looked at him.

"Good morning. It was my fault. I think I went out intending to get laid. I don't get like it often. My period must be due. I hope you don't mind me smoking in bed?"

He didn't like the bit about the period, it made him feel as if he'd been used to fulfill a function because no one else was available. Maybe that was true, but he didn't have to like it.

"I guess I needed it too, or I wouldn't have let it happen," he said, "so we're both at fault—if anyone is. You'll have to forgive me for my opening remark. It's just that I feel a little guilty, like I'm cheating on my wife. It's too recent, you understand."

"Of course. I suppose we drank too much last night."

"I never make drinking an excuse for my actions."

What had happened was that they had sat in the living-room talking for a period which Dave had intended should last about thirty minutes, but which stretched to two hours. During that time the coffee had been abandoned in favor of a bottle of whiskey, and before they realized it, they were both shelling their feelings and letting them pop out like peas.

"I loved my wife and son very much," Dave had said, "and it's hard, *very* hard, to let them go to wherever they've gone. I'm still trying to keep them here, do you know what I mean?"

"I think I understand. I lost my mother when I was nine, and I used to pretend she was still there. I would play a game, when I walked home from school, convincing myself that she would be in the kitchen, cooking dinner when I got home. I used to open the door and yell out, 'Mom!' It used to drive my father crazy."

"I bet it did. It would drive *me* crazy."

Vanessa had nodded.

"Yeah, well, I guess it was kind of rough for him."

"Anyway," Dave had said, "it was you who wanted to talk. Can I help? I mean, Danny's not here, so you can bounce things off me, if you want to."

That's when she had started depodding her emotions. Not the really deep ones, but the recent hurts. She told him about the former boyfriend, and setting fire to his bed.

"I've got a history, I'm afraid," she had said, her elbows on her knees and her shoulders hunched, "of fire-starting. I guess I'm sick."

"Not necessarily sick," he had hastened to assure her aware that her neckline had fallen forward and that he could see her pale blue-veined breasts, which had embarrassed him. "Just a little unstable perhaps?"

He had forced his eyes away, but they came back again.

"A rose by another name. I know there's something wrong with me, you don't have to be nice about it, but I'm working on it."

They had had some more whiskey and Dave had started to cry. She had comforted him, first holding his hand, and then resting his head on her shoulder, hugging him. He couldn't remember how they had got from the sofa to the bed, but he did recall how cool her skin had felt. Celia had always felt warm, plump and warm. With Vanessa, he was aware of a long length of woman beside him, her hands and feet cold to the touch. The texture of her skin was silky, not dry like Celia's. She didn't help him either, the way Celia used to, to enter her. It was all left up to him to fumble and find the entrance to her vagina, while she lay beneath him as if she were powerless to do otherwise. He did not recall his climax and wondered if he had actually made it, but he sure as hell wasn't going to ask her, any more than he was going to inquire whether she had got there or not.

Now that morning was here he felt like shit, both emotionally and physically. His head was hammering, which was understandable because he could see the empty whiskey bottle through the open doorway, lying on the living-room floor. His stomach was not too good either, but that might have been an emotional reaction.

She wasn't even his type. He liked short feisty women, with dark eyes, like Celia, not tall rangy females with blondish hair, all elbows and angles. Vanessa was thin and painfully white, with large under-full breasts that accentuated every movement of her body. Not his type at all.

"So what do we do now?" she asked, sitting up and lighting another cigarette.

"What do you mean?" he said, warily.

She looked at him sharply, and her mouth dropped at the corners.

"Oh, I'm sorry. I'll get dressed and go."

He held her arm as she went to get out of bed.

"Wait a minute, I'm sorry. You've got a right to ask what the hell is going on. Truth is, I don't know. I really don't. I'm not used to one-night stands, and at the moment I just feel drained. I think you've done me some good, listening to me talk, making love with me, but I don't know whether I want to see you again. I'm being honest. I think I like you. How do you feel about me?"

"I don't know you yet. I mean, I know a little bit about you, and I think you're a nice man . . ."

"Like Danny?"

"No, not like Danny. Danny's sweet, but I could never go to bed with him. He knows that."

Does he? thought Dave. That'll be news to Danny.

"So basically," she continued, "I like your body, but I'm not sure about *you* yet."

She smiled.

"*That's* honest enough," he said. "I deserved that. Well, any time you want to use my body just yell."

"I will."

He got out of bed and shaved and showered, then went to the kitchen to make some coffee. She followed him through the bathroom. When she entered the kitchen, she looked fresh and serene, her long face almost regal. He saw that she had tied her hair back, which emphasized her narrow features. Not his type at all, except, damn it, yes, she excited him. While they were making love was the first time since Celia and Jamie's death that he had managed not to think about them. Was that a good thing? Maybe he *should* think about them all the time? Maybe they should be an obsession, if he had loved them?

He had looked at one or two other women when Celia was alive. Not seriously. Just window shopping, wondering what it would be like. The sort of minor fantasies that any man might have, when he sees someone he finds particularly sexy. He had never felt guilty about it then, while Celia was there, feeling they were harmless secrets. Once or twice he had even told her, and she would feign anger, punching him on the arm. Now she was dead, it didn't seem right to desire other women. He felt he should be faithful to her memory for a long time, and not want anything but that memory.

But the fact was the misery had eased a little, and he was weary of the devastating nature of his emotional pain.

They had some coffee and toast together and he heard himself saying, "Can I see you again?"

She raised her eyebrows in a very effective way, making him feel like a plebeian before a patrician lady.

"I thought you didn't want to."

"I said I didn't *know*. I've decided I do want to see you, if it's okay with you."

"You know I'm on probation?"

"Sure. You want to tell me about that? Why *did* you fire your boyfriend's bed? He make you mad?"

Her eyes took on a distant look.

"No, that is, yes. He asked me to do something special for him, sexually, you know. I did, but I hated him for it afterwards, so I set fire to his bed."

Dave's brain jangled with warning bells. Each one of them told him to back off now, get the hell away from this woman, leave her to find her own way out of the jungle she seemed to be in. There was something about her manner that indicated there was an ugly hidden monster, which, when it was revealed to him, he was going to find revolting. If he got too involved with her, he would start to feel responsible for her. Maybe it was already too late?

"I'm not going to ask what this something special was, because it's none of my business, but was it so terrible that it warranted a fire?"

"Not so terrible, really, between lovers—but it was the thing my father used to make me do."

The bells were almost deafening now, but Dave found he couldn't help himself.

"To him? Your father?"

"Yes, I'm a classic case of a sexually abused child."

She gave him a wry smile. At least, he took it to be wry.

"I don't know what to say," he muttered.

"Don't tell me I've shocked a policeman. No need to say anything."

"If we ever make love again, you'll have to warn me what

that special thing is, because I like my bed the way it is at the moment."

She stared at him seriously.

"Funny thing is, I think it would be okay with you. I mean, I think I want to."

Dave didn't know what to make of all this, but it frightened him. He was a big tough cop with hoods and gangsters, but strange women scared the hell out of him. She looked like a witch. Her eyes bored into him, when she stared at him, as if she could see every stain on his soul. She seemed unpredictable, as if at any moment she might start screaming hysterically, or spitting venom at him for some imagined insult. There were people like that, who seemed more or less rational most of the time, but something else surfaced occasionally and they became monsters.

Was she one of those? Would he wake up some time to find her bent over him like some predatory bird, ready to rip open his throat with her claws?

They finished breakfast, then Dave said he had to meet Danny.

"Oh," she replied.

"What do I say to him?"

She looked surprised.

"What you like. Do you want to tell him we made love? That's okay with me, if you do, but I thought you were worried about being in mourning, what he will think of you. I don't mind. Whatever makes you comfortable. I won't say anything unless Danny mentions it to me, then I'll know you've told him. He's just a friend, you know."

"So I understand."

She went to pick up the dishes to carry them into the kitchen, and he started to say, "Leave those—" when something caught his eye. He grabbed her wrist, pulled up her sleeve. There were scars, tiny circles, on the white flesh inside her forearm.

"What's this?" he asked in his policeman's voice.

She wrenched her arm out of his grip.

"None of your business."

"I'd still like to know," he replied, modifying his tone.

Her ponytail had come undone and she was looking at him darkly, through curtains of hair. Dave could not tell whether she was angry or upset. He waited for an answer.

Finally she said, "My father did them, to punish me. They're cigarette burns."

He stepped back, really shocked now.

"To *punish* you? What, for some childish wrong?"

"He told me I led him on, made him . . . made him . . . I can't say it. He was punishing me for being a whore, he said, and the way he did it was to burn me with a cigarette—after he'd been with me."

"Christ almighty," he breathed.

Dave was appalled. He had seen some terrible things in his time as a policeman, but he had been able to detach himself from them, tell himself they were a part of the human race with which he had no connection. His was a different world, a better place, and things like that did not happen in the better place. Now here was someone he had met, liked, even made love to. Part of *his* better world. And she had been through this awful ordeal: rape and torture. And the man who had done these unspeakable things to her was her father, for God's sake, the man who should have protected her from such things.

"How old were you?"

"Ten."

He wanted to kill her father, right there and then.

"Is he still around?" he asked.

"Dead. He died in a domestic fire—our house burned down."

"You weren't there at the time?"

"I started it."

After she'd gone he sat down and had another coffee, thinking, I mustn't get involved with this woman. It's not her fault she's like she is, but I sure as hell don't want to die in a fire of my own making. I must get Danny to tell her I don't want to see her again. She's not bad news, she's the worst news I could get at the moment. My own wife died in a fire under two months ago, I can't take any more of this stuff.

He left the apartment and went to meet Danny.

After leaving Dave's apartment, Vanessa went down the passageway toward the elevator, but opened the fire doors instead, and stepped out into the quiet dimness of the back stairway. Alone now, without fear of being interrupted, she took out a cigarette and lit it, taking a long pull on it.

Had anyone caught her, they would have believed her to be a wife or girlfriend who had promised to give up smoking, but was still having the odd cigarette in secret.

For a moment she watched the smoke curling up from the end of the cigarette, then she deliberately reversed it. Pulling up her sleeve like a junkie about to mainline, she gritted her teeth and then pressed the lighted end of the cigarette against the soft white skin in the crook of her elbow. There was a sizzling sound and the stench of burning flesh.

Tears sprang to her eyes as the pain coursed through her. She put her tongue between her teeth and almost bit through it in an effort to diversify the pain. Then, at last, the cigarette was out and she threw it away.

"Oh, Daddy," she whispered, "I'm sorry."

She spat on the burn, to try to soothe it, then went back through the fire doors and took the elevator.

10

Danny licked the brown-powdered rim of his plastic coffee cup as a subconscious action, probably giving himself time to take in the monstrous confession he had heard from Dave, and then looked up. His eyes revealed his feelings and for once Dave did not protest at Danny's habit. Though his voice was low and quiet Dave could tell his partner was incensed.

"You *slept* with her? Shit, Dave. You told me to stay away from her. Why? So you could get to her? What kind of friend are you, anyway?"

Dave felt suitably guilty, and started saying all those things people say when they're desperately back-pedaling, trying to mollify an enraged friend with a justifiable grievance. He began reinventing their former conversation, to put himself in a more favorable light.

"I didn't tell you to stay away from her, I meant be careful, is all. Look, Danny, would I be telling you this if I wanted to sneak behind your back? It was an accident, that's all. She came there looking for you, and I happened to be there instead."

Danny looked mournful.

"Three weeks I been trying to get her in the sack, and you do it by accident. It isn't fair. It just isn't fair."

He turned and stared into Dave's eyes.

"Tell me something, if I had been there, you think she would have gone to bed with me?"

Dave wondered whether to lie, to bolster his partner's ego, or tell him the truth. Either way he was going to feel like the worst kind of bastard that ever partnered a cop. He finally opted for the truth.

"Danny, you're just not her type . . ."

"So you say."

"So *she* says," replied Dave. "Look, some women would go overboard for you, and wouldn't give me a second glance. This woman's a head taller than you, for Christ's sake. She's almost as tall as *me*. You want her to bend over double every time she kisses you?"

"Lotsa men have had girlfriends taller than they are. Look at Dudley Moore. Look at Billy Joel."

"Those guys are *rich* celebrities, they have something more to offer than inches. Every time Vanessa looked down on you, she'd see that bald spot. Shit, I didn't mean to say that, Danny, I'm sorry . . ." Dave wanted to laugh now, at Danny's expression, which would not have been out of place on the face of General Sherman on being told by a color coordinator that he would look good in gray.

Dave pulled himself together.

"Look, Danny, I wish she wanted to go to bed with you, I really do. I didn't mean anything like that to happen. It was the booze . . ."

Danny, who had begun to calm down, was incensed again.

"You got her *drunk* first? No wonder you call it an accident."

"She got *me* drunk. I swear, she practically dragged me into the bed and raped me. I can't help it, I have this effect on her. You don't, you little squirt, so for Christ's sake, find yourself a pipsqueak of a woman and *then* go to it."

The two men, driving through Pacific Heights, stared out of different windows of the car, Dave through the front windscreen, because he was driving, and Danny through the side window, because he didn't want to look the same way as Dave was looking. They carried on in silence for two more blocks, before Danny melted first, as he always did.

"I won't forget this, Dave," he said stiffly, "and I want you to know that."

"Right, don't forget it, but shut up."

"I will."

"Good."

Danny looked out of the side window again.

"Are you seeing her again?" he asked.

"I don't know. I don't want to get involved with anyone, right at the moment. She's not really my type, anyway. I like 'em short," he glanced at Danny, "shorter even than would suit you."

He gave Danny a grin. The other man kept a stiff face for about thirty seconds, before he broke into a smile.

"I don't like 'em short, that's the trouble. I like to have to climb up their legs to reach the goodies. I like to monkey up their willowy forms."

"You're a pervert. You got a weirdness to you."

A call came over the radio, a fire four blocks away. Dave spun the wheel and they raced to the scene.

That night Dave drove back to his apartment having finished the midnight shift. Danny had tried to persuade him to go to a bar, but he was not a barfly and let Danny go alone. Halfway to his address Dave changed his mind and drove instead to the outskirts of Pacific Heights, to a residential district where he knew he wouldn't get accosted by anyone. He wanted to be able to stroll around deep in thought, without having to keep his wits about him watching for muggers at every turn in the road.

He parked the car in a street with large houses and driveways, locked it, and started to walk, head hunched down into his coat. As usual there was a glow in the sky, created by fires somewhere in the city. The fire department, desperately stretched in manpower and resources, would be going through its usual patterns of chaos.

Dave walked aimlessly, his apartment no longer a place where he could sit and recall favorite memories. It had started to become a hall of sadness, and Dave was now revising his opinion that he would be better to stay there. He was seriously thinking now of getting a new place, perhaps a bit smaller, more in keeping with a single man's life.

There was the business with Vanessa Vangellen to consider as well. She had been good company that night, but he felt no burning desire to see her again. If she called him, fine, he would respond, but he could not summon up the enthusiasm to contact her. Not yet. He wondered if his lack of energy were due to some kind of illness: maybe he was coming down with something?

Thus immersed, he stopped and looked up at the stars. It was a clear night, with a heaven full of night suns. When he glanced along the street, he could see another man, also staring up. Only the guy did not seem to be looking vertically, but at an angle of about thirty degrees. It took a few seconds for Dave to realize the man was staring at the upstairs window of a large house.

The man had his hands in his pockets and seemed extraordinarily intent on the light in the window.

A peeping Tom, thought Dave. The guy is watching some-one's wife or daughter take off her clothes.

What should he do about it? He wasn't on duty and this wasn't his territory, anyway. He could tell the guy to get his ass out and away home. Any decent citizen would do that.

He walked toward the character, who turned at the sound of footsteps, gave Dave a casual glance, then went back to his voyeurism.

He's a cool one, thought Dave.

The man was young, with handsome features. Dave would have called him beautiful, except that he didn't use words like that, fearing their effeminacy. The guy's hair was jet black and slicked down on his scalp. His build was slight and lean, though he was of average height. Why the hell does this character need to stare at women's bedrooms? thought Dave. He looked as if he could get any woman he wanted.

As Dave approached the man, he became aware of a fragrance, the delicate sweet smell of some kind of herb.

"Hey," said Dave, "what . . . ?"

He did not manage to finish the sentence. There was a tremendous *whooomph* and the upstairs window of the house blew out, spurting white tongues of flame. Incandescence! The fire was so bright and intense Dave was temporarily blinded. He felt the heat scorching down the street like a torrent. A blistering wave of air picked him up and threw him bodily against a wall, where he slithered down the bricks to finish up in a sitting position on the sidewalk. For a few moments he lay there, too stunned to comprehend what had happened.

Gradually his senses came back to him, but not his sight.

The man who had been watching the window was a dark haze, a fuzzy silhouette in Dave's eyes. The flames were licking round him, and his clothes must have been scorched and unbearable to the touch, yet there was no indication that he felt any pain. Instead he stood stock still, allowing the fire to reach out, flaying his skin.

The figure remained watching the window, until some audible screams reached him, then he turned quickly and walked past the detective.

Dave, certain that the guy had planted an incendiary device in the house, and had been waiting for it to explode, grabbed the man's legs. The fragrance he had smelled earlier was a cloying stench now, that threatened to make him vomit. He recognized it: the scent of almonds.

Dave felt a tremendous power in the man, vibrating like the contained energy from some huge dynamo. As he clung on, groggy and half-blind, he was lifted by one hand, torn away from the leg, and thrown across the street. He struck the opposite curb, jarring bones and teeth. The impact was excruciating and knocked all the wind out of him. Incredibly he had burned his hands on the man's shoe, which had been furnace hot, yet its wearer had seemed unconcerned by the heat.

It was then that Dave first began to realize that he was dealing with something outside his usual sphere of experience.

When he came to, he was looking into a face bracketed by yellow and black. It took him a few seconds to realize it was the face of a fireman.

"You all right, buddy?" the face asked him.

Dave's limbs and back ached. He tried to sit up.

"I think so—head aches."

The fireman stood up, towering over him now.

"The medics will be here in a second."

Down the street, the fire was still raging, the flames billowing like plumes up into the night sky. There were fire trucks parked in the street, the usual commotion that went with such events. There was a crowd too, but a fairly small one: fires were so commonplace you could choose your spectacle. Dave was inside the ribbons put up to define the territory of the firefighters and that of the spectators. A uniformed policeman came over to him, out of the darkness, and said, "Suppose you tell me . . ." but Dave cut him short by flashing his shield.

Minor cracks and explosions were occurring now within the fired building, shooting showers of sparks from the flames. These were greeted with ooohs and aaahs from the crowd as if it were a firework display put on for their benefit. The heat generated was tremendous, and scorched Dave where he sat. The policeman helped him to his feet, and he allowed himself to be assisted back, out of the hot zone.

"When did you arrive on the scene?" Dave asked the officer.

"Same time as the fire boys," was the answer.

"You see anyone running away?"

"Nope. Saw plenty running toward it."

Dave nodded.

"I saw the bastard. I'll have a word with your guys. He looked like some goddamned twenties film star—like Valentino or something. And he stank of some kind of aftershave."

"You got close enough to *smell* him?" the cop said, sounding surprised.

"I got close enough to *grab* him, but he's a strong bastard—skinny, but strong. Threw me across the street. I was already stunned a bit, by the explosion from the fire. Funny thing is, it didn't seem to bother him. The blast, the heat. He walked around in it like it was a cool day in the park."

The cop shook his head slowly.

"These fire-starters, they're nuts. You can't compare them with normal people."

"I guess not," said Dave, immediately thinking of Vanessa.

The pair of them then had to back off, as a side wall came down into the street with a shrieking of stone and timber. Hot bricks went flying through the air like smoking bombs, to bounce dangerously among skipping watchers. Bits of flaming mortar fell into the crowd, though they were well back from the main conflagration. There were screams and shouts. The flames suddenly leapt upwards, having caught hold of some combustible material: a quick-growing artistic tower of red and yellow. Large splinters of fiery timber zinged into the air like tracers.

A fireman had been caught a glancing blow by a section of the wall, and staggered a few paces before falling on his face. He was dragged clear just as the ambulances began to arrive.

"Those are the devils I feel sorry for," said the cop, indicating the fire crew, "they get it night and day."

Dave stayed to watch the inferno burn itself to a black molar on the face of the street. A detective from the local precinct had told him the mansion was no great loss as far as he was concerned, it being the home of a mobster they had been trying to nail for years.

"Those beautiful colors in the fire—that's heroin going up, or coke. Makes a pretty flame." He sniffed. "You could get high around here, just taking a breath. Could be, he had some of it stashed in hollow walls . . . money, too. Nice fire. No loss, pal."

"You think it was a rival attack?"

The detective gave him a sidemouth smile.

"Bet my ass on it. He pissed a lot of people off, especially me. I didn't start the fire, but I woulda if I'd thought of it. Somebody else's godfather got tired of him and ordered a hit. This is the way they do it now. Why be different from everybody else? You want to take someone out? Burn him, let him roast along with a dozen others the same night. Give the cops a headache identifying who's who. Hide the burned trees inside a charred forest. It makes sense."

"I guess so," said Dave, wearily. The exhaustion that the adrenaline had chased away came flooding back now. He said good night to the detective and told him he'd send him a report in the morning. The guy thanked him, without taking his eyes off the smoldering ruins of the house.

Dave drove back to his apartment and climbed into bed

about six thirty, falling instantly asleep. Danny called him at eight and he roused himself sufficiently to tell his partner what had happened and that he would not be in the office before eleven. He had taken a lot of smoke down into his lungs which was exacerbating any normal weariness. Danny said he understood and would catch up on some paperwork.

Dave did not mention the smooth-faced arsonist to Danny. He was going to, but he wanted to look through the files first, to see if the guy had a record. The image of the man was printed on Dave's brain, and he wanted to get this one very badly. The newspapers talked now of "white-fire" conflagrations, which appeared to be somewhat different from "ordinary" fires. The theory was that someone had invented or discovered, and was using, a new incendiary substance that produced an initial, very violent white flash, which ignited the target building. There was a purity to this white flame that puzzled most experts, who had never seen or heard of anything like it, even among the military's arsenal of fire weapons.

White-flame fires were about one in ten, and the fire Dave had witnessed the previous evening had been of that type. So had the one reported by Foxy Reynolds, a man with whom Dave now urgently needed to talk.

More important to Dave than both of these, was another white-flame fire: the Japanese department store in which his wife and son had been burned to death.

Foxy met him in a bar, which Dave expected because the other cop had a reputation as a drinking man. Dave was therefore surprised when Foxy ordered an orange juice. They compared descriptions of the doer, though both men had been dazzled by the white fire at the time of the sightings, and neither had a really accurate portrait to recount.

Foxy said, "He looked like a mary."

"A what?" asked Dave.

Foxy then went shy.

"You know, kinda womanish, like a woman. You know. Not necessarily a gay, but pretty boy, with that soft skin and long eyelashes and stuff. A mary."

Dave remembered seeing a cowboy movie, *The Culpeper Cattle Company*, where the trail cook's helper was called "Little Mary" or something similar. It was not an expression he had ever used, or would want to use.

Finally, Dave asked Foxy if he had anything more to tell him, anything he could remember out of the ordinary. Dave knew what he wanted to hear, but he didn't want to prompt Foxy.

"Like what?" asked the uniformed cop.

"Anything, anything at all."

Foxy screwed up his face.

"I don't remember . . . wait. There was this smell, like the fish Clem grills. Like marzipan. Almonds. That was it."

Dave thumped the tabletop triumphantly, causing others in the bar to look across and shake their heads.

"That's it," said Dave. "I smelled it too. It's the same guy. Have another drink, Foxy."

Foxy ordered another orange juice. Dave had a vodka, a small one.

"You on the wagon?" Dave asked the red-haired cop.

Foxy looked at him through bright blue eyes.

"Yeah, ever since I saw that fire downtown. Well, not straight after, but then I got to figuring that I was flushing my life down the toilet, you know what I mean? I got a nice wife, nice coupla kids, why throw it all away for the sake of numbing my brain after duty?"

Dave looked at the pupils of his colleague's eyes and saw the trembling in the hand that lifted the glass of orange juice.

"So what are you taking instead of booze?" he asked quietly.

Foxy was immediately defensive.

"You think I'm taking something?"

"You might as well carry a sign."

Foxy looked down and kicked the table leg savagely.

"I can't hack this anymore. It's killing me."

"Tell me about it. No, I mean, tell me about it. I'm listening, Foxy."

"Ray. For Christ's sake, call me *Ray*. That's my name."

"Tell me, Ray."

Foxy stared at the orange juice in his hand and looked about to throw it across the room, but he didn't. In the end he placed it carefully on the table top, and then met Dave's gaze, squarely.

"I've been taking some uppers, to get me through the shifts. I'm not cut out to be a city cop, Dave. Not all of us are. I wanna do something else now, something where I don't see people with their faces smashed in, or their skin burned off, or in pieces after a traffic accident. Only, I got a problem, you see—a financial problem. Like, I have this family, who need a family house, and kids cost money . . . Shit, why am I telling you all this?"

"Because I asked you to. Go on . . . Ray."

"I've been thinking. I want to go into business, open a small restaurant. Nothing fancy, you know, just a bistro—that's a kind of French place, with these tables with cloths on and candles in bottles, kinda Boho-arty . . ."

"I know what a bistro is, Ray, I'm not dumb."

"Sorry, I get enthusiastic, and want to explain it all the time. It's my wife's idea, really, she's the brains of the family. But," he sighed, "anyway, we can't do it yet. Not for a while."

"Why not? You up to your ears?"

"Not badly. I don't play the horses or anything like that. It's just mortgage stuff and an outstanding loan."

"Ray, I'll lend you the money to start your bistro, settle your debts, whatever. We'll get a contract drawn up this week. I'll be your silent partner."

Foxy sat back in his chair and blinked.

"What the hell are you saying, Dave? You hardly know me."

"I know you well enough. I met your wife at the last Captain's Ball. She talked about your kids. How well do I have to know you? This is a business deal. Some people make business deals with men they've never even met."

Foxy looked as though he didn't know whether to laugh or to cry.

"Jesus, Dave, where are *you* going to get the money from?"

"I've already got it. I've also got several brokers on my ass, telling me how to invest it, and with who. Now I got my investment. I chose it all myself and don't have to pay a broker's fee."

Dave saw that Foxy required more of an explanation, and he didn't blame him. He leaned forward, knowing the next piece was going to be painful to vocalize. He had thought about it a lot, but he hadn't spoken to anyone, not even Danny.

"You see, when I collected the insurance on my wife's death, I didn't want anything to do with the money. These accountants and brokers, they get wind of large pay-outs, and they move in like buzzards, when you're still running around with half a head, confused, bewildered by your loss.

"I still feel a bit like that. Me and my wife, we insured each other pretty heavily, for Jamie's sake, thinking that if one of us went, the other would need it to pay for baby-sitters or boarding school." Dave swallowed a lump that was in his throat. "Neither of us guessed Jamie would go too, so I'm stuck with all this blood money. You want some of it, it's yours."

Foxy looked as if the sun had been created over again, right before his eyes.

"Shit, Dave, I don't know what to say. Sure, yes, great. You won't regret this. Me and Clem, we're not afraid of work, that's not why I want off the force. It won't make a fortune either, because I ain't gonna turn it into one of those places that catch the eye of the Mafia, and have to end up taking an offer I can't refuse.

Hell, no, this is just going to be a quiet little place on the corner—but we'll make a tidy profit, and you won't regret this."

"You already said that," said Dave, smiling. He took a sip of his vodka, and a bulb lit up in his head. "Hey, I got a great name for the place!"

"What?" cried Foxy, excitedly.

"How about 'Red's Square'?"

Foxy stared at him for a minute and his jaw dropped, then suddenly realized Dave was kidding, and a look of relief came over his features, before he said, "Yeah, great, Dave. Only don't make it part of the contract, eh? Red's Square. You bastard. You had me going there for a minute . . ."

Manovitch had followed Dave all the way to Jack's restaurant and was sitting in his car enjoying a cigar. He could see the two men through the window and was rather enjoying the idea of spying without being seen. There was a faint kind of thrill to it, similar to the feeling he got when he went to a peep show. He liked the idea of being in the darkness, looking in on a private scene, while his own presence remained a secret. There was a kind of power in it. Manny felt himself in control.

He had not, of course, made any concrete plans to get even with Peters, but he knew he would, one day. It didn't matter how long, how soon. It would be done. In fact, he liked the wait. He liked following his victim, getting to know his habits, forming a dossier on the other man's life. There was satisfaction in gathering information. It made Manny feel like a CIA agent or something. It gave the operation an official base, almost as if it had been rubber-stamped by a higher authority.

"I'll get you, Peters," he whispered, watching the other man's lips move as the policeman spoke to Foxy. "I'll string your balls on a thread and hang 'em out for the fucking sparrows to eat."

Manny enjoyed this, too. Mouthing threats. Telling himself what he was going to do to his victim, once he had him in his hands. The whole thing was exciting. It gave him a hard-on to think of killing Peters. It needed dealing with.

Manny started the car. He drove to a club he knew, where there would be broads available for the price of a few drinks and a few bucks on a dressing table afterwards. One or two of them even liked a few slaps on the ass, before he rammed his dick in them. He was willing to administer such pleasure, if it was required.

He parked outside the Silver Chalice, and crossed the foyer, through two sets of double doors, and into the clubroom itself.

It was dimly lit inside, and Manny strained his eyes against the semidarkness. There were only a few people there. A bad day of the week.

"Double Jack on the rocks," he told the bartender.

Someone nudged his elbow and Manny turned to see a fruit staring at him.

"Hi," said the fruit. "You cruising?"

"I'm hetero," said Manny. "Get out of my face."

The fruit shrugged, smiled, and sipped his drink.

"Only asking. No need to be impolite, you tragic man."

Jesus, thought Manny, you couldn't even have a drink in peace without someone wants to screw with you.

Now that his eyes were used to the gloom, Manny surveyed the rest of the club. There were two hookers he knew, sitting in the corner. Lolita and a pal of hers, what'sername, Deborah. They had such fancy names, hookers. Probably not their own. Lolita was a blonde and Deborah dark-haired. They often worked together, but Manny wasn't feeling *that* energetic. Lolita would do for him tonight.

Apart from these two and the fruit, there was only one other person there, a young guy with dark eyes. He was staring at Manny as if he were about to burst into tears. Probably another fruit, thought Manny. The guy was just a little too handsome to be true. Manny distrusted perfect looks. They smacked of hormones and facial treatments.

Suddenly, Manny wanted the john badly. All that coffee he had drunk in the office had weakened his bladder. He needed to go at least once every hour these days. He took a quick bolt of his drink and then crossed the floor to the toilets, making sure the fruit wasn't following him. He wasn't going to take his dick out in front of that creep, no matter how badly he needed a piss.

Once in the john, he relieved himself while reading the latest graffito. It was misspelled as usual, but Manny liked that. *He* could spell and that made him superior in this night world of pimps, hookers and fruits. He looked at his watch: two minutes past eleven.

When he reached the velvet-covered steel double doors to reenter the clubroom, he noticed through the smoked-glass portholes that there was some kind of commotion going on inside. Two men were confronting each other across the dime-sized dance floor. They were both similar-looking, slim young men. They didn't seem to be having a vocal argument, but it was obvious from the way that they were standing, staring at each other, that something was going down. Manny decided to stay outside in case some shooting started.

Suddenly, one of the men, incredibly, exploded into a ball of flames.

"Shit!" said Manny, stunned. "He's been torched."

Manny took one or two steps back, but went forward again almost immediately, fascinated by what was happening on the other side of the metal doors.

With a shock, Manny realized it was the too-handsome stud, the one who had been staring at him with wet eyes just a few minutes before, who was burning. The other guy must have come into the club while Manny was in the john. Funny thing was, the second guy had gone. Manny hadn't seen him leave, but he was no longer in the clubroom.

The tinted portholes in the door had protected Manny's eyes from the flash, so that he could still see, but it was bright enough in the club to startle him. Others, those inside the room, were rubbing their eyes, blinded it seemed. Only the bartender, who had been down behind the counter doing something with the glasses, appeared to have survived the flash.

The living ball of fire was staggering around the room, thrashing wildly, dripping flames on the carpet. Within the bright burning sun Manny could discern the silhouette of a man: arms and legs, torso, tottering on muscles that were rapidly being devoured, on bones that would soon crack under the heat.

Small fires were starting where he trod. Tablecloths began to trickle flame. Seat pads on chairs were ablaze. The carpet was burning. Plastic fittings began to crackle and spit, shooting out small flaring missiles like molten saliva.

The fireball lurched toward the bar.

The bartender's eyes opened wide and he picked up a drink, rushed around the counter, and threw it in the blazing man's face, probably wanting to help him. Unfortunately there was liquor in the glass. The alcohol fueled the flames, making the face crackle more fiercely.

Just as a drowning man clutches at straws, so a burning man reaches out for help. The victim staggered forward and clutched the bartender in an embrace of fire. The bartender began screaming in a high voice, trying to struggle out of the hold.

He failed.

The conflagration was redoubled.

"Jesus!" cried Manny.

The blazing pair began a strange stumbling dance across the club floor, locked together like a pair of lovers learning their first waltz. They were creatures of another world, burning as if they had been dipped in wax. An inferno of two. They stumbled into the large velvet curtains hiding the small stage and these caught fire immediately. Within seconds the curtains fell blazing to the floor and more carpet fires belched flames, smoke and poisonous gases. Lines of fire shot across the clubroom floor, like burning sulfur. Black curling smoke filled the atmosphere. There were fizzing and popping sounds as Formica tables bubbled, split and hissed gas. Chairs fell apart as the glue in their joints melted.

As Manny watched, frozen to the spot, the whole clubroom erupted in fire, inflammable items spurting fiery streaks, with every faltering step of the terrible dance. It was mostly Formica and cloth. Flames leapt from table to table to carpet to more curtains and managed to catch the clothes of patrons. Lolita, in a flimsy muslin dress, turned into a torch, her hair a fountain of fire, her face crispening quickly.

The original victim was still screaming and others had joined him in a hysterical chorus. Faces began to blacken as Manny watched. Deborah, blinded by the flash, fire and panic, tried to reach the exit, but the remainder of the incandescent curtain material fell on her and stuck to her skin, giving her the look of some creature from a horror movie.

The bar was now a roaring furnace and the bottles lined up on the shelves behind began boiling. Some shot their corks, spraying liquor like golden-rain fireworks. Others cracked and split, or simply exploded, showering glass. Formica peeled, rolling itself up, like a live creature trying to escape the heat.

Manny could feel the heat through the steel doors. The velvet had begun to smoke on his side. He started to think of getting out, but he was still mesmerized by the scene behind the glass. It was as if he was privileged to have a glimpse of hell and its terrible tortures.

The fruit came Manny's way, running, seeking escape

through the steel doors. Manny quickly bolted them against him, before the terrified man could reach the handles. The double doors were thick and lined with rubber and would keep the fire at bay until Manny could figure out what to do next. He wasn't going to risk getting burned alive, or suffocated, not for anyone inside that room.

The man's face was against the tinted glass, distorted, screaming. Manny could see smoke rising from his back and shoulders. The man's hands clawed at the red-hot handles of the doors, trying to get them to turn. Then the eyes themselves were alight. Finally the face slipped down out of Manny's sight, its owner most probably asphyxiated by the toxic gases that must have been filling the room beyond.

The metal doors began to get hotter and Manny decided it was time to look for another way out. The conflagration would rage for a long while in the room and while he might be all right where he was, he didn't want to risk it, so he reluctantly left the hellish scene behind the glass portholes and went searching.

The john had a small back window, jammed shut by overpainting, of course, which Manny kicked out. He used his shoe to knock out the jagged pieces of glass around the edge and then crawled through to find himself in a dim passageway. It led to the foyer. There was smoke pouring from the clubroom doors as he passed and he could see the manager shouting frantically into a telephone in a small office off the foyer.

Manny looked at his watch.

Nine minutes past eleven.

The whole thing had only taken seven minutes.

Incredible! What an incredible experience! He felt elated. He was a survivor. He had witnessed people dying, burning to death, and he had come through it without so much as a scorch mark. The poor fuckers. But he, Manovitch, was alive. It was like he was some kind of hero. Like being part of a combat unit and coming through a hail of bullets unscathed, while others had dropped on all sides. Incredible. He felt important, a chosen one. He was *special*.

"There's people in there," Manny yelled to the manager. "They're burning to death!"

The manager looked up and Manny remembered where he was and knew he couldn't be caught there by the media. A probation officer should not be found in places of vice. They would make all kinds of shit out of it. He waved a hand at the manager and then pointed to the clubroom.

Manny hurried out into the street, aware that he had another hard-on, which, for once, his wife would have to deal with.

I got out, but the open door slammed shut behind me with a great deal of violence, almost as if God had reached down with his hand—I suppose it was a rush of air or something, to fill the bedroom—anyway, my father couldn't open it. I could hear the fire in there, wood cracking and splitting, and the smoke was pouring through the gap under the door. I suppose the door had expanded with the heat and was jammed.

"I was still in my nightie, the corner of it was smoldering. There was a half glass of whiskey and soda on the coffee table— my father had been drinking before he came in to . . . to . . ."

"To rape you," said Dave, simply, staring at the dark ceiling.

Vanessa, also lying on her back, also looking at the ceiling, agreed with him. "Yes, yes, to *rape* me, that's what he did. Anyway, I doused the nightie with the drink, and then heard scrabbling sounds, like rats scratching to get out of a box. It was my father, trying to claw his way through the door. The paint was beginning to peel and melt off the outside now—I could hear his screams, like—God, I don't know—like a baby being tortured."

"He wasn't a baby, he was your father, an adult who had taken advantage of a child of ten."

"Yes, you're right. Anyway, the screams, the scratching sounds, they stopped. The fire had consumed him. I ran out of the house, into the street—"

He made a slight movement, but her breath was whistling through her nostrils, and she said, "Don't touch me. Not yet."

"I wasn't going to," said Dave, calmly.

"I know you only want to hug me, to comfort me, but I don't want to be touched yet."

They lay there in the dark, side by side, on Dave's bed, fully dressed, not touching each other. It was the only way she could tell him, she had said, and she wanted to tell him. She wanted him to understand why she was like she was, though he had expressed no desire to be told, on the contrary. However, he felt that if it would help her, he was willing to listen. Whether it was right, or ethical, or anything like that, from a mental health point of view, he had no idea. He could be fanning the flames of her problems for all he knew, and he was concerned about that.

After a long period of silence, she spoke again.

"So that's how I killed my father."

"That's how your father was killed. It's a different thing."

"It was me who set light to the bed. I knew he was dead drunk."

"You were only ten years old, for God's sake. The fact that he was drunk was his fault, not yours, and because of his way of 'punishing' you—burning you with a cigarette afterward—your mind naturally went to fire, I guess. It wasn't your fault. You were a child. A parent has a sacred duty to protect his child from experiences like that, not be the cause of them. The man was sick."

"Like I'm sick now?"

"Not like—your illness was the result of this terrible experience, his was the cause of it."

"The cause of his illness was the death of his wife."

"That wasn't your fault either, she was your mother as well as his wife, and if he felt he couldn't handle the bereavement, he should have seen someone, a doctor. He didn't. He let himself sink lower than a sewer rat and he died like one."

"I don't think it was the sex he wanted. I think it was something else—comfort, my mother back, I don't know. He was my father, and I did love him."

"That was the trouble, he took advantage of that. In my book he got what he deserved. You'll never see it that way, I don't doubt, but I shudder when I think of him. I won't call him evil, because you say he was out of his head and it wasn't really him, but he was certainly a sick son-of-a-bitch."

"The truth probably falls somewhere between the two of us," she said quietly.

They didn't make love that night, but sat up and talked, mostly about fires. She asked Dave what had made him call her, because she said she was sure he had not intended to, even though he said he might.

"That's true," he told her honestly. "I even said as much to Danny." He scratched his head. "I don't know. I needed someone to talk to, someone not Danny, and you kept coming back into my mind."

"It's called loneliness," she said, seemingly not put out by his matter-of-fact way of telling her he was using her.

"I guess so. And I like you."

"You don't have to say that."

"I know, but I do. You attract me, as a woman, which I find intriguing because you're not my type, really."

"You're too hung up on types."

"Maybe I am. Anyway, here we are, and it looks like I'll be calling you again."

They both smiled at each other, not knowing what to say next, then Dave remembered about the arsonist he had seen in the residential district and described the man to her.

"He's a good-looking devil, that's for sure," said Dave.

Vanessa said, "You think he's responsible for the white-fire burnings?"

"There was definitely a white flash, before the main fire started in the house. It blinded me. I've never seen anything like it, except when you watch one of those documentary movies about atomic explosions. A nuclear flash—that's what it was like, though not on the same scale, of course."

"You think someone's invented some kind of bomb like an atom bomb—a mini atom bomb?"

"No, nothing like that. An incendiary device of some sort, that explodes into whiteness. Maybe something with a phosphorus base. I'll have to ask Forensics if they've got any ideas. I want to get this guy. I want him badly . . ."

The way in which he said it chilled Vanessa to the bone. Dave had a certain amount of the killer in him: she could sense it when he spoke of such things. It worried her. She felt like she was sleeping with someone who might explode at any moment and tear her to pieces for being an arsonist. After all, it was an arsonist who had been responsible for his wife's death.

He had loved his wife fiercely, of that Vanessa had no doubt, and the panther in him wanted revenge. It was this passion for vengeance that was helping him get through the worst time in his life. It was keeping his mind locked on something other than his loss, though she wondered what was going to happen once the white-fire maniac was caught.

Somehow he had fixated on this particular arsonist, which made her feel a little safer in his company, but when she had watched him pace the room earlier in the evening, his eyes burning, his hands clenching and unclenching, she was afraid for her own life. Though tall and lean, he was immensely strong, and he had a kind of righteousness which added to his strength. He would be a very difficult man to defeat, if he were your enemy and in the right, she thought to herself. He would rather die than allow a bad person to get the better of him. For Dave, she realized, the world was not like that: bad people did not win. She thought of him as some kind of modern-day Roy Rogers, or perhaps Superman. No, not Superman. Superman was an alien, after all, from another planet. Dave Peters was a home-grown hero, an American knight. Maybe Roy Rogers, after all.

"Have you ever done anything bad, Dave?"

He was at the sink, washing the dishes of the meal she had made for them both earlier.

He turned to stare at her as she leaned on the door-jamb, her arms folded.

"Those damned inquiring eyes," he muttered, looking into her face. "Yes, I've done something bad."

She smiled.

"What, stole your friend's lollipop at school?"

She thought he would be angry with her for making fun of him, but he simply looked away, quickly.

"No, I killed someone."

When she saw that he meant it, she felt a chill come over her. She had been right! He was at heart a killer. She turned to leave him to finish the washing up, but he was leaning stiff-armed on the sink, staring out of the window into the darkness, and he said, "Don't you want to hear how it happened?"

"Not really," she replied quickly.

"You opened the can of worms."

She stopped and then turned.

"All right. You want to tell me?"

"Yes, yes, I think I do. I hadn't even told this to Celia, so I don't know why I should want to tell you, but I do. Danny doesn't know. You'll carry my secret alone."

"I'm actually flattered. I'll look on it as a priest does a confession—for my ears only."

"Thank you."

He stopped talking then, and she waited for a long time, wondering if he was ever going to start again. When she was about to turn and leave, thinking he had changed his mind, he suddenly blurted, "I was seventeen at the time, and I ran around with this street gang . . ."

Her eyes widened.

"You were in a *street* gang? I imagined you were a choir boy."

"Don't interrupt," he said, sharply.

"Sorry."

"Anyway, this was no east-side kids gang—we were all from good homes. We were just bored, out for a bit of fun mostly, and we thought we could compete with the real hard cases, the Italians, the Puerto Ricans, the Blacks and the Irish. They would have made mincemeat of us, except they didn't want our turf and we never strayed in theirs. I don't suppose they knew we existed, and if they had they would have laughed us into the gutter.

"The leader of our gang, which we called the Puritans—how's that for a First Family gang name?—was a guy named Wexley Hunterman, a blonde kid born with a muscled frame and an arrogant streak as wide as a six-lane highway. Hunterman was contemptuous of most of the gang members, except one or two he was afraid of, but he looked down on me as a real worm. I was a skinny kid, a bit goofy in those days, not much meat on me at all."

He began to wash the dishes again, slowly, even the clean ones, but she didn't interrupt him.

"Anyway, Hunterman's father was a lawyer, which he was always ramming down our throats, lawyers being superior to anyone else in his eyes, and this lawyer's son had a cruelty in him you would not believe of your average Gestapo torturer. He loved to have the weaker members of the gang bound and at his mercy, pushing broken bits of razor blades up their nostrils . . ."

"Didn't you bleed?" she said, shocked.

"Of course, but if we went home with a bloody nose, our parents used to say, tut tut, fighting again? and that was it. He was a clever bastard, young Hunterman, he knew what he could get away with. He had a dozen good ideas like the one with the razor blades, some of them to do with the sexual organs— I'm not going to go into details."

"Why didn't you leave the gang?"

"I'm coming to that. I wanted to, but like most street gangs the Puritans ran on fear, no one was permitted out. Still, I decided, what could they do to me that they hadn't done already? One day I didn't turn up at our usual meeting place after school, or the next, then they came to get me and met me out of class.

"I was taken to an old abandoned water tower on the vacant lot of a factory site."

Dave hesitated and she wondered if he was going to go on.

After a long while, during which she kept absolutely still, he continued the story.

"One of them lit a fire. Hunterman put the blade of his knife into the fire until it was red hot then he . . . he threatened my eyes with the tip of the blade. He pretended he was going to burn out my eyes.

"I kept my mouth shut tight. I was damned if I was going to give them the satisfaction of screaming. That's what Hunterman wanted. He needed a scream out of me. He needed fear. He finally got it.

"He was pissed at me for not responding, so they took off my shoes and socks and Hunterman pushed the knife blade under one of my toenails, then another, and another, till I screamed like hell."

Vanessa felt the blood drain from her face and she felt giddy and sick.

"Good God," she whispered.

Dave gave her a grim smile.

"Oh, I screamed then. I—can—still—smell—the—burning—flesh. My own flesh. I can still feel that blade peeling my big toenail off. It was fucking *agony*, I'm telling you. Couldn't walk properly for weeks.

"Once he had his scream, Hunterman kissed me full on the lips and said, 'Cry, baby. Don't cry, baby. Poppa's not mad anymore.'"

"They forced me up the water tower, blindfolded me, and tied my hands behind my back. Then they tied a rope around my ankles and pushed me over the edge. I was left hanging upside down, sixty feet above solid concrete."

"Good God . . ."

"I was terrified. After it was dark, Hunterman came back with his two closest cronies, and they pulled me up and untied me. I felt sick and exhausted, but they weren't finished with me. They told me it was time to throw me off. I was so scared I wet my pants. Then the two cronies waved a hand at me and said to Hunterman, he'd better do it, on his own, it didn't need three of them to toss a wimp like me from a tower. So they left, and climbed down, leaving the two of us."

Dave had stopped washing up now, but his arms were still immersed in the suds.

"I was lying on the top of the water tower's tank, a huge hollow oblong made out of steel, and Hunterman was standing beside me, arms folded, looking down on me. I remember he said, 'Kiss my ass . . .'"

Dave paused, stirring the suds with his fingers.

" 'Kiss my ass and maybe I'll let you go.'"

"Instead, I lashed out in fury with both feet, caught him on the shins."

He looked at her now, full in the eyes.

"Hunterman went over the edge, somersaulting through the air, to land *splat*," he slapped a wet hand down hard on the Formica countertop and the sharp sound made her jump, "on the concrete down below. I heard screaming till the sound of the crunch, then the screaming stopped. Still shaking, I climbed down.

"I was so scared then—can't remember feeling remorse at that time, since, yes, but not then. Maybe I was too frightened to feel anything at all. I blurted out to the other two what had happened, but they didn't believe me. They thought Hunterman had slipped, and that I was trying to scare them or maybe grab a bit of glory. They told our parents and the cops that they had seen Hunterman start to climb down from the tower and then his hands just came away from the ladder. I never confessed to anyone but those two, and they never believed me, thank the Lord. In turn, I didn't squeal about what they had done to me. We just said we had all climbed to the top of the water tower to see what the view was like."

He paused again, before saying, "I think I'm telling you this because of the torture bit. We've both been through something as kids, though I realize your experience was far more traumatic than mine—it can't compare—but I thought you'd like to know."

"Thank you for your confidence," she said, wondering whether she really wanted it.

"Well," he wiped his hands on a towel, "you asked me whether I had ever done anything bad. The answer's yes, the worst. I murdered someone."

"Not without cause."

"Never mind the cause. There is no excuse. I murdered a fellow human being in cold blood and, worse still, I got away with it. Maybe what happened to Celia and Jamie was punishment for that, I don't know. If it was, then someone up there has a terrible sense of justice because they didn't do anything."

"God would never punish you in that way, he's not a punitive God, anyway."

"He is in the Bible."

"Only the Old Testament. We've progressed since then. He's a forgiving God now."

"He can change?"

She smiled.

"The universe is *about* change, all things change, even God. Nothing is immutable. Don't you read Keats?"

"Who?"

"Never mind, just rest assured that Celia and Jamie died because of something someone *else* did, not you."

"If you say so," he said. He put his arms around her neck and kissed her. "I love intellectuals—they're so . . . *intellectual.*"

She laughed.

12

Danny and Rita were sitting up in bed together drinking coffee. Their clothes were scattered around the room, draped over chairs, bedhead, lampshades, floor. They had come in drunk early this morning and had a sudden consuming passion for each other, so hot that Rita forgot she was a whore and for the first time in many years, money wasn't mentioned. She had enjoyed it as much as he had, not having to fake her orgasm.

Now her mouth was grim as she sipped her coffee.

"You gonna confess about me tonight?" she asked.

Danny put on his reading glasses, the ones he kept a secret from the boys at the station, and looked into her plump but pleasant features.

"I guess so," he said. "I can't see what difference last night makes. It's still a sin." He paused, recalling their unbridled lust for one another, both of them yelling dirty words as he was plunging into her. He began to go hard again as he thought about it and smoothed down the sheet self-consciously. "In fact, it was probably worse last night than usual."

"I don't like you confessing about me," she said. "It makes

me feel dirty. I mean, don't I have a say in whether God gets told about what we do?"

Danny thought about that and conceded that she had a point.

"I don't mention you by name, if that's what you're worried about. I never say it's you. I just tell the priest I slept with a woman."

"Didn't you enjoy it with me, Danny?"

He went harder still beneath the sheets and was glad she could not see.

"Yeah, sure," he said, feeling abashed.

"Then why have you got to confess about me? We're two young people in love . . ."

He sat up straight.

"We are?"

"That's what you said last night, at the moment of truth."

"When's the moment of truth?"

"You know, Danny."

He did not, in fact, remember saying anything about love, though he well might have done. He could have said *anything*, the state he had been in. Could he promise her that he would not confess this one? It might leave him with a cardinal sin staining his already besmirched soul.

"Rita," he said, "why don't you move in with me? We don't have to get married or anything, not for a while. If you moved in I could tell the priest I was half-way to becoming an honest man. This apartment's small, but we could manage okay. What do you say?"

She took his face in her hands and stared into his eyes.

"You really want me to, don't you?"

"Yeah, yeah, I do."

"And what would I do for a living?"

"Well, I earn. What did you do before you became a hooker?"

"Waitress, then I was a secretary—that's what they called it anyway, but it was just filing things—oh, and I was once a receptionist."

"Receptionist. There's a good job. You get to meet lots of people, have an interesting day. Why not try that again?"

Rita stared down into her coffee.

"I could do that, I suppose, sign up with some agency."

There was a gentle ripple of excitement in her voice now, and he knew he had her on the hook. She had told him she was sick of the street life now. It had first been a way of making money, meeting the bills. Then it became a way of life. Finally, it had her trapped, so that she could do nothing else. Her pimp took most of her money, anyway.

"What about Span?" she said.

Danny knew her pimp, who was a loner, not connected with any big mob, and he knew he could handle him.

"Let me worry about Span. When I leave word that you're with me, he'll stay away. The guy's a gutless little shit when it comes down to it. He'll cut up a girl, but he'll keep well clear of me."

"Tough guy," she sneered.

"Yeah," he sneered back.

So, it was settled, Rita was to move in with him. Now that they had made up their minds, it seemed like a great idea. It might even work for them.

"Shall we consummate our togetherness?" he asked.

"Do what?"

"You know."

"After last night you still got some left?"

He lifted the sheet and showed her, shy in his unusual sober state.

When he dressed that day Danny put on a dark suit, plain tie, and pinstripe shirt. He wore black leather shoes: the kind his father had worn before him. This was the conservative in him, finding it necessary to dress formally because he was taking a lady to lunch. He had a date with Vanessa. Dave wasn't invited because they both wanted to discuss him, for reasons of their own.

During the shift, Dave expressed surprise at the smartness of Danny's outfit, but Danny told Dave he was going to meet an aunt of his for lunch and needed to feel right. Dave told him he would meet him later in a burger joint.

Danny was in the small bistro that Foxy had opened after leaving the force. A few of the guys took their wives or girl-friends there on special occasions, but since it wasn't a bar, it was not, in general, a watering hole for thirsty cops. Foxy kept it that way on purpose. He had left the police force, and didn't want to take half of it with him, like so many guys who still craved the camaraderie after they had hung up their uniform and called it time. Foxy had given his badge and gun back, and now he was an ordinary citizen, with the right to protection from the men in blue, without having to socialize with them.

He liked to see some of his old friends, but not the assholes he used to get smashed with in Stokey's Bar, who would be falling all over his shirtfront at two in the morning, remem-bering old times, and bumming free drinks off him, and mak-ing passes at his wife in the crude universal language of the macho drunk, which never varied in its so-called humor, and was about as funny as soggy cigarette butts in a urinal.

The only alcohol Foxy served was wine, which was not an off-duty cop drink.

The bistro was called Clementine's, after Foxy's wife, and they seemed to be doing okay, with their Maryland crabs and minute steaks and oyster soup. Foxy did the cooking, while Clementine and another woman did the waiting on the tables. They had the menu chalked up on a blackboard fixed to the wall, flowers in used Paul Masson California wine carafes, and candles in Portuguese Mateus Rosé bottles. French bread in a basket was free, and the idea was to make as much mess of the Irish linen tablecloth as possible, as if the object was to feed wild birds. It had an atmosphere that was duplicated in a thousand other bistros, but that, Clementine argued, was what people wanted: familiarity without contempt.

Danny got there at one o'clock sharp, and Vanessa arrived just a few minutes afterwards. Danny stood up to hold her chair.

"Hello, Danny, how are you?"

She was wearing a loose black dress that made her look more blonde than normal. She also had on black lace gloves and black stockings. Her eyes were heavily made up.

"What's this, Gothic day?" he joked as he sat down.

She looked down at herself and her mouth dropped. Danny wished he hadn't made the remark. That was typical of him and women, always saying the wrong thing at the wrong time. He tried to retrieve the situation.

"Just kidding, you look great."

"No, I don't, but I look better than usual," she replied. "That's what Dave is doing for me. I feel good. I don't care if it doesn't meet with your approval."

He wasn't sure whether she meant the way she was dressed or her new relationship with his partner.

"Look, Vanessa, I don't want to fight with you. I can't say I fully approve, but that's probably because I'm envious of him. I saw you first. I know, I know, it doesn't work that way. It's not an end-of-season sale. Just the same, I can't control my emotions. I feel hurt. I offered you my friendship, I thought it might lead to something stronger, and the next thing I hear you've jumped into the sack with my partner."

"It wasn't like that."

"The way I hear it, it was *exactly* like that. Now I'm not blaming the chemistry here—it happened. But you can't expect me to just smile and say well done."

Danny broke a bread roll which disintegrated into dry crumbs and snowed onto the white linen cloth. The butter was straight from the freezer and brick hard. He made one or two attempts to spread it on the crumbs, then decided to cut it into chunks each the size of a thumbnail and balance a piece on each crust.

"So," said Vanessa, "what are you going to do about it?"

Danny shrugged.

"Nothing. I just wanted us to get together and find out where we were. Actually, I'm living with a girl called Rita at the moment."

"A *woman* called Rita, unless she's under age, in which case I'll kick you in the balls."

Danny was offended.

"Please, don't use that kind of language in here, this is a respectable restaurant. No, she's not under age. In fact, she's none of your business. I only mentioned it to show you I'm not heartbroken. And if I want to call her a *girl*, and she wants to call me a *boy*, we'll damn well do it without asking your permission first. You look after yourself, let Rita look after herself, she's quite capable of it."

"Is she?"

"What—are you going to patronize her as well?"

"I think it would probably be '*ma*tronize' if I did it, but never mind that now. Tell me about Dave. He loved his wife and child, right?"

Danny nodded.

"Ferociously. Lived for them both, and when they were killed, he came apart. You better be careful with him, because he's a pretty fragile guy inside. On the outside, tough as a thick-shelled crab, but inside emotionally delicate, all pink and mushy."

"I don't want to hurt him. He's not in love with me, in any case. He likes me, likes my company, but there's no overwhelming passion there."

"Probably the best way. He couldn't handle anything more at this time. Tell me, how is he when you're alone together? Don't look at me like that, I don't want to know the sex part. I want to know if he's stable, if he's pulling himself back together again, or does he . . . you know, cry in his sleep, or anything like that? He's more likely to do it in front of a woman than he is a man, even though we're the best of friends."

The soup arrived and Vanessa picked up her spoon and began sipping. Danny wiped his own spoon on the table napkin first, much to the annoyance of Clementine, before joining her.

"He doesn't cry in his sleep, he cries on my shoulder," she said, "and it's quite normal. Things trigger it off—a piece of music, a snatch of a late-night film, or maybe just a memory flash. It doesn't mean he's unstable."

As she was raising the spoon to her mouth, Danny reached across and grabbed her by the wrist. He turned her forearm over, so that he could see the underside.

"What's this?" he snapped.

She tried to pull away her arm, her mouth sullen.

"Scars. Old cigarette-burn marks."

"Crap, that one's not old," he said pointing, "and neither is that one. These are fresh marks."

She succeeded in retrieving her arm.

"What would you rather I did, set fire to his bed?"

Danny stared at her, knowing her history, and guessed what was happening. He was not a detective for nothing, and he had been on the streets since he was twelve. He knew what the bottomside looked like.

"You're burning yourself," he said matter-of-factly.

"Yes," she admitted.

"When?"

"I don't think . . ." She drew herself up haughtily, but he snapped back again, "When?"

She seemed to collapse from the inside, and slouched over the edge of the table.

"After we've made love. My father used to do it, to punish me after he had used me for sex. I do it myself now. I don't know why."

Danny winced.

"You're punishing yourself for being a naughty girl?"

"I guess that's it. In a funny kind of way, I need it. I feel cleansed afterwards. It scours my soul."

"It's not necessary, Vanessa. You're not doing anything wrong."

She looked up and smiled at him.

"Look at who's talking. Who goes to confession the evening after sex?"

Danny tried not to feel nettled.

"It's not the same thing. I'm not mutilating myself. If you do feel bad, why not come to confession with me?"

"The priest would have a field day, wouldn't he, dashing from one box to another, listening to our sordid stories and trying to hide his hard-on."

Danny was shocked and almost choked on his soup.

"You can't talk about priests like that."

"Don't be so naïve, Danny, they're men, aren't they? Listen, I will try to stop doing this. I hate being addicted to anything, but it's very difficult. You must understand that. I can't always help what I do. Please don't tell Dave."

Danny considered what she had said, and decided that Dave already knew about the bed firing, and if she kept up the masochism he would eventually discover that as well. What he would not welcome was interference from Danny. So he decided he would say nothing.

"My lips are sealed."

She smiled at him.

"Thank you, Danny."

They talked some more about Dave, themselves, and the situation, before deciding it had worked out for the best, whatever that meant. The soup plates were whisked away, and the main course arrived. Danny tucked into his veal, with only a passing thought for the milk-fed calf that had provided it. He was not a man who looked very far into anything. Vanessa ate her trout, wondering how long it had been since the fish had been swimming around in a clear Canadian stream. She was the kind of woman who always looked behind a screen.

"You a Catholic?" asked Danny.

"Lapsed," she replied.

"Uh-uh, fires of hell," he muttered without thinking, then instantly regretted it. He tried to retrieve the situation, failing miserably for the ten-thousandth time in his life, and was glad when the time came to ask for the check.

Just as they were leaving, Foxy came out of the kitchen and remonstrated with Danny for not telling him he was there. Danny said he thought Foxy didn't like cops in his place, but Foxy replied that some cops were always welcome, so long as they called him Ray. They were introduced to Clementine, who was busy and could only manage a smiling "please-tameecha" over her shoulder.

Foxy insisted they have a brandy with him, and they left after another half an hour with Danny feeling warm and good inside. It didn't matter that cops hated the force, like Foxy had: once they were off it they missed it.

Human beings, thought Danny, are the most contrary creatures on earth. You give them something, they want something else. They go to live in Ohio, and they want to live in California. They finally get to California, and they can't stop talking about Ohio. You let them into a club, and they want to be in a different club. You let them out of the club, and they wish they were back in again. Danny had once heard a famous mountain climber say, "When I'm climbing mountains, in cold miserable conditions, I want to be home with my wife, by a roaring fire. When I'm home, I long to be up a mountain . . ."

Span was six feet two inches tall, with a magnificent upper body which he had developed through years at the gym, and a miserable skinny pair of legs with feet the size of which most women would have envied. Span's problem was that he found leg exercises boring, and had only ever concentrated on his arms and torso, and consequently he looked like an exclamation mark. Whenever he had his photograph taken, he insisted that it be only from the waist up.

Span ran a stable of seven girls, of which Rita was one. He looked after his whores, giving them at least ten percent of the take, and making sure they weren't hassled by freaks and weirdos, mobsters and street gangs. The vice cops for their stretch of sidewalk were on his payroll, and he had been a lieutenant's snitch for many years. The lieutenant protected him from extraordinary busts. Span also shelled out to the local Mafia, ensuring his own protection. Straight cops he could do nothing about, except complain in a high whining tone about being black and racially oppressed. Actually, he wasn't of African origin, his parents had come from Mauritius, but years of sunray lamps allowed him to pass for black. If anyone asked, he told them he had a touch of the whitewash brush in him.

Like most pimps, Span was primarily concerned with his image, and had developed the walk, the dress, and the manner of his colleagues, with a seriousness that would have gained him honors if taking a college degree. Anything that threatened that image was both hated and feared.

When Span learned that one of his girls wanted to leave, to live with a cop, he was highly aggrieved. He had given those girls the best years of his life, then they went and ran out on him. He tried cajoling Rita, then persuading her, and finally he threatened to carve his name on her face with a razor blade. She seemed to understand that.

That evening, Span went to the gym as usual, and pumped some heavy iron with grim determination. He was Arnold Schwarzenegger on top, and Stan Laurel down below, but he was respected among his own kind as being a man who took no shit. Span was prepared to suffer injury, even death, to protect his image in the world of pimps, pushers, gamblers, conmen, and other middle-class underworld types. His image was his ego, and it was all he had, apart from plenty of spending money.

After his workout, he took a shower, then went into his favorite cubicle to do his toilet. He was sitting there, dropping his load, humming songs from his favorite musical *Kiss Me Kate*, when someone kicked the door off its hinges.

"What the fuck . . . ?" he yelled, reaching down to his ankles for the switchblade in his pants pocket.

"Leave it, Span."

A cop Span recognized as Friar Tuck stood there pointing a gun at him with one hand, and a do-everything automatic camera in the other.

"You gonna shoot me?" snapped Span.

"Not if you do as you're told," Friar Tuck replied. "Now, reach up slowly, and flush the toilet."

The toilet was one of the old-fashioned overhead cistern kind, with a dangling chain. Span tried to stand up, but Friar Tuck waved him down again.

"Do it from a sitting position."

"What the fuck is this?"

"Do it, or I'll shoot you with your pants down and your ass dirty, and drag you out into the middle of the gym."

"You wouldn't do that."

"Try me."

Span stared at the muzzle of the gun, looking like a small

black hole in the center of the universe. He was incensed at this cop before him, who was threatening his image. Still, he didn't want to die like that, with his ass out of his pants. You never could tell with these straight cops, sometimes they went off the rails, and looped the loop. He reached up and grasped the chain.

"Pull it," Friar Tuck ordered.

"Listen, if there's a bomb in there, we both go to hell . . ."

"Do as you're goddamn told."

Span sighed and pulled the chain. There was a grating sound from above and the heavy iron cistern began peeling away from its rusted mountings, falling on the head of the pimp.

Span yelled and threw himself forward, just as the cistern began to hurtle down on the ceramic toilet. Span saw several flashes of light as he was traveling through the air, and then he heard the loud crash behind him, as the ceramic bowl shattered into a hundred shards.

When the debris had settled, he looked up at the cop.

"You bastard—," he began, but Friar Tuck cut him short with a sharp-toed kick to his hip.

"Listen, you freak," said the bald-headed cop, "I've got your picture here, pants round your stick-insect ankles, ignominiously avoiding death from a falling cistern. When it's developed, it won't be a very noble portrait. I'm gonna have it blown up, lifesize, and post it on every wall in the neighborhood. Your image will be shit, you understand me? Unless . . ."

Span sighed.

"Unless I lay off Rita."

"Bright boy. Do we have a deal?"

"What choice do I have?"

"I knew you'd cooperate. I said to my partner Dave, 'Span is a reasonable man. He'll cooperate, once I show him the advantages of the deal.'"

"Funny guys, you two."

"Not really. We just like to get our own way. I mean, we're the good guys, and you're the bad guy, so traditionally we always win in the end. Don't feel bad about it. And don't expect me to put in any words for you, when Vice finally gets your ass, which they will one day."

"I'll remember you're not on my side."

"Good. Take it easy, Span. Enjoy the rest of your crap."

13

Dave and Danny were driving along a downtown street, each lost in their own thoughts. Danny was at the wheel, and Dave was staring at the burned-out shells of buildings, which were almost everywhere he looked. They looked sad places, some with weeds already growing on the site, their charcoaled timbers and warped steel girders testimony to the fierceness of their brief moment of brightness. They were the city's dead stars, that had gone novae, and were now igneous debris.

Dave had to admit that even though they were making more arrests than ever, Reece was still gnawing at their asses, telling them to find the white-fire perpetrator that everyone wanted nailed. He was the leader, the messiah of the firestarters. They used him as a beacon for their cause.

Suddenly, Dave broke his reverie, and looked back at the people on the sidewalk. He gave an excited yelp, and shouted, "Danny, pull over."

"What? What is it?" Danny steered the car to the side of the road and crunched up against the curb, scraping the hubcap. He was peering over his shoulder, trying to see what had excited Dave so much. "Robbery in progress?"

"No, goddamn it, it's *him,*" hissed Dave.

"Him?"

"The white-fire arsonist. There," Dave pointed, "strolling along the sidewalk."

"The pretty boy?"

"That's the son of a bitch. Don't look at him now, he's glancing this way. When he's past the car, we'll follow him."

"Don't you want to pick him up?"

"We don't have anything on him yet. I want to find out where he hangs out. If we can just get him in the right neighborhood, let Forensic get to his hands . . . Shit, I'd like to do him right now." Dave reached for his gun.

"Dave!" cried Danny, in a warning note.

"Okay, okay. Look, he's turning the corner."

The two detectives jumped out of the car, just as a traffic cop was coming along to tell them to move it. They flashed their badges quickly, and he nodded and turned away. The two cops scuttled up to the corner, and fell in behind their suspect.

He led them to a greasy-looking restaurant on a street that would have welcomed demolition crews with open arms. The man went inside and Dave decided to follow. He knew it was the wrong thing to do, but he was excited. Danny fell in behind him, willing to trust his partner with everything except his women.

There was one other customer, an old black man with a grizzled beard, sitting in the corner. The pretty boy was about halfway down the narrow room, facing the counter, behind which was the kitchen. He was being served with a cup of coffee by a short-order cook with tattooed forearms the size of a tennis player's and a paunch like a kangaroo's belly. He looked like a navy man, gone to land.

"Two coffees," Danny called, "black."

The old man looked up with rheumy critical eyes.

"That's without milk," Dave amended. "Two."

Pretty Boy stirred his coffee slowly, without turning around at the sound of the voice.

Dave sniffed the air. There was that damned aftershave he had smelled the night the mobster's house had been fired. Almonds. The smell of almonds. The excitement built up in his chest. This was *definitely* his man. Without saying anything to Danny, he got up and went to Pretty Boy's table, sitting opposite him.

He stared into the man's face.

"Hello," Dave said.

Pretty Boy looked up mildly with light-gray eyes that could have belonged to a baby. Despite the contained anger that he felt for the man, a chill went through Dave. They were mesmeric eyes, inhuman, perhaps even *un*human. For some reason Dave felt very vulnerable, insignificant, like a snail about to be crushed by a giant foot. Yet the man he was confronting was slim and of slight stature: Dave towered over him.

Dave said, "You mind if we have a few words?"

Danny joined him now, sitting beside him. Dave sensed Danny's discomfort on being appraised by those mild gray eyes, and felt his partner stiffen under the gaze.

"Two of them?" said Pretty Boy.

The cook was placing the coffee in front of them and he said, "Cops. It's wrote all over their fucking suits."

"Okay," said Danny, having found someone he knew how to deal with, leaning back in his chair, "get back to your kitchen, meathead."

"This is my joint, I say what I like in here."

"Not to me you don't. If I get any more crap from you, we'll be calling in every day to check your cockroaches for track marks."

The cook wiped his hands on a dirty apron.

"Smart-ass," he muttered, but drifted off to the rear.

"So," said Dave to Pretty Boy, "you got a name?"

"I have no time for silly games."

The man's self-assurance began to get under Dave's skin.

"Plenty of time to light fires, though?" he snapped. What he really wanted to do was grab him by the throat and grind his face into the grease on the tabletop, but something told him this would not be an easy thing to do.

The man smiled and leaned back, adopting the same posture as Danny. His smooth flawless features were an anathema to Dave. They were incongruous with the fiend he believed lurked beneath. This was the lizard that had killed his wife and child, he could feel it in his heart. He wanted to shoot into that face right now: six rounds of solid lead from his .38. He wanted to smash the smile with bullets, watch the flesh and bone disintegrate as he pumped metal into it. It took all his strength of will not to take out his police special and do just that.

"You do have a name?" said Dave, evenly.

"If you want to call me something, Jophiel will do."

"Jophiel," said Danny, letting his chair come forward with a bang, "that's a pretty fancy name. Italian?"

Jophiel sighed.

Dave studied him intently, wondering how to react. Either the guy had convinced himself they had nothing on him, which called for one kind of approach, or he knew they had his number but had decided to bluff it out, which called for another. Jophiel, if that was his name, looked as if he believed in himself. He was too cool, too much in control. It was going to make it all that much tougher.

"Okay, Jophiel, where do we go from here?"

"You tell me, Sergeant Peters. I'm the one being accosted."

Dave was taken aback.

"How the hell do you know my name?"

Jophiel smiled at him.

"You are so . . . transparent. Not only that, you are lacking in knowledge, woefully ignorant. You believe I killed your wife and son, Jamie. I think I probably did.

"They are dead, sergeant, gone to another place. Forget them."

Dave reached for his gun, but Danny grabbed his wrist and held it in a strong grip.

"Leave it, Dave, this joker's not going anywhere. You, where do you get your information?"

Danny still kept hold of Dave's wrist, even though his partner's muscles had slackened.

"What are you, some kind of a terrorist?" he asked.

"There's nothing you can do to me—no one on earth can touch me. I come from a place which is beyond your understanding. I am a warrior of the Lord, sent here to hunt his enemies." He gazed toward the rear of the restaurant. "There's one in here now, cowering in the storeroom behind the kitchen. He knows I am here, and he knows I know he is here. He is trapped, waiting for me to obliterate him."

"What has this man done to you?" asked Danny.

"Man? He is not a man. The body, like mine, is that of a man, but the spirit within . . . You would call it *demon*."

Danny shook his head, distaste for this lunatic evident in his expression.

"A demon hunter. You from the Bible Belt, boy? You don't have a Southern accent."

"You are like small children, you have pictures in your head that bear no resemblance to the truth. Pictures of creatures with wings, hands clasped in prayer, a circle of light around their heads. Pictures of red fork-bearded beings with tails, horns and hoofs."

Despite his revulsion, Dave wanted the man to keep talking. He desperately wanted to know what made him tick. He wanted reasons.

"If the guys you're chasing are *demons*, what the hell are you?"

"I am what you would call *angel*, though the term belongs to your language, not to ours."

Danny interrupted triumphantly with, "What about 'Thou shalt not kill'?"

The penetrating gray eyes took on a look of impatience.

"You're confusing me with a mortal. *Thou* shalt not kill, as you so quaintly observe, but not me. The Ten Commandments were given to men, not to my kind. You're wasting my time and yours. I am here to hunt. It is not my concern if humans die in the process—they will die anyway, at some time. Death is a natural end," he said mildly, "and in the hands of such as myself is not an evil act. Our morality is quite separate from yours, quite different, we are absolved from mortal sin, just as we are above worldly desires.

"We are, quite simply, divine."

"Okay," Dave said, the anger in him intensified, "we've heard enough of this crap."

Jophiel stood up quickly and walked to the door before either of the detectives could jump to their feet. Then he paused and glanced significantly toward the rear of the restaurant.

"I suppose the term you would give it would probably be something like 'holy fire,'" he said.

In that moment there was the muffled, sickening sound of inflammable material igniting, bursting into flame. A soft explosion occurred in the back room. There was one single piercing scream, like that of a cat in agony, then incandescent flame gushed through cracks in the hardboard wall, devouring it almost instantly. The thin storeroom door was consumed in a moment, and flames belched three feet past the counter. Dave, already on his way toward the door, felt the fire scorching past him, and the hair on the back of his head was singed. Danny was right behind him and the pair of them staggered out into the street. They battled against a strong wind, as air rushed in to take the place of the oxygen that fed the fire. There were popping sounds as blisters appeared on the counter, and swelled, and burst.

Since they had had their backs to the kitchen, the two detectives had not been blinded by the white-fire, but the sudden exposure to great heat sapped their energy, draining them to the point of exhaustion.

The back of Danny's suit was smoldering. He ripped off his jacket and began beating the back of his pants with his hands. His hair was smoking and the back of his neck was scorched.

From inside the restaurant there were terrible screams of agony and when Dave looked back, he could see the cook with his clothes, skin and hair ablaze, blindly trying to scramble over the bubbling counter. Sizzling cooking oil erupted in streaks of flame from a pan of French fries at his elbow, like lava from a small volcano. The old black man was also burning, slumped over a table, convulsing wildly. The gut-wrenching stench of burned flesh came from inside the restaurant.

Dave attempted to make his way into the flames, but cooking fats had flash-fired and sprayed the room with burning blobs, and the whole place was aflame with the sudden intensity of napalm. Grease-covered wallpaper formed a box of flame around the two bodies, and Formica peeled and rolled as if it were alive, running lizardlike across the tables until it caught fire. Aluminum began to melt, dribbling silver flames, rivulets, down the melting counter. Dave was forced back out into the street. A minute later the window exploded, showering glass onto the gathering crowd—people screamed and ran.

Toxic fumes were now belching in waves from the blazing restaurant: dangerous gases from the Formica, plastic, and other synthetic substances. The odor stung nostrils and eyes, and caused coughing and retching in those too near the area.

Neighboring shops were beginning to burn as the intense heat forced combustible materials behind the thin walls above their flash-point temperatures. Bricks turned to powder, crumbled, and plaster burned brightly as the fire reached with greedy fingers through the ceiling of the room, finding new softwoods to eat beneath.

While the fire raged, Dave dragged Danny backwards, out of the heat bubble surrounding the restaurant. The pair of them found a doorway some way down the street, and huddled behind it, out of the channel of fierce blistering air. Thick black smoke was climbing around the skyscrapers, bringing office workers to the windows.

Dave could hear cans of soft drinks exploding inside the restaurant as their liquid contents boiled and turned them into small bombs. There were sounds like gunshots as iron griddles cracked apart and bottles shattered. Glowing bits of carbon filled the atmosphere, and wires began to melt on the poles directly outside the restaurant. A long slim blue flame hissed out halfway across the street: a gas pipe had melted and was now a dragon's tongue.

Sirens began cutting through the noise in the street.

Suddenly another explosion sent debris raining into the street. As Dave turned his head, he saw someone standing in the alley, directly opposite. Incredibly, it was the man who had caused the inferno, Jophiel, watching the fire from a safe distance.

Dave drew his gun and, leaving Danny, ran across the road, narrowly escaping being hit by a fire truck. When he reached the entrance to the alley, Jophiel was walking swiftly down the dark passage. He was almost at the end and out into the light when Dave went down on one knee and aimed his .38. There was a distance of about thirty yards between the gun and its target. He knew he was going to lose his badge for this—gunning down an unarmed man—but he had murder in his heart. This man had admitted to killing his family, and his death was worth any future punishment.

One last chance.

"Freeze, you bastard!"

Jophiel turned and gave him an infuriating smile.

The anger and frustration was choking Dave so much he could not repeat the challenge, and as Jophiel once more turned to walk away, Dave squeezed the trigger. He pumped five shots into Jophiel's back, feeling the gun buck in his hand. The satisfaction of revenge warmed his stomach.

It was replaced almost immediately by disbelief. He had seen the jacket flick and jump where the rounds struck their target, but there was absolutely no reaction from the retreating figure. A dead man was walking away, as if lead missiles were nothing but gnats.

Dave thought: *He's wearing a protective vest!*

Jophiel hadn't even paused in his stride. At the end of the alley he turned and stared. In desperation Dave took careful aim and squeezed the trigger. The bullet struck Jophiel on the forehead. Jophiel left with a contemptuous wave of his pale, waxy hand.

Six shots, all squarely in the target, and nothing to show for them.

Dave went down on both knees in a position of genuflection. A sick feeling dominated his stomach. In that moment he knew he was dealing with something completely outside his control. He wanted revenge, but how was he going to get it if the murderer would not lie down and die?

"Oh, God, Celia," he whispered, "I'm sorry."

14

"WHO THE JESUSINHELL SET FIRE TO MY RE-PORT BOOK?" screamed the desk sergeant, Bronski. The benches were full of fire-starters, and they all cheered hoarsely. Somehow one of them had managed to sneak over to the desk, throw lighter fuel on the report book, and match it.

A uniformed cop rapped the counter loudly with his night stick. The cop threatened to crack some heads, while Bronski poured a glass of water over the flaming pages of his precious book in disgust. For the rest of the day people would suffer, for when Bronski was not happy, those around him became unhappy too.

Captain Reece shut the office door to try to keep some of the noise on the outside. Since the glass from which half the office was made was not double-glazed, it was a futile gesture, and only served to rattle Bronski, who had been a cop twice as long as the captain, and did not see why the higher ranks should not experience the same everyday hassle, including the noise, as dutiful old-timers like him. It was part of the job, and if you wanted to be cushioned from the harassment of the world, you became a manager for a soft furnishings store, with a hush-hush carpeted office and a whispering pneumatic secretary.

Facing Reece's desk were Dave and Danny. Danny was swathed in bandages around the shoulders and hands. Dave kept feeling the back of his own neck, where the hair was short and crinkled from the fire blast in the restaurant.

"Let me get this straight," said Reece, coming round to his side of the desk and resuming his seat. "Let me get this absolutely facking straight. You had this guy in the restaurant, you're sure he's the white-fire perp, but you didn't arrest him right away because you had nothing on him. Then the bomb goes off in the storeroom, planted by this same guy, and you—you let him go."

"We know what he looks like. We know he's a nut. We know the district where he hangs out. We'll get him again."

Reece turned on Dave.

"You fired your weapon?"

"Yes, sir. I squeezed off a couple of shots," he lied, "but I'd just been through a hell of a fire. My hands had been scorched, my eyes were sore from smoke. I was in no real condition to shoot someone at a distance, and I should have left well enough alone. It was a waste—I missed with both shots."

"You missed with both shots. You endangered the public for nothing? You say the doer wasn't armed?"

"I thought I saw something, at the last minute, and there weren't any bystanders around to get hit. Just me and him, at either end of the alley."

"You thought you saw something."

"A weapon—something glinted in his hand. I just told you, captain, I was half blinded by the smoke, and I'd just been through a hell of an experience. Have you ever been in a room when an incendiary bomb goes off? You don't know whether you're on your ass or your head. The flash is enough to wipe your eyeballs clean."

Reece calmed down a little, though he was clearly frustrated and angry at having missed the opportunity of capturing the target of that anger by such a very small margin. At such times he was wont to take it out on his men, as he was doing now. Desk workers and field workers universally believe each other to be lazy and incompetent.

"Damnit, Dave," said Reece, surprising Dave by using his Christian name, "this is the second time you've come within touching distance of this guy."

"I know. Don't you think I don't want him too?" Dave gritted his teeth. "I want this perp so badly I'd lose an arm to get him."

Danny cleared his throat and finally spoke.

"This might be no ordinary guy, captain."

Dave was electrified. He had a premonition of what Danny was going to say and it wasn't good. Danny knew about the six shots. Dave had told him that all six struck the perpetrator somewhere on his body, and the guy had not even flinched. Both cops knew they were dealing with someone out of the ordinary, maybe a nut with the abnormal mental strength to ignore excruciating pain—there were crazy people like that—or maybe something more, something beyond normal understanding? It was possible that the first five shots had hit nothing vital, but the last one had gone through the guy's face, just below the left eye, and still he had not flinched. Danny had been in time to see that one. Danny felt they were dealing with something so strange it was giving him nightmares.

"What do you mean?" asked Reece.

"This guy may be different from . . . from anyone else."

"You mean he's got connections? With who?"

"Whom," corrected Danny, probably without thinking.

The captain looked as if he was going to blow.

He said slowly, "What the hell are you talking about, Spitz?"

"He said his name was Jophiel."

"So?"

Danny looked extremely uncomfortable, but Dave could see he was going to go through with it. Inwardly he winced for his partner. He knew Danny hated leaving loose ends.

"Well," said Danny, "Jophiel is the name of an angel."

Reece looked mystified, and Dave knew that the captain was wondering whether he was missing something. No doubt Reece was running some street language through his mind, wondering where the word *angel* connected.

Finally he said, "What's an *angel*?"

Danny said, "You know, a heavenly angel, an angel of the Lord? You know what an angel is, Captain."

Reece's eyes started from his head.

"This guy told you he was an angel of God?"

"He *implied* it, and I looked up Jophiel when I got back to my apartment. Jophiel is a minor archangel. Now, Dave says he's a nut, and Dave's probably right, but . . . but I *felt* something when he looked at me." Danny seemed almost in tears now, as if he were a small boy desperate for Reece to believe something he knew adults would wave away with a disbelieving hand.

Reece said, "Look at me, Spitz. Look right into my eyes. You know what my first name is? Eh? *Michael*. My first name is Michael. Michael John Reece. You know where Michael comes from?"

Danny looked miserable.

"He's one of the archangels."

"Right," nodded Reece, his nostrils dilating with annoyance, "one of the archangels. Do I look like a facking archangel?" Reece always pronounced fuck as *fack*, like some people say *frigging* or *freaking*, fooling themselves that their vocabulary did not include sexual swearwords. "Do I? Get the fack outta here. Look, I want this guy nailed. I want him crucified, you understand me?"

"We'll do our best, captain," replied Dave.

"I want more than your best, I want everything you've got. I need this guy's skin on my wall, you understand me? He's wanted in seven continents. He's like some kind of phantom, here, there and everywhere. This morning I got a faxed description from the French of their white-fire starter." He picked up a piece of paper and handed it to Dave. "Read it."

Dave read it and nodded. It was a description of Jophiel.

"That's him all right."

Reece said, "How does he manage to be in two continents over such a short space of time?"

"Concorde?" suggested Dave.

Reece nodded. "Well, we'll cover the airports. You two get out there on the street and bring me something back, preferably this creep in cuffs. And you, Spitz, you're becoming a religious maniac. You want to see the police shrink?"

"No, captain."

"Then get out there and do some work."

"Yes, captain," said Dave, steering Danny toward the door.

They left the office and went through the chaotic squad room, giving each other a look as they walked. Once in their car, Dave said angrily, "What the hell did you do that for?"

Danny still looked miserable.

"I don't know, I'm confused. *You*'re the one who said he walked away from six direct hits. Maybe we ought to keep an open mind on this one."

"Danny, listen to me. There's no such thing as fairies."

"We're not talking about fairies, we're talking about angels. Angels are real."

"Not in my book."

"You're a fucking heathen."

"Don't get personal."

They both fell silent for a moment, then Dave said, "You *really* believe in that stuff?"

"Naw, no, not like that, but I just think we ought to keep an open mind, that's all. Don't let's close ourselves to any possibilities."

"So what do we do next?"

Danny leaned back in his seat, lit a cigarette, then spoke.

"He seems to be able to start a fire, instantaneously, just by thinking about it. A fire hotter than a furnace for melting pig iron. If we can't shoot him, and we can't arrest him, what the hell *are* we going to do? How do you arrest someone like that?"

"Maybe he planted the incendiary bomb earlier in the day?"

"Then why go back just as it's about to go off? And Forensic went through the debris. They said there was no bomb. Same as all the other white fires. The fire started in the corpse of the man they found out back, the one he said was a demon, the one he'd come to kill. Other fires have reportedly started the same way. What do you think's happening, Dave? An outbreak of spontaneously combusting humans? Eh? An epidemic of overheating internal organs? C'mon, Dave, I'm willing to accept it may have a scientific cause behind it, and not a supernatural one, but something definitely weird is going on here, definitely."

They stared at the dashboard of the car, trying to find some answers there.

Dave said, "He had to be wearing a protective vest when I shot him."

"You told me he didn't even flinch. Even with a vest, thirty-eights hurt like hell. I saw you shoot him in the head with the last one. His brains must have been scrambled inside his skull. What about that?"

Dave gripped the wheel and said angrily, "I'm not reliable at the moment. Maybe I'm going crazy. Celia's death, Jamie's, these things take their toll. Maybe I haven't worked out my grief properly, and my mind's going. How the hell do I know what's going on? All I know is, you can't stop a thirty-eight with your face, so I must have missed, or it went through his cheek or something. I must have been mistaken."

"About everything?"

"Everything."

Danny said slowly, "Look, Dave, you're not going crazy. I've seen crazy people."

"All us crazy guys act differently."

"No, you don't get out of it that easily. You *know* there's something strange here. You know it. I understand you too well. You can't just block your mind to it. Find out more. Do what you normally do—investigate. Don't turn your back on it."

"You want me to look at the possibility of this guy being a supernatural being?"

Danny was almost shouting now.

"Why not? You know everything? You a walking encyclopedia? You an expert on the paranormal?"

Dave could see how this whole business had affected Danny, in an adverse way. His partner was definitely shaken. If anyone was going crazy, it was Danny. So was he, for that matter.

"I'll have a word with Vanessa. She's an expert on religion. That satisfy you?"

"Good idea." Danny sounded relieved that the problem had been put aside for a while, perhaps even passed over to someone else. "Find out what she thinks."

That evening Dave called Vanessa and met her at an Austrian restaurant called Schule's at eight o'clock. They planned to go on to Clementine's afterwards, but Vanessa said she did not want to eat there every time she was taken out, and both Danny and Dave had taken her there once. Neither of his friends knew Dave had a part share in Clementine's. He saw no reason to tell them. Foxy would be upset when he just turned up for coffee, but then, Dave thought, what the hell? They couldn't live their lives around the bistro.

Dave was dressed to impress Vanessa, in a midnight blue suit, a tie with a bit less color than he would have worn for Celia, and a sober shirt. Vanessa did not like anything loud, whereas Celia would have accepted a quilted poncho with bells around the fringe. Dave didn't mind either way. He dressed to please other people, not himself.

Vanessa had on a black dress and a choker of freshwater pearls. Her hair was wrapped in a coil at the back of her neck. She had obviously taken a lot of trouble with her makeup, sparse as it was, and her eyebrows were perfectly arched. She looked regal, even quite beautiful, but severe, like a queen about to sentence a man to execution.

"Hi," she said, arriving just after him, "how are you?"

"I'm okay," he replied. He tried to get up, but the tables were very close together, and he could only half stand. She waved him down.

"That's okay, you made the effort," she said, taking her own seat. "I appreciate it. Say, I hear that Danny is living with a woman. Someone called Rita?"

"Yeah, they've known each other for some time."

"What, old school friends?"

"Hardly." Dave saw no reason not to tell the truth. "It seems to be working okay. She's got herself a job in a department store. I hope she sticks with it and doesn't get bored." Dave paused.

"Now, you know the reason I asked you here . . ." He saw her mouth drop at the corners and knew he had made a mistake with that line. "Look, I do have a reason, but it's really good to see you again. You look terrific. A bit like Dracula's sister, but terrific."

That made her laugh.

"At least you didn't say like Dracula's *mother*."

"Seriously, I've been looking forward to it, ever since I thought up the excuse to call you. You got to understand, it's going to take me a while to get Celia out of my system. I don't *want* her out of my system at the moment. I'm still in love with her and I see no reason to fight that. I like you—I like you a lot. And I think you like me. But I'm still walking around in a daze half the time. I find myself looking at my watch and thinking, 'I've got to get home before Celia puts Jamie to bed,' and then pull up short. It's not that I forget they're gone, I *know* they're dead, but there's habits in these bones that work in spite of that knowledge. A sort of double-think—two systems working side by side. Can you understand that?"

She smiled.

"Perfectly. I once heard a story about a farmer who rose at five-thirty every morning, for eighty years, and when he died his bones were so ingrained with the rising habit they got up of their own accord and frightened half the country folk to death.

"Seriously, I'm quite happy to take things slowly, and if they come to nothing, well, we can't say we haven't tried."

He felt relieved, the anxiety fled. He reached across and touched her hand.

"You're a nice person, Vanessa."

"No, I'm not." She looked at her scars.

"That's not you, that's someone else who we've got to get out of you."

They ordered drinks and then chatted about mundane things.

Finally Vanessa asked, "I suppose, apart from wanting my scintillating company, you asked me out because of that matter we discussed on the phone today?"

"It's difficult to believe, isn't it? You're going to get up in two minutes and walk out of here, convinced I'm crazy."

"That'll make two of us, anyway."

"Listen, something funny's going on. It's worrying me because I think I'm going out of my mind."

"Okay, run over it all again."

"This fire-starter, the white-fire maniac, we encountered him yesterday. I remembered him from the mobster's house—you remember I told you he threw me bodily across the street? Same looks, same smell of almonds. So Danny and I followed him, to a joint in Bellam Street, and when we cornered him he told us . . . told us . . ."

"He told you he was an angel."

"Yes. He as good as told us he was some kind of spiritual warrior. I mean, he didn't use those words, but he said he was hunting down demons, and other stuff." Dave began to feel embarrassed and played with his table napkin, until Vanessa reached across and touched his hand. "An angel, he said."

Dave stared at Vanessa, who looked him squarely in the eyes. Finally, she said, "Go on, tell me all of it, and let me make up my own mind."

Dave realized he had been holding his breath, and he let it out with a long sigh.

"Fact is, Vanessa, he did things we can't explain. He blew the kitchen of this joint just like that, without having placed a bomb of any kind. He didn't have time, and Forensic found nothing afterwards. He just told us that he was going to do it, and it happened. Killed an old black guy and the owner of the place: burned them both to death. Me and Danny got out, but Danny was burned. He's still in bandages. I just got singed a bit.

"He told us his name was Jophiel, which Danny says is the name of some archangel."

"Danny's right about that, though opinion varies regarding the names of the archangels," she said.

"I scoffed at him, of course, but after the fire I chased him down an alley. I put all six shots from my gun into that bastard and he turned round and grinned at me. One of those shots went smack into his face. It just passed through, leaving no marks. You can't stick your face in the way of a piece of lead coming at you and just laugh it off."

"Why would the angel Jophiel be down here?" she asked simply.

Dave stared at her expression, searching for signs that she was mocking him, but could detect none.

"He says he's down here because the demons are running from some battle—Danny guessed it was Arma-something. I'm not religious. I haven't been to church since I was a kid."

"Armageddon. The final battle between Good and Evil."

"That's the one. Anyway, these demons or fallen angels, they're deserting to earth, and trying to hide. This Jophiel has taken it on himself to follow them here and hunt them down—destroy them with holy fire. Maybe he put some kind of self-destructing incendiary in that restaurant earlier in the day, but I can't explain why he would go back to watch it going off, putting himself at risk. And he didn't seem to care whether we knew who he was or not. He admitted to firing the department store which killed my wife and kid. He knew who I was, my name, Danny's name. He could've got those somewhere else, but we came across him by chance, you know what I mean? He seemed *prepared* for us. And how does a man stop six pieces of lead, without flinching? Finally, there's an ex-cop named Foxy. He saw Jophiel start one of his fires three months ago, from *inside* the building, and he watched him walk out unharmed while everyone else burned to death. I'm going nuts, Vanessa, I need a lot of help."

"Take a breath," she said, "and calm down. Now look, have you considered the fact that you don't *want* to believe that this person is a supernatural being? If he is, then you might not get the revenge you want so badly. So you'd rather believe you were crazy, right?

"We have to begin by assuming that this man is not what he purports to be. He must be an ordinary human being. On the other hand, you don't seem crazy to me, and Danny has been through the same experience and, if I read you correctly, is having the same problems with his perspective of things."

Dave nodded.

"The answer may lie somewhere between the two. Jophiel has got you thinking you're going insane, but he may be an extraordinary person—one able to convince you that what you see and hear is actually happening. There are some powerful manipulators of minds in this world, Dave, people who can hypnotize you into believing anything. Jophiel may be nothing more than a very good hypnotist."

Dave thought about that, and it made a lot of sense. He remembered how Jophiel had held them with his strange eyes, and how mesmeric his voice had been. Dave also recalled watching a hypnotist on stage, and how a shy young Celia sitting beside him had suddenly leapt to her feet and cried, "We're going to a party," and had skipped down the aisle with a dozen others from the audience, and when she was told later to wake up, remembered nothing about it, and kept asking Dave why she was out front.

"Maybe you're right," he said at last. "Danny said we ought to keep open minds. This is probably what he meant. What do you call it, lateral thinking?"

"I'm inclined to agree with Danny. Keep an *open* mind. Don't settle for my explanation, there may be half a dozen more. Don't shut your mind completely to the supernatural, either," she said, surprising him. "Keep everything simmering until you find out the truth. If you start shutting down theories, before you've got the right answer, you'll end up in blind alleys."

Dave said, "You look as though you know what you're talking about."

Vanessa shook her head.

"I'm saying this because I have a friend who's a medium. She told me a number of people in her profession, the genuine clairvoyants, have been experiencing disturbing psychic vibrations, almost amounting to metaphysical quakes. There's a balance to spiritual things, as with everything else, and that balance has been upset by some cosmic agitation. The ambience of the spiritual environment has recently altered—it's become unstable. It's been in a lot of newspapers and magazines. Theories to explain this phenomenon have been aired on TV programs. You must have had your head in the sand."

He coughed.

"In the normal way of things, I wouldn't bother to read such articles. They wouldn't interest me."

She shook her head in a sad way.

"My friend says there's something very big going on in the psychic world, which is intruding upon the real world. Now I know you're a policeman, and a pragmatist, so you find these things difficult to swallow, but don't be a bigot. Don't push things aside because they don't fit in with your idea of what the world is like. I'm psychically very sensitive myself. We live in the same world as you, people like me, and we see things differently from you pragmatists. Do you see what I'm saying?"

He leaned back in his chair.

"Yeah, you're saying I'm a narrow-minded redneck."

She smiled.

"A very nice narrow-minded redneck."

"Touché," he said, "for the Dracula crack."

They ordered their main course, and kept to ordinary chat while they waited for it to arrive, both glad of a respite from their previously rather heavy conversation.

Over coffee they began to discuss angels again.

"I'm all mixed up," said Dave, "I mean, let's keep an open mind on this," he mocked himself, "and say that Jophiel *is* an angel, whatever. Everything I learned as a kid told me angels are good creatures, who bring you messages of joy, not arsonists who burn people to death. Surely that's *evil?*"

"There's evil and there's evil."

"What does that mean?"

"Well, what you and I would regard as evil, is not what, say, a Bible-thumping fundamentalist from Alabama would call evil."

Dave said, "If I hear of someone raping, killing, or something in that vein, to me that's evil. Hitler was evil. Pol Pot was evil. This Jophiel is evil, because he murders innocent people."

"Exactly, to you *evil* means evil deeds, but there are some who believe in evil as a supernatural energy. They talk about people who have been taken over by evil spirits. A person might not need to do anything at all, yet still be regarded as evil, because he renounces God, or blasphemes, or simply gives an impression of being evil. There's this vague horror that's in the air, that invades bodies and makes their owners do bad things, that shapes the lives of the damned. It's called EVIL and it lurks around corners, waiting to pounce."

Dave snorted. This was the kind of thing he hated, these airy-fairy theories that no one could prove or disprove, but which fueled the fundamentalist preachers and gave them power over their adherents.

"Jophiel told us," said Dave, "that the Ten Commandments didn't apply to angels, they were given to *men*. According to him, angels can kill as many mortals as they like, in the course of running down demons, and God will pat them on the head and tell them they're doing a good job."

The check came and Dave paid it and heard himself asking Vanessa if she would spend the night with him.

She gave him a faint smile and said yes.

In bed afterwards, Dave had pursued the subject of the angel. He plumbed her knowledge of angels, a vast and vague subject gathered from many sources, the least of which was the Bible.

Scholars, poets and writers had gathered around them, like a patchwork cloak, a mystical array of supernatural creatures, ambiguously documented, equivocally reported.

"This angel, what do you think he is?" asked Dave. "I mean, as I remember it, there are angels and angels."

Vanessa was on home ground here.

"There's supposed to be three triads of angels: High, Middle and Low. The highest triad consists of Seraphim, Cherubim and Thrones. The middle, Dominions, Virtues and Powers. The lowest, Principalities, Archangels and Angels. All together we know them as *angels,* the generic term."

"I thought Archangels were the top brass."

"No," she replied, "they're second to lowest in the triad structure, but no authority agrees entirely with this hierarchy any more than it agrees on who the archangels are. Islam has only four Archangels, for example, and Christianity has seven. Anyway, God is at the center of things, his illumination absolute, and around him are the triads, the Seraphim in the brightest light, and so on."

Dave shifted in the bed beside her.

"Seraphim and Cherubim? They're just babes with wings in the pictures I've seen."

Vanessa smiled.

"Yes, they've been reduced to that through the ages, but actually they're supposed to be terrible beings. In some documents they're described as having millions of eyes, thousands of wings and vicious claws. Cherubim are the awesome guardians of East of Eden, wielding the Ever-turning Sword. Seraphim are endowed with the Fire of Love, whatever that is— I doubt it's benign, though."

"Maybe our angel is one of those?"

"Well, maybe, but fire is attributed to many of the angels. Chasmal, one of the Dominions, is called the 'Fire-speaking Angel,' but interestingly, White Fire is said to be the prerogative of the Thrones. The Angel of Death is supposed to be a Throne."

"The Angel of Death," muttered Dave, "the first serial murderer."

"Isn't that a bit harsh? After all, the Egyptians were oppressing the whole Hebrew nation."

"I'm a cop." He smiled. "I'm concerned with the law, not justice."

"Typical," she snorted.

They left it at that.

When Dave finally fell asleep beside her, his breathing slow and regular, Vanessa was able to think. She had been lying next to him, almost able to hear the wheels turning in his mind, as he twitched and turned in the bed, fighting the monsters of his id. Vanessa knew she could never have Dave, not like Celia had had him, wholly and completely. Even if she and Dave were to become partners for life, there would always be the ghost of Celia lying between them. This had to be accepted, and many women, many men, managed to have happy relationships in such circumstances, so why not her?

It was two o'clock in the morning as Manovitch drove his BMW car along Pratt Street, the road that ran past the rear of Clementine's. In the trunk of his smart European automobile, which he loved more than his daughter and certainly more than his wife, were four gallons of gasoline, with which the probation officer intended to burn down the new bistro. Like most others connected to the local police station, he had been there, had stayed late enough for Foxy to get out his cognac, and had got thoroughly smashed with the ex-cop. Clementine had been there too, but she never minded her husband drinking "at home": it was when he stayed out visiting bars that she did not like it.

Foxy had revealed, during a long drunken speech, that he

had a partner in the business, a silent partner, and that man's name was Dave Peters. Manovitch had to sit and listen to a list of Mother Teresa's virtues, until he was ready to throw up in disgust. It was halfway through this revelation that the probation officer had the bright idea of firing the bistro. Friar Tuck he could deal with at any time, and would do so, one of these days, but Mother Teresa was the man he hated as a self-righteous dickhead who needed deflating. Both cops had paid him a visit over that bitch Vangellen, but Peters had played the avenging angel, with his high moral tone and menacing threats.

Manovitch switched off the lights to the BMW and cruised slowly along the curb edge, until he was a few yards from the rear of the bistro. He sat there for a long time, letting one or two other cars go past, just staring at the building, making sure there was no movement from within. When he was satisfied all was quiet, he took the keys out of the ignition, and had just put his hand on the door handle, when a shadow fell across him from a figure who leaned on the roof of the car.

"What's happening, Manovitch?"

Manovitch looked up fearfully, to see Mother Teresa staring down at him with a grim hawklike expression.

The probation officer quickly clicked down the lock to the door, and wound the window down an inch.

"What do you want, Peters?"

"Get out of the car," said the detective.

"No."

"Why not?"

"Because I'm staying in here, is why. What the fuck do you want? Can't a man with insomnia take a peaceful drive without being hassled by you people?"

Mother Teresa's expression remained grim.

"Most people, but not you, Manovitch. Get out, I want to talk to you about something."

"What?"

"Your treatment of a certain client of yours."

"None of your business. That's confidential. How the hell did you come to be here, anyway? This is no coincidence."

"No, it's not. I followed you. I've been watching you, and I'll keep watching you, until you treat a certain lady with a little more respect."

"That whore?"

Peters made a sudden movement and Manovitch screamed and covered his face as the windshield shattered under the impact of a two-pound hammer. Shards of glass, like a shower of diamonds, covered the probation officer. He felt himself being gripped by the hair, pulled forward over the wheel, his throat poised over the jagged edge of the broken glass pane. He gulped in air as terror overtook him.

"Now, you listen to me, you fat shit," snarled Peters. "If you so much as blow cigar smoke in her face again I'll personally come and tear your head off."

"My car," groaned Manovitch.

Peters twisted Manovitch's face upwards, so that he could look into his eyes, and then brought the hammer down onto the hood, making a large dent in the gleaming metal.

"Do—you—understand—me? This is your last warning, you dumb excuse for a human being. You're supposed to look after these people, not take advantage of them. They're placed under your trust. You ever heard of that word? Trust? You're scum, and one day soon I'm going to find someone who'll testify against you in court, and then I'll put you away." The hair was wrenched, painfully. "You hear me? I got a good mind to run your gullet along the edge of this window. It could be a nasty traffic accident."

"Don't do it," whispered Manovitch, hoarsely, the driving wheel painful against his chest. "Please don't do it."

The terror was bobbing in his throat, like a fisherman's float on the still surface of a pond.

"What the hell are you doing out there, at this time of night, anyway? This is Foxy's place."

Manovitch could hardly breathe through the fear. If Peters looked in the trunk of the car, and found the gasoline, he would put two and two together. The cop wouldn't be able to prove anything, but he would know, and Manovitch knew Peters would not allow him to leave the spot without some sort of injury, perhaps even death.

The tall willowy detective was known to be a man of ethics, but there was something behind those eyes lately which told you he could no longer be trusted to remain calm and rational in all circumstances. There was an edge there, over which he could so easily be pushed. Since his wife died Peters had been a different man. He was out for blood, the arsonist's blood, people said, but maybe he would settle for that of another man, if the situation got out of hand? Peters was a latent maniac waiting for the right time to go out of control.

"I'm sorry," croaked Manovitch. "I'll treat her right from now on. Please."

"I asked you a question. What are you doing here? This is no coincidence either."

"I came to . . . to see if Foxy wanted to go for a drink or somethin'. I get this insomnia. Foxy and me, we used to down a few together, at Frank's Bar. I was just seeing if there was any lights on."

"Why not go round the front?"

"Because I came round back. Foxy sometimes has a poker game going in the back room, and you can see the lights."

Mother Teresa's eyes bored into his own, and Manovitch squirmed, seeing the suspicion fade from them. He started to use mock indignation as a weapon, knowing that the detective was vulnerable in that direction.

"Look, you can't do this to me. I'm an officer of the court. You got something on me, then book me. Otherwise let go my hair."

The hard fingers gripping his hair relaxed a little.

"You better treat people right, Manovitch, because just one more complaint, from any of them, and I'm going to come down on you like something out of the *Enola Gay*. You get it?"

"I get it."

Peters let go then, but while Manovitch was fumbling with the ignition, the hammer came down rhythmically on the hood of the car, *bang-bang-bang-bang,* until the vehicle was finally started, and Manovitch sped away from the scene, the cold wind blasting his eyes, and pieces of windshield flying like bullets into his face as they became detached by the wind. Before he had driven two blocks, the weather turned against him too, and it began raining hard, the water driving in, stinging his skin, soaking the expensive upholstery of the car.

"I'm going to kill that son-of-a-bitch," screamed the sobbing Manovitch, the dents in his precious BMW rippling under the street lights. "I'm going to get him."

The wind and rain rushed in, shoving the words back down his throat, forcing him to eat his own threats.

15

Danny told the priest he did not want confession tonight, he wanted something else. What? asked the priest, warily. Nothing terrible, Danny told him, I just want to talk. I need to discuss something: an experience. I can't handle it on my own, I need spiritual advice.

The priest, Father Feiffer, told him to come to the back of the church, where they could speak without being interrupted. Father Feiffer led the way.

"Well, what is it?" asked the Father. "Have you got yourself into trouble?"

Danny wasn't sure whether to be indignant or not, but decided to brush it off.

"No, not trouble. Do I need to be in trouble to come to you, Father?"

"You don't *need* to be, but people usually are, before consulting me. If they came here *before* they got into trouble, they might not get in it in the first place."

"Well, not this time. This time I have a troubled spirit, not a troubled life. Now, I want to ask you something. Father, don't be angry at this question, but—can an angel be evil?"

Danny's distress was obvious to the priest, for he took Danny's bandaged hand in his.

"Why do you ask such a question, my son?"

Danny felt uncomfortable with the soft-skinned hand enveloping his own, but he didn't pull away.

He explained, "There's a man—at least he's not a man, he's something else—and he calls himself Jophiel. He implied he was a soldier of God, down on earth to destroy demons escaping Armageddon. Me and my partner tried to arrest him, but he burned us both, and killed two other people. Dave, that's my partner, shot this creature six times, and he walked away as if nothing had happened. I saw it, Father. He just smiled and walked away."

"You believe this man is a supernatural being?"

"Yes, no, that is, I don't know. I felt something, you know, something in here." He tapped his chest. "I'm scared, Father. I don't know what to think."

Someone came into the church, went down to the altar, and lit a candle, placing it in a sandbed of already lighted votive candles. The newcomer, who appeared to be an old woman, found a pew and kneeled in prayer. Danny could hear her muttered orisons, though he was not close enough to understand what was being said.

Father Feiffer squeezed Danny's hand, presumably to comfort him, but Danny felt only pain.

The priest said, "Would an angel of the Lord come down to earth to *destroy* life? Of course, there have been bad angels, hell is full of fallen angels, including Lucifer—Satan. But if they came to earth they would be devils and demons, my son, not angels. There must be trickery involved. I have been called in to exorcise houses, to establish the authenticity of mediums, and always I have found deceit. The world is full of charlatans, my son."

Danny began to get annoyed and pulled his hand away.

"Yeah, I know that, but a thousand charlatans don't mean there's no genuine mystics around."

"I'm just saying that I would be very wary of such a claim. We read and believe that messengers came down from heaven in the form of angels, but this is a more practical age. These are symbolic areas of the Bible . . ."

Danny's eyes widened.

"You don't believe in angels?"

The priest's own annoyance began to show in his voice, which took on a hissing tone.

"Yes, yes, of course I believe in the *principle* of angels, but I also have an opinion as an individual, which is that things of the spirit remain of the spirit, they do not take on fleshly form, they do not prowl the streets creating havoc."

"You don't believe in angels," Danny stated, flatly. "My own priest doesn't believe what he preaches, for crying out loud. Who am I gonna go to if I can't go to you?"

"I want to help you."

"Well, first you got to *believe* what I'm telling you. You think I'm some kind of liar?"

The priest shook his head.

"Not a liar, Danny, but you may be persuading yourself that something special is happening to you for some subconscious reason. Perhaps you need more attention than I can give you? Why don't you have a word with a friend of mine?"

Danny smiled sardonically.

"A shrink, you mean?"

"An understanding man, Danny, who will listen and try to find out what's troubling you."

"I know what's troubling me. I saw a guy laugh at six lumps of lead as they slammed into his body," shouted Danny. "That's what's troubling me. I saw a guy start a fire by just thinking about it. That's what's troubling me."

"Keep your voice down," said Father Feiffer sharply, as the old woman looked up from prayer and stared into the gloom at the rear of the church. "We know what's troubling you, what we must find out is the *reason* for those troubles."

"Jesus Christ!" Danny moaned.

"Don't blaspheme in here!"

"I'm not blaspheming, I'm calling for help," Danny cried. "You can't give it to me, so I've got to ask somewhere else."

"Then do it in prayer, with reverence."

Danny realized he was getting nowhere, and he kneeled down at the pew, virtually dismissing Father Feiffer by cutting him out of his sphere of attention. He stayed on his knees with his eyes tightly shut, trying to think of something to say that would help him connect with God, but failed miserably. When he opened his eyes, the seat next to him was vacant, and the priest had gone up to the altar.

Danny remained in the church for another ten minutes, then went outside into the rain.

Despite the downpour, the sirens were going, and the sky behind the city had a backdrop of light. There was a fire somewhere, blazing away, rain or no rain.

Danny sloshed through streets running with water, his overcoat soaking through within minutes, the downpour penetrating his jacket to his shirt. His mind was in a turmoil. He went over and over the events of the previous day, looking at every tiny detail in his mind, trying to figure out how Jophiel had fooled them. He couldn't see it. He just couldn't see it. But then again, he remembered that when he was a kid and a magician came to his eighth birthday party, he saw some amazing things, things which he spent days afterwards discussing with his friends, lying awake at nights trying to figure out. He hadn't seen it then, either.

So maybe the priest was right, maybe the guy was some kind of illusionist. You saw these people floating in midair, hoops passed around them: the impossible performed right before your eyes. They weren't real, they were tricks.

But what about the way Danny had *felt?* That was what worried him the most. He had been acutely aware of being in the presence of someone very powerful, someone with immense psychic energy. He had definitely experienced that feeling. Of course, he hadn't allowed his inner turbulence to show in front of Dave, who would have started wondering about the reliability of his partner, and clearly Dave hadn't experienced those feelings himself. As far as Dave was concerned, it was all in what you saw and heard, rather than feelings.

Was it possible that Jophiel and those feelings were separate from one another? That Danny had been in the path of some powerful force, but that it was unconnected with what happened inside the burger joint? If so, it was a big coincidence, that someone should claim to be a hunter from heaven, and while you were being told this, your spirit was crawling with electricity.

Danny walked back to his apartment. He passed a wall covered in posters advertising a forthcoming pop concert. The group called itself Firestorm, in keeping with the times. Danny considered how easily the public had taken on board the idea that fires were inevitable. When the fires first began to become more than a nuisance there had been concern, then outrage, and not so long after that, acceptance. From outrage to acceptance was one small step for mankind. Nowadays street talk reflected the obsession with fire. If someone "got cremated," it meant several things from losing heavily on the track or in a poker game to being murdered. *He got cremated.* Then the latest phrase questioning the sincerity of a deal was "Are you trying to kindle me?" *I got kindled.*

The human race was good at adapting. In the beginning, that had been to its advantage. However, adaptation had its downside. It meant that when humans finally built huge cities, which at the center became jungles, they quickly adapted to the idea that their possessions and themselves would be subject to violation from time to time. They quickly adapted to the idea that murder was a commonplace crime, and that more people would die violent deaths on the streets of a city than in a foreign war.

Now, they had accepted that at least one major fire would occur every single day in some city. A year ago it would have been unthinkable, and people in authority would be asked for their resignations. Today, the fires came and went with a shrug of the shoulders. *Another fire? Seventeen dead? So what else is new?*

Danny reached his apartment and found the lights out. Rita came home pretty tired these days and if he wasn't in by ten o'clock she would go to bed without him. He had once thought that hookers were nightlifers, staying up all hours partying, but since Rita had moved in, he realized that here, at least, was one that was quite a homely soul. He liked it. He liked the domestic-serenity bit. The streets were full of shit and violence, but at least his apartment was an island of peace.

He crept into the bedroom and noted with satisfaction the long lump in the bed.

"Is that you, Danny?" said a sleepy voice.

"Yeah, it's me."

He liked the way they stated the obvious to each other.

He took off his shoes, quietly laying them down beside the chair he sat in. Then the rest of his clothes. He crawled in beside the soft warm body, putting an arm around her, and holding her to him.

"I like it when you cuddle me," she murmured. "How did I do without it before?"

"Tonight I got an ulterior motive," he said, placing a hand on her breast.

She turned in the bed.

"I ain't arguing. I been waiting up, but you took so long I came to bed. Only been here five minutes."

He could feel her breath on his face.

"Yeah, sorry, I called in at the church. I wanted to see Father Feiffer about something, but he was about as helpful as I expected." He thought of something, and added quickly,

"Nothing to do with living with you. It was something else."

"No deal, eh?" Her voice came out of the darkness.

He wanted to see her eyes when he talked to her.

"Listen, you mind if I turn on the light?"

"No, go ahead."

He twisted round and snapped the bedside-light switch.

When he turned to face her again his gut turned over and he jumped out of bed with a scream, his heart drumming wildly, and his temples hammering. There was a hairy shape on her neck, with a lolling tongue, and yellow fangs. Its mouth opened and snarled at him.

She had the head of a dog.

"TAKE IT OFF!" he yelled, his voice cracking with fear.

"What's the matter?" she shrieked, obviously as terrified as he was himself.

He blinked and the dog head was gone.

"What—how did you do that?" he cried.

"How did I do what?" she shouted, looking frightened and probably wondering what the hell was going on herself.

"I . . . I'm sorry. I thought—I thought I saw something."

She looked around her wildly, crying *"A spider?"* having her own dreads to submit to or conquer.

"No, no, not a spider, I thought you had—had someone else's face. It's okay, I'm seeing things. Don't worry about it, I'm sorry, I've been working too hard."

But he still could not go near her for a while and watched her warily out of the corner of his eye for signs of more changes. Had it been an hallucination? Ever since he had been bitten by a German shepherd as a child, he had been terrified of dogs. People had told him it was a phobia, but when he looked the word up in the dictionary he found that phobia was an "irrational fear" of something. Since dogs had jaws full of sharp teeth, which they used unpredictably, he considered fear of the beasts reasonable and sensible, not irrational in the least.

He made them both a cup of coffee, and soothed her with calm words while sitting on the edge of the bed. She kept asking him if it was a joke, but he assured her that he had seen something, even if it was a product of his imagination. His own nerves were still twisted and wrecked and it was all he could do to drink his coffee without shaking and worrying her further. What the hell was this? How come a *dog's* head? He really was cracking up. Maybe it was a nervous breakdown. The whole thing was getting to him, pressure, stress.

By the time he climbed back into bed he was feeling better, but neither of them wanted to make love now. They settled down into their former position, she with her back to him, and he with an arm around her, like two spoons lying together.

In the middle of the night he woke in a sweat, feeling hair in his face, but it was human hair, not that of **a dog**, and he went back to a fitful sleep again.

16

Dave was driving Vanessa back to her apartment after work. On the way there, he asked her if she was managing to keep Manovitch in his place, and she said the man was a creep but at least he hadn't tried to touch her recently.

"I report to him when I have to, and he still tries to intimidate me by blowing cigar smoke in my face, and childish tricks like that, but at least he hasn't tried to put his hand up my skirt recently."

"He'd better not," said Dave, incensed. "I'll break both his legs."

"A lot of good that would do the pair of us. It's best you stay away from him, Dave, and let me handle anything that comes up. I know how to look after myself."

He didn't press the point and he didn't tell her he had threatened Manovitch round by Foxy's place. But he felt like driving round to Manovitch's apartment and grinding the guy's ugly face into the toilet pan. The man was a disgrace to his profession. Once Vanessa was off his books, Dave promised himself he was going to sort Manovitch out once and for all. Until then, as Vanessa said, it would do neither of them any good to cause trouble.

When they reached her apartment she made drinks for them both and they settled down to talk again.

She seemed to want Dave to do the talking, so this time Dave told her about his childhood, rather than continue with what they had been discussing at the restaurant. He told her he had been a regular churchgoer in his younger life.

"I thought you were an atheist," she said.

"Am now, I guess, but once upon a time I was very religious."

This kind of talk pattered on, into the early hours, until they were tired enough to go to bed. Once between the sheets they made love and fell asleep holding each other. Dave did not like to continue touching her when he was trying to sleep, because he needed space after lovemaking, but he did not dare to let her go. He thought she might sneak out of bed and burn herself. So he kept a tight hold of her, and she responded through natural affection.

In the morning, however, they were two feet apart. Dave woke first and crept out of bed and into the bathroom to shower before she woke. Then he made a cup of coffee, because he liked something to drink while he was dressing. It helped him think about the rest of his day and plan his workload hour by hour.

He took two coffees into the bedroom, putting one on the shelf by her side of the bed. She still had the sheet pulled over her head, and he whipped it back, with "C'mon, sleepy, time to say hello to the—"

He stopped in midsentence with a choked gargle, and stepped back toward the window, cringing in horror. The body on the bed was moving of its own volition, like carrion being eaten from the inside out by scavengers. He tried to catch his breath as Vanessa sat up and stared at him with what was left of her eyes. He wanted to vomit.

"Dave, what's the matter?"

The skin on her face had degenerated into a mass of writhing maggots. There were large pits in her chest full of wriggling corrugated blowfly larvae, and they were dropping out onto the sheets with little plopping sounds. When she opened her mouth to talk, they spilled out of there too.

He was about to throw up, when they disappeared. One minute her flesh was crawling with maggots, the next it was clean, unblemished. He still couldn't speak.

"Dave?" she repeated. "You're scaring me."

Dave took a minute to catch his breath, and when he did, all he said was, "I don't feel well. I think I'm coming down with something."

"You look as white as a ghost. Why did you look at me like that? Have I done something?"

"No, no. Nothing. I—I don't think I was staring at you. I was just . . . staring. You know, into space? I just had this terrible feeling wrenching at my gut, as if I'd eaten something bad. It's gone now. I'll be all right."

He didn't want to tell her what he had seen, for fear of upsetting her. It seemed to be all in his own head, for she had obviously felt nothing. It made his head spin with apprehension. What the hell was the matter with him? Although he had no fever, he was obviously sick.

"Could you get me something to drink?" he asked, sitting on the edge of the bed.

She was solicitous and went to get him a glass of water. He kept watching her, out of the corners of his eyes, expecting another change to come about just as suddenly. Nothing happened. The water came and he drank it. Then he got dressed. She put on a robe. They went to the kitchen, but Dave did not feel like eating any breakfast, so he had a second coffee and left.

He picked up Danny and the pair of them sat in the car outside Danny's apartment block. Danny did not appear inclined to move anywhere either. He looked thoughtful, distant.

Finally, he broke out of his trance, and turned to his partner.

"Mother Teresa, you don't look so hot today."

"Neither do you, Friar Tuck."

They permitted each other to use the nicknames occasionally, when they were feeling low. Any other cop would get a mouthful of fist.

Danny said, "I had a nasty experience."

"So did I," replied Dave.

"Not as horrible as mine."

"Worse," said Dave. "How would you like to wake up in bed and find the woman beside you is crawling with maggots?"

Danny winced.

"Vanessa? Vanessa is covered in maggots?"

"No, but I thought she was. I pulled the sheet back from her face this morning, and there was a ghoul there, like in one of those horror movies, writhing with these . . . things. I hate maggots. Of all things, I hate maggots."

Danny's eyes narrowed.

"You hate maggots. You have a phobia about maggots, right? Something happened when you were a kid."

Dave looked at his partner in surprise.

"Yeah. Well, not *startling*, or anything like that, but my old man was a Sunday angler. He loved to take me fishing. Any other kid would have been ecstatic, you know, but I *hated* it. I hated it because he would make me put the maggots on the hook—these ugly blowfly maggots. He kept them in a square tobacco tin, and he would open the tin and shove it under my nose, saying, 'Take one, David, bait your hook, son. Boy, we're gonna catch some fish today, you wait and see,' and there, not two inches from my face, was this mass of crawling things hatched from blowfly eggs. I tell you, Danny, I was shitting my pants, but I didn't dare say anything to my old man, or he would've made a big thing about it. He'd have kept me at it, telling me that familiarity bred contempt and if I stuck my hand in a jar of them, and kept it there, I would have nothing but contempt for the little parasites."

Danny's eyes were still narrowed, a sure sign that he was thinking hard, and Dave said, "What?"

"We're being set up," said Danny. "You have a phobia about maggots, and I'm scared to death of dogs."

"So?"

"So, last night, when I turned on the light, Rita had the head of a dog. I freaked out, I can tell you, and I scared her too, screaming my guts out like that. I put it down to over-tiredness in the end, working too hard. But now you come up with the maggots. It's like a repeat of my experience last night."

They both stared out of the front windshield.

"Jophiel," said Dave.

Danny said, "Why? How?"

"It's obvious. He's trying to scare us off. He planted one of those posthypnotic triggers in us. He put this in our brains while we were sitting staring into those mild gray eyes of his. It's a kind of warning. Lay off. He set it up, to come out when we were with our women."

"What if we didn't have women to go home to?"

Dave said, "I don't know all the answers. But he seemed to know all about us, remember? This guy is trying to scare the hell out of us, get us to drop the thing. Well, he's got another think coming, if he thinks we're just gonna walk away from him. I'm going to nail this bastard if it's the last thing I ever do on this earth."

"Don't use phrases like that," Danny said. "So, what you're saying is, he didn't change the people—Rita and Vanessa—it was all in our own heads. He hypnotized us for a later time, when he wasn't around, and when we were least expecting it."

"That's it."

"Look," said Danny, "we're both skeptical about the su-pernatural angle, right? You more than me. We're cops, right? And we like life to be plain and simple. But somewhere inside us we have these voices saying, 'Something's really out of kilter here, something's lopsided,' right?"

Dave conceded this.

"I sort of believe sometimes but dismiss it as nonsense at other times. I keep changing my mind. I keep going over events until they're spinning around in my skull like fireworks."

"Right," said Danny, "me too. So we gotta *do* something. I got an idea. Maybe we can flush the bastard out."

"How?"

"If the angel's out there, then so are the demons. I've sort of jumped ahead of you here, Dave, but I've contacted two or three high priests . . ."

"Priests?"

"No, *high* priests. Black magic. People we've pulled in from time to time, on charges like corruption of minors and public decency violations. They hold these black masses, in derelict churches and stuff . . . I know what you're thinking," said Danny, "but we've got to use them. They'll know where to find a demon, if anyone does."

"What do we want a demon for?"

"Information. We need all we can get, Dave, and these are the guys, the creatures who'll give it to us. If we can get hold of a demon, we can find out what the hell is going on—if you'll excuse the expression. If we can't find one, then maybe we are barking up the wrong tree."

"So what do we do? We sit and wait for one of your black magic priests to set up a meeting?"

"You got it," said Danny.

Dave stared at his partner, trying to gauge the depth of seriousness in the crazy plan. From the look in Danny's eyes it would appear that he meant what he said.

"And if you're wrong, you'll black your face and sing 'Ole Man River' standing on one leg in front of the Aryan National Army Hall?"

"Those sons of bitches?"

"Well, that's the deal. You got to be mighty sure of your ground here, Danny, because even letting you go ahead is going some way to agreeing with your point of view. I mean, if our patriotic brothers do anything to you, like lynch you, at least we can bust 'em for it. I haven't made a decent collar in weeks."

"You're shitting me."

Dave nodded. "Yeah, I'm shitting you."

"Trust me, Dave, I'll find a way."

Dave said, "What do we say to Reece?"

Danny looked startled.

"Are you kidding?"

"Well, the captain goes to church on Sunday, with his family, I've seen him. He should understand what you're doing here, being a fellow believer."

"Don't mock me, Dave, it doesn't suit you. Reece goes to church because it's good for him politically. He wants to make chief."

"I know that, you know that, but do the demons know that?"

"Fuck you," said Danny, hitting his partner over the head with his notepad, just as Rita was leaving the apartment for work. She stared at the pair of them, still sitting in the car, and shook her head slowly. Walking over to them she leaned in through Dave's side window.

"I always knew cops didn't do any work," she said. "You gonna sit here all day, or what?"

"Naw," said Danny, "we got to eat, don't we?" He glanced at his watch. "In about an hour we'll drive over to Mario's for a focaccia and coffee."

She nodded as slowly as she had shaken her head.

"Just as I thought."

Dave protested.

"We've *been* working, Rita, here in the car. It's the only

place we can get some peace. At the precinct house they all drop their pens to watch us coming in, saying, 'Gee, there's the famous team called D&D, I wonder if I can get their autographs?'"

She smiled and stepped back from the car.

"Nah, what they say is, 'Here come those jerks Friar Tuck and Mother Teresa. I wonder what they'll screw up today?'"

With that she walked away, swinging her purse, leaving them grinding their teeth and trying to think of something clever to say.

17

There was a cold Irish-fine drizzle over the city as Dave pulled back the curtains to reveal the day. Raindrops stuck to the window like oil from a highway stuck to the windshield of a car. The air pollution went to the heart of the stormclouds overhead, and the rain came down dirty to cling to dirty glass in a dirty atmosphere. It might have looked dismal to someone from out of town, but Dave was used to it, and would have been surprised had it been otherwise.

He didn't like the rain, of course. Rain hampered police work.

The phone rang. It was Danny.

"We got something, Dave."

"What?"

"An answer from a high priest."

"When I last checked we had a dozen answers. They were all cuckoos."

"This one's the real baby. It feels right."

"Yeah, yeah, you wish. Okay, I'll be with you in thirty minutes."

He went into the shower, then shaved and put on a shirt

and tie, slacks and shoes. Left to himself, his choice would have been for casual clothes, but Reece liked his cops dressed respectably, even though it might hamper their street work. He would rather lose a bust than have a scruffy cop under his command. Of course there were the "bearded weirdos" as the captain called them, at the station, but they were the night shift. Reece didn't have to see them that often.

So, Dave wore a suit. His partner Danny liked the clothes they were expected to wear because, given the choice, Danny would wear a suit anyway. He was a rigid dresser. Danny had been two years in the army, and instead of turning him against uniforms, it turned him on. It was probably one of the reasons why he had joined the cops. Only he found himself back in civilian clothes within a very short time. A suit was the closest thing to a uniform.

Dave picked up Danny, who took over at the wheel and drove to McLaren Park. They sat in the car looking out over dingy-green grass, if not verdant pastures. What they were doing was unofficial. There was no way they were going to tell Reece they were looking for a demon.

"So tell me," said Dave.

"There's a guy who calls himself the Grand Inquisitor. He called me this morning. He's set up a meeting with a demon here. He'll meet us at nine—the demon, that is."

"Just like that," said Dave, in a sarcastic voice. "You want to meet a demon, Mr. Peters, well, just go to the park at nine o'clock. He'll be sitting on the third bench from the old oak. Oh, yes, you'll recognize him instantly—he's got these little horns sticking out of his skull, and a long red tail with a barb on the end—"

"It isn't like that," snapped Danny. "The guy looks like you and me. Or to be more precise, he looks like the angel."

"Why should he look like the angel?"

"Because that's what he is, you dickhead. A fallen angel. Now, are we on or not?"

"What choice do we have?" grumbled Dave. "But why the park?"

"It was my choice. He wanted to meet in some pighole downtown."

"Okay, let's wait."

They were reading their papers when the guy sat down on the bench Danny had mentioned in his call. They watched him take out a cigarette, light it, and then stub it out underneath his foot directly afterwards.

"That's the signal," said Danny. "Let's go."

It was still drizzling slightly as they walked across the park and approached the man, intending to sit on either side of him. Even as Dave was walking toward the guy, and could study him more closely, he knew that he was going to have to open his mind a great deal wider than he had until now.

The guy could have been the younger brother of Jophiel. He was dark and lean, and very good-looking, in the way of many young Latin males. He had the kind of masculine beauty that made women tremble at the knees: the sort that lured them away from confident, muscled, athletic husbands, leaving the jocks shocked and uncomprehending. There was an easy grace about him, as he lit up a second cigarette, and Dave would have marked him down as some kind of dancer or circus artist. His indefinable effeminacy would have rednecks scoffing but unsure of themselves, though Dave, a trained judge of other men, could detect that he was mean and hard underneath his natural stylishness.

"So," said Dave, after they had sat down, "we're the guys that asked for your help."

"Who are you, exactly?" asked the man.

Dave said, "You tell us first."

"You're the ones who contacted *me*."

"You must need us, or you wouldn't have agreed to this meeting."

The man sighed, as if tired of the game.

"Okay, my name is Malloch. There's someone after me,

someone who wants to . . . kill me. I would like to see this person taken care of in some way." He flicked the ash off his cigarette. "Frankly, I'm desperate. I'm clutching at straws. So what have you got to offer?"

Danny spoke for them.

"We're cops, and we're after the same guy that wants you."

Malloch nodded.

"We want this guy badly," said Dave. "Very badly. Maybe neither of us has anything to give the other, but we can at least pool what we've got. Now, this arsonist who calls himself Jophiel, he maintains he's some kind of freak of nature," said Dave cautiously.

Malloch smiled and drew on his cigarette.

"You mean it calls itself an *angel*?"

"Yeah," said Dave. "That is, he didn't say he was one, but he implied it."

"Well, let me put your minds at rest."

"Yes?" said Dave, expectantly.

Malloch said, "It's everything it claims to be. We don't use words like *angel* where I come from, but since we're here on earth, we've got to use your terms. You would call me me"—he looked a little wistful—"a *demon*. I rather like the word. It has depth to it. A fallen angel, I don't like. That's a bit negative, a bit like *angel* with a line through it. Demon is much more positive."

Danny said abruptly, "Can you prove it?"

"Actually, I don't need to prove it, because it doesn't matter to me whether you believe me or not. Right at this moment I have no desire to be a demon, because my position in the Great Chain of Being means that I have a vengeful angel on my ass, ready to burn me to gray ash."

"Do you have any special powers?" asked Danny, hopefully.

"None that can help me avoid being obliterated by my enemy. I have a physical strength probably ten times that of a mortal. I can only be destroyed by some corrosive agent that will corrupt my flesh, like acid or fire. Here on earth we have none of our spiritual powers. Think of me as a kind of meteor, entering earth's atmosphere: a giant when I began, but a smouldering rock not much bigger than a house brick when I landed."

"So," said Danny, "we can't kill you, any of you?"

"We can be dismembered, disfigured, crippled, but there will still be life in us. Fire is the purest form of annihilation. It wipes the slate clean."

Dave said, "How come Jophiel has superpowers?"

"I wish you wouldn't encourage the creature in that name. It doesn't belong to it, it belongs to an archangel. This one has no name."

"But he's very powerful," protested Danny.

"Only in comparison to mortals, who are so weak that the most retarded demon could snuff one out like a candleflame. This angel retained its powers in the descent precisely because it is what it is. Angels have a mandate to visit the earth—as messengers among other things."

"You keep saying *it*," said Dave.

Malloch nodded. "Angels are asexual, they are neither male nor female."

"And demons?"

Malloch smiled.

"We're what we look like."

There was silence between them for a moment, then Dave spoke up. "Let me explain something here. I'm the one you have to convince about all this angels and demons stuff. My friend here is already a believer. Do something for me, to convince me that you're worth getting wet in the rain for."

"I told you, I have no interest in proving my identity."

Dave said mockingly, "Aw, come on, be a sport . . ."

Malloch shrugged, then his hand flashed out in a snake strike. In an instant he had disarmed Dave and held Dave's .38 police special in his hand. Before Danny could move the demon pressed the muzzle of Dave's gun against his own stomach and pulled the trigger. Pain disfigured the demon's face for a few moments, but this was very brief.

Malloch then handed back the fired weapon to a shocked Dave.

"Jesus Christ!" whispered Danny. "He shot himself."

"You asked me to prove myself," said Malloch, "and apart from a feat of strength, which you might dismiss as merely extraordinary, this was the only thing I could think of. Not having done it before, I wasn't sure how much it would hurt. I might add that it hurt like hell, but fortunately not for very long. The bullet's lodged somewhere inside my gut, but apart from that, the wound has healed itself."

Dave returned his gun to its holster.

"Let me see the point of entry," he said to Malloch.

The demon opened his shirt and showed the two policemen where the bullet had gone in. There was a puckered dent in his skin, but no raw flesh and no blood. It looked like a scar from a wound caused years before.

"Now," said Malloch. "You asked me here for a reason. Let's get it over with. I don't like to stay in one place too long. It's already got close to me once."

"The wound *has* healed," said Dave. "I don't know. I was sure you weren't anything special before, now I'm confused. I admit, I'm having credibility trouble. This angel, if he is what you say he is, and Danny thinks he is, then how do we get rid of him?"

"You can try prayer, but I don't think it'll work. You see, you won't receive any divine help. He won't interfere in things, not now. You've got free will, you have to sort out your own problems, decide upon your own destiny. If the divine hand comes down once, it might as well come down a billion times, and sort out every trouble in the world. You'd be slaves to benign interference. Nothing you did would matter any longer, because as soon as you made a mistake it would be corrected.

"So, God won't help you, any more than He'll help us. The angel is down here without authority. The others, well, you can't communicate with the angel's immediate superiors. And the only way of stopping the creature is to get word to them. How you might do that, I have no idea."

Dave said, "What are you doing, you—people?" He couldn't bring himself to call them demons. "Are you getting together?"

"The time for that is past. We were together on the battle-fields, and we fled, deserted. We're in full retreat now, and re-treating armies don't 'get together' or turn and fight. They keep running, as individuals. I've managed to avoid it this far, and I'll keep doing so. I don't think you can help me. You can hardly help yourselves. I thought it would be this way, but it was worth a try."

"Get together," said Danny. "Together you might figure something out, find some form of defense against this holy ma-niac."

"Yeah," said Dave.

Before they parted, Danny said to Malloch, "What I don't get, what puzzles *me*, is why demons are *evil*. I mean, what have you done that's so terrible? Do you kill people?"

"No," said Malloch, "not really. I mean, we would in self-defense, just as you might, but not out of gain or for reasons of malice. What would be the point?"

"Do you rob, steal?"

"No."

"Do you rape women—or men? Sexual crimes?"

Malloch laughed openly.

"Do you think, looking at me, that I *need* to force myself on anyone? In any case, it wouldn't do to draw attention to our-selves. Sure, we frequent places of vice, but that's our camou-flage."

"That's it, that's what I mean, you're not evil at all."

"You're confusing morality with criminal law. We are evil because we followed Lucifer."

"Who did what? Defied God?"

"Yes."

"I know people who defy God every day, and no one considers them evil. No one chases them out of the light and into the darkness. No one hounds them to hell. Something's got turned around here, somewhere."

Malloch left them then, walking quickly toward the far side of the park.

The drizzle was soaking them through.

"Let's get out of here," Danny said. "I feel kinda strange. As far as we're concerned, the bad guys are the good guys, and the good guy is the bad guy. Don't you find that weird? I mean, the angel is destroying our people, therefore he's the evil one to us, while the demons, like Malloch, who come from legions of the Devil—well, they're the underdogs, the downtrodden, helpless ones. They're the good guys because they obey the law. They're on our side.

"I mean, it turns the whole concept of good and evil on its head."

Dave said nothing in reply. He walked back to the car. He was thinking that Malloch was strong—very, very strong. A superhuman strength. The power behind Malloch was like nothing Dave had ever witnessed or felt before. If these people were not angels and demons, they were certainly something not-of-this-world, and if Dave was admitting that much, he might as well go all the way, and accept them for what they said they were.

An angel had killed his wife and child, and was burning others to death, every day, simply to take revenge on a few spent demons. He had to be stopped. The angel had to be stopped. There was no other way around it.

But how in hell were they going to do it?

18

The angel moved through the city streets, never resting, never needing rest. It was tireless in its efforts to track down and kill its enemies. The angel enjoyed a great potency among the mortals, able to move between places easily. This was not its first visit to earth, which was one reason why it could follow its enemies down here without the guidance or knowledge of its superiors.

Yes, it had been here before, as a messenger: the messenger of death, the Angel of Death. Men had talked of the shadow of its dark wings ever since. In that time it had gorged on death, passing over the houses with lintels dripping in blood, seeking out the firstborn of a nation, sucking the breath from their lungs, watching them turn blue, then gray, leaving them with staring eyes, contorted bodies. Bed after bed, life after life. Mothers screaming, fathers wailing, bedlam in its wake. The mission had been one of dark energy, a task of many decisions, the blood-smeared dwellings eventually passed over reluctantly, with difficulty, for it was like a fox among chickens, a necessary duty turned to lust with so much death.

It was work for many angels, but only one could be spared, and this was solely its chore.

After a night of killing, death had become a drug, difficult to assuage except with more death. The angel had gone back to the battlefield full of death, ten thousand deaths in its mouth, the taste of which though initially bitter was now sweet, to throw itself into the fight with fresh fury.

Its energy was an infinite universe of sunpower. It was light within light. The angel was supercharged with the power of Good, able to draw on a furnace fired with suns enough to fill a forever. Here on earth, it was invincible, though his name was not Jophiel. The angel had no name. On the spiritual plane it was hardly noticed, but on earth they would reckon ill who ignored its presence.

The angel believed the remaining fallen angels hiding somewhere on earth were numbered in hundreds. They could be anywhere, but, of course, they were more likely to be in the cities. And, of course, they were still arriving, deserting from the battlefields where they were being overcome by the forces of the greater Good.

The demons were in the cities, as opposed to the deserts and jungles, for the simple reason that down here they had the frailties of mortals. Only their former physical strength survived the journey from other planes, not their superpowers: their shadowy magic, their shape-changing abilities, their invulnerability when opposed by physical forces, all this was lost on the terrible voyage through layers of light and darkness, leaked from their fleeing forms like energy from a fractured star. Wasted. By the time they reached the physical world, they had nothing left but the weak spark of life which dwelt in all mortals.

There were routes along which demons could travel but they had to be invited to use these channels by practitioners of sorcery and devil worship. They could not set out of their own volition, but needed guidance and an entrance to the physical world, provided by those familiar with the black arts.

Thus they were subject to the same rigors of climate as any human being. They needed food and water to fuel their corporeal forms. They had to protect the weak flesh that held their spirits within them from fire and other excoriating agents. In the deserts and the jungles they would quickly become prey to the angel. In the jungles and deserts there was little evil to shield their own wickedness. Their flesh had healing properties beyond that of human flesh but they were weaker than men in some respects.

So they ran to the cities, which were jungles in themselves, full of corruption behind which they could hide their own iniquity. They haunted dens of vice and sin, where they felt more at home, and could use the evil they found there as a barrier against the angel's radar mind. In hell they swarmed like cockroaches in a sewer, but that was where demons were expected to be, for hell was no place of comfort even for fallen angels. It was the metaphysical equivalent of a cramped pit full of unbelievably foul filth, in which the demons had to wade, fighting for room to rest their negative souls.

And hell would eventually be destroyed.

The fallen angels had fled to earth to escape death, a demon's death of turning into nothingness, not even darkness, not even airless space. But here they were still finding that same death from the hand of the angel, whose power stretched over every part of the globe.

If its superiors discovered the angel's presence on earth, it would no doubt be recalled and asked to account for its actions, but unlike the Master they served, who held Himself aloof from the frenetic activity of His free-willed creations, these creatures were not omniscient.

The angel swept through the streets, shadows folding about it, its human form a necessary encumbrance on this physical world.

It was on the track of another demon, Hedrag, who had been eluding it for hours, the trail of evil weaving through the clubs of Amsterdam's red light district, like the silver path of a snail.

Finally, the angel entered a brightly lit dive in the Teggen area, and sat at a table. It scanned the room, leaving nothing to chance. It located its victim, standing with his back to the bar, hiding in a crowd of young revelers.

The angel allowed a human smile to cross its face.

It stood up. The demon Hedrag turned, the terror on his countenance a gray creased film. There was a last desperate effort to avoid the angel. Hedrag clutched a woman to him, as a hostage, and pointed.

"It's going to kill me!" Hedrag screamed.

The angel flash-fired his victim from within, a combustion which resulted in a burst of incandescent flame that devoured not only the fallen angel, but also the human in his arms. Several other people screamed in agony as the white fire leapt toward them and consumed parts of their bodies. So powerful was this holy flame, that it instantly reduced to ashes anything combustible, and seriously ruptured the stability of more fire-resistant materials.

A woman was rushing toward the exit, her dress blazing, her voice a piercing whistle in her throat. She fell among some blinded patrons, crashing over a table, sending glasses, bottles and other objects flying. With the intense heat coming from the giant white flame by the bar, the temperatures were high enough in the rest of the room to make flash-points easily reachable, and her dress set fire to other inflammable fabrics just waiting for the touch of a spark.

Almost everyone in the room was covering their eyes, blinded by the effulgence from the burning demon.

Hedrag's form was like a giant candle flame, reaching as high as the ceiling, as the remains of his spirit burned away, adding its own colors to the white fire. The flame was white not simply because it was pure, but also because of the heat which it generated. A steel cigarette case just a few feet away melted to a dribble.

The fire was so fierce, so potent, that almost immediately tables and chairs began blazing furiously. The bar caught fire, and the smoking face of the bartender was charred black as charcoal, as if suddenly wiped by a hot tar brush. He fell backward, dead before he crashed into the shelves of melting glasses and bottles, and the released hard liquor roared throatily into flame. The chandelier over the bar came down with a massive clatter and splintering of crystal, as the chain holding it up melted and snapped.

There was a sizzling and smell of cooking flesh, as more victims got caught in the conflagration. People were panicking, screaming and clawing to get to the inadequate fire exits, some of them still blinded by the white flash. They stampeded, tripping over objects, some falling into the heart of the flames, where they were trodden on by others. The fumes from synthetic materials were choking the atmosphere, and patrons were dropping where they stood, clutching their chests, writhing like wounded rats on the floor. There were asphyxiations and heart attacks.

The angel was concerned by none of this.

It stepped over the bodies, away from the fire of its own making, and out of a side exit. There in the alley it considered its next move. There was London to visit. One of them was there, in a Soho tenement.

Then back to America, and the city where those two foolish policemen were fumbling around looking for it. Their efforts were hardly worth concern and the angel tried to put them out of its mind, but found it difficult. They were an irritant. The angel had already wasted time and effort in planting within them hypnotic warnings, which they would have done well to heed. They were becoming bothersome in their pursuit of it, like mosquitoes in the room of a half-awake man.

If they persisted, for its own peace of mind, the angel would have to destroy them. They were causing it to doubt itself, which for an angel was dangerous. If it did not believe in its own righteousness, then it fell under the scrutiny of those who were its superiors. They constantly monitored the souls of their subordinates, and sparks of spiritual doubt were always investigated. Its superiors might not know or be interested in geographical locations of angels, what dimensions or planes they were on, but they were always concerned with the condition of their spirits.

One revolution in heaven was enough to last an eternity.

These two mortals were causing the angel to question its own zeal. Why should it be concerned with the lives of a few animal humans, who were going to die the next instant in any case? The lifespan of a mortal was but a single knot in the silk-thread timeline of an angel, so where was the sorrow, where was the concern? A year, a decade, a century: these were but moments in the vast tides of eternity.

At their meeting in the restaurant, one of the two mortals had opened up his mind and revealed his grief for the death of his wife and child. This had startled the angel more than it liked to admit to itself. Such raw emotion was not part of its experience, and it was like a private viewing of a bloody wound in the heart of a fellow spirit. The shock was instantly brought under control, but the angel did not like being shown such things. It had no wish to know or understand the sorrow, the terrible spiritual and mental agonies, of a bereaved human being.

So, if these two creatures persisted in bothering it, the angel would have no choice but to seek them out, and rid itself of them. They were impeding the work of a warrior, interfering with the holy duties of a soldier of God, and preventing justice from falling on the unrighteous.

How the angel was to discover their whereabouts, it had not considered, for its power was now such that it could reach out among the swarming millions of mortals and find their minds. They had to be physically close for that, and open to it. Nor was it familiar with the ways of men, and their methods of communication and transport. It knew of few things that were part of the world into which it had ventured. One was gasoline, and its inflammable qualities, because a demon had tried to use this substance against it, failing miserably. Little else had come within its limited experience.

It merely smelled out the evil of its enemies, tracked them down by their foul odor, and destroyed them. It had its own method of travel, perfected on that night when it had moved from house to house, killing the firstborn. This manner of movement did not involve material things, and the angel used speech only when necessary.

The creature knew of its inadequacies, but deemed them unimportant until the time came when it might have to learn.

Dave spent that evening sitting in a bar, drinking steadily and staring into space. He had at last come to terms with the fact that he was in a situation which could not be solved by the law or by the gun. Whether he fully believed in God, angels, demons, or any of that stuff did not matter. What mattered was he knew he was dealing with something outside his understanding: something paranormal or supernatural. He had never had much to do with mystical things before, and he didn't know how to begin. He had the vague idea of bringing a priest into the equation, but that would have meant more explanations, convincing the priest of what was going on.

Danny had already had a run-in with one of his own three priests, and the outcome had been remarkably unsuccessful. There were Danny and Dave, two down-to-earth cops, who were aware that they were involved with the supernatural world. Then there was this priest who was supposedly in contact with the spiritual world every day who rejected any idea of the paranormal. That in itself didn't seem to make sense.

Naturally, neither of the two cops had any thought of going

to Reece, who would have blown his stack. So they were left on their own, the three of them—or maybe four if you counted Rita—to solve the world's arson problem. If they could get rid of the angel, then the copycats might gradually be erased or disappear. It was the angel who was fueling their imaginations. The lunatics and others would soon slide back into some other crazy game, less destructive, if left to their own devices.

Malloch had said that the only way to get rid of the angel was to get into contact with its superiors. Who were they? The archangels, presumably. And how were they supposed to do that? Danny said he would try prayer, but then added that one didn't pray to archangels, only to God, His Son, and the Holy Spirit. Any one of the Trinity, but nothing below it. God would do nothing. Dave understood that.

So, how to get to the archangels?

"You want another?" asked the bartender, breaking Dave's train of thought.

"No, no thanks. Gotta be going, Al."

He pulled on his raincoat and put some money on the counter.

Al said, "Okay, Dave. See ya."

Dave went outside. It had stopped raining, but the sky was a murky yellow as evening came in like a cloud of sulfur. Danny had the car, so he took a cab to Vanessa's.

She wasn't home when he entered the apartment, using the key she had given him earlier. He made a cup of coffee in the tiny kitchen, which was no more than an alcove off the living room, then settled himself in a chair, to wait for her.

When she finally came through the door, she jumped on seeing Dave sitting in the gloom.

"Damn," Vanessa said, "you scared me."

"Sorry," said Dave.

"Why didn't you switch on the light or something?"

"I didn't think to. I was busy trying to figure something out, and I hadn't noticed it had gotten dark."

She took off her coat, switched on the light, and busied herself with some papers.

"Have you eaten, or do you want me to fix you something?"

He climbed to his feet.

"I can do it, just tell me where the stuff is. An omelette will be fine—can I do one for you?"

"I ate at the college. Look, sit down. I don't mind cooking, it was just that you frightened me, and I take time to settle after a scare. I'm not used to finding people in my apartment without they call first."

He nodded.

"I can understand that. I should've called. I'll do it next time."

She melted rapidly.

"So what is it?"

"That night at Clementine's, I told you I didn't believe in the supernatural? Well, some things have happened, and I think I do now. I think this guy we're dealing with is a creature—an angel I suppose I'm going to have to call him—from wherever such things come from. Heaven? Hell? Who knows? I met a guy today that says he's a demon, and unless there's some kind of worldwide conspiracy to fool Dave Peters, I have to believe him. He knew things, said things. Not only that, Vanessa, I *felt* the truth. I felt it, here."

He tapped his heart.

"And here."

His head.

"Sometimes you've got to go with your instincts, with your emotions, with your *feelings*. This guy, Malloch he called himself, says that the angel is after him—"

"Jophiel?"

"Well, Malloch says that this is not Jophiel, but a minor angel impersonating the archangel, something like that. Malloch says that this one hasn't got a name, that he's a nobody.

Which is probably why he's down here, creating havoc, trying to *make* a name for himself. Back where he comes from he's insignificant. Down here, though, he's an army, and he's destroying our world, Vanessa. Malloch says there's not much we can do about it. The only way we can get rid of this monster is to bring him to the attention of the archangels, because he's here without higher authority.

"Now, what I want to know is, how the hell do we do that, Vanessa? There's Danny, down at the church, praying his guts out to a God who won't listen because he doesn't want to interfere. We've got to figure some way to get rid of this bastard, and send him back where he came from. Personally, I'd like to see him burn, like he made my family burn, but if I can't have revenge I'd settle for a disappearing act."

Vanessa sat down, her face turned toward the window.

"Listen," she said.

Dave listened.

There was the usual disturbing traffic noise coming up from the streets below and from the apartment next door could be heard the sounds of a bitter argument in progress. There was a multitude of other sounds below these two main noisemakers which, once he concentrated, made him edgy. The city was a place of pressure, stress, but who could live in the country, unless they were born to it and knew how to survive there? You had to be where people could make a living, and clustered people generated a tense environment.

Dave could see the glow through the window, of the city, which like all cities, never fully rested. Anxiety prowled the sidewalks, lurked in the alleys.

"What?" he asked her, after a while, becoming impatient.

"Is it a wonderful life, or not? Is this a good world to live in? Will you be sorry to see it go?"

"It's got its drawbacks, but, yeah, I don't want to die, any more than the next man."

"Will you be sorry to leave all this behind, or are you just afraid of death?"

He thought about that for a while.

"I guess a bit of both," he finally replied.

"How much of it is *fear* of death? Worrying what might be on the other side? Concern about disappearing forever, without a trace, into nothingness?"

Dave couldn't see where this was leading.

"What is this? Question time? This is too heavy for me, I've got other things to think about."

"What I'm getting at," Vanessa said, "is that not everyone is of the same mind as you. I don't mind dying. I'm not exactly looking forward to it, but it doesn't bother me as much as it does people like you. There's a hell down here on earth, too, and some of us live in it. I've even tried committing suicide once, though I'm a Catholic. Have you ever read Sylvia Plath?"

Dave felt extremely uncomfortable with this conversation.

"Who's she?"

"A poet, somebody you should read some day. She wrote about suicide, and then finally did it, and it was a triumph."

"How the hell do you know? She didn't come back from the dead, did she? How do you know she didn't bitterly regret taking her own life, once she'd done it? Come on, Vanessa, stop twisting things to suit your argument. What are you getting at? You want to commit suicide, because you've had a rough time down here. Because you've suffered. I know you've had some bad breaks—"

She interrupted him with, "Not suicide, I've told you, it's against my religion. But to die? Sometimes that sounds like a wonderful escape to me. We *should* be allowed, you know, to have the choice."

Dave was exasperated. He hated talking about euthanasia, things like that. The subject bothered him. When women came on too strong sexually, or started talking about death, or the monstrous violations perpetrated by men, like rape, or even just the *failings* of men and the emotional sufferings undergone by women in times of adversity, he felt inadequate, unable to deal with it. He could understand that they had wants, felt anger, hurt, anguish, fears, jealous rages, loathing, lust, love, but *he* couldn't *feel* them, or relate to them, because they didn't sound like the same emotions he had himself.

At such times women became strange oceans, with great depths, with alien tides and currents, which threatened to drown him. At such times he was afraid of women, afraid of that vast sea of feelings he could only guess at, afraid of what was to him a darkness. He knew he had to stay away from those waters with their maelstroms that would suck him down into a nightmarish world of female emotions.

"What are you *really* saying, Vanessa?" he asked, pleadingly. "Don't play games with me."

She leaned forward, looking into his eyes.

"I'm saying that if we have to get a message to the right quarter, there has to be a messenger to carry it."

When it sank in that she was talking about one of them dying, he was horrified.

"Good God, what are you saying?"

"You know what I'm saying."

"I *think* I know, and I'm shocked. It's a crazy idea."

"Is it?"

"You think that one of us has to die, in order to carry the message to the archangels?"

"I'm convinced of it. And what's more, I would seem to be the logical choice. I mean, you couldn't go."

"For the sake of argument, why?"

"Because you believe you're a murderer."

He was about to protest, sharply, when he remembered that he had told her the story of his youth. He had never thought of himself as a murderer, but she was right, he was. The word pierced his heart with its significance.

"You've killed too," he riposted.

"I didn't mean to kill my father, but you say you intended to kill that boy, though I doubt you actually did it. I have a feeling the other two boys may have been right, that the kid fell, but somehow you've convinced yourself that you were responsible, because you *wanted* to be the cause of his death, you needed revenge for what he had done to you. Our minds sometimes give us what we want, Dave, whether it really happens or not."

"I was responsible—"

"The circumstances are debatable, but the fact remains, *you* believe in your guilt, and you planned a murder, while you hung upside down from the tower."

Dave's mind was in conflict, between belief and nonbelief in God and an afterlife. He had accepted that there was a supernatural creature in their midst, and it might seem to follow logically that if an angel was abroad, then it meant that there was indeed a Supreme Being. If there was a God then, without doubt, there was an afterlife.

But challenging this was Dave's entrenched belief that dying was like switching off a light. You went out, and that was it. Nothing else. Why fool yourself? Why not face up to the fact that death was empty, as empty as life before conception in a mother's womb? Only cowards clung to the idea that there was another world beyond this one.

And the angel? Well, he was now a fact, but who knew where he came from, what his role was, and who were his masters? Perhaps there was another plane, on which creatures like the angel existed, but this did not automatically mean that humans were going there, or that it was a place of peace, a place of refuge beyond death. There might, for instance, be life on other planets, but this had nothing to do with the immortality of the soul.

He was on the razor's edge of belief and unbelief. Though he did not want to join those complacent people convinced of life after death, he desperately wanted to believe he would meet his wife and son again.

Was it possible to believe in an afterlife, and also *not* believe, both at the same time?

He shrugged his shoulders, trying to rid them of the weight of his burden.

"This is all academic," he said to Vanessa, "neither of us is going to kill ourselves. You said yourself that suicide is out. Suicides don't get to heaven. The messenger wouldn't get to meet the intended recipient."

"No, but if you killed me, that would be different."

It took a little while for the meaning of this, though it was plain enough, to sink in. When it did, a strange anger overtook him. It filled the crevices of his heart and mind, and thickened his blood.

"What are you saying? There'll be no more of this talk. It's dangerous. People get caught up in things like this and can't get out of them," he said. "I won't listen to this kind of talk."

"Fine," she said quietly. "Let's relax, then, and watch some TV."

She turned on the television set, leaving him drained and limp, like a used dishcloth. For a while the pictures on the screen flowed in front of his eyes, the sounds past his ears, without anything registering in his mind, until gradually, the voices began to make sense, and he managed to fight his way up to the surface once more.

Joey Cabeza was a Puerto Rican youth who scorned the street gangs, preferring instead to be a lone tiger in the concrete jungle. There were advantages and disadvantages to this choice.

The advantages were that you didn't get involved in senseless gang fights, in which you might end up dead; that you weren't labeled and harassed by the cops as often as you would be if you wore a jacket with a symbol; that you didn't have to follow some dumb bastard's orders; that you could run or stand, fight or not, when you chose to, without some stupid council telling you what you should have done afterward.

The main disadvantage was that you didn't get protection from numbers, if you happened to fall foul of a gang. It was easy to fall foul of a gang: all you had to do was be on their turf.

What Joey had done, like most lone tigers had to do, was establish himself as a bad man who took no sides. He had a reputation of being absolutely independent, was no snitch and would not interfere with individual gang members, or groups, at any time. However, if you messed with him, he had no hesitation in using a piece. He was the man with the gun, unafraid to use it.

Also essential to his lone-tigership, was a belief in his connection to the mobs. In fact the local syndicate did not know that Joey existed, but he managed to be seen talking to the lower members of the hierarchy from time to time, thus instilling in any potential enemies a strong sense of his mystique. Joey would stop Freddie Pinnella outside his barber's, and in a conspiratorial whisper ask Freddie if he had any tips for the next heavyweight fight. Freddie, always flattered to be asked his opinion, though it was invariably wrong, would give the kid a few moments of his precious time. Joey would nod gravely at receiving the tip, and hurry off, as if on some mission for the mob, leaving any street gang watchers in no doubt that Joey was a hit man for the big boys, and not to be messed with.

Joey's haunts included the street on which Vanessa's apartment block stood, and from time to time he passed her on the sidewalk. Joey was a ladies' man, who never failed to give the girls a nod and a smile, even fire ladders like the babe with the stringy blonde hair. So you'd have to climb up the legs to get to her? That was okay with Joey, so long as she paid him for the work. He didn't mind them tall, short or any shape but square. Once, he had allowed his windbreaker to drop open, so she would see the gun sticking out of his waistband. He knew it gave the women a hard-on, to see a weapon on a guy. Hell, it gave *him* a hard-on thinking about it, and since he was wearing skintight jeans at the time, she could see that too.

He knew her name, Vanessa Vangellen, from sneaking a look at her mail. Joey liked to know what was going on in one of his streets. It was a classy name, so he was a little surprised when she stopped him one day and asked him if he would do something for her, in her apartment. She was obviously one of those older women who liked lean young Spaniards like him, with tough bodies and plenty of energy. He knew he had a reputation among the older women as being a guy who could keep going where others would be wilting, and women talked to each other about such things. They were worse than men, when they got together on their own, without their husbands and boyfriends around. Joey could make the bitches yell for Jesus several times in succession, and still not come himself. They loved his tight little buns, they said, and his smooth hairless chest.

"Sure," he said, smirking. "How muchu payin'?"

"I'll let you know," she replied.

20

Bronski was the desk sergeant that morning. An overweight cop closer to a heart attack than he was to his pension, he had, in his heyday, boxed for the city's police against other organizations, even against the cons when the penitentiary got a team together.

That was in the old days, before San Francisco was full of fire-starters, with not a decent puncher among them. Your average arsonist squealed and ran when it came to fisticuffs, having long slender fingers good only for striking matches. In the old days, they had mostly muggers and murderers behind bars, some of whom were pretty handy with their mitts, and Bronski used to enjoy mercilessly slugging them, until they dropped to the canvas. He said he was getting his own back for the bumps and bruises received on the beat, when making arrests among them.

Sergeant Bronski was standing at the desk when the fancy guy came in and asked if detectives Peters and Spitz were in the building. Bronski was a naturally belligerent man, who believed in being aggressive first, and if it was required, polite later.

Bronski had also had a bad day up to that moment, having been bitten on the hand by a hooker. He was worried about the bite: anxious about whether he might be infected with some disease, one kind of which he didn't even want to think about.

"Who wants to know?"

"I want to know," said the smooth-looking weirdo.

Bronski said, "Could be they're on duty, but I still want to know who *you* are."

Bronski knew that the D&D were off-duty, but he wasn't handing anything out unless he got a name.

The pimp was wearing some kind of fancy aftershave, which offended Bronski's nostrils. Bronski believed people should smell natural. He picked up a report book and began writing in it, knowing it was one sure way to irritate someone who was waiting for an answer to a question.

The pimp—Bronski was sure he was a pimp because he looked like one—leaned on the counter.

"I want to know *now*."

Bronski loved it when they were hostile. It gave him the excuse to insult them. He didn't even look up from his writing as he spoke under his breath.

"Well, fuck you, sir," Bronski said. "No name, no game."

The man's hand flashed out and grabbed Bronski by the necktie, dragging him halfway across his counter. His hat went rolling under the legs of the hookers and pimps on the benches. Two other cops in the room just stood there, transfixed, wondering what to do about it.

Bronski did what he always did in such situations. He swung his meaty fist, hitting his assailant full in the face.

Unfortunately, the result was not what he expected. Pain went shooting up his arm, to his elbow and shoulder. He felt jarred. It was like striking a solid metal statue. A hand took hold of his fist and crushed it. Bronski heard his own bones cracking, and felt the blood trickling down his knuckles. He screamed in agony and anger.

He reached down and across with his left hand, trying to draw his gun, but the man grabbed his wrist and snapped his forearm as if it were the rotten bough of a tree. The sergeant screamed again. Then he was lifted up and thrown bodily toward the doors. He landed heavily on one ankle, dislocating it, causing a fresh wave of pain to go coursing through him. He knew when he was beaten, and even if the guy looked like a wimp, he had strength that outmatched Bronski's.

The other two cops in the room unfroze. They both pulled their weapons, shouting, "Hold it, hold it, mister, don't move, don't even breathe," and equally original phrases, which the man ignored.

Bronski just wanted to get away from the guy. He was obviously a maniac, and everyone knew that psychopaths had the strength of ten men. They were likely to kill you, just as soon as not, and Bronski would bet a twenty the bastard had a sawed-off under his coat. Bronski wanted to collect his pension in two years' time, if the blood pressure didn't get him first, and he didn't want to lose his face in a lead rainstorm before that happened.

The desk sergeant crawled through the main doors and out onto the steps to the precinct. There were two heavy ceramic plant pots, too large to be stolen by the local populace without a crane and a truck, on either side of the doors. The plants had gone long ago, and the soil in them was hidden by a layer of stubbed cigarette butts. Bronski crawled behind the one on the left-hand side, his great bulk hidden by the bulging urn.

Some shooting was coming from inside the precinct house now, and Bronski was thinking, Nail the bastard, I want to stamp on his frigging face. He broke my hand. He broke my arm. He broke my leg. I want to see him gutted.

There followed a soft *whoomph* from within, and then the high-pitched screams of hookers pierced the air. Someone came running through the doors, clothes blazing, and fell, rolling down the steps and out into the street. A truck was thundering along the road. Unable to avoid the burning man, the truck struck him, sending the body slamming into a parked car.

A few moments later, the smooth-faced pimp came through the doors. He turned and stood on the top of the steps before descending, and seemed to concentrate for a moment. There followed the sounds of heavy but muted explosions coming from within various parts of the building, as if a series of incendiary bombs had been activated. Bronski reached with his crippled hand for his .38, but with broken fingers there was not much he could do with it. His other hand dangled uselessly from the broken forearm.

The pimp looked down at Bronski and gave him a tight smile, before walking off down the street. The guy didn't even glance in the direction of the crowd, which had gathered around the burning body of the man hit by the truck.

Traffic was jamming up now, behind the halted truck, and horns were going. Nothing was moving either way. Some of the drivers in the front cars, realizing that there was a serious situation, had got out of their vehicles and were adding to the numbers milling round the burning man. A storekeeper had run from his shop with a saucepan full of water, which he threw ineffectually on the corpse, creating hissing and steam, but not putting out the flames.

In the middle of it all the truck driver was pleading with people to listen to him, saying, "I didn't stand a chance, he just run out like that with his clothes all on fire, how was I supposed to stop . . . ?"

The attention of those on the edge of the accident vultures had now been captured by the sound of the explosions from within the police station, and many of them were pointing to the windows, some backing away and crossing the street. Flames were licking under the thick glass doors near Bronski's feet.

Bronski could feel the heat through the walls of the building, and fire started roaring from a washbasin drainpipe to the side of him. He crawled down the steps, to where the crowd were moving like a confused herd of cattle, spreading outward away from the fire. His leg had gone numb, but the pain in his arm was eye-watering. When he looked down, he could see the bone just piercing through his skin. He felt sick.

A young cop came running from his black-and-white, which had been trapped in the traffic jam.

When he looked back, Bronski could see that the whole precinct house was on fire, flames at every window. The main doors, which had to be opened inward, had people jammed against them, desperately trying to open them. Unfortunately, those at the front were being pressed from behind, by a crush of hysterical men and women, and there was no room to pull the doors open. One of the men at the front was hammering at the thick glass with his fist, trying to break it, while the face of another was squashed against the pane, distorted, eyes bulging with fear.

The young cop who had run from his car wrapped his coat over his head, then ran up the steps to smash the glass with the butt of his .38. It took three hits before it shattered, then he came running down again, his facial skin blistering with the heat. A woman managed to crawl through the hole he had made, but lacerated herself on the jagged glass. She slid down the steps and was dragged clear by members of the public, leaving a red trail like that of a wounded turtle.

Bronski was now up on one leg, propped against a car on the far side of the street. He yelled at a gaping store assistant to phone the fire department. The man, his eyes fixed on the conflagration, said it had already been done.

A body landed on the far sidewalk with a thump and remained where it was, limbs and torso at grotesque angles. Someone had jumped out of a sixth-story window. There were faces at other windows, dark silhouettes with stark staring eyes that disappeared and reappeared every few seconds.

Bronski could see people trying to open windows, to get to

the fire escape, but most of them were stuck shut, having been overpainted a dozen times by a series of underpaid workmen anxious to get the job done. The air-conditioning made it unnecessary to open windows in the summer, and in the winter no one wanted cold air coming into their office. One trapped policeman managed to rip open a second-story window, tearing it away from its adhesive paint, only to be swallowed from behind by a roaring belch of fire that might have come from a flamethrower. In opening the window he had fed the blaze with a sudden blast of oxygen, and it had thanked him by consuming him.

"God," cried Bronski. "Do something, somebody. Everybody's in there. Do something."

It was a holocaust, the inferno raging through all six stories in the time it took for a man to run down one flight of stairs. The fire was unnatural, too fierce and fast for a normal fire, and white, very white. It consumed everything it touched within seconds, the glass on the windows blowing or melting, and when the air fed its voracious appetite, it refueled itself, its energy seemingly limitless. People were driven out of the area altogether, to the far ends of the street.

The first of the cars, closest to the flames, then began exploding, showering the neighborhood with burning bits of material. By the time the fire trucks managed to force their way through the jam of vehicles, the chaos was complete. The firemen contented themselves with watering the two buildings on either side of the fire, to keep it from spreading further. The precinct house itself was gone: a hollow shell containing a raging furnace. Those in the street who had been happy at the thought of a police station going up in flames, were now struck with the horror of it. Not only had cops been burned to death, but dozens of citizens from the area, friends and relatives, who had been awaiting attention or had been trapped in the cells. It was a disaster, a tragedy that reached out over the whole district.

Only two people escaped the inferno: Bronski and the black woman who had crawled through the broken glass. Even she was in terrible shape. She kept muttering something about a man being shot several times, and walking away unharmed.

"He didn't even fall down," she murmured. "He just kep' on standing there, making people burn."

Bronski was weeping when the ambulance took her away: not for her, of course, but for all his pals, who were just charred lumps of coal among the smoking ruins.

"What the fuck?" he kept crying. "What the fuck?"

Among Bronski's first visitors were the D&D, Mother Teresa and Friar Tuck.

"What happened?" asked Dave.

Bronski felt miserable, but these were two guys he really wanted to talk to.

"This motherfucker came in asking for you two. I tried to tell him to fuck off. I got the feeling he was bad news, you know how you do. That feeling you get when you look into their eyes and see a skull full of shit behind them. He got nasty then. Busted me up. Then he set fire to the place, don't ask me how, I didn't see no gas can or nothing. It just went up, like a fuck-ing bomb went off or somethin'."

"He busted *you* up?" said Danny.

Bronski turned his face away in embarrassment.

"Yeah, he was one strong pimp."

Dave said, "Why do you think he was a pimp?"

Bronski shook his head.

"Just his looks, you know. He was either a pimp or a fairy. He was smooth-looking, maybe a bit Spanish, but with these soft gray eyes. I dunno. He smelled too. Some kind of stuff that made me want to puke."

"Almonds?" asked Dave. "Did he smell of almonds?"

"I dunno," said Bronski, "yeah, I guess."

Then the big ex-boxer, afraid of no man's fists, found he was crying, and tried to get out of bed, to hide somewhere, but D&D got hold of him and forced him back down onto the sheets.

"He killed them all," wept Bronski. "He burned everybody. It was terrible, Dave, I never seen nothing like it. People just burning to death before your eyes. Friends of mine. Buddies from way back, standing at the windows with the flames eatin' them up. You could hear them screaming. *Please, please, God help me.* The typist, that little girl from the sixth floor? She jumped. She hit the sidewalk like a hunk of meat, Dave.

"And when that bastard walked away, he laughed at me. He *laughed*, the son of a bitch *laughed*." His voice changed to anger and the tears dried out. "If I get that bastard, I'm gonna tear his arms out. Danny, you hear me? I'm gonna break his fucking back for him."

"Sure, Bron, sure you will. Right now you get some rest and leave things to Dave and me. We know who the guy is—he's the white-fire perp. We'll get him, don't worry about that."

"He was asking for you guys," repeated Bronski. "He wanted to see you. I think he was gonna waste you. I think that's why he burned down the building, he got mad because you weren't there."

Danny shook his head.

"No, Bron. He burned it down because he thought we *were* there. He wants us dead."

Bronski went up on his good elbow.

"You mean he killed all those people, Captain Reece, the little typist, all the guys, just to get you two?"

"We think so," said Danny.

Bronski lay back down on his pillow.

"He must want you real bad."

Danny shook his head.

"No, he was probably just passing by, and thought, 'I'll go in and burn those two cops that bothered me the other day.'" This guy is a mean one, Bron. He doesn't need to kill us, because he knows we can't touch him, but we irritate him, like a fly irritates a man. He just took a little time out to swat us, that's all. That's what makes it all so senseless—it wasn't even necessary."

Outside the hospital, as they were walking across the car park, Dave said to Danny, "Do you really think that's why he burned the place? Because he thought we were in there?"

"You heard Bron. He was asking for us."

"You don't think there was a demon in there somewhere, maybe in the cells?"

Danny shook his head.

"He was after us. If he was after someone else, he would have asked for that guy's name. I tell you, Dave, he's getting far too confident, far too casual. I think he's making mistakes. *He* probably doesn't think so, but *I* do. There don't *seem* to be any rules, but there sure as hell are, Dave. In this universe there are always rules, laws which govern things, even the supernatural. Everything moves in cycles. There's a balance to everything. You upset that balance, and you bring it all down on your own head."

Dave opened the car door with his key, and then let Danny in the other side. Danny flopped into the passenger's seat.

Dave said, "I can't see that, Danny. This angel, whatever he is, can get away with murder, literally. I can't see what's going to stop him."

21

When Dave and Danny parted company in the late afternoon, Dave was still in shock. It was difficult to take on board the fact that most of his fellow cops had been massacred. He felt rudderless without the precinct house, and Reece gone. He hadn't liked Reece much, but, then, that wasn't a requirement of the job. What was important was he had been able to count on his boss for backing, and Reece had never been frightened of making decisions, even those that might jeopardize his career if things went wrong. The worst kind of boss was an insecure one, with an inferiority complex, for such captains often made irrational decisions, stupid judgments, which put men in danger. Reece had never appeared inferior. Men called him an asshole because he jumped on them and bawled them out, but never because he was weak.

For the moment, Dave had nowhere to go. He could do what he liked until they found a temporary building. The old one wouldn't be in commission for a long time yet, and when it was, it would have to be a brand new place.

While wandering the backstreets of the city, he came across

a small Protestant chapel. Dave had been raised a Calvinist in the Presbyterian church, in contrast to the Catholicism of Danny and Vanessa. Were he at all religious, he told himself, he would still prefer the austerity of his parents' sect to the lavish ritual of theirs. On an impulse, he entered the building, and sat in one of the wooden pews at the back.

There was a simple altar, below the Norman-arched windows at the front of the church, with a brass crucifix. In the window itself, a leaded stained-glass pane, was a scene of a shepherd guarding his sheep. There was a starkness he liked about the interior, which helped him to pare down the clutter in his own mind to the important considerations.

A rogue angel. That's what the creature was, a rogue, a runaway. Maybe Danny was right? Maybe the angel had overstepped the mark at last? After all, until now the mortals who had perished as a result of the fires he caused had died by accident, not by his design. The torching of the police building, however, had been a *deliberate* action, carried out purposely to rid himself of these mosquitoes, Peters and Spitz. Surely, even though the Ten Commandments did not apply to angels, that kind of destruction of innocent lives could not go unnoticed. It was one thing for humans to die accidentally in fires intended for the enemies of the angel hosts, but quite another to change the quarry from demons to mortals themselves.

The angel was at war, hunting down his enemies in a foreign land. If civilians were killed as a result of demons hiding among them, it was an unfortunate consequence of a combat condition. The blame could be attributed to the circumstances of war, rather than to the angel.

However, if attacking soldiers began slaughtering civilians, simply because they were an irritating obstacle to the liberators, then the whole aspect of the war changed from a righteous cause, to a cruel, murderous one.

The angel had indeed become a rogue invader. His arrogance had outstripped his integrity.

Dave began thinking over the conversation he had had with Jophiel, and subsequently with Danny. *Armageddon.* What if this war between Good and Evil—this supernatural conflict, as Vanessa called it—had resulted in the defection of demons for many of earth's centuries? Perhaps, Dave thought, they've been among us for a long while, *our* time.

We can protect ourselves against demons, with our religious beliefs and practices, but we have no defense against angels.

Dave stared at the stained-glass window, wherein the shepherd watched over his sheep, protected them against wolves. Although they did not appear in the scene, the shepherd would have his dogs, to help him keep his charges safe. But what if one of the sheepdogs went crazy, and began slaughtering the sheep?

Christ, he thought, *you are the shepherd. Please, Lord, do something about this rabid guard dog that is among us.*

The weight of Danny's faith was behind this request, and Vanessa's convictions, as well as Dave's anger.

Dave left the church, needing to talk to Vanessa. She was the brains of the trio. She had read Milton and Dante, guys like that, who knew where they were when it came to battles between angels and demons. They were poets, sure, but the supernatural wasn't an area where you dealt with facts.

On the way to her place, he called in at a library, hoping to arm himself a little first. He hated his own ignorance in certain areas. He found a Bible dictionary and looked up ANGELS. The entry told him the word came from the Greek *angelos,* meaning messenger. ("Los Angeles," he said to himself, "yeah.") In it he learned that angels were instruments of God's judgment, with three main functions: one, to deliver His messages ("Mailman," grunted Dave); two, to watch over His people ("Shepherd"); three, *to punish His enemies.* There was the crux. The divine retribution, on God's foes, Satan and his demons. Dave's eyes went back to the first reference to function, before the listing, and read it over again. *The main purposes of angels are to praise God, watch over his people and carry out God's will as an instrument of God's judgment.* But had God willed that mankind should be destroyed in the process?

Before he left the library, he took out a couple of art books, and studied various representations of angels, such as those in Leonardo's *The Annunciation* and *The Virgin on the Rocks*. Both were beautiful angels with wings, the former a little more masculine than the latter. In Foxy's terms, a mary. Raphael's angels were too pretty. However, Verrocchio's *Baptism of Christ* also had an angel painted by Leonardo, which had no wings, and would easily have passed for a man. Without the halo, it was very much like Dave and Danny's enemy. Perhaps this vain creature had imposed himself on Leonardo's subconscious? Or maybe all angels looked alike? These were questions which were only answered by questions.

When he reached Vanessa's apartment building, it was late and the building was quiet. The super happened to be passing through the main hallway, as Dave was letting himself in with the keys Vanessa had given him, and recognized him. The super was one of those people who believed that life continually dealt him severe blows, when he deserved better, and he had a dim view of the rest of humanity. Everybody else was much better off than he was because they were assholes who trod all over people like him. Whenever he could, he scored from these people. It was the only thing that made him feel good. It pleased him to cause dissension among his fellow human beings.

"You goin' to number twenty-seven?" he said to Dave.

"I might be. What's it to you?" Dave answered.

The super sneered.

"Nuthin', 'cept maybe you oughta know she's already got somebody in there. Young guy. Younger than you."

The super smiled again, then shambled away to his own rooms, knowing he had done his job of destroying someone's night.

Dave watched the old man shuffle out of sight and wondered whether he was just dealing out crap, or whether Vanessa really did have someone in her room. She was entitled to, of course, and he was surprised at the pang of jealousy that stabbed him on hearing the words. Of course the super had laid it on thick. *Young guy. Younger than you.* Maybe it was somebody that Vanessa didn't want up there?

You wish, he thought, and turned to go. Before he reached the main doors, however, the jealousy built in his breast, and he turned and took the stairs to her apartment. On reaching it, he glanced around at the other closed doors, before putting his ear to the wall. He could hear low voices from within, one of them a male. Dave felt himself growing steadily more angry.

He slipped the key in the lock and turned it, opening the door quietly.

The place was in semidarkness. Voices were coming from the bedroom, the door to which was ajar. Dreading what he might see, and hating himself for the compulsion which drove him to look, Dave crept over to the doorway and peeked through the two-inch crack, gradually pushing the door open wider.

Vanessa was sitting on the edge of the bed, fully clothed, and standing near her was a young man of about seventeen. The guy was lean, and dark, with slicked-down hair. He had on a purple jacket with a tiger on the back, jeans, and dirty tennis shoes. The young man had something in his hand, and though it wasn't what Dave had been expecting, it was just as electrifying.

His fist was full of gun, and the muzzle was pressed against Vanessa's temple. The youth's hand was shaking violently.

Dave was stunned for a moment, and stood staring through

the widening gap, his thoughts in chaos. If the youth had turned at that moment, Dave would have been almost helpless. His brain had seized and his body had locked into immobility.

Gradually, his mind unwound itself, like an overtightened clockwork spring unraveling, and movement returned to his limbs. His brain turned over a dozen different remedies to the situation, some learned by experience, some garnered from the tales of other cops. Any action was potentially dangerous, and knowledge of the assailant's personality was essential, but that was something Dave did not have. The boy was a complete stranger to him. Dave decided to instill the kid with the absolute certainty that if he shot the woman, he would die in the same second himself. So long as the boy wasn't a complete sociopath, but had regard for his own life, it should work.

Dave eased his own gun out of its holster, thinking: *Don't shoot yet, sonny. Hold it. Hold it.*

He swung the door wide open, and said softly, "Pull that trigger, boy, and I'll decorate the walls with your brains."

The kid jumped about six inches in the air, and Vanessa gave a startled cry. Unfortunately the gun was still pointing at Vanessa, though the muzzle had dropped. If the kid fired now, the bullet would take her in the chest. It flashed across Dave's mind that the finger on the trigger might have tightened since his unheralded entrance.

"Just put the gun down, slow and easy," said Dave. "If you so much as twitch I'll kill you."

An eternity passed before the words seemed to register on the youth. Dave's experience told him that the boy was so high on adrenaline, and maybe something else, that he was half out of his head. The boy's hands were shaking, his face was sweating, and his pupils were dilated. The kid was wired for action, every sinew, every tendon, taut and straining. One mistake, one external factor like a siren out in the street, or a ring on the phone or doorbell, or even a yell from the next apartment, might cause the trigger finger to jerk. Everything had to be done with the utmost care and consideration, like picking a delicate flower, or catching a butterfly in one's hands.

"Where are you, kid? Come down from there, slowly—slowly. Relax yourself, take it gradual. Let the gun drop to the floor, let it fall."

But the slim fingers remained locked in a tight grip around the butt of the gun. Dave silently cursed him, knowing he was dealing with a highly strung hoodlum here. You could bully some of them, their heads were like blocked drains waiting for a plumber to clear them, but this one had too much bore, and the blood and adrenaline was rushing through him in a torrent.

"Easy, kid, easy," Dave crooned. "Excitement's over. Put the gun down carefully. Nothing's going to happen if you do it right, do it now . . ."

The kid expelled air noisily, frightening even himself with the sound, and Dave realized the boy had been holding his breath, ever since Dave had first yelled.

"Don't shoot . . .," said the boy.

That was a good sign. He had recognized at least that his life was in danger. He didn't want to die. Whatever he had expected to get out of this situation, death was not on the list, that was sure. Suddenly, the muzzle dropped, turned a little. Now the kid's gun was pointing at the dresser, and Dave was tempted to shoot him then, before he could swing round and pull the trigger. Another cop might have done just that, and got away with it in court, but Dave was Mother Teresa.

"Just drop the piece, sonny. *Now.*"

The youth finally did as he was told.

Dave stepped forward and kicked the gun, a small-caliber Italian pistol, into the far corner of the room. It struck the wall and spat a bullet into the plaster with the noise of a Chinese firecracker. Dave realized it must have been on a hair trigger.

"Jesus," he said.

The youth looked at Dave out of the corners of his eyes and seeing the fury in Dave's expression he cringed, obviously expecting immediate punishment, like a small boy who gets smacked around when he accidentally knocks over a cup of coffee at the breakfast table. He said, "Uhhh," as he ducked away, his hands over his head, protecting it.

Dave was sweating badly, his hands slippery, but relief washed through him. It was the relief of not having to kill, especially a minor. There was nothing worse, to Dave, than being responsible for the death of a kid.

"Step over there, by the wall," he barked.

"She made me do it," the kid cried. "She made me."

"Step over by the wall!"

This time the kid did as he was told, facing the wall. He was starting to cry. Vanessa came to his rescue. The words came out in a rush.

"He's right, Dave, I asked him to help me do it. You know, we talked about this, and you wouldn't help me, so I went out and found somebody who would."

Dave's head jangled.

"What are you saying?"

"We talked about it, Dave. One of us has to die, to get to the angel's superiors, and that someone has to be me. It's the only way to stop him."

The boy turned and looked at them, his cheeks tear streaked.

"You're nuts," he cried, "both of ya. Crazy bastards. What ya gonna do to me?"

Dave kicked him lightly on the backside.

"Get out of here. If I see you again, I'll break your legs, you understand me?"

The boy looked at Vanessa, obviously still not sure that he was going to get off scot free.

"Go on, Joey," she said.

Joey didn't need a third telling, he went through the door like a rabbit with a dog on its tail. They heard him slam the door to the apartment behind him. It sounded as if he were taking the stairs three at a time.

There was silence between them for a while, then Dave put away his gun and shook his head. He was furious with her, not only because she had tried to have herself killed, but because she had used a juvenile to do it. But this was not a good time to go through it with her. She looked worn and sleepless. Now that the certainty of death had been taken from her she was going through the torment of having to face life again: the pain of blood pulsing through arteries that had been numbed by lack of circulation. Her frozen mind had thawed.

"Vanessa," he sighed, "why do you want to kill yourself?"

"Because . . ."

"No, *why*? Really, why?"

She flopped back on the bed and stared at the ceiling. She began a long monologue, saying, I don't know, yes, I do know, I've been happy lately, with you, and I know it can't last, it never does, it always gets taken away, look (she bared her forearm) I've even stopped burning myself, you cured me, no more setting fire to beds, or stubbing cigarettes out on myself, you're the only one who can make love to me without that happening, and it's strange, because you're a lot like my father in some ways, you'd think that would be a trigger, wouldn't you, you'd think that anything that reminded me of him, would make me worse, but it doesn't, maybe it's because he's already dead, he's already been burned to death, and it can't happen to the same person twice, I don't know, I just know that I'm happy at the moment, and that's the best time to do it, to go out when you're winning, rather than depressed and hating the world . . ."

He stopped her by touching her cheek.

"Vanessa, I nearly killed that boy. I nearly shot him."

She looked at his face.

"No, you didn't. You don't do things like that, Mother Teresa."

He stiffened.

"Where did you hear that name?"

She smiled now.

"Manovitch."

"Oh, *him.*" Dave nodded. "Well, I suppose you're right, but that's a red herring. What we have here is you trying to commit suicide, whether it's by your own hand or somebody else's doesn't make any difference. Nobody says it's going to last forever, you and me, but for crying out loud, don't cut it short. I'm enjoying it too."

"You do . . . need me?"

"Right now I need you more than anyone I know. It wasn't until the super told me you had someone in your room with you that I realized . . . I realized how badly I want you to be with me—to be mine. You have no idea how jealous I felt. I frightened myself. I didn't think I was that kind of man—the kind that can think like that. I wanted to kill that boy even before I saw the gun in his hand. In fact I was *relieved* to see it. Like the old joke, I expected something worse than a life or death situation. I expected to see you two . . . never mind."

She smiled weakly and gripped his hand.

"All right, I know."

Thinking about it, of her lying there on the bed naked, her long legs wrapped around someone else's hips, aroused him. He was ashamed of himself, that such thoughts acted on his sexual subconscious, but they did, and he asked her hoarsely if they could make love.

She said of course, and undressed for him, then tenderly and with much feeling they moved together, and afterwards, she cried. He knew better than to ask *why,* what the tears were for, because from experience he guessed she didn't even know herself, but just held her until she stopped. He had accepted long ago that there were not always answers when it came to human emotions.

They lay together in the darkness, talking.

"The station was burned today," he said.

"I know, I heard on the news."

"Most of the guys . . ."

"I know, I know."

"He's made a mistake, Vanessa, I *feel* it. Danny said it first, but I agree with him for once. The creep has overstepped the mark. There was no demon in the building. He burned it simply to get at Danny and me."

"You really think so?"

"Yes. I hope it may lead to something . . . I dunno, some notice from above."

"What about your revenge?" asked Vanessa.

"Screw the revenge. Let's just get rid of the bastard, send him back to where he came from. Let them discipline him in their own way. All I want is for the destruction to stop now. We have to pick up the pieces, calm the population down, start damping down the fire-starters once their mentor has gone."

"What about all the demons? Won't they go on the rampage now?"

"I figure they've been here for years anyway, and maybe one or two of them cause trouble from time to time, but don't forget they're hiding out. They need to keep their heads down. They're like the Nazi war criminals who disappeared into South America, they need to keep a low profile, behave themselves, no matter how vicious and cruel they were on their home ground. They're not just hiding from the angel, but from the eyes of heaven."

"You've really thought this out, haven't you?"

"Tonight, at a church. Maybe someone did the thinking for me. Put it in my head. You know?"

"You'll be telling me next you talked with Jesus."

He didn't reply to this, not knowing the answer to it.

Manovitch was feeling relaxed. He had been cruising around in his car, along Fisherman's Wharf, but now he had stopped to stare out across the bay. In the distance he could see the lights of the tourist attraction, Alcatraz, where the voice of Leon "Whitey" Thomson, once a long-term inmate, now told visitors of the terrible and infamous days of the island prison's past. Whitey was famous throughout the world. The Japanese, the Chinese, Europeans, Australians, New Zealanders, people from Raratonga, Tahiti and the Maldives, Africa and South America, had listened avidly to Whitey's taped voice.

It just shows you, thought Manny, that you never know how the chips are going to fall in the future. Yesterday Whitey was a two-bit crook, despised by society, and today his voice was alongside those of his correctional officers, as acceptable to society as the President of the United States. It just showed you that history is history and yesterday's hood can be today's hero, thought Manny. If you did something really bad today, you could be lauded for it tomorrow. Nobody thought of Whitey as a bad man now. They thought of him as yesterday's victim.

If Manny turned his head ninety degrees to the left, he could also see the lights of the Golden Gate Bridge. An automobile was burning in the middle of the bridge—a pyre, for Manny had just heard on the car radio that a woman had been trapped inside the vehicle when it exploded into flame. It lit up the girders and cables around it. There was something beautiful about fire, something quite magical.

Manny was feeling relaxed and relieved.

He had heard about the precinct house being burned down, and he was glad that those sons-of-bitches Peters and Spitz were not in their office. That meant they were still alive. Manny didn't want the two cops to die in a fire that had not been of his own making. He wanted to kill them both himself, with his own device.

"Those bastards," growled Manny to himself. "I'll get 'em one at a time. That way I'll get twice the satisfaction."

He already had another plan figured out, after the aborted attempt on Foxy's bistro. The fuckers didn't get away from him that easy. Time, though. Plenty of time. If he killed them too soon, he wouldn't be able to savor it. Once they were dead, they were dead, and the fun would stop.

Suddenly Manny felt very miserable and sorry for himself as he thought about the wrongs that had been perpetrated upon him. People had been always out to get him, humiliate him, emasculate him. Especially women. That bitch Vangellen, she was going to suffer too, but slowly. Manny was going to fuck her goddamn eyes out, then slit her throat and watch her bleed. No quick burn-up for Vangellen. A slow draining away, with her eyes open, and her mouth trying to speak.

"I'll show 'em," sobbed Manny. "I'll show 'em all."

22

To men, the ways of angels would be strange and diverse, their methods of communication without parallel or comparison. A sense, a feeling, might carry as strong a message as the sound of a trumpet. The angel had experienced the need to return to its home, a feeling which came from deep within itself, yet it ignored that call and cried out in anguish.

The mortals had been busy trying to find ways of reaching the angel's superiors, to inform them of his crimes, yet this was in fact a waste of energy.

What the mortals did not know was that an angel is its *own* judge. It examines its own motives, especially for allowing a call to return home to go unheeded, and decides its own fate. What it has done unknowingly can be forgiven, but what it has set out deliberately to accomplish, if subsequently judged to be wrong, must be met by its own sentence.

When the angel felt the call it agonized over its untimeliness, over the unfairness of having to leave before its work was finished, and before it had settled accounts.

Frustrated, full of rage, the angel delayed the departure,

knowing that such deferral would be to invite punishment, a penalty that would be according to its own assessment of how far it had transgressed, how deeply it had stained itself.

Procrastination itself was even more serious than the original trespass. The order to return home had come and the angel remained on earth. Yet *still* the angel did not obey, for it was bound in its own undoing, caught within an obsession that spelled its destruction. The inevitability of its downfall was perhaps a predestined event. The angel wanted to go, to save itself from the fall from grace, yet it *could* not go, for its anger anchored it to earth.

Finally, it had waited too long. It was too late.

Disobedience. The one unforgivable angelic sin. Lucifer had fallen because he had disobeyed. He had put personal desire before the certainty of feeling, had raised himself above himself, and his arrogance shone brighter than the essence of his being.

The angel knew then that it had argued itself into an untenable position, for it was aware of its own iniquity in these actions and it knew its punishment should be severe.

Angels *fall*, they are not pushed into the void.

This angel was not cast down: it had thrown itself over the edge. It had set out unconsciously to destroy itself, without wanting to, and this it had accomplished. Such are the terrible spiral contradictions of power over oneself, where a being is its own guardian, and its own harshest judge. A tiny seed of self-aggrandizement begins the rot from within the core, until the spirit loses enlightenment, and is indeed, endarkened.

It was true that the Commandments given to Moses applied to mortals not angels, but this angel had been fighting a war on earth, which was without precedent. There was a mandate for visitors. The angel could have argued zeal, begged forgiveness, offered mitigating circumstances: the heat of the battle, the chase to the edges of heaven and hell, the crossing without knowing—but not now, now was too late. The angel could never convince itself, now, that it was in the right. It had been on earth too long, caused too many deaths among the feeble shadows that were mortals.

In truth, it had to admit, it had always been a little haughty, a little bit too arrogant. It had chastized itself more than once for its obvious pride. At one time its pride told it that it was destined for higher things, and impatience had led to its overzealous behavior, both above and below. Now it was facing the fall.

The angel sat naked on the bare floorboards of a disused house, shoulders slumped, back rounded, head hanging low. Its beautiful face was in its hands, covered by the slim tapering fingers. Its legs were crossed, drawn up, beneath its buttocks. It was like an egg, waiting.

Suddenly, there was a stirring in the creature's loins accompanied by dreadful, unbearable pain. The hurt began in its abdomen, in that smooth area between its legs, and spread outward until it penetrated its very brain. Needles of pain rained upon its flesh, as if all the nerve ends in its body had been torn from their roots and replanted.

For the first time *he* felt this agony and hunched even more tightly into himself as the terrible burning of quickened growth, of flesh swelling like heavy buds, ripening, bursting into flower between his legs, made him squirm in terror.

His screams of torment pierced his own skull as he suffered the horrors of transfiguration.

Physical pain, spiritual pain.

A change was coming over the spirit, as well as within the body. While genitals blossomed grotesquely, growing into large ugly fruit between his thighs, his soul was stained with a canker that burned like acid within him. While the *thing* between his legs grew to enormous proportions, thrusting forth like the branch of a tree, accompanied by its wrinkled sack, his spirit within him withered like skin on dead meat.

Emotions that had not been present within him before now flooded through him.

There was horror and hate, fear and sullen suspicion, spite and malice, and many, many more strange, unwelcome feelings. He felt the ugly, distended horror of lust, the nasty taste of unbridled desire, the frustration of unslaked revenge. He had needs to fulfill, excesses to indulge, urges to satisfy. They crowded his mind and body like tiny demons themselves, competing with him for control over himself. They were small voices that screeched for his attention, making him take notice of them, and they were repulsive to his former nature.

The agony of the change lasted for many mortal hours, during which he shrieked for mercy, spat and snarled with rage, screamed hate upon all men and angels, called death upon his enemies, cursed and made many terrible promises and oaths, and when it was over he found himself a disgusting, loathsome creature, without purity of soul, without purity of flesh. In physical appearance, he had changed very little. Except for the oversized male genitals, there was no apparent blemish. Yet he felt he was a hideous, grotesque monster.

He was bitter about how things had turned out. He had to admit that in the beginning he had had no intention of disrupting things on earth to the extent that he had done so, gaining the enmity of a vast number of mortals. All he had wanted to do was destroy demons, which had been his task since Lucifer had fallen and the war had begun.

When humans had died in the fires too, he did not think this was so terrible. After all, death released the spirit, the soul, from the body prison. Surely that was a good thing? What he had not taken into account, because as an angel neither meant anything to him, was the physical suffering he had caused, and the emotional grief left in the living. Angels felt no pain, either emotional or physical, so he had been ignorant of both aspects of his destruction.

Was that his fault? Should he have known? The *knowledge* of pain was there, but he had dismissed the need to examine it. His preference for ignorance was his downfall, and yes, he was bitter about it. The rankling in his breast was severe.

He still blamed those two mortals, the policemen. His own fatal error had been in deliberately seeking them out and attempting to destroy them. This intentional action had destroyed his soul within him.

Damn those policemen, damn their souls.

Yet damnation was not his to bestow, and was, in fact, the policemen's gift to the angel, for they had unlocked the truth of ambition hidden deep in himself, and had stolen his light from him. He was bound for darkness—his punishment for his disobedience—and those he had been hunting were now his traveling companions, his comrades in arms. He had become what he loathed—a fallen angel, a demon—and he now realized that it was the only thing they all had in common, that loathing.

Demons do not love, they hate, and most of all they hate what they have become: they despise their fellow fallen angels and the Devil. They follow Satan, but they hate Satan. They hate the world, the flesh, and all except God, for God cannot be hated, only feared, a distant entity, untouchable by anything except love.

He had fallen from Grace.

He had become a demon.

He now realized he had a name.

Nethru.

He was called Nethru.

His power of speed through the darkness and light, swift movement through space, was gone. He was much more vulnerable now, his body substantial flesh, bone and blood.

And he was afraid of fire.

That which he had used as a weapon could now be used against him.

Nethru walked down to the harbor in the gathering purple of the evening. He deplored the slowness of his movements, growing angry with himself. Still faster than the fittest human, it was a snail's pace compared to his previous speed. The mist was drifting through iron grids, around the stanchions of the bridges. He leaned on a parapet and gazed into the swirling waters of the flow. His immediate concern was to find Malloch and take his revenge on the demon, but then to seek out the two policemen, David Peters and Daniel Spitz.

"Hey, you!"

Nethru turned, to find himself confronted by three young men in loose jackets. Each of them had some kind of weapon in his hand. The tall black youth held a hunting knife with a broad blade and a tassel on the hilt. The broad-shouldered one had a short length of lead piping. The remaining one—white, long-limbed, with a face like a monkey—held a small gun in his fist.

Monkey, obviously the leader, said, "Whaddya think ya doin'?"

Nethru sighed and turned away from them, not even considering it worth answering such a question.

"Hey!"

Nethru turned.

"Go away before I have to hurt you. I have no time for such things."

"No time?" said Monkey. "Shit. Just throw over your wallet and watch."

"I don't have either."

Lead-piping stepped forward, swinging his stubby weapon.

" 'M gonna break your arms, mister."

Nethru now lost patience with them. He grabbed his assailant's swinging arm and snapped it in two. Then before the youth could scream, Nethru's hand clamped on his jaw and closed, the talons sinking deeply into the facial flesh. The mandible cracked and splintered as the strong hand crushed the jaw. White slivers of bone, like fish needles, poked through the flesh.

With one arm Nethru lifted the youth from the concrete walkway and threw him over the parapet into the water. He hit the water with a splash, sank, then bobbed to the surface again, the wrong way up. He stayed that way, bound on course for the open sea.

Monkey rushed over and looked down into the water, to see his companion being carried away on the current, face down.

"Jesus H, you killed 'im!" the boy cried, his voice cracking with emotion. "You fuckin' bastard, you stiffed Joey. He was a good kid, and you . . ."

The youth's voice degenerated into some choked sounds, which might have been words, but they were so distorted they meant nothing to Nethru.

"I did tell you to go away."

"Fuck you."

Monkey turned and fired in one movement, the bullet striking Nethru on the cheek and passing through the back of his head. A lightning strike of pain coursed through Nethru's skull. His eyes widened involuntarily. He did not like it. His anger flash-fired to a high intensity.

In a moment he was next to Monkey and had torn the gun from his hand and crumpled it. He struck the youth on the temple with his fist and the boy's skull shattered and collapsed in on itself. The head went the color and consistency of mashed strawberries. Monkey was dead before his body hit the floor.

The remaining member of the trio, the tall one, turned and ran. Nethru reached down and tore up a flagstone, skimming it after the fleeing youth as if it were a piece of slate. It struck the boy just below the right elbow, taking off the lower part of his arm. Wisely the youth kept running. He was screaming and spurting blood, but he kept running just the same.

Nethru let him go, but reached down and picked up the second body, tossing it, too, into the river.

When his fingers explored his face, the wound was already almost healed.

"Violent people," Nethru muttered. "Why are these humans always so violent?"

Nethru headed off into a district, where he hoped to immerse himself in the same kind of society that had protected the demons fleeing from him. He was not concerned that he would be recognized. Although he had been an avenging angel, he was now a demon. His fragrance was gone: the aroma he had exuded as an angel, which had helped him combat the nauseating stink of the world into which he had come, was no longer necessary, for the smell of the world was now his odor. He would not be so easily recognized by the demons he had been chasing, for they had not previously identified him by his features, but by the aura he emitted. In any case, they would be relieved that he had ceased to chase them, would hate him the way they hated everything else, but they would not put themselves out to destroy him. Most of them were fairly apathetic creatures, content to wallow in their own muck, rather than go chasing around destroying their enemies.

There were advantages to being a demon, then. Not many, but a few. Nethru would make the most of them.

He walked quickly, but of course his swiftness of flight was gone, and the quickest walk was like the pace of a stranded turtle to him. His former luster had fallen from him: he had shed the light and now carried darkness.

The streets were puzzling to him, and he took many frustrating wrong turnings, until finally he came upon a burned-out warehouse, a building he himself had torched. There would be no other demons here, for the place stank of the death of one of them. He found a place among the damp ash, where he could rest, away from the eyes of the world. There, with the sodden trash, and the dirt where the rats freely ran and the cock-roaches made their homes, he wept for his former splendor.

He could no longer speak with the tongues of angels, and he cried out, many times during the night in the harsh voice of a demon, for retribution. His inner beauty had left and in its place was an ugliness that its bearer despised. Where his mel-lifluous and marvelous spirit had been was now a shriveled thing, like an ancient dried walnut locked in its shell. It was hard, bitter and useless.

"Give me back my glory," he cried.

But there was no one to hear except the feral cats, who spat at this creature of darkness from a safe distance, their fur stand-ing on end, and their lips curled back in disgust.

"You have stolen my light."

The light had gone, not stolen, but thrown away.

23

Danny's phone call woke Dave from a strange fitful sleep, both deep, yet punctuated by sudden awakenings throughout the night. The illuminated digits of his bedside alarm clock appeared brilliant in the darkness. They said 3:31. It took him a while to surface, but he finally croaked, "Yeah, yeah, I'm here. What's up?" There was something about the short silence which followed this remark that warned him something bad had happened.

Then Danny's voice came through, cracked and pregnant with distress. "He's . . . he's killed Rita."

Dave didn't need to ask who Danny was talking about. He lay back on the bed again, and stared at the ceiling.

"Danny," he said eventually, "I'm sorry. How'd it happen?"

"She was in a cab. It exploded. Burned both her and the cabby to cinders. Caused a big crash too. Other people died."

Dave's mind was awash with other possibilities.

"You sure it was *him?* Maybe it was an ordinary incendiary device which some other joker planted. Maybe it was just a freak accident. They do happen, you know."

Danny sounded disgusted.

"It was him, I know it was him. Witnesses reported a pillar of white fire. He killed Rita to get at us, let's stop fooling ourselves. This is one son-of-a-bitch angel we got ourselves here, and he doesn't give a damn who gets hurt, so long as he gets his own way."

Dave nodded, forgetting Danny couldn't see him.

"Danny, are you okay? I mean . . ."

The voice at the other end sounded dull, the way he knew he had sounded, when talking about himself after Celia's death. A kind of leaden tone which, when you heard it, made you think that the person using it couldn't give a damn about anything, anything at all. If you told him the world was going to end, he would say, okay, fine, what time?

"Yeah, yeah, I'm all right. I just feel kinda dead inside, you know. I mean, at the moment I just want to curl up and go to sleep, forget everything. I remember reading about some guys on an expedition to the Antarctic, I think it was. They got so cold they wanted to fall off to sleep and drift away, never wake up. That's how I feel, I guess. Very cold, very tired. It's times like this I wish I smoked crack. I'd have some place to go. Some fantasy land where people you get fond of don't go and die on you . . ."

There was a choked sound from the receiver.

Dave said, "Danny . . .?"

There was a long period of silence. Dave thought the phone had been left dangling.

"Danny?"

Now the voice was rigid with anger. Danny could hardly get out the words. Dave could imagine his face, stiff and red with fury, like the time they had found that six-year-old girl that had been raped, her throat cut to keep her quiet, her body crammed in a trash can.

"I want to get that freak if it kills me. Me and Rita, well we weren't in love—not like you and Celia—but we were getting that way, know what I mean? She was a great kid, and that bastard is going to pay for this, somehow, or I'll put my head through a mincer."

"We'll get him, Danny. We'll get him for Celia and we'll get him for Rita. Somehow. He's got to have *some* weak point somewhere."

"When I get through with him, he'll have more than one weak point."

"It'll happen, it'll happen."

Dave could sense Danny calming down now, getting himself under control. The smaller man was slow to anger, but quick to defuse. That was why he made such a good partner. He didn't lose his head in an emergency, and if something did make him mad, that anger would have cooled to a chilled resolve before leaving the scene of the crime.

"Yeah, well, I got to arrange for Rita's funeral, what's left of her. And I got to phone her mother. I'm not looking forward to that."

"Okay, catch you later."

"Yeah."

Suddenly, Dave thought of something, and leapt out of bed, alarmed.

The fat student in the back row of Vanessa's "The Nature of Evil" lecture had fallen asleep again, but his antithesis with the wispy beard trying to grow into manhood through his chin was as wide awake as usual. Between them this pair always gave Vanessa a headache because one of them paid no attention at all to her lectures and the other too much. Wispy Beard was one of those who sat in the front, arms folded, ready to challenge anything and everything his tutors told him. He knew better than any mortal on this earth about every subject.

"Surely," said Wispy Beard, "evil is what we, as a society,

say it is. If we call murder evil, and believe it, then murder is evil. But if murder was an accepted form of culling an overpopulated world, or some ritual sacrifice—such as the Aztecs used to carry out—well, then, it's not evil, is it? I mean, what about war? Men are heroes for killing in war."

"We're not talking about just *killing* here, we're talking about *murder,* which is *unlawful* killing. Anyway, don't you believe that we have an instinctive feel for morality? As you say, killing in war is encouraged, but does that mean the men who do the killing don't suffer any kind of guilt or remorse? Personally, I think if *Homo sapiens* didn't have an intrinsic knowledge of what was right and what was wrong, we'd be in real trouble."

The student looked smug.

"Lady, we *are* in real trouble. Don't you read the newspapers? There are about a dozen wars going on right now, and probably a murder a minute."

Her voice chilled and tried to frost him over.

"I am not *lady.* I'm Ms. Vangellen to you."

The youth shrugged and looked around for support from the other students, which wasn't forthcoming but didn't change his expression or his attitude.

"Fine, *Miz* Vangellen. Sorry I touched a raw nerve."

She walked over to his desk and leaned with both arms, so that her mouth was close to his ear, and none of the other students could hear what she was saying.

"Listen, you little shit, my boyfriend is a cop, a sergeant detective, and I think he would be grateful to know what you've got stashed between the pages of that book on tropical fish—you understand what I'm saying?"

The youth went white and the fine hair on his chin quivered.

"I don't—," he began, but she cut him off with a conversational tone, saying, "Listen, cokehead, even if he doesn't find it, he'll work you over when he knows I want him to—so what's it to be? A little cooperation, or a knee in the groin? Simple choice."

He nodded, briefly, and she went back to her original position.

What Wispy Beard had been saying was relevant and made sense, but the way in which he said it made her want to knock his skull against a brick wall. He was too self-satisfied, he sneered too much, he was too goddamned arrogant.

She posed another question for her class.

"We have a problem with religion and evil, in that if God is omnipotent and omniscient, and He created everything, including Himself, then he must have created evil, right?"

Wispy Beard looked about to argue, then obviously remembered her threat, and sank back in his seat and twiddled his pencil. He performed a trick they all seemed to know of twirling the pencil like a propeller with their fingers. Vanessa had tried it and failed, and concluded that they must have spent literally *hours* practicing this useless pastime.

A female student, a girl in brown horn-rimmed glasses, said, "Maybe it was an *indirect* creation, a spinoff? Maybe *mankind* invented evil? Okay, God made man, but he made him imperfect, so that he could make mistakes, learn by them, and use freedom of will—and in using that freedom, man invented evil."

"Good," said Vanessa. "Any other ideas?"

Wispy Beard took this as an invitation to go in again.

"Evil isn't something that's *invented*. You make it sound as if it's a tangible thing, or something like a gas, that's in the air. Evil is doing evil things."

Vanessa sensed a more respectful tone in his voice and let him enter the game again.

"Ah, but is it?" she said. "Is an evil act by a good man worse than a similar act by an evil man?"

"That's what I mean," said the youth looking pained. "You're calling someone evil without defining what evil is."

"Okay, let's put it this way. You have a choirmaster who all his life has helped people, the old and infirm, the poor and needy, and then suddenly he goes off the rails and robs a bank, and a teller is killed. Before this act, he's been a pillar of respectability and good in the community, and is loved by all those with whom he comes into contact. He blames this one bad act on a temporary aberration, and says it will never happen again.

"With him, an accomplice to the murder, is a guy who's spent his life gambling away his mother's savings, until she's been left destitute. He has a history of street gang warfare, petty thieving and sexual offenses, and shows no remorse over anything. He laughs at the judge and court officials, and threatens the jury with violence if he gets convicted.

"Is the second man *more* evil than the first? Should the choirmaster be given a lesser sentence, when the court convicts both men of the deed?"

Wispy Beard was adamant.

"If they were both responsible for the bank teller's death, a single deed, they should be punished equally. It doesn't matter about their history, or how they feel about what they've done. It's the deed that matters, nothing else. You do evil, you are evil."

"Ah, but—," began Vanessa.

A voice from the doorway interrupted her.

"I agree with the kid. In fact, I think the good guy should be punished more severely, because he's the more evil of the two."

She turned, furious at the interruption, to see Dave standing there, leaning on the doorjamb.

Dave said, "For instance, say you have this angel who goes rogue and comes down to earth and starts burning people alive.

Is he any less evil than a demon who does the same thing? I reckon he's *more* evil, because he's supposed to be a guardian of good, and should uphold the principles of what's right. An angel who's gone rogue is like a cop with a dirty badge, he's violated his trust. You don't ask for trust from a demon or criminal, and they don't promise it, but an angel and a cop both promise to fight evil, not join with it. We relax our vigilance with angels and cops, because we *expect* them to be trustworthy, and if they desecrate that trust they're not only as bad as demons or criminals, they're *worse*."

Vanessa looked at the floor and smiled.

"Thank you, Sergeant, for your input."

"You're welcome."

Vanessa turned to Wispy Beard.

"John, I want you to meet Dave Peters, the detective I told you about."

Wispy Beard colored up and looked nervous, pushing a book into the sports bag under his desk.

"Pleasetameecha," he croaked.

"Mutual," said Dave.

"Okay," said Vanessa, looking at her watch, "it's only five minutes to break. You can go out now, if you creep away. Don't wake Jefferson"—she nodded to the sleeping fat student —"let him dream on."

The kids gathered their books quietly and moved toward the door. First through it was Wispy Beard, who glanced fearfully into Dave's face before disappearing into the corridor.

When they had all gone, except Sleeping Beauty, Dave asked her, "What was all that about?"

"What?"

"The kid with the fuzz on his chin. Has he been putting his hand up your skirt, or what?"

"Dave Peters, you have a one-track mind. He's a pain in the

ass, that's all, and I threatened him with the bogey man if he
didn't shape up. You're the bogey man."

"Gee, thanks."

"Don't mention it. Actually, he's very bright, that boy, but
he has an attitude problem. I hate know-all little creeps who
think their brain is on the same axis as the earth."

"You would've hated me as a rookie cop, then."

She smiled.

"I expect I would've done. Anyway, to what do I owe the
honor? You've never come here before. And at ten in the morning?"

"Rita's dead."

Her smile went.

"Oh, no. What happened?"

"Danny's convinced it was the angel. He's moving in on us,
and you could be next. I came to collect you."

The funeral was a somber affair, appropriately late in the afternoon on a dark rainy day. The minister was a tall thin man, who
bent in the middle as he read the service, bobbing with the
words. His voice was harsh, almost condemning, as he went
through Rita's accomplishments and good points, as supplied
by Danny.

Rita's mother came up from L.A., wearing a black dress and
gloves: a plump woman who strained her underwear. Vanessa
could see the lines of her foundation garments making em-
bossed geometric patterns through her frock. Her cosmetics
were sixties: pale lipstick, heavy mascara. There were carpet
bags under her eyes, and doggie jowls on her jaws. She spoke
softly to Vanessa, thinking she was her daughter's best friend,
and the look in her eyes showed she was impressed when she
learned that Vanessa was a college lecturer.

"Rita always made friends with proper people," she said,
squeezing Vanessa's hand. It was meant to be a compliment,

to herself as well as to Vanessa. After all, she took credit for raising her daughter right.

She stayed only long enough to see the coffin go into the
ground. She sniffed her way through the service, toying with a
small lace handkerchief, and nodded when the preacher said
what a good daughter Rita had been.

"She sent me money, you know," she whispered to Vanessa,
"and always wrote such nice letters."

The mother refused Danny's offer of lunch, and seemed to
disapprove of him.

When Dave asked about it, Danny said, "She knew we
weren't married. She thought I was taking advantage of her
daughter. She thought Rita was a buyer, you know, for one of
the big stores. I saw no reason to change her mind. Most of
those girls have got mothers and fathers who think they're
business women."

Vanessa said, "Well, they are."

"I guess so," said Danny.

"Let's go for a drink," Dave said, "and talk about our next
move against the bastard that's responsible for all this."

The three of them trooped down the street, away from the
red-brick Presbyterian chapel to a bar nearby. There wasn't a
great deal to talk about, however. None of them knew where
the angel was, and had nothing to offer even if they did. They
were still as helpless as before.

They stayed until eight in the evening, then all went back
to Dave's place for coffee, after which Vanessa excused herself,
and took a cab to her own apartment.

Tom Shimchak was waiting in the darkness. He sat in the arm-
chair, smoking a cigarette, enjoying the quiet sensation of being
there, in a woman's apartment, without invitation. He studied
the glow of his cigarette as another man might study a star, considering its beauty. Tom had always enjoyed smoking, but with

him it was a necessity: he was a lawyer for a tobacco company. He was expected to smoke.

Tom was the grandson of a Polish immigrant, his father's father having fled Warsaw in 1939, during the extermination of the Jewish ghetto by the Nazis. In those days the family name was spelled Szymczak, but Tom had changed it when he went to Harvard. It was okay to be Polish, he was proud of that, but it had been a pisser to keep spelling the damn thing three times, to registration clerks and their ilk.

Tom had come to the apartment because he was missing Vanessa, now that they had split up. He had phoned her probation officer, and talked with him, then decided to visit her on spec. She would be surprised to see him, and now he had got over the shock of the fire, and knew what it was all about, he could handle it better.

He heard her key in the lock, and put a smile on his face.

Vanessa came in, fiddling with her purse, and switched on the light. She had walked several paces into the room before looking up and seeing him, and she jumped visibly, some two inches in the air.

"Shit," she said with anger in her voice. "What are you doing here?"

He stubbed out the cigarette in an ashtray.

"I'm missing you," he said. "I thought you might be feeling the same way."

She put down her purse and took off her coat.

"I'm seeing someone else."

A hand went down inside Tom's chest and grabbed his lungs, squeezing them tightly. He stared at her. She had on a crisp white blouse and tight blue skirt. Her eyes, as always, were owlish, but pretty. She looked ravishing. He had not had a woman since they had split up, having been too nervous after all that shit with the fire to go into a bedroom with a female in it. He was a sensitive man.

He took off his opalescent-framed glasses and pretended to clean them, to hide his embarrassment and anger. Then he put them on again, knowing he looked anemic without them. His milky face needed adornment to give it strength and color.

"You—you're what?"

"I'm see-ing some-one else," she stated, pronouncing the syllables very deliberately, as if he were six years old, which made him madder than ever. "Is it hard to understand?"

"No, no, not hard to understand. There's no need to make me feel small. It's just a bit quick, that's all. Who is it?"

Her voice softened a little, but she said, "None of your damned business, Tom." She folded her arms under her breasts and stared at him. "Look, Tom, I'm sorry for what happened. It was a terrible thing to do, and I wish I could go back again and *not* do it, but you turned me in, you know. You had your revenge, or your justice, whatever you like to call it. Now it's all over. If you'd been a little more understanding, tried to get to the reasons *why* . . ."

He stood up and touched her elbows with his fingertips.

"I *want* to. I want to understand."

"It's too late. It's over."

She tried to move away from him. His anger turned into something else, and he grabbed her, pinning her arms to her sides, feeling her breasts against his shirtfront. It wasn't fair. He needed her. He had an erection.

"Please, Vanessa, for old times' sake."

"Tom, let me go."

She struggled, sounding a little scared. Instead of making him ashamed of himself, it fired him. It made him worse. There was a hot feeling coming over him.

"Keep still, damn it, I'm not going to hurt you."

"You're not going to do *anything*, Tom."

Her glasses fell to the floor as he tried to kiss her and she jerked her head back.

Incensed, he threw her onto the carpet and fell heavily on top of her, tearing at her blouse, ripping the front away. He was like a madman now, his head full of buzzing noises. He tore her bra off, bit into the soft white flesh beneath. The piercing scream brought him round again.

He was staring into her narrow features, into her eyes. There was a bright red mark on her breast, where his teeth had been. He blinked rapidly.

"Tom," she sounded as if she were panting, "don't do this, please, Tom."

"You want me to," he said.

"No, no, I'm not excited. I'm scared, Tom. Don't make this mistake. Dave will kill you if he finds out."

He gripped her harder.

"Dave?"

"He's a cop. He'll kill you."

"No, he won't. He won't know. You don't have to tell him."

Tom reached down and wrenched at her waistband, making the skirt pop open. He held her down by the throat with his right hand, and pulled off the skirt with his left. Then the panties and tights, ripping them away. He was surprised at his own strength. He had always thought of himself as physically weak, but in fact he was quite strong.

"Oh, God," cried Vanessa. "Please don't do this, Tom."

"Don't make such a big thing out of it. We've done it before, dozens of times. Remember? Just think yourself back. It's only the same thing. You used to *ask* me for it. You used to ring me up and say let's do it today, anywhere—"

"That was *then*, that was—let go my throat, Tom. Let go. I'm choking. Okay, you can do it. I'll let you do it. We'll do it together just one last time."

He relaxed his right hand. The strong smell of her perfume was in his nostrils. It was driving him crazy. Expensive brand.

He, Tom, had bought it for her. A gift when they had been going together. It had been purchased at the airport, when he had flown in from Florida that time.

"That's better. It'll be okay. You'll see. You'll like it, same as you always did."

She stroked his hair.

"Tom, will you do to me . . . you know? You know what I used to like. You were the only one who would do that."

He smiled.

"Sure, baby. I know what to do."

He slid down her body and began kissing inside her thighs. Suddenly her legs scissored, gripping him round the neck. He felt his chin go back, her mound against his neck, the hairs coarse and rough on the smooth skin of his throat. He could feel her pelvic bone grinding into his Adam's apple.

"Hey," he tried to say, but the sound was strangled.

She swung sideways improving her grip, so that they were at right angles to one another, his face staring at the ceiling, she on her side, her right leg on top of his throat, her left leg on the back of his neck. She began increasing the pressure, so that his head was forced right back. He tried grabbing at flesh, twisting it, to make her let go, but the more pain he inflicted the harder she squeezed with her strong legs, until he thought his spine was going to snap.

"Please," he said, scrabbling at her thighs, trying to force the legs apart with his hands. "Vanessa."

"You bastard, I ought to break your back."

Her vulva was hard against the side of his neck, but it was not a pleasant feeling. She was strangling him. He began to get weaker. He was getting a little air, but her bone was on an artery running up behind his ear. Bright spots of light appeared in front of his eyes. The room began to fade away. He knew he was going to die, if she didn't release him.

Then he felt the legs relax. He was pushed aside by one of

her feet. He rolled and coughed, the dizziness overcoming him as blood rushed to his head. She kicked him again, hard with her bare heel, probably unaware how close she had come to killing him. Eventually he sat up and looked at her.

"Get out," he heard her say. "Get up, get out."

She gave him his glasses, which had fallen off during the struggle. Sitting there, his shorts felt wet in front, and looking down he saw his pants were unzipped. When had he done that? He zipped them up again. Finally, he staggered to his feet, allowed himself to be pushed toward the door.

"I'm sorry," he whispered hoarsely. "Sorry."

"Don't come back, Tom. I don't ever want to see or hear from you again. You understand? I won't say anything about this, but I want you out of my life for good."

She opened the door and gave him another shove.

He nodded, stumbling through the doorway into the passageway.

Out in the street it was cold. He lit another cigarette, inhaling it slowly, staring down the empty street. He could still smell her perfume on his clothes, but the previous image of her had changed. The picture of her which he had carried earlier in the evening was now marred by a savage expression. It was as if he had been carrying an icon around with him that had been slashed, mutilated, scarred by some vandal.

Nethru scanned the alleyways and streets, trying to find some sign of the woman. He had followed her to this place, and had lost her on the last corner. She had to be nearby somewhere. But where? The blocks of apartments housed hundreds, thousands of mortals. How was he going to find her in this multitude of dwellings? Had she been a demon, and he an angel, it would have been relatively easy. He could have followed the scent of evil to its source.

But she was no demon, and he was no angel. Nethru had

not realized how difficult it was going to be to find ordinary people when you were a stranger with little knowledge of how things worked in this world of mortals. He had come across her by chance. It was not likely to happen again. As an angel he had had no need of transport, or a place to sleep, or protection from the cold night air. Now he was a demon, all these things were necessary, and he had no idea how best to get them, how to use them once he had got them. He was going to have to learn, very quickly, if he wanted to find the policemen.

A figure came along, walking past the end of the alley where Nethru was standing contemplating. Nethru caught a fragrance wafting on the draft coming down the alley. There was a stirring in his loins and an unfamiliar sensation. His penis was erect. There was something he could do to the woman now, before he killed her. He hurried after the figure.

When Nethru emerged from the end of the alley, however, he saw that it was not her, but a man. He went after the man, quickly, catching him up on the next corner.

"You have been with the woman," he said. "You have her smell on you."

The man looked startled, guilty.

"What?"

The man blinked rapidly, his blue eyes had a frightened look in them, set in the wan face. He rearranged some loose cloth-ing with shaking hands. Nethru was aware that some act had taken place, but he was not sure of its nature.

"The woman? Where is she?"

"I don't know what you're talking about. What woman? You don't look like a cop to me. Who the hell are you?"

Nethru clutched the man by the throat, driving him up against a wall. The mortal's face grew livid in the lamplight.

"—the fuck off me!" screamed the man, kicking out sav-agely with his feet at Nethru's shins.

"I want to know where the woman is."

"I don't know what you're talking about, you freak. I'm a lawyer. I'll have your ass for this."

The man was soft to the touch. He had nice fair skin. Nethru's lust, which had been aroused by the perfume and subsequent thoughts about what he would do to the woman once he found her, had not abated. Perhaps this fair-skinned man would do for the same thing? He touched the man in an intimate region of his body.

The man screamed again.

"What the hell are you doing? Leave me alone, you faggot!"

"Why?" He gripped the man in an embrace and pressed him up against the wall.

Fear came to the man's face from some place deep within him. Nethru had unlocked some dark terror which made the man struggle far more intensely than the threat of violence had done. An unusual strength came to the man, and he began thrashing and kicking in Nethru's arms, biting the demon on the cheeks and nose with a mindless savagery of which Nethru had not thought the creature capable. The fear of being raped drove the man out of his head and he began to butt Nethru in the face with his head, smashing his glasses in the process. There was no thought process there, only an insane terror, driving the human to supernormal acts of potency.

It was useless. These creatures were all useless to him. They never had any help to give him. Maybe all women smelled the same? No, that wasn't true. But a lot of them might. Nethru decided he was wasting his time with this creature.

Nethru quickly cracked the man's skull against the wall, fracturing it in several places, and the body went limp in his hands. He then went out into the street, lifted a metal sewer cover, and dropped the corpse down into the stream below. It would be carried to some other part of the city, and probably remain undiscovered for some time. He did not want to alarm the woman. It was best she remained unsuspecting until he found her. If the mortal was known to her, and was found dead in her district, it might put her on her guard.

He gave the streets another cursory inspection, before hurrying away.

24

The three of them met in Dave's apartment and tried to rationalize their predicament.

"The way I see it," said Danny, "is we don't stand a snowball's chance in hell. If this creature wants to get us, it will. There's nowhere to hide, nowhere to go that he won't find us. We have no weapons we can use against him—none that we know of, anyway. What can we do?"

"We can keep hoping for something to happen," said Dave, rattling the ice cubes in his glass. "Keep circling him. Moving around him. Something might happen. Anything."

Out of habit, once he had quenched his thirst a little, Dave got up from his chair and stepped over to his telephone answering machine. He pressed the PLAY button. There was a message from Celia's parents, just a keep-in-touch thing. Then Malloch's voice came out of the box.

"I need to see you," said Malloch. "I don't want to talk about it on the phone. Meet me at this address . . ." and the name of a warehouse in a local street followed.

"Bingo!" cried Dave.

Vanessa said, "Aren't you being a little premature? It could be anything."

"You think he would bother to call us with bad news? What could be worse than what we've already had. Hundreds of people burned to death. Each of us has suffered the loss of someone killed like that. We don't just throw in the towel because we've failed a couple of times. This fiend has got to be nailed, somehow, and we won't get anywhere by sitting on our asses complaining that nothing can be done."

He picked up the newspaper lying near the magazine rack where he had thrown it.

"Read that! We have no police station, no cops in this part of the city. In three days' time they're going to open a temporary headquarters for us, in a derelict gymnasium. They're going to draft in cops from other parts of the city and try to create some order out of the mess our friend left behind.

"In the meantime, the city's trash is collecting here. It's like the blackout in New York, everybody rushing around trying to get as much crime done as they can, before the boys are back on the job. People are getting hurt here."

"Okay, okay," mumbled Danny. "Let's go and hear what Malloch has to say."

"What about me?" asked Vanessa. "I don't want to stay here alone."

"She better come with us," said Danny.

Dave nodded.

"Yeah, I guess you'll be as safe with us as without us. Rita was on her own, and now she's dead."

When they got to the warehouse, it was in darkness. The only sounds to be heard were the background noises of the city. They had passed two fires on the way, but there was no point in stopping to investigate. If the angel had started them he would be long gone. Besides, they still had no plan of what to do when they finally caught up with him.

Dave cut the motor's engine and stared around for a few moments. There were no cars in the parking lot and nothing appeared to be stirring except some empty fast-food cartons being blown along the street. Otherwise the place was still and, it had to be thought, a little eerie. Peering out into the near darkness, Dave felt no great desire to leave the vehicle and go searching black corners for demons. It had occurred to him that the angel would be a brilliant mimic: it had the power of light and darkness and there was no reason to suppose it did not have the power to manipulate other physical laws. To imitate the sound of Malloch's voice on the phone would be easy for such a creature. Dave shivered involuntarily and for the first time in his life his fear overcame his sense of duty.

The other two had remained as silent as he was and it seemed they were waiting for him to make the first move, or at least suggest what it might be.

Dave said to Danny, "One of us has to go in and look for him."

"You go," said Danny. "I hate dark warehouses."

"Well, that's a great excuse," snarled Dave. "I don't much care for them myself."

"It was your idea."

Vanessa interrupted.

"Is this the way our city is normally policed? Two cops arguing about who's going to sit in the car and who's going to make the arrest?"

"Nobody's making an arrest," said Dave, "otherwise we'd both go in."

Dave sighed, swallowed his fear, and took a flashlight out of the glove compartment. He got out of the car and switched on the light. Danny remained in the vehicle and Dave wondered whether his partner was going to follow him out. He didn't look back because if Danny was gathering his reserves of courage then such an action might serve to humiliate his partner.

Dave walked to the main doors through which the trucks drove during business hours. When he tried them they seemed locked. He rattled them, testing the bolts, but they refused to open.

He skirted one corner of the building and looked along its wall. There was no opening on that side. Then he went round to the far corner. Here he was in more luck. His flashlight beam found a small door swinging open in the draft.

He walked along and stepped inside. The place was empty, except for some cardboard boxes stacked in one corner. He looked around for a light switch, but couldn't find one.

"Malloch?" he called, the sound echoing through the empty warehouse.

There was a sound like a door creaking, and Dave shone his light up into a raised area of offices that overlooked the whole warehouse. The beam glinted on the glass of the windows, making Dave jump for a second, until he realized what it was. His heart was pattering in his ribcage like that of a small mammal within pouncing distance of a predator. He could feel his hands sweating.

Dave called, "You up there, Malloch?"

Still no answer, unless, perhaps, that was not a door creaking at all, but some other sound. He concentrated hard and his imagination turned the noise into a low moan from a human throat. Human? Or otherwise? It was all he could do to stop from running out through the door. Whereas if there had been a gang of violent hoods in the warehouse Dave would have continued with determination, perhaps even eagerly, now that he was dealing with supernatural forces he was loath to take even a step toward the area from which the noise came.

Dave swapped the flashlight to his left hand, then took his gun out of his holster with his right. The weight of it made him feel more secure. It might not be of any use to him, but he felt more comfortable with it in his fist.

A door swung open, somewhere on the raised platform above him, and he could smell something now, quite strongly. An odor like burned rubber. Its distinctness wafted down to him, settling around him, setting his nerves on edge.

"I'm coming up there, whoever you are," cried Dave, trying to keep the tremor out of his voice.

He took the stairs slowly, his .38 straight out in front of him, ready to pull the trigger. The sound of his leather soles on the steps seemed monstrous to him: like some giant clumping around on a drum. This was the way caretakers got shot, he told himself, but he couldn't worry about that now. He was sweating heavily, concerned about dying. In a few seconds he was likely to be flash-fired: he wanted to get a few shots off, at the very least, to show he was going out with rage in his heart.

When he reached the top, the sound came again, and this time he recognized it as the groan of someone in pain. Was that a trick? If it was Malloch, why didn't he call, reveal that it was him, knowing Dave was coming? It didn't make much sense.

At the first door, Dave stopped, and pushed it open with his foot. It swung back swiftly, hit the half-glass wall and shuddered, rattling its glass pane. Dave swept the room with his flashlight beam, taking in a desk, a filing cabinet with the drawers empty and stacked beside the frame. Nothing else, apart from a few pamphlets scattered on the dusty floor.

The smell was stronger than ever, and it wasn't smouldering rubber. It was the same smell that filled his apartment when he set the timer wrong on the oven, and overcooked a joint, or left a steak in the frying pan when he answered the phone, forgetting about it. It was *burned* meat. It was charred flesh.

He wavered then, the sense of terror about the place reaching down inside him and tugging at his guts.

Maybe he should go back for Danny?

He didn't. He went on. The next office was much the same as the first. Then he reached the third room. When he swung the door open, the odor almost knocked him on his back, and he knew he'd found the room that held the burnt meat. He swept the floor with his flashlight. A table and a filing cabinet.

Nothing else.

Then something clicked in his mind.

He played the beam back on the filing cabinet, and sticking out from the other side of it was something black and nasty. The something black and nasty moved, sent ice-water trickling down Dave's spine. He really did not want to look at whatever that black and nasty something was joined to.

There was another of those low groans.

Dave walked slowly around the room, on the far side from the cabinet, and shone the flashlight into the space between the filing cabinet and the corner of the room. The sight, though in some respects expected, made him jump and want to run screaming from the building. Instead he swallowed hard, taking down the bile that had come up to his mouth.

There was a black charred mass, from which the stink was coming, jammed in the space. The mass had stick-like projections that used to be arms and legs, and a ghastly bubbled blob on what used to be shoulders. Remnants of clothes, still black and smoking, were hanging from the torso. The eyes had burst with the heat, and dribbled down the bared bone of the cheeks.

Again, the groan.

"Peters."

This time Dave's brain jangled as it registered what the sound was intended to convey. *It was his name.* This grisly thing that used to be a live creature was whispering his name.

It took all his strength of will to cross the room and kneel by the dying figure.

Dave gagged as he spoke and asked hopefully, "Angel?"

"Gone," came the whisper.

"What is it? Who are you?" Dave asked, swallowing rapidly as the salt taste kept returning to his mouth.

"Peters," croaked the figure, "this is—this is—is . . ." it sounded like *mallet*. Malloch?

"Malloch? That you?"

A nod came from the creature.

"Who did this? The angel?"

Another nod, then a crisp stick-arm jerked out, grabbed him by the collar. Charcoal fingers, remarkably strong, pulled him down toward those scorched lips, as if to kiss him. Dave pulled back in revulsion and let out a cry, ripping his shirt in his attempt to escape the demon's clutches, but the fiend would not let him go. Finally, Dave relented, going down with his ear close to the blistered mouth.

"The angel," croaked Malloch.

"Yes, that's what I said."

"Not anymore."

It took a few seconds for this statement to sink in. The angel wasn't the angel any more. What, then, was he?

"Is he human?" asked Dave.

The dark head with the frizzled skull shook from side to side.

"Fell," croaked the lips.

Dave was allowed to pull back then, to savor this word. There was no doubting what it meant. *Fell*. The angel had fallen. He had fallen from grace, that direct line from God to all the beings He had created. The angel was now a demon, like all those he was—*had been* hunting.

"Can he die?"

"Not usual way," whispered Malloch. "Fire, only fire. Holy fire best. Use holy fire."

Where in the hell did one get holy fire?

"Okay, I've got it. He's now a demon, who can be destroyed by fire. Did he do this to you?"

A nod from the terrible head.

"What did he do it with?"

"Gasoline bomb."

"Oh, how the mighty have fallen. His wings have been clipped neatly this time, eh? What about you, Malloch? Can I do anything for you?"

A shake of the head.

"Leave me."

"Will you die?"

"Yes, soon. Skin gone. Flesh burned. Dying now, in great pain."

Dave felt sorry for the demon.

"Can I . . . can I help you along, get it over with quicker? My gun?"

A shake of the head. No, there was no way to speed up the death of a demon. He had to fade away in his own time. Malloch had information he still wished to impart. His lips opened once more.

"Demon called Nethru," whispered Malloch.

"Nethru?"

25

Nethru was surprised at the lack of satisfaction he gained from the death of Malloch. He had imagined prior to his success that a feeling of great elation and triumph would follow, and now that it was over, and Malloch had been destroyed, all he experienced was a flatness of spirit. He wondered if, now that he was a demon, anything would ever give him satisfaction again.

He tried to raise his spirits with some optimistic forecasts regarding his future operations.

It will be different, he told himself, when I kill the two policemen. What is the destruction of another demon, compared to the deaths of these interfering mortals? The sweetness of revenge must surely come with the highest prizes. Spitz and Peters were his real targets.

But first he had to find them.

Humans were, he conceded, probably easily tracked down, if you were a human yourself. The one time he had wanted to find two humans their occupation had been his guide. He had simply gone to the place where policemen were to be found.

Even then he had failed. Humans left their workplaces in order to rest, but Nethru had no idea how to go about finding these nests where men sometimes ate and slept.

He would need weapons: they weren't foolish enough to let him get in close. He was vulnerable himself now, to the very weapon he employed against others. The policemen were not stupid. They would know what would be effective against him.

So weapons were essential, but Nethru didn't like the idea of guns. Guns were complicated mechanical things, distasteful to a spiritual being. Nethru still retained a preference for the ethereal over the physical. It was in his nature: his supernature.

And when it came down to it, they did the simplest of jobs. They sent out a missile at great speed, to penetrate the flesh of the victim. These missiles were not always effective, sometimes passing through the body without causing a mortal wound. Nethru could do as much with a stone by flinging it.

It was difficult to get away from the idea of fire, for that had always been his weapon. To burn. It was clean. It was artistically destructive. It was the way of the angel. He loved the idea, the concept of fire. You found your target and you razed it to the ground. Ashes to ashes. Smoke to the wind. He had washed the legions of the unholy in fire-rain, had watched them sizzle to nothing under the heat of his flames. He had bathed them in death, bringing light to the heavens, sending evil back into the smoky regions of hell.

Was it only yesterday that he had had the power of holy fire at his fingertips? He mourned its loss and wondered how he was going to replace it. Any device he created would always seem coarse beside the ability to produce fire naturally.

The firestorm he had created to destroy one demon in Tokyo, for example, had cleared a whole area of the landscape. A thousand or so mortals had died in that fire: clean, sweet deaths. He had watched them burn, with disinterest, finding within himself only a fascination with the fire, with the flames that licked the bottoms of the clouds. Fire was *light*.

Fire was fire.

The instrument Nethru eventually, and somewhat reluctantly, chose was similar to that which he had already used with great effect against Malloch. Humans called it a Molotov cocktail: a bottle filled with gasoline with a rag wick. It was a crude device for a fallen angel, this fire-grenade, but it was effective. Somehow the idea of it was a kind of tribute to Lucifer, the bringer of light, now Satan, the lord of darkness.

He filled the inside pockets of his raincoat with some half-dozen Molotov cocktails.

He had fashioned them from small stubby beer bottles whose glass was thinner than most other containers and which were easily obtainable from trash cans. The gasoline he had siphoned from cars, tearing off the gas tank cap with a single bare-handed twist. The means of ignition was stolen from a passerby who was startled and indignant at having his lighter snatched from his grasp just as he was lighting a cigarette, but Nethru's speed did not even allow time for the victim to shout for assistance.

Now he was armed. And he was ready to send a message to his enemies.

A uniformed policeman was walking home after a night shift, and took a shortcut down an alley.

Binny Wilson, black as a brick of tar and proud of it, was always happy to get night shifts behind him. The first part was all right, when you were feeling warm and comfortable with the sleeping world, feeling kind of special because you were awake and watchful.

But later, around four-thirty, when the darkness was hauling ass, and the gray began to filter in like slow smoke, the world took on the color of cigarette ash and it was different.

Your blood sugar got low, the hump of the tiredness weighed you down, and you thought you would never make it through without keeling over. At that point in the shift he could go to sleep on a cutthroat razor's edge.

Then around six you got over the hump and you started wondering whether your girlfriend would still be in bed when you got home. You started to imagine the smell of those slept-in sheets, and the quite different aroma of perfume lingering on the pillow. One a warm body smell, the other a scent to send you into dreamland ready armed with fantasies.

Then, afterward, the fried steak and eggs.

Night shift didn't seem so bad after six.

Halfway along the alley one of three winos sleeping there got to his feet and confronted Binny, shattering his mellow mood.

"Going somewhere?" said the wino, his raincoat flapping open. He was standing there like one of those gunslingers in spaghetti westerns, with their long dustcoats. He looked as if he were about to draw his Colt Peacemaker and blow someone to kingdom come.

"Home," said the cop. "Now get out of my way, I'm in a hurry. Unless you want me to book you?"

He rested his hand on his .38.

"Go for it," said the wino, nodding and smiling. He had a gas cigarette lighter in his hand, which was already burning with a long hissing flame.

The cop was nonplussed. Jesus, thought Binny, I have to go and get a nut on my way off duty. Why couldn't it have been during the shift, when I could have used some distractions? You could humor these drunks, or you could frighten them away with threats. He was too annoyed to use the first method.

"You freakin' shit, I ought to kick your ass," he said, wondering what the lighter was for.

The wino smiled.

"Go for the gun. In less than a second I'm going for mine, and if I go first, it won't be fair. Ready?"

Binny looked into the freak's eyes, and saw that he meant it. The streets were crawling with nuts, some of them homicidal. Maybe this asshole had got a weapon from somewhere, and had decided to get even with society? Binny wasn't just going to stand there while some psycho blew a hole in him.

He reached for his .38.

Nethru's hand was swifter than any western gunslinger's. It reached into an inside pocket of the raincoat. It came out with a bottle filled with gasoline. He lit the gas-soaked wick with the lighter, and flung the grenade straight at the wall above the cop's head. It struck, raining fire upon the policeman's head and shoulders.

Binny, whose hand was still fumbling with the strap over his weapon, screamed in pain. His fingers went to his eyes, trying to claw out the burning in them.

Nethru took out a second Molotov cocktail which struck the cop hard on the skull, and again shattered, covering the blue uniform with flaming gasoline. The policeman went up with a *whumph*. The two drunks suddenly woke up, as renewed shrieks hit their ears.

What they witnessed was a pillar of fire, staggering around the alley, bumping into walls. The pillar had flaming arms and legs, which it waved, screaming loudly now, waking up the whole neighborhood. The drunks looked on in terror as the human torch stumbled into a trash can and then fell over, twitching and convulsing.

The other guy, the one who had been sleeping in the alley with them, was on his feet.

"Tell Peters it was Nethru . . . tell them it was *the angel,*" he said.

Then the guy walked from the alley. He seemed pleased with himself. Maybe he was one of those arsonists who like flames, but it didn't seem right (said Jake) to enjoy watching a *man* burn. No (replied Deke), it damn well didn't.

They told the same thing to the other cops, when they arrived some minutes later, and then started arguing with each other when they were asked to describe the man they had seen walk away, one saying he was blonde with a moustache and the other saying he was dark with rimless glasses.

The two winos were hauled up in front of the arson team, D&D, in their new temporary offices.

"You're Mother Teresa, aintcha?" smiled Deke through a mouthful of rotten teeth.

"Detective Sergeant Peters to you, Deke," said Dave.

Deke drew himself up.

"*Mr.* Deke . . . Trindall to you, Detective."

"Your name isn't Trindall, it's Turner."

Deke nodded.

"I know, I just forgot, so I made one up. Close, though, wasn't it?" He smiled.

Dave put up with the smell coming from the wino long enough to get a rough description of the killer. Deke told him that there had been another wino in the alley at the time, who called himself Jethro, and he knew the detective.

"He said he knew me?"

Deke nodded. "Yep. Said to tell you Jethro done it."

Jake, being interviewed by Danny, snorted at this.

"Didn't say *Jethro*, said *Ned Glue*, the angel, thass what his name was."

"*Nethru?*" snapped Dave.

"Thass what I said," retorted Jake.

Forensics called Dave on the phone and reconstructed a scenario for him.

"We found bits of glass on and around Officer Wilson's body," said Dermot of Forensics. "Our guy was burned to death by a homemade bomb—two of them, both made from beer containers. Lobo, it's a Mexican beer, uses squat bottles made of thinnish light-green glass. The killer knows what he's doing. If I wanted to make Molotov cocktails, it's the kind of bottle I would choose. Thinnish glass that would break easily on impact. One was thrown with such force it smashed on the victim's skull."

"How do you know that?"

"There are slivers of glass embedded in the officer's head."

Dave said, "How come the officer didn't shoot the guy?"

"That's really your job," said Dermot, "not mine, pal. I just give you the jigsaw pieces, you have to put 'em together yourself, but my guess was the first bomb was intended for the eyes. That's the way the Chinese used to do it, during the Tong wars, though the weapons were a little different. They used light bulbs filled with sulfuric acid taken from car batteries. First the eyes, then the killing stroke—knife, chopper, whatever. In this case, fire."

"That's very helpful of you."

"Donmenshunit."

Dave filled Danny in with the details.

"*Two* Molotov cocktails?" said Danny. "Isn't that a little excessive? What do you think's going on?"

"I don't know, but Dermot reckons he needs an initial demobilizer, in case the victim uses his own weapon. There's a possibility that he might object to being burned to death and get you before you can strike the match."

"Dermot is a brain."

"Yeah, must be his age," said Dave. "You suddenly get wise when you reach fifty-three."

"You wish," said Danny. "Anyway, we'll be lucky to see our next birthday, if we don't nail our guy. Why all this Molotov cocktail business?"

Dave nodded, sighing.

"You know, the thing I really hate about this is we can't play it straight. We can't arrest the bastard, and haul his ass before a judge. We'd be dead before we got two yards. We have to kill him, Danny."

"*Destroy* him. Would you read a rabid dog its rights before you shot it?"

"No."

"Well, there you have it, Dave. We got to get to him before he gets to us, because what Officer Wilson got this morning, Nethru intends to serve us this afternoon, or tomorrow at the very latest."

26

Dave and Danny cruised the night streets in their unmarked car. There were dozens of drug users and pushers out among the crowds, one or two of whom the two cops could identify, but tonight the D&D were not interested in booking junkies or pushers, pimps or hookers, street gangs or burglars. They were looking for the hardware merchants, who sold the tools of the killing trade.

They curb-hauled the neon district, then the backstreet bars, and finally, around midnight, the nightclubs.

They were parked outside Smiley's Place, a downmarket joint which only kept its head above water because the mobs used it as an exchange house, where certain items were traded for other certain items. No one, except perhaps a misinformed out-of-towner, went there for entertainment. Smiley had bought the place out of his pool-hall winnings in the nights when he had played for serious money and finally ousted Rick "the Felt" Foley as Number One. The club had never had a good show.

Smiley had been dead for years, killed in a nearby pool hall by an immigrant hustler with a hot temper and a pocketful of Colt. Smiley had outhustled the guy for kicks. He died with that famous grin on his face, which had never been an expression of humor, just the frozen residue of a teenage muscular disease.

His wife ran the place now, occasionally taking a singing spot when one of the girls went sick, and driving the customers crazy with her warbled distortions of songs from *West Side Story*. The police raided the club, from time to time, but since she never allowed drugs or weapons in the house—there was a bouncer called Adam, built like a bulldozer, doing the searching at the door—all the cops ever hauled in were a few fences with stuff they swore they thought was legitimate.

At seven minutes past twelve, the D&D struck a rich vein. A guy called Swanton Morely, someone Danny recognized as a dealer in hardware, came up the steps from the basement and made his way to a parked car just down the street. He was alone.

The D&D took off from the curb with a screech, and pulled up alongside Morely just as he was opening his car door. With fear in his face, Morely instinctively ducked, his arms going up around his head. There wasn't any doubt in the cops' minds that the gun dealer thought it was a hit.

Danny jumped out of the vehicle and waved his .38 over Morely's crouched form.

"In!" he ordered, opening the back door.

Morely started to say something, but Danny shrieked, "Get inside or I'll cut a canal through your head!"

He got inside.

Danny got in with him, and Dave took off with another screech, leaving a layer of hot rubber on the road. They drove along in silence for a while, during which Morely sneaked a look at his abductors, and decided with relief that this was something other than a hit. On noticing the dashboard transceiver, he muttered, "Cops," but left it at that. He relaxed, deciding that he would be told what it was all about soon enough. In the meantime, what else could he do? He had the muzzle of a police special in his ribs. One thing was certain, he was not being arrested. They were driving in the wrong direction.

When they got to a waste lot, he started panicking again, thinking that maybe it was a hit, after all. There was no reason why they couldn't be cops *and* work for someone.

"What's going down?" he asked.

No one answered him. The two cops looked grim.

"Hey," cried Morely, the hysteria rising to his throat, "what's going on? Who wants me cremated? I ain't kindled nobody. I been straight in all my deals, you ask anybody."

"Out," said Danny.

The driver had come round to the side door now, and was dragging him from the car. Morely's leg bones turned to water, and he found it difficult to stand. He suddenly wanted to open his bowels. If someone had taken a contract out on him and this *was* a hit, he knew he could not talk himself out of it. Professional hit men, especially if they were cops, were not in the listening business. They had a job to do, as quickly and as efficiently as possible, and nothing on earth would make them change their minds. You could more easily persuade God that he should give you a few more years.

The empty lot was ghostly, lit up from behind by a fire in a nearby street, where arsonists had been at work just half an hour earlier. The two men walked Morely to an abandoned car, the wheels of which were probably now on some runabout driven by a seventeen-year-old punk, and the engine parts of which had been scattered around the local population, swallowed by various aging heaps their owners called vehicles.

"Hey, look," croaked Morely, desperation getting the better of his tongue, "you're cops, you can't do this."

There was no reply.

He was pressed against the side of the wreck, his nose against the cold metal roof, his hands on the guttering. They kicked his legs apart, to keep him off balance, and then not one, but two guns were placed gently one behind each ear, right on the hairline. Morely was sure he was about to die.

"Mother of God," he whispered.

One of the cops, the guy that had been in the back of the car with him, finally spoke.

"You a Catholic?"

Morely grasped at the straw.

"Yes, yes. A practicing Catholic. I need my last rites."

One of the guns was removed, though the other remained.

"Aw, look, Frank," said the cop, "I can't waste a Catholic. You'll have to do it on your own. I'll wait for you in the car."

Morely heard the footsteps leave.

The silence was excruciating, and he wanted to scream, but instead he said, "Can't we come to some sort of deal? Please?"

"It's no good," said the remaining cop called Frank, "I'm a Presbyterian."

Morely almost blurted out, *So am I,* but realized how stupid that would sound.

"I don't mean that, I mean money."

"Money?"

"Anything."

"Anything?"

"What is you want? Anything in the world, so long as I can give it you. If I can't, I'll get it."

There was another interminable silence, during every second of which Morely expected to hear the roar of the gun in his head, and experience the final experience of all living men. The cold metal of the muzzle was boring a hole of its own behind Morely's ear, as he waited for an answer. Then the unbelievable happened. The guy had actually been deliberating over Morely's offer. He spoke in the accents of hope.

"I want some hardware," said the cop, "tonight."

Was that all? Jesus, was that all? Morely felt like wetting his pants in relief. They wanted some tools. That was what this was all about. Christ, cops! They couldn't just come in and ask for the stuff, they had to pump your guts full of fear first, so that you were close to a coronary.

"I'm fifty-three years old," said Morely, "you know what this night has done to my heart? What is it you want? Maybe a machine gun? Something heavy, eh?"

He got his answer.

"A flamethrower."

Morely almost exploded, his eyes on the distant building that was now a glow on the skyline.

"A fuckin' *flamethrower*? Where the fuck am I gonna get one of those at this time of night?"

"Okay, fine."

Morely sensed the finger putting pressure on the trigger.

"All right, all right," he yelled. "Just give me time to think. Can't I just complain a little? Okay, I got it, I know someone. Let me make a call."

"You better be sure about that, because if you're not, we're going to string your throat to your heels, mob style, and watch you strangle yourself slowly."

"Okay, okay. Fuck the threats. I'll get you your flame-thrower, but you got to let me make this call. I can't do it out here, freezin' my balls off on a piece of waste ground. Get me to a phone."

He was marched back to the car, where the short bald-headed cop was sprawled over the hood, finishing a smoke. The cop threw away the lighted cigarette, and jerked himself up-right.

"What the hell is this, Frank?" he cried. "We were told to incinerate this joker."

"Incinerate?" said Morely.

"Yeah," replied the cop named Frank. "I was going to slug

you then burn you in the wreck . . ." He waved his gun at the car's trunk. A gasoline can was standing there.

"Jesus," whispered Morely.

He could feel the fire on his body now, creeping up from his genitals, down from his hair, the two places which would burn first.

"Look, Rico," said the Frank cop, "he's promised to get me a flamethrower."

Rico cop slammed his fist on the car roof, the sound making the nervous Morely jump a foot off the ground.

"They told us to smoke him," snarled the Rico cop, "I think we got to do like they say, Frank. I think we got to burn this freak's ass to cinders."

"Listen, he's a hardware merchant . . ."

"I don't care who he is. That's not supposed to influence us, Frank. He knows our names now—he can put us away."

"I don't know your names," blurted Morely, wondering if he was really off the hook yet. "I never heard of you. I forget names so quick, they go in and out my head, never leaving a goddamn trace, so help me. You want a flamethrower? Get me to a phone. I'll have a flamethrower for you, quicker than that, I swear."

"I want one with a full tank," said Frank, "I don't want to go begging for fuel in the middle of the night. You get me one with a sealed tank, okay?"

"What? How can I . . . ?"

Frank snapped, "Listen, Morely, there are guys who set fire to their own warehouses every day, and you supply them with the equipment. Now, get me one with a full tank."

"All right, all right, I hear you."

Dave and Danny, hardly able to contain their mirth, drove Swanton Morely to a phone booth, where he made a quick call. Then they all got back into the car, and drove to an address which Morely gave them. A guy was waiting on the corner, near the address, and there was a big black sports bag at his feet. Morely got out with Dave, while Danny stood by the car, gun in hand and watching the man with the bag.

There was no trouble. Morely opened the zipper and checked the contents of the bag. He paid the man with the bag, picked it up and carried it back to the car, with Dave behind him. They put the bag in the trunk and drove away.

Danny said, "Stop the car, let's look at the goods."

Dave stopped, Danny got out, and went to the trunk, taking out the bag.

Morely was saying, ". . . it's a good piece of equipment, never been out of its wax-paper wrapper, believe me. There's even a book, an army book with instructions. You can get the hang of it in no time."

"I was in the army," said Dave, "I know how to use one."

"That's good, that's good."

Dave and Danny rummaged through the bag, and Dave swore and muttered, "A World War Two job."

He said to Morely, "Couldn't you at least get me a Soviet LPO-50? Something with a bit more range? This one is only good for fifty yards."

"You talk as if I've got a big choice. I take what they get me, and pass it on. This is what's coming through. Anyway, this one has some advantages. It's American for a start, so the instructions—yeah, I know, you can work the sucker standing on your head—anyways, the LPO-50 only gives you three two-second bursts, one from each tank. Then you got to throw the fucker away. This baby'll whack out *ten* two-second bursts from the four-gallon tank."

"Fifty yards," grumbled Dave.

Morely shrugged.

"How far away do you wanna get? I mean, a hunert an' fifty feet is a fair distance, hey?"

They wrapped up the flamethrower, returned it to the bag, and put the bag back in the trunk.

As they got back in the car, Danny nudged Dave and said, "Hey, that's a good piece of equipment we've got back there. We could use it to burn this freak, and still collect for the contract."

"You don't need to do that," said Morely, going white. "I carried out my part of the deal."

"Yeah, but we're not to be trusted, see. We're cops. You ever heard of a cop with integrity?" said Danny. "I mean, honor among thieves—but cops?"

Dave thought they had tortured the man enough.

"Okay, Morely, get out."

"What?"

"Out. Walk. Don't let me see you again. My advice is to retire. Go to the Bahamas. Go to Bermuda. You can afford it on what you've made peddling guns. If I see you again, I'll run you in, you got that?"

"You—you ain't gonna shoot me in the back, when I walk away from the car?"

"Us?" said Danny. "We hand out sweets to Sunday School kids on our way home from work."

"Yeah, I bet, but once you cops turn dirty, you're the worst of the bunch."

"Out!" shouted Dave.

Morely opened the door, stepped out into the cold night air, and began running. They knew he would hate them for what they had done to him tonight, but they weren't worried. They had what they wanted, and it was touch and go whether they would see him again. He might even take their advice.

They drove to a nearby hotel, where they intended to spend the night. It would have been beyond stupidity to go back to either of their apartments. Vanessa was already at the hotel, holding the room for them. It was the kind of place where the man behind the desk didn't even blink when two men and one woman registered and said they would sleep in the same room where there was only one double bed.

They parked the car and removed the flamethrower from the trunk, carrying it up to their second-story room in the black bag. The bag clunked against the metal banister as they went up the stairs. Danny glanced back at the desk, then followed Dave who was hauling the equipment.

The septuagenarian desk clerk hardly stirred an eyelash as they passed him, his attention glued to the sports page of the evening news. It crossed his mind that there might be slave manacles, chains and whips in the heavy-looking bag, but what the hell did he care, he'd seen it all before. He'd done some of it himself, one time. Sex. It was nothing special, not to a seventy-eight-year-old with a walleye and a caved-in chest full of phlegm. Sports page, now that was something important.

27

In the room of the sleazy hotel, the trinity formulated its plans. This was the final showdown.

They had left a note in each of their apartments, believing that eventually, no matter how difficult it was for him, Nethru would find out where one of them lived. He was not stupid, far from it, merely unused to the ways of the world. There would come a point where he would find that asking questions of people got him further than roaming the streets, hoping to come across one of them by chance. Eventually someone would show him how to look up an address in the phone book.

The notes they had left all said the same thing:

SEE YOU IN CHURCH.

Below these bold words, they had left the address of the city's cathedral. It was their intention to lure Nethru there, and use the flame thrower on him. A gruesome but necessary task, if they were to save themselves. It seemed an appropriate battleground; a contemporary OK Corral. There was space to maneuver, in the graveyard and around the cathedral grounds, where there was little likelihood of innocent bystanders being caught in the crossfire. Especially in the dark early hours of the morning.

As a weapons instructor, Dave had trained soldiers in the use of a flamethrower when he was in the army, but he wanted Danny to do the burning. There had to be a decoy: someone who would show himself and present a target for the demon to attack, so they could get him close enough. Dave knew that was the most dangerous part of the plan, and he didn't want to expose Danny to the vengeful Nethru's incendiaries. Dave saw it as his job to be the decoy, to expose himself. So he carefully tutored Danny in the use of the flamethrower.

He began with his standard lecture, delivered to all his classes during his days in the army.

"Fire has been used as a weapon for thousands of years. Assyrian carvings show towns being attacked by armies with blazing torches, and the ancient Greeks developed 'Greek Fire,' an incendiary mixture difficult to extinguish. It had a base of naphtha, but the exact formula still remains a secret—"

"Cut the crap, Dave," said Danny, "we haven't got time for all that."

Dave shook his head, looking at Vanessa for support, but none was forthcoming, at least, not from her eyes.

"I want you to understand what you're dealing with here, Danny." He unzipped the bag. "There is a terrible weapon. It can turn on the user, and I want to instill its dangers in you before you start playing with it. I know you and weapons—you're a goddamn cowboy at heart, a gunslinger. They're toys to you."

"No, you're wrong," replied Danny, looking hurt. "I know the importance of handling weapons with respect."

"Well, this one needs a hell of a lot of respect, because it's inefficient, hazardous to the user, and when it was used in battle, it was *hated*. If you got caught wearing one of these on your back, the enemy would blow your brains, no questions asked. If you were lucky. It's a morale buster. Men who would go against bullets and bayonets, withstand hours of artillery pounding them, would turn chickenshit when told there was a flame thrower about, and anybody who's faced one wouldn't blame them."

"I get the message," said Danny quietly. "Come on, Dave, this isn't the classroom."

"Yes, it is," said Dave, levelly.

He took the weapon out of the sports bag and placed it almost reverently on the floor: the black nozzle like a pig's snout, the backpack tank and their connecting tubes. He went through the different parts of the weapon, demonstrating in theory how pressing the trigger ignited a magnesium cartridge, which lit the jet of fuel forced out of the nozzle using the pressure created by a cylinder full of inert gas.

"Probably nitrogen," said Dave. "There's something like two thousand pounds per square inch of pressure in there, which a spring-loaded diaphragm reduces to a working pressure of two hundred psi . . ." Vanessa's eyes had glazed over, though Danny was still attentive, "and that'll force out the gasoline gel from the nozzle, past the igniter which will create a blanket of fire. This is a little napalm kit, Danny—essentially the same stuff our troops used in the Nam war—I'm guessing that though it's an old weapon, it's using modern fuel, and if so it's got an alloy mixed with the gel to keep it burning, right down to the bone, even if the victim douses himself with water, by jumping into a river or whatever. Try not to drip any down your shirt front."

Danny's eyes widened at this flippant remark, obviously realizing that he was dealing with something that required all the respect he could muster.

"Are you sure you can handle it, Danny?"

"I think so," said Danny. "Help me strap it on, will you, Vanessa?"

Vanessa looked startled, her eyes taking in the black tank and the stumpy nozzle, worn in places to reveal the silver beneath. There was something about it which would revolt anyone of any sensibility. The nozzle had a grotesque snouty look to it; the tank, a humpbacked gnomish appearance.

"I'm not touching that ugly monster."

Dave nodded.

"Yes, it is, isn't it? And it does an ugly job. Still, we've got no choice. It's him or us."

After Danny was fitted out with the flamethrower, Dave passed Vanessa a handgun, a spare .38 that Danny owned. He gave her a quick lesson on how to use it, and then loaded it for her.

"It probably won't be of much use against Nethru," said Dave, "but you never know."

They each had a drink, to calm their nerves, before setting out on their mission. Vanessa was strangely quiet, until Dave asked her what she was thinking. She flopped back on the bed and stared at the ceiling.

"Oh, I don't know," she said. "I guess it's because we've come to the crunch time. We really do have to get him this time, or we've had it. You two, at least. He'll probably want me as well, by now, knowing I'm associated with the pair of you."

She stubbed out her cigarette in the bedside ashtray, before continuing.

"I guess I was thinking about fire again. It's dogged my footsteps all my life. Did you know there are over three hundred references to fire in the Bible? Have I told you that? From the destruction of Sodom and Gomorrah, to Abraham's near-sacrifice of his son, to Moses's burning bush and pillar of fire, and on and on. Then there are all the other fires, Rome, London, Alexandria, Dresden, I know them all. I used to think they were my friends." She smiled at Dave. "You've been awfully patient with me, haven't you? I know I'm screwed up, but I'm coming out of it, I think. The angel has done that much for me. I no longer want to be burned at the stake, like Joan of Arc, or some medieval witch. And now we are going to destroy a demon, with the agent that I've used to cleanse myself, all my life . . . fire."

Danny quoted, " 'And the beast was taken—and the false prophet. These were taken and cast into a lake of fire burning with brimstone.'"

"Revelation nineteen, verse twenty," said Vanessa.

Dave shook his head, looking at them sadly.

"A couple of intellectuals. I need Ninja warriors to fight demons, and I get a pair of nerds."

"Just because we have brains," said Danny, "doesn't mean we haven't got brawn."

"That's a nerd's answer," said Dave. "Come on, academics, we need to get to the church on time."

The other two nodded.

Dave said to them, "Look, you two, before we leave I have something to say."

Danny and Vanessa gazed at him.

"What I'm trying to say is . . ."

"We know what you're trying to say, Dave," said Danny, "and it doesn't need to be put into words. This time tomorrow we'll be sitting in Clementine's celebrating, and the only smell of burning will be coming from Foxy's roast. Let's get it done."

They drove to the cathedral, wary of any movement out in the night. When they arrived at the great building with its twin spires, and Kennedy Window, they vacated the car and approached the place through the back way, slipping silently between the gravestones.

It was dark, clouds obscuring the moon. The cathedral was

always open, its treasures stored during the night hours in a safe at the Dean's residence, abutting the cathedral grounds. Danny, with the flamethrower at the ready, checked the cathedral grounds, jumping at every shadow, while Vanessa and Dave went inside, and searched nooks and crannies.

Dave explored above, around the sacrarium, his only light that of the altar and votive candles, which had not yet burned down to their prickets. There had been a midnight mass at the cathedral, followed by prayers for those who had died in recent fires, including the tragic police deaths. In the sandbed near the altar, over two hundred votive candles were alight.

Vanessa, less concerned by the blackness than Dave, went down to the crypt below the stone flags, and used a penlight to find her way through the dark. There was nothing down there but dead priests and benefactors of the cathedral.

Both were aware that should Nethru be discovered by either of them, they would probably die, but a scream would be enough to warn Danny, the man with the weapon.

Their individual searches revealed nothing, and they knew they had arrived before Nethru. So far, everything was going according to plan. Danny was stationed out in the graveyard, behind one of the headstones. Dave hid himself in the shadows, below a flying buttress, ready to reveal his position once Nethru entered the cathedral grounds.

Vanessa, armed with the spare .38 Danny had pressed on her, remained inside the cathedral, behind a pillar near the altar. She knew the weapon was of little use against Nethru, but its weight and feel was comforting, and she needed *something* to fill her hands. Dave had closed the doors behind him, leaving her feeling isolated from the two men.

While she waited, the moon came from behind the clouds, and illuminated the cathedral interior with colored light from the great circular window high above the altar.

It gave the place an eerie atmosphere, and Vanessa settled down on her haunches, still gripping the gun with both hands. She wondered how Danny was feeling at that moment. He was the one who had to administer the deadly fire, the one who had to destroy the fallen angel. If he failed, they all failed, for there was no other way to get rid of the creature. Nethru would surely kill them all without compunction, probably with some relish, if the flamethrower did not get him.

Vanessa stared around her, at the cathedral interior bathed in muted colors. The tabernacle was lit with light from two sides, from the altar candles, and from the moonbeams striking the John F. Kennedy memorial window above it. There seemed to be a kind of hopeful peace about the scene. It was then she began to wonder: would the demon *dare* to come to a church? It was, after all, the house of God. Perhaps in here there was sanctuary from the creature?

Then she realized, that was exactly why Dave had put her in there.

Damn that man, she thought. Why did he have to be so protective all the time? He was so old-fashioned in that sense, still clinging to macho values. Why couldn't he be like the renaissance men that she usually went out with? Because he was a cop? No, she had to admit it to herself, it was because he *loved* her. Not that there was anything exactly wrong in that, perhaps, but love shouldn't get too protective, or it became stifling. Still, she would have to pry that out of him, over the years they had left together. *By the time we're sixty,* she thought ruefully, *he'll have some modern ideas about women.*

While Dave was waiting in the shadows of a flying buttress, under the hollow-eyed stares of the gargoyles, he thought about the kind of angels and demons on which he'd been raised. They were nothing like Nethru had been or was now. Dave's childhood angels were like the stone one he could see in the moonlight, standing by a nearby grave: beautiful women without busts, in white Greek robes and with tall feathered wings sprouting from their shoulderblades. His childhood demons were cloven-hoofed creatures, with narrow faces, goat's eyes, bat's wings, and of course, the forked tail and horns.

Evidently, Nethru had not changed in physical appearance. As an angel he had been a good-looking young man. As a demon, he remained the same.

Dave wondered whether, when he saw Nethru, to say something like, *"You're laughing at my mule. My mule don't like to be laughed at,"* but decided against it. The truth was, right now he was practically pissing his pants.

The other man wetting himself was Danny, crouched down behind a gravestone and ready to lance the air with a deadly tongue of flame. He felt bulky, piggy, and vulnerable. Right now he wished he was snuggled up in bed with a plump lady called Rita—but there would be no more comfortable nights with Rita, only more confessions to his three favorite priests, after nights on the town.

Shit, thought Danny, *I wish the bastard would come, and we could get it over with, one way or the other.*

28

Manovitch found the note as he was dousing David Peters's apartment in aviation fuel, soaking the furniture, carpets and drapes. He had come in by the fire escape after forcing open a window. The note was pinned to a broom handle propped up in front of the entrance to the living room. He scanned it by the beam from his flashlight. The message on the note was short. It read:

SEE YOU IN CHURCH.

An address followed.

Manny broke out in a sweat, stuffing the piece of paper into his leftside pocket. How the hell had they known he was coming? He had been planning this for months, but only in his own head. No one else knew he was here. He hadn't breathed a word to a soul.

Then he got to thinking that perhaps he'd been a bit hasty in his initial assessment. Maybe the note was not for him? Maybe Peters was expecting someone else to call? All Manny could hope for was that the detective came home first, before the visitor.

Manny had obtained the aviation fuel from a friend of his, a maintenance guy who worked at the airport. Avgas vaporized on contact with the air. It was a hell of a lot more inflammable than ordinary gasoline, with a highly sensitive ignition flashpoint. Just a spark would be enough to gut the whole apartment with a fire ball.

The first thing to do was fix the light switch by the door.

He examined it in the beam of his pencil flashlight. Then he unscrewed the fitting plate from the wall, and puffed a handful of powder-fine steel filings inside among the works. This would ensure at the very least a healthy spark when the light was switched on. Manny then replaced the fitting plate.

He splashed avgas around liberally, soaking the furniture and carpets. The fumes quickly filled the room, so that it became difficult for Manovitch to breathe.

When Peters came home the spark from the light switch would ignite the fumes and burn the bastard to death.

Manny stood in the dark room, surveying his work by the sliver of brightness from his flashlight. The whole room was now reeking with the deadly fuel. The explosion would, of course, be blamed on some ex-con, or even better, on the slut Peters was sleeping with. Then Manny would have the whore where he wanted her. She was going to open her legs for him, if it took him until hell froze over to pry them apart.

Perhaps someone other than Peters was going to come waltzing through the door, to switch on the light and fry themselves to crisp potato chips? It didn't matter too much, as long as Manny wasn't there. Maybe they would even accuse Peters of laying the trap. That would suit Manny fine.

Manny gulped for air in the thickening atmosphere of the room and made for the window.

He was only halfway there when the front door burst off

its hinges and flew into the room with such force it knocked him off his feet. His squat body went flying over the back of the sofa, where he cracked his head on the wall behind.

He lay there dazed for a brief moment, sucking the avgas fumes down into his lungs, then his eyes sprang open, and he screamed at the top of his voice, "DON'T TOUCH THE LIGHT SWITCH! DON'T TURN ON THE LIGHT FOR CHRISSAKES! LEAVE THE LIGHT ALONE!"

A voice from the doorway snarled, "I could smell the gasoline from a hundred yards down the street. Do you think I'm stupid, or what?" The tone suddenly became accusative. "You intended to burn me."

"Not you, not you."

Manny struggled to his feet, rubbing his face. His hand came away wet, and he realized his nose was bleeding. He took out a handkerchief and wiped it several times. His head hurt, both back and front, but his nose had taken the brunt of the door, and the pain from it was making his eyes water.

He asked the silhouette with the hall light behind it, "Who the hell are you? What're you busting doors down for?"

"Where's the policeman?" asked the figure, quietly.

Manny remembered the note, and put two and two together. This guy, maybe an ex-con with a grudge had come looking for Peters, and the cop had known he was coming, and left a note. There was going to be some kind of showdown at the city cathedral.

"He ain't here," replied Manny.

"Where is he?"

"Who wants to know?"

Anyone else but Manovitch would have taken the hint when the door was kicked in. Anyone else would have thought to themselves, *That's one strong motherfucker out there.* Anyone but Manovitch.

The figure stepped into the room and gripped Manny by

the throat. He felt the fingers tighten, squeezing into his voice box. "Hey," he grunted, letting go of his handkerchief and trying to pry the fingers open. "Hey," he said again, with more panic in his voice, only the word came out *Hugghhh*.

His hand scrabbled into his trouser pocket like a frightened crab, and came out with the crumpled message, which he waved before his attacker's eyes.

He was released, left to stroke his neck, while the other man read the message by the light from the hall.

"Where is this place? How do I get there?"

"Jesus," grunted Manny, "show it to a cab driver, for fuck's sake."

"Cab?"

"Taxi. Where you been?"

The man nodded his head. "The hire cars."

Manny tried to sneak a look at the creep's face, but the light was still behind the man, and all he could see were the eyes glaring at him. There was some kind of decision being made, in which Manny had no say, and he suddenly felt a surge of panic.

"Hey, listen, mister, I don't—"

But his arms were already gripped, held fast by his sides, and a knee came up into his groin. He was released, his hands going down to his balls, as he groaned in pain. Then a fist smacked him between the eyes. His brain exploded in a burst of agony, and the floor came up and whacked him in the face. He lost consciousness.

When he came to, Manny felt sick and dizzy, and even though the room was dark he instinctively knew his vision was impaired. He was lying right next to the half-full can of avgas, and his lungs were pulling on the fumes. His throat was raw, his balls felt like they had been crushed by a steam hammer, and his head still hurt.

He yelled, *"Hey, help, someb—"* and then stopped abruptly, when he remembered the light switch. He could see no haze of light anywhere in the room, as he stumbled to his feet, and guessed the door had been jammed back in its hole. Whoever came through would instinctively switch on the light and burn them both to blazes, literally, and it was wise not to yell for help. The gas fumes filled the room. He wouldn't stand a snowball's chance in hell. Manny broke out into a cold sweat just thinking about it.

He decided to try to find the door by feeling around the wall, but when he walked it was with a sickening feeling, and the dizziness threatened to send him crashing to the floor with every step. Unfortunately, during his first few steps he managed to knock over the gas can, splashing it over his legs. He ignored this, and left the can glugging onto the carpet. Bit by bit he managed to work himself closer to the wall, and began feeling around the edge, banging into furniture, and knocking things over. A ceramic lamp crashed in a corner of the room, and shattered noisily. Manny panicked, thinking someone would come, and fell backward into the room again.

When he had recovered his feet, he stumbled off in another direction, only to fall across another chair. He began weeping, the tears rolling down his fat cheeks, and then, mercifully, he felt wood, and the door handle was in his hand. Pulling, he found it opened easily, and then began whining, realizing it was the door between the rooms, not the way out of the apartment.

The whole episode was a nightmare, and as he lurched giddily back into the living room, he was thinking what a fool he was to ever try such a plan. He wanted to be back home, in bed, next to his bulky wife Pearl. At home. Safe. Out of this crazy place of swooning darkness, and imminent death.

Next, he tried to find the window where he had come in, but he had pulled the drapes so that those on the outside would not see his flashlight. Now he wished he had left just a chink, so that he could locate the exit to the fire escape, somewhere out there in the swimming blackness.

All he hit were blank walls, which fell away from him when he tried to use them as supports. Twice he went toppling over backward, as if he had been blown by a breeze, when his head spun.

Then, as he was giving way to despair, he heard footsteps going along the hall outside. He held his breath until he was sure that no one was going to enter the room, then he crawled toward the sound. He found the can again, and managed to wet his jacket, but refused to be deterred, and continued his journey, finally reaching the far wall. He felt along this, careful not to press too hard in case his hand found the light switch accidentally, until finally, limp with relief, he found the door.

As he had suspected, it was jammed.

He tried pulling on the handle at first, but it wouldn't budge. It turned in his fingers, all the way round, without the slightest effect. Next he tried kicking at the door and was weeping with frustration after five minutes in which the door had only moved an eighth of an inch, showing a crack of light down the left-hand side. He wanted to get to that light, then he could let that sickening dizziness take over, and swoon away into the state of unconsciousness his mind was urging him toward.

He continued kicking and using his shoulder, growing more frightened and excited by the second. In his head he could hear the roar of the avgas going up, and it became more urgent with every moment. Manny didn't want to die, not like that, not like a piece of barbecued pork left on the grill for too long. In his head he could smell the burned meat, hear it crackling, hear his own curses for not attending to the cooking more diligently.

Then finally as he kicked the bottom panel savagely, the door gave way. Contrarily, it fell inwards, striking his head and shoulders, and he wriggled out from underneath.

He felt the triumph surge through his breast, knowing that

in a few minutes he would be in the hallway, and shuffling himself out of danger.

It was at the very instant when he relaxed, thinking himself home and dry, when there was a click from somewhere in the room. It was not a very loud sound, but to Manny it was like a nuclear bomb going off. In the minuscule moment during which he was poised between life and death, Manovitch realized the apartment's heating was on a timer switch.

It only took one tiny spark.

In another second Manny would have been in the hallway, round the corner, *safe*.

But he didn't have a second, or even a fraction of a second.

Manny didn't even have long enough or breath enough to call himself an asshole.

The fire roared through the apartment, entering all the crevices, all the corners, until it had filled every tiny pocket, even Manny's lungs. It belched in a T-shape down both sides of the hallway outside, stripping paint from the doors, curling linoleum, and popping lightbulbs. Then it withdrew again, into the apartment, as if there were a dragon there, inhaling the fire back into his chest. The half-can of avgas exploded, showering what was left of the furniture, and hard flames now took hold and seriously began to devour the contents of the living room.

One of the first things the fire ate was the remains of the creature that was writhing, lizardlike, on the floor by the door.

29

The Dean was a hopeless insomniac.

His sleeplessness these days was to do with his job, which in the main was concerned with the cathedral's financial situation, though there had always been some reason on which to pin the cause. When he was a young boy of fifteen, as then only dreaming of the mysticism and distinction of priesthood, he had been kept awake at nights by his fear of catching some dread venereal disease. The other boys at the boarding school had told him he could catch VD from public toilets, and sometimes he would go all day at school without urinating, bearing a pain like someone was pushing a hot needle into his crotch. He came to hate pain.

In those days he was terrified of the shame, for in his imagination he knew that no one would believe he had not been with a prostitute. It had kept him awake, sweating in the dark, for hour on hour. Once, he worked himself up into such a state of terror that his thigh muscles cramped and cut off the circulation to his legs. When he tried to get out of bed and stand, his legs would not support him, and he screamed for the school matron, convinced he had caught a virus in the swimming pool.

Nowadays, the insomnia had a less melodramatic parent.

The cathedral, he had been told, was sinking slowly at the northeast corner, and a lot of money was needed for underpinning. The Dean's quarters were in a large brownstone, near to the cathedral itself. He visited the cathedral in the middle of the night, and stared at the corner where the stone met earth, to see if he could notice some movement.

It always looked fine to him, as solid as a mountain, but they told him it was sinking. He had marked the stonework, just above the turf, with an indelible pencil. The distance between the mark and the turf did not *seem* to grow any smaller. It always looked the same. He had thought that perhaps God had answered his prayers. Yet when the experts had visited only just a week ago, they told him it was still sinking. A secret movement that only the experts could discern. When he told them about the mark they just looked at him, but in their looks were words, *Don't meddle in things you don't understand.*

He wanted to tell them, *I don't understand the mystery behind the Creation, or the enigma of Death, or the ways of the Lord. Should I give up meddling there too?*

They told him patiently that the next movement could be sudden, or slow, that earth movements of any kind were unpredictable. They said there was always uncertainty attached to such things. What was certain was that the cathedral was slipping, and while they didn't see any harm in prayers, it was best to make sure with reinforced concrete and steel.

Visiting priests told him not to worry. The cathedral had lasted for a hundred years, hadn't it? Why shouldn't it last a thousand? Ten thousand? Why, look at the Leaning Tower of Pisa! Still standing, after how long? Eight hundred, nine hundred years? They knew, at least they had heard of, another monument, somewhere in Asia or in South America or in the Pacific, which had been condemned for centuries, yet had survived the experts.

There were the so-called experts, and then there were the visiting priests, like the boys at school, ignorant yet convincing.

The experts doubted, of course, that religious faith was strong enough to support a thousand tons of granite. They preferred to put *their* faith in steel girders. They didn't understand that the Dean believed his faith to be stronger than steel. God had created the earth and stone in the first instance; He could do with it as He liked thereafter. If God chose to drive the cathedral into the earth with His fist, he would do it. If, however, he was willing to grant the Dean's prayers, the building would remain stable for eternity. Never mind a thousand tons, He kept billions of tons suspended in a vacuum, spinning in space, and had allowed it to flourish with life. He had created the planet which freewheeled in nothing, was balanced delicately in a void, without even a thread to hold it up. He had created countless such worlds: a whole universe of them, neverending.

The Dean's arguments would have been listened to by the experts, tolerantly, patiently, and received gentle agreement, then be countered with, *Yes, but, Dean, we're dealing with a major fault here . . . this is San Francisco. This is earthquake country. Even a tremor . . .* There was a deep-seated underground stream apparently, running across and under that corner, which had been eroding the foundations, he was told, since the cathedral had been built in 1883. It might last another year, ten, perhaps a hundred years, maybe even five hundred, without falling down. Geological time was vast. There might not be another quiver from the San Andreas fault for another thousand years.

But this was a cathedral. It was supposed to be in place *for ever*. It had withstood the 'quake of 1906, and others since, but between the stream and the earth movements the experts believed its days to be numbered and they spoke about small figures.

Then there was the roof, and the new school that had been

promised, and a multitude of other expenses, both running and standing.

The Dean had not reached his present position just through being a good man, although he *was* by most standards, a very good man and spiritually sound. But he was also a wheeler-dealer, who knew how to juggle people, knew how to get them pushing him from behind, instead of blocking his way. That was why he was no longer a parish priest, like Father Morgan, along-side whom he had been ordained. He couldn't help having this gift, and though he used it in the service of Christ, one of the spin-offs was his own elevation up the status ladder. It worried him, and kept him awake sometimes, this easy fulfillment of his ambitions. He felt the Lord should make it tougher for him, harder, so that success came with difficulty but more satisfaction.

The Dean wandered around the cathedral grounds, locked in the constant internal struggle which twisted him so much he could rarely manage more than four hours' sleep. At first, he did not see the man hiding in the shadows, below the flying buttress, but then a slight movement caught his eye. He stopped, and stared, his heart pattering faster in his chest.

"Who's there?" he called. "Who's that at this time of night?"

He was a little frightened of physical harm, and did not feel he had to apologize to God for that weakness, if it were such. Many people were concerned about pain: you weren't sup-posed to enjoy it. (If you did, that in itself might be a sin.) And if you were worried about pain, there was no reason not to be frightened by it.

"Come out of there!"

A tall man with a narrow face moved out of the shadows, and spoke softly to the Dean.

"I'm a policeman. We have reason to believe there may be some criminal activity here during the night. Are you the Bishop?"

"The Dean, but I still don't understand."

"My partner and I are waiting for an arsonist, a murderer, and there may be difficulties. It would be better if you weren't around, Dean."

The Dean could see the other man now, by the gravestones. He had something on his back which looked like one of those spraying devices for killing garden insects. You occasionally saw the gardeners in the city parks, spraying the shrubs with one of those . . .

Suddenly, a long thick plume of fire tongued out into the night, over the tops of the graves, from the snout of the man's device. It lit the whole cathedral close. There was a strong smell of gasoline in the air, which stung the membrane inside the Dean's nostrils. There was black smoke in his eyes.

The Dean clutched his face, to stop the smarting. His heart was jumping from his chest into his throat, and he could not speak for a moment.

The man himself let out a yell.

"He's here, Dave. I missed him with the first burst."

The policeman beside the Dean shouted, "Where is he now, Danny?"

"He went round back."

The Dean was petrified. They obviously had a madman on the grounds. But why were they using that weapon? Surely they should be using revolvers or something, shotguns at the most? Why the fire?

The Dean began running, stumbling between the masses of headstones, toward the wall around the graveyard. Once there, he crouched down, hidden by the forest of markers of the dead. Everyone wanted to be buried at the cathedral, and they packed them in the earth like canned carrots. There were crosses, flat-stones, angels and obelisks, with hardly a few inches between them. The dead would protect him, hide him, as he had looked after them, cared for their remains.

The Dean was very frightened. He could feel something, deep down inside him—something terrible was out there, on the consecrated ground of his cathedral. The Dean was a very psychic man, more spiritually sensitive than most of his colleagues. His soul was on fire with anxiety. Some horrible creature was desecrating his holy place. It put fear into the Dean such as he had never known before. He pushed the knuckles of his right hand into his mouth, and bit them, to stop himself from screaming. His mind was awhirl with prayers, *Mary, Mother of Christ* . . .

What was that weapon? A flamethrower? He peered over the top of the marble forest as the man let out another plume of fire which eerily lit up the cathedral. Now his target was there, just thirty yards in front, but the creature had ripped out a huge headstone, and was holding it in front of itself like a shield. The fire licked at the stone.

"He's out of range, Danny, save it!" cried the first policeman. His voice sounded tight, full of fear. But if he sounded afraid, the second policeman beat him on any scale of terror the Dean liked to use.

"I know. Jesus, he moves fast. I can't keep track of him, Dave. He's like a snake . . ."

The Dean, now that he had seen the creature, knew it for what it was. He *felt* it, deep in his soul. They were hunting a demon out there: a creature from hell. A foul monster that had somehow escaped the environs of its real home, and had come to earth to destroy his cathedral. No wonder they were using fire. No wonder they were terrified.

The Dean gagged on his own fear, bit harder on his knuckles, and let out a low whine. He tried to bury himself in the brickwork of the wall. He wished the marble stones would spring out of the turf and form a barrier between him and this evil creature that was fouling the sanctity of his home.

It was then he felt a slight movement beside him, and

looked up, to see the creature's incandescent eyes, staring into his own. The Dean gave a little cry, but the slender creature took him in its immensely strong hands, and held him up, using him as a shield. The psychic stench from the demon's body was putrefying and the Dean vomited immediately. The creature took no interest in him at all: the Dean was a tool, nothing more.

"Drop the flame machine," growled the demon, "or I'll snap his neck like a twig."

The policeman with the flamethrower came out from behind a tomb. He was about twenty yards in front of the Dean and his assailant. The nozzle of the flamethrower was up, pointing bluntly toward the Dean, its ugly black snout ready to belch death, and turn him into charcoal. The Dean prepared himself to die, murmuring his prayers, hoping to live long enough afterward for the Bishop to administer him his last rites.

He tried to anticipate the pain involved in being burned to death like one of those protesting Buddhist monks he had seen on the news from time to time, and the vision was horrible, more than he could bear to contemplate. To sear the skin from the body caused unbearable, unbelievable agony to the victim. The Dean had a near memory of burning one of his fingers on a votive candle, in the cathedral, and the pain had been incredible. Just a tiny patch of skin on his forefinger! How would he feel with his whole body alight, sizzling like candle wax under a grill? The pain would be so intense he would be able to hear it, like the sound of cicadas. Not that. Anything but that.

He struggled in the demon's arms, hoping his neck would be broken and he would die with only a snap of sharp pain.

"What do I do, Dave? I can't burn him. He's got the priest."

Suddenly, the Dean was surprised to hear his own voice, ordering the policeman to do the opposite of what he actually wanted.

"Burn him, don't worry about me. Burn the evil—"

A hand was clamped over his mouth, squeezing his lips into his teeth until he could feel blood trickling down his chin.

"Quiet, or I swear I'll break your neck."

The policeman called Dave said, "Let him go, Nethru. It's us you want."

Nethru was unsure of what to do next. He had guessed right: they would not kill the priest. Equally, he could see they were not going to relinquish the flamethrower. Why should they? They would not burn the priest, it was against their laws. So he had to hold on to the priest, to use him as a shield.

But he could not stand there forever with the man struggling like a fish in his hands. He had to do something. He was not going to leave without killing these two. That was what he came to do, and he was going to do it. What he had to do now was get them somewhere they would not be able to use their weapon.

Inside the cathedral?

Danny did not know what to do. He was on the point of dropping the flamethrower. But if he did, he knew he would die, and Dave too, and possibly the Dean. Yet if he *didn't* do what Nethru said, the Dean would have his neck broken. Danny would never forgive himself if the Dean was killed. It would be his, Danny's, fault, and he would blame himself for it for the rest of his life. Being responsible for the death of a priest was like hitting a child with an automobile. You couldn't live with guilt like that. It would drive you crazy.

Now they had this Mexican standoff, and Danny wished he were somewhere else, somewhere like Philadelphia.

Dave felt helpless. He had no idea what his next move should be. He could see Danny was strung tighter than a Flushing Meadow tennis racket. Dave had no idea what was going through Danny's head at this moment, but he knew that he was either on the point of dropping the flamethrower, or pressing the trigger. He knew Danny well enough for that. In some respects, he knew Danny better than Danny knew himself.

Then there was the Dean, whose fear could be smelled from fifty yards away. Yet the man had enough courage. No doubt as a religious man, he had come to terms with death. The Dean was afraid, as anyone would be, but what was he afraid of? The demon? Being tainted with the evil of the creature that held him? Or was he really scared of death, despite his beliefs?

Finally, there was Nethru, who was unpredictable but whose practical aims could be assessed. Nethru wanted to kill the two policemen. He wanted revenge. Killing the priest would not give him that, because he would be destroyed by fire moments afterward. It must have been obvious to the demon by this time that Danny was not going to drop the flamethrower, or he would have done it already. So Nethru, too, was caught in the deadlock.

"Don't hurt me," Dave heard the priest say, "I can't stand pain . . ."

Then and there the answer came to Dave, and he smiled.

He drew his spare automatic out of his holster, and began aiming. Nethru sneered, but then he did not know what was about to happen.

The priest stared into Dave's eyes and there was an understanding between them.

Dave said, "Danny, get ready with the thrower. I'm going to kill the Dean with a single shot. The Dean isn't afraid to die, are you, Dean?"

The Dean shook his head in affirmation.

"Kill me," he said.

Nethru felt the priest relax in his arms. No, the priest was not afraid to die. Everything about him protested against pain, but not against death. Would this policeman kill the priest? Yes, Nethru believed he would, to get at Nethru, the killer of his wife and child. This policeman would sacrifice his friend and himself, so why not some stranger?

Nethru had left himself an escape route, however, which the two policemen would have overlooked.

He let the priest go, and instantly did a high backflip, over the wall, landing on his feet on the sidewalk at the other side. The sidewalk and roadway were about seven feet below the surface level of the graveyard at this point, the cathedral being on a slope. Nethru was now out of the immediate reach of the two policemen, who had to climb a six-foot-high wall, then drop thirteen feet to the ground.

Nethru could at this moment have made a run for it and got away, but that was not why he came. He was here to kill them and the flame machine was not going to deter him from his purpose. They were going to die, by his hand, tonight.

The demon had brought his own weapons. There were six Molotov cocktails in the pockets of his raincoat, and he took one of them out now. He lit the rag fuse and tossed the bottle over the wall, hearing it shatter, probably on one of the tightly packed gravestones. The satisfying sound of a scream followed the *whumph*.

Nethru had aimed for the spot where he had left the priest.

There was a drunk standing some way down the street.

The drunk's name was Billy Dranton, and he was on his way home to his wife after running out of money and booze. Billy desperately needed just another few shots, before he could face Maria, who was one hell of a bitch when he had been out drinking with the boys. Last time she had taken the bread knife to him, though she was sorry for it afterwards, when he had bled all over her clean kitchen floor.

Billy had stopped in midstride on seeing someone fall out

of the night, and land on the sidewalk in front of him. He had looked upward, bemusedly, at the stars, expecting that there might be more. Then the person who had dropped out of the sky took a bottle of booze from one of his pockets—a *full* bottle by the look of it—and lit the top.

"Hey!" he said to Nethru, his senses instinctively tweaking his brain at the sight of the stuff of life. "Hey, whatcha doin' with that there?" The bottle sprang a flame from its neck.

To his amazement and chagrin, the man threw the bottle away, into the graveyard. Just *threw* it away. Crazy bastard. Crazy fucking shithead. A *whole* bottle.

It must have been good stuff, because it exploded on the other side of the wall, in a fountain of flame.

"Whatthefuck? Whydintchagiveit*me*?" screamed Billy, incensed at this stupidity.

The other man, a skinny bastard with a woman's face, came running toward Billy, and Billy instinctively crouched ready to take the guy with a football tackle. Maybe the skinny shit had *another* bottle of booze on him? Billy needed a drink badly, so Billy was going to find out.

Nethru ran toward the drunk and struck him in the chest with his shoulder. The drunk clutched at Nethru's coat, and clung on to him for a moment. Nethru struck him in the face with his elbow, and the man went spinning out into the road, slipped on some trash, and went down on his backside. His nose was bleeding profusely.

"Hey!" he said again. "Hey!"

However, the drunk was holding something in his hand. It seemed he had gone into one of Nethru's pockets and had stolen a Molotov cocktail. Nethru made a move toward him, but the drunk quickly pulled out the rag cork and swilled down some of the gasoline before Nethru could reach him.

The drunk went, "Ha!" in satisfaction.

Then the man's eyes suddenly bulged and he began coughing and spluttering, squirming in the road clutching his throat. The bottle fell to the street and rolled away, glugging a trail of gasoline to the gutter.

Nethru paused just a moment to light this trail of fuel, before running on. A moment later he heard the sound of the cocktail going up, and then another muted noise, probably the drunk's lungs exploding.

Nethru ran swiftly along, under cover of the brickwork, to the back of the cathedral again, where he climbed the wall. Then he slipped between the gravestones, hunched over with marble angels watching his every move with impassive eyes.

He began to scale the back wall of the building.

Danny shrieked, "Did you see that?"

Dave had indeed seen it. The move had been incredibly fast. One moment the demon had been standing there, his arms around the Dean, and the next second he was gone, using some acrobatic movement to leap the graveyard wall.

Danny ran to the wall, just as the Molotov cocktail came sailing over the top, and shattered on the concrete path close to the Dean. He ducked and crouched behind a headstone, knowing that if fire got to his backpack, he would go up in a pillar of flame so high it would dwarf the cathedral's spire.

The priest was showered with flaming fuel, and screamed as it burned his skin. Dave rushed across to him, removing his jacket as he ran. He wrapped the garment around the Dean's upper body and head, where the flames were, effectively smothering them. Then he pulled the priest out of the ring of fire, where the gasoline was still burning. The Dean groaned and after a moment climbed to his feet.

"I'm all right," he kept saying, "don't fuss over me. I'm all right. I'm all right."

The Dean used the repetition of an hysteric, who is trying to convince himself more than others. Dave inspected him quickly in the beam of his flashlight, and discovered only superficial burns. Luckily, the Dean really would be all right.

From the other side of the wall came shouts, then the sound of another explosion. Danny pulled himself up, looking over the wall, and called back to Dave.

"He's fired somebody else. Jesus, that poor guy . . ."

The next shout came from the Dean.

"There he is!"

The Dean pointed to the back wall of the cathedral, his wounds forgotten for a moment. Nethru was scaling this swiftly, fingers and toes in the cracks of the stonework, like some giant black spider going up the side of a cliff. It was almost sickening to watch. The demon could move with the speed of a striking snake, and climb sheer surfaces with his clawlike hands.

Some rock climbers Dave knew could go up vertical walls, so long as there were tiny ledges, cracks, projections, as any block-built wall must have. But never this fast. A rock climber's ascent was deliberate and careful, not this rapid scuttling movement, faster than a crab over seashore stones.

Danny began running toward the cathedral, fumbling with the nozzle of the flamethrower, but before he could get within range, Nethru had reached the high Kennedy window. Clinging onto a gargoyle with his right hand, he shattered the circular stained glass window with his left fist, and then he was gone, through the hole and into the cathedral itself. He seemed to drop inside, not climb.

"The fall will kill him!" cried Danny.

Dave knew it would be otherwise. Nethru was not like the Dean. Nethru did not mind pain. It was destruction *he* feared. And the demon could only be destroyed by fire. A fall might fracture a bone or two, which in Nethru would heal within a very short time, maybe seconds.

Now the demon was inside the cathedral. Dave could see why he had gone there. He wanted to draw them in. The flamethrower would be difficult to use in the tighter space, and the hiding places were many. Dave would have to position Danny by the doors, and flush the demon out from wherever he was hiding, the crypt, or one of the many small rooms with Latin names that chambered Catholic cathedrals.

Then Dave remembered.

"My God, Vanessa's in there . . ."

30

Vanessa had been listening to the shouts outside, and guessed from what she heard that the demon had not been burned. They were the sounds of frustration and chase, followed by silence. There was a scrabbling noise on the back wall, and more urgent yells. Then suddenly the window above the altar shattered, the sound making her start in fright. Lead-framed stained glass hurtled to the floor and smashed on the flagstones around her, breaking into smaller pieces that skated over the surface of the sacrarium.

She looked around and upward from behind the pillar where she was crouched. A figure was coming through the gap in the circular pane. It had to be Nethru. She saw the demon drop from an enormous height, his raincoat billowing like a cloak. He landed like a cat on all fours, behind the altar. There was the sound of a bottle breaking: a muted crack, as if the glass were wrapped in cloth. She smelled gasoline. The fall had broken one of his Molotov cocktails. He would have more, of that she was certain, in the pockets of that voluminous flapping raincoat.

Her heart was pounding against her ribs, and a cold terror had overtaken her, as she waited for him to emerge from behind the altar. He was there for what seemed to her to be an eternity. There was the thought that, even if Nethru was not hurt, perhaps the trappings of God's house had immobilized him. The crucifix, the statue of Mary, the consecrated ground, the sanctified surroundings, perhaps all of these were neutralizing agents to the demon, robbing him of his powers. Outside, among the graves, there were few potent holy symbols. Just a few stone angels, a few stone crosses. Nothing with any force. In here, there were sacred objects, holy water, hallowed books.

This had been her first glimpse of the creature, and his dramatic entrance had done nothing to quell her fears. What she had seen was a dark, slim shape, very feline, very agile, come hurtling through the broken Kennedy Window, and drop to the ground in an arched attitude. Vanessa hated cats. They had eyes that looked down into your soul, and sneered at the sins that were staining it.

Just as she began to think that perhaps the fall had hurt the creature, he stood up, his pale features caught by the candles burning on the altar. Vanessa quickly ducked her head behind the pillar and gripped the .38 with both hands. It offered a little comfort—not much—but a little. She peeked again after a while, and saw him disdainfully knock aside the processional cross, which took care of her idea that the sanctuary might rob him of his devilish strength. He glanced around the cathedral, his dark eyes catching the light of the candles. Again, she ducked out of his sight.

A shadow flickered on the wall she was facing, and she jumped. He was walking about, yet she could not hear his footfalls. That worried her. He could walk right up to her and she would not know he was coming. Then she heard something fall, a stack of hymn books or Bibles, and she knew he was on the far side of the aisle.

Vanessa tucked the gun in the pocket of her thick woolen skirt, and squirmed from her pillar to the next, hoping to snake her way to the altar, intending to hide behind it. He had already been there once, and would probably not bother to go back again, even if he guessed she was in the place.

"I can smell your perfume," said a voice.

She stopped all movement, frozen with the horror of that tone. It was as she imagined it would be, harsh, discordant, thick. The creature had smelled her, knew she was there.

"I know it's you. I have smelled you before, when I followed you through the streets. You have no idea how close you came to being burned that day. I had to compensate with the death of another. There was a man, a thin pale man, with weak eyes. He wore glasses that changed color in different lights . . ."

Tom.

". . . and he had been with you. I smelled your perfume on him. I crushed his face with my hand. Then I threw him down the sewer. The rats have eaten him by now."

He had killed Tom, the day Tom had tried to rape her. Poor silly Tom, with his values all topsy-turvy, was a fool, but he hadn't deserved to die. What was the demon telling her all this for? Did he expect her to come rushing out, screaming defiance, looking for retribution for the death of her former boyfriend? It was possible. It was possible that he was trying to flush her out with what he thought to be a cunning method. No doubt he had established in his mind how much the two men wanted him destroyed for killing their women. Why shouldn't a woman feel the same about her man?

Except that Tom was no longer her man, and she certainly wasn't going to expose herself for the sake of his memory. Nethru had miscalculated there, badly, and if he could make mistakes like that, he was vulnerable. There was hope yet that he would be destroyed.

"Are you going to come out, or do I have to tear the place apart to find you?"

Just at that moment, there was a scraping sound, down by the doors, and Vanessa knew that someone was trying to enter, quietly. She hoped it was Danny with the flamethrower: she had to distract the demon.

"Why do you want to?" she said, her voice echoing in the hollowness of the room.

"Because I can use you," he replied.

He began to move toward her, just as Dave and Danny entered. They stood framed in the doorway for a moment, two dark silhouettes against the backdrop of the moonlit graveyard.

"Vanessa?" cried Dave. "Are you all right?"

Danny lifted the nozzle of the flamethrower, aiming toward the striding demon, but Dave shouted, *"No!* Vanessa's in here somewhere."

Just then Nethru reached the spot where she was trying to hide, and grabbed her by the throat. He dragged her out and showed her to the two men. Vanessa felt the utter worthlessness of trying to struggle. This man, this *creature,* was so strong he could snap her spine in a second. She went limp, allowing herself to be carried by the demon.

"I have the woman," Nethru said simply.

Danny lowered the flamethrower.

A stale silence followed, then Dave said bitterly, "What do you want us to do?"

"Take off the weapon. Throw it outside."

"Danny, don't—," Vanessa shrieked, but Nethru squeezed her throat, robbed her of words. She tried to pull the gun from her pocket, but the hammer had caught itself in the cloth, and she was getting weaker all the time.

Then Nethru swiftly reached inside his raincoat with his right hand and pulled out a Molotov cocktail. He lit it from a nearby candle, and hurled the gasoline-filled bottle-bomb.

Dave instinctively ducked, his hands over his head.

Danny took two paces backward, his mouth open, knowing, of course, that when the bottle struck, smashed and showered the area with flame, the pack on his back would explode. He would go up in a ball of incandescence, taking Dave with him.

The gasoline grenade did not hit the flagstones, nor any of the pews. Instead, it struck Danny a glancing blow on the side of the head, knocking him cold. The bottle was deflected by Danny's skull, through the open doorway, and onto the steps of the cathedral. There it shattered and billowed into flame, filling the night with brightness.

Fortunately for the two detectives, only small amounts splashed back through the doorway. Some landed on Danny's shoulders, after he had gone down with a crash on the flagstones, but Dave quickly beat them out with his hands.

Then Dave turned to look at the demon.

"Let her go," Dave said to Nethru. "You can have us. Just let her go."

Vanessa tried to show her anger with Dave, telling him to get out, run for it, fetch help. Dave stayed where he was.

"Why don't you *run?*" she cried.

"I just can't let it happen. Not twice."

And she knew he was talking about Celia.

Nethru laughed.

"This is easy. This is too easy."

He let go of Vanessa and was beside Dave in a dozen strides. The demon took the policeman, lifted him up, and threw him the length of the aisle. Dave landed on his side and went skidding into the altar, bringing everything down with a crash. He lay there and groaned. Vanessa ran to him, kneeled by him. Dave was still breathing, still alive, though his left arm was twisted in an absurd way.

Nethru wrenched the flamethrower from Danny's inert form, twisted it into uselessness, and threw it out into the night.

Then he walked down the aisle toward Dave.

"I'm going to burn you," he said.

Vanessa ran to the far side of the cathedral and crouched there. Here, at last, she managed to wrench the .38 from her pocket, and hid it behind her back, like a child with a secret. When Nethru reached her, he grabbed her by the hair, pulled her to her feet. She felt no pain, only a racing adrenaline, which coursed around her body. Her hand was steady. He started to drag her to where Dave was lying, half-conscious on the steps to the sacrarium.

Suddenly, she pushed the gun into the demon's face, and pulled the trigger.

The gun went off, point blank, bucked in her hands and fell to the floor, with a clatter. The sound of the shot was absolutely deafening, like an explosion, the hollow confines of the great cathedral amplifying the noise tenfold. She was left with her ears ringing.

Nethru's head snapped backward sharply, and he had to let her go. He grunted in pain. His hand went up to his face.

The bullet had taken out his left eye.

"You . . ."

The anger in that single quietly spoken word was terrifying to her. She knew then that she had hurt him, that he had experienced great pain. She knew that, even though he would heal, he could not replace what had been taken from him. She had stolen one of his eyes, and he was going to tear her apart as if she were an insect.

Dave, one arm obviously broken and useless, tried to grab Nethru's ankle with his good hand, and received a savage kick in the face, knocking his head back.

Vanessa snatched the gun from the floor, and ran back to a pillar.

Danny, at the other end of the aisle, was now on his feet, and was staggering groggily toward Nethru. Danny had his own gun out. His face had a wild look.

Vanessa shrieked, "Aim for his right eye!"

Danny stopped, blinked, and then she knew the message had got through. The short bald-headed cop went down on one knee, took careful aim, and squeezed the trigger six times. The explosions thundered through the stone channels of the cathedral, and Vanessa saw Nethru's head jerk back. When he turned to look at her, there were two holes in his right cheek, and one just above the good eye.

Danny had missed.

Nethru picked up the brass altar cross, and hurled it the length of the aisle. It struck Danny on the right shoulder, and he went spinning round, and fell on the floor by the door. He lay there, groaning.

Vanessa backed away, as Nethru came toward her.

"You have caused me pain," was all he said.

Vanessa backed up against the pillar.

The demon moved toward her.

She raised the .38 again, this time using both hands so that it would not jump out of her grasp. There were five shots left in the gun. Her mind had gone cold. There was no longer any fear in her. She squeezed the trigger, the way Dave had shown her, earlier in the evening. Four times she fired, trying to hit Nethru's face. Each time, she was either too high, or too low. It would have been a miracle if she had hit his good eye from that distance, with no experience of firearms.

Three bullets missed, one hit him in the throat. Then she pulled the trigger one last time and struck him in the forehead.

He was driven backward just a little by the force of the last shot that hit him, up against the blazing bed of votive candles, some of which were down to the bottoms of their stubs, and beginning to sputter.

Nethru's raincoat had been soaked in gas after his fall from the window. It fluffed into flame. The gasoline had all but evaporated, but there was enough to allow a thin blue streak of fire to leap up his left side.

There was just a flicker of apprehension on the demon's

face. He stepped away from the votive candles and swatted at the faint fire which seemed to trickle over his body, through his fingers. Vanessa could not understand why the demon was so worried about a little blue flame. She had seen worse brandy flames on plum puddings. It did not occur to her that he was in a highly dangerous and vulnerable position.

But a policeman's mind works quicker in such situations. "Nethru!"

The demon looked up at the sound of Dave's voice, and Vanessa saw his expression go from controlled panic to unrestrained terror. Dave had his own .38 in his good right hand, pointing at Nethru, who had at last realized where his vulnerability lay. His own weapons were his weakness, his worst fear. The detective also knew.

Dave was smiling, but it was not a pleasant smile. It was deadly. He spoke softly, as if afraid his breath would put out the gentle flame that licked around the demon's coat.

"Still got some gas on you, pal?"

At the same time as speaking, the detective squeezed the trigger six times. He carefully placed the shots over the demon's torso. There was a look of pained surprise on Nethru's face, as bottles shattered inside his pockets.

Then he flowered into a single bloom of flame, that almost reached to the cathedral's ceiling.

There was a crackling, sizzling sound, accompanied by the stench of burning meat, as the heat of the fire drove Vanessa away, toward the windows. A high distant screaming began. It seemed to come from another world. It was the scream of an animal in intense pain. It was the scream of a dying creature whose skin has been seared from its body. It was loud and shrill enough to puncture eardrums. It was the scream of a tongue on fire, a throat full of burning flesh, a set of lungs that were bubbling with heat.

The force of the rounds hitting him hard in the chest had

driven the demon backward, and now he toppled onto the blazing bed of votive candles. There he burned, like a figure made of wax, writhing and struggling against invisible agonies. He was consumed by holy fire, from the holy candles of the devout, his pale flesh burning furiously. His one penetrating black eye stared at Vanessa in rage, before it melted under the heat from the blaze. He staggered toward her, reaching for her with blackened smoking fingers. Vanessa stepped aside, watching him thrash around in flame.

Then he ran, the high-pitched sounds of agony still coming from somewhere deep in his throat. Somehow he managed to cover the length of the cathedral, and then stumbled out through the doorway.

He lit the night for a moment before it swallowed him.

Vanessa ran outside. There she witnessed the demon, still ablaze, rapidly scaling the tall steeple. He was an incandescent creature, scrambling blindly up the brickwork, miraculously finding toeholds, handholds. It was as if he were trying to reach heaven by a ladder, climbing up the wall of the sky, to what he believed was still his rightful home. At the pinnacle of the spire he ran out of stonework and clutched the wire cross which crowned the tip, his weight tearing it from the masonry.

For a moment he seemed to hover in free space, only his feet touching the spire.

Finally he plunged to earth, the rush of air fanning the flames around his body, spreading them wide, whipping them into trailing sheets. They streamed out like wings of red feathers on either side of him. It was a beautiful if terrible sight, this fiery-winged figure falling to the ground.

For a few brief moments Nethru was an illuminated letter from an ancient manuscript.

Vanessa saw him strike the ground, then went back inside to help the men.

The pain in Dave's broken arm, he told her, was only mar-

ginally worse than that from the broken nose. Vanessa helped
him to his feet. Danny had managed to sit up, and was holding his shoulder, which looked badly injured. He tried to grin,
but it came off as a grimace.

The three of them limped out into the night, looking round.
They sought the remains of the fallen angel.

Nethru's charred figure was not far away.

His agony-twisted form was lying on a tombstone, curled
and smoking, like something that had been dipped in molten
lava. Standing over him, balanced on a headstone, was a tradi-
tional concrete angel: a beautiful feminine-looking creature
with a broad sweep of feathery wings. Her head was tilted to
one side, her arms forming a graceful tulip shape above her
head. Her features, though lovely, were expressionless.

She stared down on the heap of ashes with unsympathetic
eyes: cement in place of compassion.